# LIVE AND LET RIDE

# LIVE AND LET RIDE

RIDGEMORE BOOK 3

LUCÍA ASHTA

Podium

Cover design by Amanda Shaffer

ISBN: 978-1-0394-7858-9

Published in 2025 by Podium Publishing
www.podiumentertainment.com

*For my devoted readers.*
*I'm so grateful that you share all these wild and wonderfully strange adventures with me, that you fall in love with my characters as much as I do.*

*For all the ride-or-dies out there.*
*Let's keep fighting for each other.*

*And for my personal ride-or-dies: my husband and daughters.*
*I'm so thankful I get to do this life thing with you at my side.*

# LIVE
AND
# LET
# RIDE

# 1

# Boss and His Bitches, Psycho Murderer and His Underlings

The priest droned on in a nonsensical monotone of Latin I probably would have understood had I been inclined to listen. I wasn't. I was too busy willing my eyes to shoot laser beams to slice every lying, fake motherfucker at this ruse of a funeral into so many tiny pieces that the coroner's office would never finish sorting what parts belonged to whom. Regrettably, though I'd been trying for a solid ten minutes, my eyes weren't sparking anything deadlier than a molten, furious anger—pretty much a constant since Griffin's Mustang, Clyde, erupted into a fireball. I was certain I'd never recover from the horrifying sight, no matter how long I lived.

For fuck's sake, our faux parents didn't even believe in religion! They condemned it as global-scale brainwashing for the weak of mind, worshipping science and its "concrete, verifiable explanations" instead. Yet here we were, at Ridgemore's largest cemetery, beside a gaping hole in "consecrated" ground behind a church, which waited to be filled with the remains of the man I loved.

<*If not-Mom gives me one more sympathetic look with those stupid, puffy eyes of hers while she clutches not-Dad and pretends to cry her cold, icy heart out,*> Layla growled into the telepathic group

chat that only Brady, Hunt, and I could currently hear, <*I swear, I'm gonna rip this veil off and shove it down her throat till her eyeballs pop. Give her something real to cry about.*>

Although the unrelenting afternoon sun beat down on our heads, making my scalp prickle hotly, Layla remained beneath a dense black veil that concealed the anger tightening her features, contorting her face into something bordering monstrous. Certainly murderous. It was the same combustible anger I wore, only I did so openly. I was beyond hiding that I wanted to kill every single sonofabitch here, playing their quaint little roles in Magnum's farce. They could all die for all I cared, all of them with their fake tears and faker sympathy. I'd cavort on their still-fresh graves.

On my right, with the imposing presence of a hulking volcano, stood Brady, with Layla at his other side. His face was unnaturally flushed, as if he were sunburned. The tendons in his neck bulged, his shoulders, arms, and hands tensing in a dance of ink and corded muscles. Even as our classmates and teachers of Ridgemore High pretended to brim with sympathy as they joined us in mourning Griffin, they gave Brady a wide berth. He was a rabid animal in the body of a man, who wore *danger* like a cloying cologne. All he needed were some cute blue shorts that showed off his ripped legs, plus a gun or two, and he'd be ready to go postal on everyone here.

I'd never been the cheerleader type, but that . . . that I would cheer. Shit, I'd don a face-splitting smile, a microskirt, high kick my legs, and chant Ridgemore High's cheerleading squad's favorite: *Be aggressive. Be-e aggressive.* I'd do it till Brady ran out of bullets.

Hunt stood to my left. In stark contrast to the rest of us, he'd never looked more stoic, more solemn. He didn't twitch and barely appeared to breathe for long minutes at a time. I imagined it was because he was barely holding himself together.

If he did anything to distract from keeping himself in one piece, he'd explode into a million shards of bloody, pulpy gore—like Griffin had.

Or maybe I only imagined he felt that way because it was how I felt.

According to everyone here but the three of us, Griffin Conway was dead. Dead as dead got, really. Blown into so many bits that the mere thought of his beautiful body ripped to shreds like that threatened to still my heart. For the first time in my life, I believed it was truly possible to die of grief, to feel a part of you missing like a crumbling, gaping chasm that could never be filled. Without Griffin, I didn't think I'd ever be whole again. I didn't think my friends would be either.

His was a loss I wasn't equipped to bear.

It wasn't like when he'd gone over the side of the cliff at the wheel in Clyde. Then at least Magnum had shown the decency to leave his body whole. Dead from a snapped neck, yes—for an agonizing while. But at least intact.

This time around, Magnum hadn't just killed Griffin. He'd committed sacrilege. He'd taken something precious to me and my crew and decimated it.

*Him.*

When we'd finally managed to extinguish the flames, Clyde had settled into several heaping, smoking mounds, and Griffin's body—his wondrous, gorgeous body—had been smeared all over Clyde's charred skeleton.

Brady had tugged on Griff's burnt arm to slide him from the wreckage. It had come free with a crackle of blackened, crispy flesh. Brady had puked until he dry heaved. Layla, who under normal circumstances probably couldn't shut up for an entire day to win a million-dollar bet, hadn't uttered a word for the rest of the night. Hunt, already thin, had appeared gaunt, his face drawn into harsh, haunted angles.

And I . . . I seesawed between feeling unbearably much, or nothing at all. I was a raging inferno fueled by hatred and a pulsing need for revenge—or a desolate ice cave, where nothing thrived, nothing lived.

<*She's doing it again,*> Layla growled into our minds, but also aloud, a guttural rumble that puffed out her veil, drawing the scrutiny of football coach Mr. Lauderbeck and his wide-receiver star, Duncan Mills. Brady glared at them. The men hastily averted their gazes, pinning them on the skinny priest with the too-narrow nose who was still intoning his religion's rituals for the dead.

But Griffin Conway, the man I loved, wasn't truly dead.

He couldn't be.

I wouldn't allow it. I'd rip him out of the embrace of Death itself.

<*She's looking at me like she gives a fuck,*> Layla said. <*Like she's not responsible for killing Griff.*>

<*Griff's not dead,*> Brady grumbled while the tendons in his neck bulged. <*He's not.*>

We were silent for long beats filled only by the rustling of the dozens of people who'd come to pay their respects—actors, all of them, it seemed—and the rote Latin I feared might actually never end, another form of torture for our already tortured minds.

<*Brade, heads up,*> Layla said, <*I'm gonna strangle not-Mom in her sleep tonight. She does* not *get to look at me like that. Like she* cares.> Even threading through my own thoughts, Layla's voice caught, nearly broke. <*They don't get to pretend they care.*>

According to a recent memo that went out to our faux parents, my crew wasn't supposed to know we were capable of dying and coming back to life. We were supposed to be unsuspecting dumbasses without a clue that most of our high school, if not the entire fucking town of Ridgemore, was in on whatever plan Magnum Chase, megalomaniac gazillionaire, had concocted this time around. We were expected to be wholly ignorant, to believe there was nothing extraordinary about us beyond our usual high intelligence levels. We were the butt of an ongoing joke that wasn't even remotely funny.

<*If you strangle her,*> Brady said into our minds, <*then I'll take Dad.*> Even tangling with my own thoughts, his words were gritty asphalt, the kind that tore up your knees so they wouldn't stop bleeding. <*The assholes aren't even telling us Griff is alive. They're letting us go through . . .*> He swallowed loudly enough that I heard it with my ears. <*They're letting us mourn him when they know he's still alive.*>

<*What if . . . what if he's not?*> Hunt asked softly, as if he didn't want to speak the words into existence.

<*Don't you dare even suggest that,*> I bit out harshly, when surely Hunt didn't deserve it. But everything that came out of me since the doomed race at the crossroads was harsh. Whatever softness I had, if any remained, was beyond my reach, even for the friends I knew to be suffering as much as I was.

<*He's alive,*> I insisted. <*He's gotta be.*>

<*But that's the problem, isn't it?*> Hunt said. <*That's the only reason we have. He has to be alive 'cause we need him to be. Maybe . . . maybe that's not enough.*>

<*It is,*> I insisted. <*It is enough.*>

Again we settled into a disturbed quiet. Every cough or cleared throat, every rustle of the uniformly black attire of the other "funeral" attendees, grated on my nerves like the touch of an open flame.

<*Oh, thank fuck. I think it's almost over,*> Layla said, dipping her hand under her veil to itch her nose. Or maybe it was to blot it. My girl didn't like to let on when she cried, especially not around her brother.

So far, I'd caught Brady crying more than she had.

As for me, I was too empty to cry. Too dry to have anything to unleash beyond anger. Of that, I had enough to burn down every single building in Ridgemore, including the entirety of Magnum's pretty new institute. Oh yes, I'd roast marshmallows as it burned. But first, I'd trap him inside the sleek modern design I'd been foolish enough to admire.

From the relative privacy afforded by my dark sunglasses, I studied him. Taller than our fake parents, he stood out as he nestled among them, as if they truly were all chums from way back. Not the boss and his bitches. Not psycho murderer and his underlings. Crazed maniac who wanted actual superpowers for himself and didn't care how many people he had to mow down to get them.

Dressed in impeccably tailored black, he stared back at me despite the anonymity of my lenses. Ever so subtly, his head tipped. He was dissecting me from afar, always seeking more data, more advantage, more rewards from his highly unethical experiments.

Magnum possessed more money and resources than sanity, and enough charisma to convert zealots to his cause, making him very, *very* dangerous.

<*I should've never let Griff race,*> I offered miserably into our group bond. <*I should've insisted.*>

Layla shook her head, her veil swaying. A warning not to betray that we were having private conversations slid to the edge of my tongue, where it withered. What did it matter anymore? Whatever advantage we'd worked so hard to preserve was meaningless when we couldn't even save one of our own.

<*Griff was his own man,*> Layla said. My body stiffened so abruptly that Magnum may have noticed. <*No matter what you'd said, he still woulda raced.*>

<*Griff* is *his own man,*> Brady corrected. <*Is, Lay. Fucking* is. *Don't you fucking dare give up on Griff.*>

<*I'd never,*> she snapped into our chat. <*I absolutely have not given up on him. We're gonna figure out how to get him back, I know we will.*>

Some of the tension drained from my body, leaving behind that constant anger, and a bone-deep weariness I wouldn't succumb to. If I did, it would feel too much like surrendering.

I'd give up on Griff over my dead body.

<*We gotta make moves,*> I said. <*No more waiting for the lying assholes to deliver him to us with a Miracle Kid explanation.*>

<*Damn right,*> Brady snarled. <*No more waiting. We get our brother back. Tonight.*>

*Yes.* I could absolutely get behind the Get Griffin Back Tonight Plan. There was just one huge, major problem.

<*How?*> I asked. <*How the fuck do we get him back?*> I chuffed darkly, brazenly, uncaring that several of our pretend parents joined Magnum in studying us, all while keeping their faces poised in careful masks that said *We care. We're heartbroken too.*

We were glaringly outmatched. We'd actually stashed defibrillator paddles in Clyde's trunk, laboring under the illusion that they'd make a difference, that we had a backup plan.

What we'd had was fuck all. You can't exactly defibrillate lumps of flesh—even if the paddles had survived the explosion, which they surely hadn't. Nothing had survived.

*Just Griffin,* I reminded myself urgently, forcefully. *He survived, dammit. He did!*

Before my friends could encourage me with a hitherto unthought-of yet sensible course of action to retrieve Griffin's body—which surely *wasn't* in the coffin despite appearances, since Magnum and team would never give up all that coveted biological material that they could perform tests on—the priest finally shut his yap. A heavy hush blanketed our gathering as the coffin, gleaming in the sunshine, was lowered into the hole that was intended to hold Griffin's body for eternity.

Despite my unwavering assurance that the man I loved lived—*he's alive, he is*—my shoulders trembled as the shiny wood inched below ground level.

Hunt wrapped an arm around me, tugging me against him. Brady hugged Layla, who for the first time in years didn't shrug off her twin's touch, slumping into him. Brady shuffled them closer to Hunt and me.

When the coffin settled with a muffled thud, my shoulders shuddered another time. Suddenly, all the tears I hadn't shed crowded against the back of my eyeballs, like a torrent rushing a dam too weak to hold back the storm.

Hunt pulled me closer, held me tighter. My face burrowed against his chest, though it wouldn't be shield enough from all the busybodies here to watch the show of our hearts breaking—courtesy of Magnum fucking Chase, yet again.

Behind my sunglasses, I blinked furiously, refusing to reveal weakness before the flock of circling vultures. Hunt ran a soothing hand along my back, though his shoulder shuddered beneath my face, not much, but enough for me to understand he was breaking too.

What if Griffin, who meant everything to the four of us, was beyond our reach?

The five of us were an unbreakable crew.

A family bound by a link greater than blood.

We'd been tight since always.

We were never meant to be four. Five, always five. Only then were we complete.

<*Can we just fucking leave already?*> Layla snarled. <*If I've gotta hug "Uncle Magnum," I'm gonna puke in my mouth, then kill a bitch. And there'll go our angle of surprise.*>

I glanced up from Hunt's chest, and sure enough, Magnum was angling our way, our fake parents behind him, a line starting to form around Orson, Griffin's pretend dad, and us.

Anyone who'd ever seen us together knew we were Griff's real family.

With Magnum twentysomething feet away from us and closing in fast, and his asshole nephew Rich drawing to his side, I barked urgently into our bond: <*Let's go. I can't do it. I can't pretend, not now.*>

No more discussion was needed. However many of us remained, one thing didn't change: We had one another's backs.

Without explanation or so much as an apologetic grimace, the four of us spun and, arms threaded together, stalked rapidly to Brady's Mustang, Bonnie. We were pulling out in a spatter of gravel before I looked back. As one, as if they were part of a single organism, every single person there was observing us making a getaway. Magnum stood at the head of them, a stark reminder that he was the master puppeteer, and potentially every person in Ridgemore his puppet.

Even us.

<*The only way to kill this beast is to cut off its head,*> Hunt said, still speaking through our telepathic bond despite the presumed privacy of the car. We'd learned the hard way it was a luxury Magnum didn't have the courtesy to offer us. And why would he? According to him, we were his *property*, the results of lab experiments he'd funded.

<*So let's hack off his head already,*> Layla hissed, sounding perfectly vicious. <*With a blunt saw.*>

<*Yes,*> I said. <*Def. But first we have to find Griff. We can't tip them off that we know what they're up to before he's with us.*>

Brady glanced at me through the rearview mirror, eyebrows raised. <*Do we know what they're up to?*>

Not specifically. <*We know they'll keep trying to kill us and study us until—*>

<*Until we stop coming back to life,*> Layla said.

My heart thudded.

<*Aw fuck,*> she said in a high pitch that sounded a lot like panic. <*How the fuck are we gonna find him? I need to see him alive, like right the fuck now.*>

<*I hear ya, girl. Do I ever hear you,*> I mumbled.

<*We hack into our parents' computers,*> Hunt said.

Brady whipped his head toward him in the passenger seat. <*You can do that, dude? On your own, I mean? Griff was always the one to do that kind of shit with you.*>

Hunt's eyes glittered with determination, drying up any weakness that had been threatening to leak out of me.

<*I can do it,*> he said. <*Step one: We get in there, start figuring shit out. They keep crazy amounts of records on us. They'll say something about Griff, for sure they will.*>

I found myself nodding along, leaning forward to be closer to the momentum that would lead us to Griffin.

<*What's step two?*> Brady asked.

<*We'll figure that out after step one,*> Hunt said with confidence I was gobbling up.

<*Okay. Okay, yeah,*> Layla said. <*We've got this. After they go to bed tonight, we hack their shit.*>

I didn't know how we'd do it, only that we had to. So we would.

I pushed my sunglasses onto my head and leaned back in my seat, rolling my neck, saying aloud for the invisible audience that constantly trailed our every move, "I'm in the mood to beat shit."

"The treehouse it is, then," Brady said, and he gunned Bonnie. The sleek blue Shelby surged forward.

*We're coming for you, Griff. Just hang on a little longer.*

# 2

## I Do Love It When You Get Murderous

Dear ol' thoughtful "Uncle Magnum" had told Homer, Yolanda, and Armando—collectively our "ninja instructors"—to give us a few days off from training to recover from Griffin's death.

As if a few days would cut it.

As if any amount of time would soothe over our devastating loss.

Since our ninja instructors, along with every other fucking weasel of a person in our small hometown of Ridgemore, were in Magnum's back pocket, they didn't show up this afternoon to kick our ever-loving asses like they had for the last several days—that we remembered. Who knew how many reboots we'd forgotten? How many times we'd trained with them over the years that were pocked full of holes vast enough to swallow entire months of our lives?

I carried a constant morass of disgust deep within my gut. Every day I woke it was with the same churning sensation, as if a strange creep were in bed with me, his curdling leer and hard-on attesting to the fact that I'd experienced a violation of the worst magnitude.

Brady, Hunt, Layla, and I had vented our despair on our punching bags and dummies, sparring till we were bruised and bloodied, chests heaving as if our instructors had led us through one of their grueling workouts after all. And afterward we'd gone for a long, fast run until our lungs had burned and Layla had bent over, begging us to stop. All that hadn't done much to ease the wrath seething inside us. But it had helped to pass the time.

Under the cover of darkness, with Hunt's "mother" Alexis, aka scientist-superspy Marisa, asleep in her room on the second floor of the house, the four of us huddled atop a twin mattress in the sleepover room. When we dragged our usual mattresses from the walk-in closet, we didn't have the heart to leave the fifth behind. All five of them lay spread out across the large room, as if Griffin had just stepped out for a minute and would be returning soon. Since we were young kids we'd had countless sleepovers here. Always the five of us. The whole crew.

We sat with our backs against the wall, low in a corner, where we were likely concealed from whatever cameras the room hid.

Layla leaned her head on my shoulder and said aloud, "Pull up that vid I sent you last night. It's fucking hilarious. The orangutan drives a golf cart like a fuckin' boss while he's playing with his dick and flippin' off his caretakers, who're chasing after him the whole time. It's the best, and I know I could use a laugh."

"Me too," I said on cue. "Def me too."

"You got it." Hunt pulled up the video on the laptop he cradled across his legs. It would play in the background as a decoy while he walked us through our parents' secret files.

For hours, he'd been typing away in a flurry of keystrokes. After he and Griffin had busted through our not-parents' security when we'd discovered the secret lair in my house, they'd beefed up their defenses.

While Hunt hacked, the rest of us did our best to pretend we weren't about to jump out of our skins. It had been one thing to wait a few days since the race under the assumption that Magnum and our parents would unveil a healed and resurrected Griffin—*ta-da!* It was quite another to wait after realizing we'd been dolts for assuming Magnum and our parents would have Griffin's back, if for nothing more than he was one of their precious, irreplaceable experiments.

We knew Magnum was testing the limits of our immortality. Maybe being blown to fiery bits exceeded those limits. Maybe we'd been wasting time while sitting on our hands, time Griffin didn't have.

Hunt's industrious hacking seemed endless. But then—he broke through.

He stopped just before unleashing the mother lode so we could do it together.

Always together.

Forever together.

The grunting of an ape flared to life through the laptop's speakers, though I saw no sign of him, his golf cart, or his agile fingers. A black background with strings of code layered across it covered the screen.

<*Ready?*> Hunt asked us.

*Come on, Griff. Be alive. You've gotta be alive.*

<*Yeah,*> I said into our private chat after Brady and Layla had already agreed.

With his finger poised above the enter button, Hunt sucked in a ragged inhale, another, and yet a third before he finally tapped that command.

The black screen vanished, instantly replaced by a bland desktop with a workflow neatly organized atop it that appeared entirely ordinary for a team of eager-beaver scientists, except for the folders that bore our names in big, bold letters.

I blinked at the blatant evidence of our parents' betrayal while the orangutan *eee-eee-eee*ed off-screen. By now, I shouldn't be surprised.

<*It shocks me every time,*> Layla said.

<*I feel like a dumbass about it, but me too,*> Brady said. <*Like, how much proof do we need before my brain finally stops thinking of them as our parents?*>

<*Apparently still more,*> Layla said miserably.

"Isn't he hilarious?" Layla asked aloud, making a show of pointing at the screen and laughing.

With answers about Griffin's fate potentially mere clicks away, I didn't have it in me to feed the ruse. I left Brady to guffaw, amazed the twins could put on such a convincing performance when my insides were quivering. I could literally feel my organs vibrating for the answers that could either pulverize me or release the band that hadn't stopped cinching my heart since Clyde had erupted into arching flames.

In addition to folders labeled with our names, there were many others with scientific nomenclature. Hunt skipped those, clicking on the one labeled GRIFFIN CONWAY.

My breath snaked in with a hiss and my body froze. The master folder contained dozens of others. Hunt eventually settled on one titled ENTRY LOG.

A tense exhale hissed out while Hunt scrolled to the most recent update. My eyes jumped around the page, scanning the text without actually reading it, too desperate to get the answer I needed more than I needed my next breath.

"Oh holy fuck," I exclaimed before dissolving into unhinged, hysterical laughter that had a few sobs mixed in there.

When I laughed, so did Layla, and together the two of us sounded like loons.

On Hunt's other side, Brady didn't make a sound for several seconds, entirely still.

"This video . . . is so fucking awesome," Hunt breathed for the recording that was undoubtedly being made of us. His voice cracked.

We were all staring at the same string of words:

*Griffin's progress has been remarkable, beyond what we have seen previously in any of the test subjects. His body is nearly finished reconstructing. He received no resuscitation or aid beyond our retrieval of his parts. It appears possibly necessary for them to be placed in close proximity for the bonding to occur. The damage was severe. It is possible we were unable to recover every single part. However, we did recover every piece over two inches in size.*

*Suggestion for further experimentation:*

*Will his body still be able to regenerate if it is missing some of its vital parts? Perhaps omit an internal organ required for sustained life.*

*T.A.D.*

<*T. A. D.,*> Brady said. <*That's Tobias Andrew Dole. Orson.*>

<*Right,*> Hunt said.

Our scientist-parents signed their notes with their real initials, not the fake names they'd fed us all our lives.

<*Guess I'm finally gonna need to make sense of the name jumble I've got goin' on in my head, then,*> Layla said.

I would, too, but I couldn't get that out.

Brady finally laughed, loud and boisterous. Hunt's muscles relaxed some of their tension. And Layla was speaking aloud, some stupid shit about the ape reminding her of Brady.

I was unable to register all of it. My chest cavity felt simultaneously both unbearably full and terrifyingly empty. A flood of relief warred with the fear that had scooped out my insides, that hadn't yet released me from its vicious, clawed grip.

Griffin was alive.

He was *alive*.

*Alive, alive, alive!*

I didn't have to be afraid any longer.

At least, not until Magnum and our faux parents pulled more shit like this—all in the name of science and the betterment of humanity. *Right. Of course.*

The terror of losing Griffin had chilled me to the bone. All at once, I began shivering so hard my teeth clattered together.

My friends' heads whipped in my direction.

"OhmyGod, Joss, what's wrong?" Layla asked aloud, wincing at her slipup.

"No-othing," I stuttered over a vibrating jaw.

Hunt wrapped his arm around me, pulling me close to his side. "Lay, get her a blanket."

"That-t'd be good."

I tried to explain but couldn't get the words out until after Layla tucked a blanket tight around me. I smiled my thanks at her.

She grunted. <*Girl, that smile looks like shit. Are you okay?*>

Brady leaned forward to better study me.

"I . . ." I sucked in a steadying inhale, sank farther into the blanket and Hunt's warmth. "It's just . . . really hard to try to have fun when Griff's gone." *Not dead. Absolutely not dead. Just temporarily gone.*

"Aw," Layla said. "I know, honey." She *never* used sweet endearments. "Losing him's been really rough on all of us."

<*I'll be okay, guys,*> I added privately. <*Just need a minute. I'm getting whiplash from all the back-and-forth. They're toying with us like we aren't real people. Like we don't have real feelings. Like . . .*>

<*Like we're nothing more than lab experiments,*> Hunt supplied with every ounce of bitterness I felt too.

"Cue up another funny vid for us, Hunt," Layla said for our spies.

Hunt complied while Brady growled into our joint mindspace: <*Did you read that shit about suggesting Griff come back again—without some of his important parts? I mean, how many times am I gonna have to murder them all to make up for this shit?*>

My shivering subsided but I continued to lean into Hunt.

<*I never pictured us killing our parents. Just Magnum,*> Brady said. <*But that was* Orson *who said that about Griff. Orson. His*

dad. *What the fuck are we supposed to do with that shit? Orson's okay with torturing his son!*>

<*Not his son,*> Layla said. <*And not his dad.*>

<*Yeah, yeah. Semantics. I want to kill Orson—excuse me,* Tad—*just for that little experiment suggestion alone. I'm . . . I'm fucking* disgusted *with them.*>

<*I am too,*> Hunt said.

<*We have to get Griff out, wherever they've got him stashed, before they go planning any more experiments,*> I said.

Brady met my eyes. <*If we spring 'im, the jig is up. After that, then we'll have to go on the run.*>

I sat up, patting Hunt's shoulder in thanks. <*Then we grab Bobo and we go on the run.*>

The three of them stared at me, the glow of Hunt's screen casting their faces in grim, gray light. It suited our vibe perfectly.

<*Magnum's got endless resources,*> Layla pointed out.

<*I know. But what's our other option? Just sit back while they do all this horrible shit to us? We can't do that.*>

<*If we run, they'll eventually find us and* then *bring us back and kill us.*>

<*Wow, way to keep an optimistic outlook, Lay,*> Brady said.

She shrugged and frowned darkly. <*Just being realistic here.*>

Somebody howled with laughter in whatever video Hunt was playing in the background. I ground out a laugh that hurt.

<*It's why we haven't run already,*> Layla persisted. <*'Cause the only advantage we've got right now is that we know what they're up to—*>

<*Only some of it,*> Brady reminded.

<*Sure. But at least we know something. Better than nothing like before. If they reboot us again, we're so superfucked,* and *they still get to just keep killing us.*>

<*So we run as long as we can. We grab Griff and Bobo and run far and fast.*>

<*He'll find us, Brade. You know he will.*> Layla let her warning hang for a few heavy moments. <*For fuck's sake, he's got a whole team of G.I. fucking Joes working for him—who, by the way, bought into his little savior of the world act. Jaggar would shoot us in the head a thousand times over if he thought it had even a tiny chance of helping his precious, perfect psycho Magnum. I'd bet money Jaggar gets off while he fantasizes about reaming Magnum's asshole.*>

I cringed at the unwelcome imagery.

<*If we run, they* will *find us,*> Layla insisted. <He *will find us. Then our advantage will be wiped out. And who knows if we'll ever get one again. Plus, we don't have enough money to run.*>

<*We have some,*> I said.

<*Some, when Magnum's got more than God.*>

I sighed loudly.

<*Where would we even go?*> she asked.

I shrugged. <*To find Hunt's dad? He knew stuff.*>

Layla scoffed. <*Stuff about "Sky People" and "ancestors" and dreams. How's that gonna help us not get murdered day in and day out? Besides, do we even know if he'd want to help us? He was a sperm donor.*>

Hunt's shoulders slumped on an exhale. <*We don't even know where he is. He might still be locked up at the institute or . . . wherever. A guy like Magnum might have a hundred places like the institute spread out across the globe.*>

<*We could go to the Aquoia res and hope somebody there will want to help us,*> Brady suggested weakly.

Layla just blinked at him until he eventually argued, <*Joss is right. We can't just keep doing what we've been doing.*>

<*Oh, I wholeheartedly agree. But we also can't be morons. We bide our time. Play their stupid, awful game. Look for another advantage. And when we have the shot, we pounce. We take out Magnum and anyone else who stands in our way.*>

<*You do mean we kill him, right?*> Brady asked.

<*Fuck yes I mean we kill him. We kill the fuck out of him. No need to change the only part of our ongoing plan that's solid. We kill the bitch, kill him good, and then we'll be free. Until then, we figure out what we can about ourselves and our powers, we hold the fuck on, and we wait for our chance to murder the rich fuck.*>

Brady nodded along. <*I do love it when you get murderous, baby sis.*>

<*Oh, fuck you. I'm not your baby anything. We're* twins. *A five-minute lead out of our mom's vajayjay . . .*> She pinned a suddenly wide stare on Hunt. <*See if you can find out who our surrogates were.*>

<*A surrogate will be no more mom to us than Celia is,*> Brady said.

<*Probably. But I'd still like to know.*>

<*Me too,*> I said, leaning toward the screen. <*Work your magic, Hunt. Show us. And find out where they've got Griff.*>

Hunt's fingers went to work until I stopped him with a gasp. Everyone looked at me.

<*You haven't noticed yet?*>

I pointed at a simple, seemingly innocuous set of dates.

Layla shook her head with a fierce scowl. <*You've got to be motherfucking kidding me!*>

# 3

## I Got You, Babe

Joss. Joss, honey . . ."

The words were gentle yet persistent as they wove into a deep sleep that was trying to drag me back under its lulling oblivion.

"You need to wake up."

A hand landed on my shoulder, shaking me awake just as I registered the source of the voice.

It was my dad's. No, *Reece*'s. No, that wasn't right either. Judah's. *Jude.*

I should call him *Judas*, perhaps the most notorious traitor in all of history—and a fitting nickname for this asshole.

"Honey, you overslept again. You're going to be late for school if you don't get up and get moving right now."

His weight lifted from the bed—*my bed*, so familiar in feel and scent—as he rose. Completely emotionally spent after hours of scouring the files our faux parents had kept on us since before our conceptions, I'd fallen asleep in Hunt's sleepover room, next to my friends . . .

Not here. Not in this house. And not in this bed.

Thus the cloying grogginess that hung heavy in my muscles and head had nothing to do with a possible few too many beers, and everything to do with the lying, scheming scumbags we were forced to share houses with.

Our faux parents must have drugged us—again—then transported us to our own beds—also again—where they were back to pretending nothing untoward had happened. As if good parents in wholesome, quaint neighborhoods like our Periwinkle Hill drugged their kids and pretended their lives were completely different *allllll the time*.

I half expected the song "I Got You, Babe" to begin blaring through my alarm, marking the start of yet another *Groundhog Day* loop we couldn't escape.

Another weight shifted on the bed and Bobo's wet nose pressed to the crook of my neck, snuffling. For my sweet pittie, I opened my eyes and smiled.

"Hey there, boy," I cooed down at him, my voice a telling rasp.

How many times had they drugged us with who knew what? We were apparently some kind of immortals, sure—crazy as crazy got, but the concept was growing on me—and we had superior healing, my friends especially—but that was no justification for exacting such a heavy toll on our bodies on a regular basis.

It was all just so majorly fucked-up.

I leaned over Bobo, kissing his head and scratching behind his ears and under his chin, two of his main favorite spots. "You're such a good boy, aren't you?"

Bobo's tail wagged in eager agreement, even though he was theoretically supposed to sleep in his bed at the foot of mine instead of next to me. Lately I hadn't been able to resist the comfort of having him beside me. There was a very short list of people whom I could count on never to betray me, and he was one of them—dog or not.

My breath hitched. As the effects of whatever drug receded, I grew more alert. Which meant my thoughts speared toward Griffin. Did this morning's bait and switch have something to do with him? Had he finished . . . regenerating?

I disguised my sharp inhale with noisy kisses for my dog and glanced up at *Judas* leaning casually against my threshold. His hair was damp, his cheeks flushed, suggesting he'd recently returned from his morning run—in time to wake his pretend daughter from her pretend sleep, of course.

None of us had ever accused our parents of not giving their all to this charade. Had the hypnosis not glitched and failed to properly "reboot" us, I didn't even want to consider how long it might have taken us to discover what was really going on. There was that terrifying chance that we might have never caught on, at least not to the full scope of the deception.

Maybe it was true that our parents hadn't started out with the intention of deceiving us, but they'd been embodying their communal lie for so long that they were pros at it. We hadn't stood a chance.

"Don't dilly-dally," *Judas* said. "Griffin will be here to pick you up soon."

My heart thudded. Bobo stopped licking my arm to jerk his head up, canting it to one side, observing me, as if he sensed the change in me.

"And you'll probably want extra time with him before classes today." *Judas*'s expression drooped. Sympathy brimmed in his eyes as he sighed and pushed a hand through his damp hair. "You remember what day today is, right?"

*This fucking bullshit again?*

"Yeah, I do. The day Mitzi abandoned Griff and Orson."

I was quick to stuff my face into Bobo's fur to hide my disgust. Griffin had never had a mom. They'd made one up just to add some tragedy to his backstory.

"That's right," he said. "Griffin will need all your support today."

*Play the game, Joss.*

I slapped matching sympathy on my face and smiled sadly up at him. "Are you gonna be hanging with Orson today?"

"Yeah. Porter and I are going to take him out to a late lunch, grab some beers, play hooky from work. He needs it."

"That's real good of you, Dad." I listened for signs of my lie and detected none. Maybe all it took was practice. Our parents had decades of it.

*Dad* shrugged humbly. "That's what friends do for each other." His eyes danced with mischief. "Though you and Griff are more than friends, huh?"

For an instant my jaw went slack. But I pulled myself together quickly. When he waggled his brows teasingly at me, I pretended to blush while shooing him from my room.

He scooted out with a trail of laughter so convincing I briefly wondered if our parents had missed their calling. They would have killed it as actors.

I bolted from bed so quickly that Bobo leapt off after me with an excited bark. I whipped around toward him.

"Bobo, no!"

He stilled, confused.

I wasn't supposed to remember that Bobo and I had leapt from a rapidly moving Clyde, hitting the pavement hard before rolling. But his body would. He'd broken his leg and recovered without the benefit of paranormal healing abilities.

He stared up at me, tilting his head from side to side, and whined.

My shoulders slumped. I squatted next to him, scratching again behind his ears.

"You did nothing wrong, boy. You're such a good dog. I just don't want you to get hurt, that's all."

He whined again. I gave him some more good scratches, then stood. Excited tingles already raced through my body.

"I've gotta hurry for Griff."

I got ready for school in record time. When the growl of a well-tuned engine drew near—not the one I recognized as Clyde's, since the most recent version of Clyde had been blown to bits along with Griff—I bounced while rubbing absently at my bicep. No doubt the unexplained soreness was from last night's nonconsensual shot.

Too anxious to wait, I started walking up my long drive, and when Griffin drew to a stop beside me, I was far enough away from the house that I didn't have to worry about my superspy not-parents reading into my expression—I didn't think, anyway. Maybe they'd hidden cameras in the car's interior, but probably not on the outside.

As far back as my memory went, Clyde had originally been a shiny silver. Then the car was black. This replacement Mustang was silver, but a more matte paint job than what Griff had used.

The passenger-side window was already lowered, and Griffin leaned across the gearshift to gaze up at me. His smile was vibrant and devilish and absolutely fucking gorgeous. It lit up his face, making the many forest shades of his hazel eyes dance. Man, Griff was the hottest dude I'd ever seen in my entire life.

"Hey, baby," he said in that deep rumbly voice of his that made my toes curl that morning. "You're looking especially fine today."

I had so much I wanted to say to him. All that slipped out was a squeak as I gawped at him, unable to stop taking in the radiance that was Griffin Conway come back to life in one glorious, stunning whole. The man was making my insides smolder simply by existing.

His brow furrowed. "You all right?"

That was my cue to put on a show for anyone listening. After swallowing, I nodded. "Yep." But I sounded like I'd just sucked the helium out of a balloon.

I cleared my throat. "Just happy to see you is all."

He hummed appreciatively, eyeing me up and down. "Before you ask if that's a rocket in my pocket or I'm just happy to see you too, it's both."

He winked, and I swear I fucking swooned. My vision actually wobbled for a fast second.

Me, swooning. Who even was I anymore?

I finally managed a chuckle and lowered myself into shotgun. I was stashing my bag alongside my feet when Griff shifted Clyde into neutral and tugged on the emergency brake. I was about to ask him what he was doing when his hands wove behind my neck and guided me toward him.

His lips were on mine before I registered he was about to kiss me. His lips were full and soft, warm and absolutely freaking delightful.

A growl slipped from me, buzzing against our joined mouths. I wrapped my arms around his shoulders, tugging him closer. Slid across the leather of my seat as I parted my mouth, inviting our tongues to dance, and kissed him and kissed him and fucking kissed him. I kissed him until I could almost forget watching his car explode into nauseating flames, until my heart felt less broken and we were both panting. The cool fall day felt hot, my skin flushed beneath all the stupid clothes that separated my skin from his.

He groaned without breaking our kiss. I moaned back, dragging myself onto his lap, uncaring that the fit was tight. I ran my hands over his shoulders, chest, and back. Wove my fingers into his hair, tugging on the strands, holding him tightly to me.

*Mine, mine, mine*, grumbled a feral part of me I was only now coming to recognize.

I shifted my legs to better straddle him. He moaned again, kissed me even harder, and rolled his hips up to meet mine. His dick was gloriously hard through his jeans.

Breathing heavily, he pulled our mouths apart, pressing his forehead to mine.

"Fuck . . . Joss," he breathed. "I was joking about the rocket in my pocket, but damn, not anymore. Let's skip out on school. I can think of way better things for us to do today than sit through boring classes."

In case I missed his message, he palmed my ass and squeezed appreciatively.

"Fuck yeah, let's skip," I said without hesitation.

His eyes were matching embers alight with passion as he stared at my swollen lips. "All right, then. This sucky day just got loads better."

"Oh, yeah, that's right. I'm really sorry about your mom."

"Thanks. Good of you to remember."

"What she pulled was total shit."

Griffin sighed so that his shoulders rose and fell. I didn't think it was an act.

"Yeah. Thanks."

I groaned loudly.

"What?"

"We can't skip today."

"Why the hell not? We skip all the time. And we've got a really good fucking reason to skip today." He rolled his hips against mine again, running his hands up and down my back, playing with one of the several thin braids I wore today.

"The others will wanna see you." I couldn't be that selfish. I couldn't keep Griffin from them when the last sight they had of him was Brady, desperate to save him, accidentally snapping off his charred arm.

"They also remember today's the anniversary of Mitzi abandoning you guys," I said. "They'll want to be there for you too."

"I know," Griffin said, but his stare had settled on my boobs. "Still, maybe they could be there for me later . . ."

He dipped his head, dragged the tip of his tongue along the swell of one breast, then the other. The length of my spine shuddered, and I suddenly couldn't remember a single good reason why we had to go to school. School could suck it. The others would be down to play hooky.

Noticing my reaction, without warning and in one swift move, he tugged down the neckline of my shirt and the cups of my bra until they hooked beneath my breasts—completely naked and exposed.

I gasped.

The crisp chill hardened my nipples in an instant. Griffin licked his lips like he was about to gorge.

"You're so fucking gorgeous," he rumbled, and my core clenched.

Griff slowly circled one nipple with his tongue, then the other.

"OhmyfuckingGod," I breathed as sensation rocketed from my tits to my core, getting hotter with every passing second.

When he pulled a nipple into his mouth and sucked, my mind went blank and I started grinding across his lap.

"You drive me fucking crazy, woman," he murmured, then sucked my other nipple into that hot, scorching mouth of his.

My vision went hazy. All I could feel was him.

All I wanted was so much more of him.

I didn't even care right then that we'd skipped over the baby steps of courtship. Bypassed the tender, timid kisses, the lingering, hopeful looks, the precious snuggles, and gone straight for the gold.

*The gold*, that's what I wanted right now. I would be pissed at our parents for robbing us of the early stages of our relationship later.

"Griff," I whispered, his name part prayer of gratitude, part automatic reaction, part caution.

He was squeezing my tits and dragging his tongue back and forth across both of them. I hazily wondered if it was possible to black out from pleasure.

"Griff," I tried again.

"Hmm?" he asked without ceasing his ministrations. His cock was like steel beneath me.

"We . . . can't do this . . . right now."

"Why not?" He lapped his tongue up and down one nipple.

"Fu-uu . . . I dunno."

Huskily, he chuckled, and it was the sexiest sound in history.

"I know what you like," he said, and that comment made its way through the fog that consumed me.

How did he know what I liked? Revealing that I loved having my tits sucked and licked wasn't exactly the kind of info shared between platonic friends, not even ones as close as we all were. Sure, Layla might try to get us to reveal our deepest, darkest desires, but we didn't go for it.

Which meant either Griffin and I had gotten hot and heavy during other reboots I had no memory of—in which case, fuck the not-parents superhard for robbing me of that—or Griffin was going off info from a recent hypnosis I hadn't received, which seemed likely, given that he genuinely seemed saddened by "Mitzi's" abandonment.

"Griff, stop."

Instantly, he released a nipple with a *pop* and looked at me, waiting.

"I . . . shit, just know I only want you to stop doing that right now for this one limited exception. Otherwise, don't ever stop, please, never ever."

The confusion slipped away, and the sparkling embers were back in his eyes. He gave me a sexy-as-fuck smile that lifted only one side of his mouth.

"Why stop now, then?"

"Well, for one . . ." I blinked away more of my daze. I was drunk on Griffin Conway. I blinked some more, tried again. "For one, we're parked in my parents' driveway."

"Not ideal, I'll give ya that."

"And two, the others will be waiting for us."

*<And we've got a whole hell of a lot of catching you up to do.>*

At hearing my voice inside his head, Griffin's eyes startled wide, and he jumped enough for me to bounce across his lap and smack my head on Clyde's ceiling.

"Oh shit! Are you okay?" he asked immediately, his eyes losing their shock and filling with concern for me.

I rubbed at my head. "I'm fine."

*<But you gotta play it cool and not let on that you can hear me in your head, or you'll blow the only advantage we have.>*

He was back to breathing heavily, now for an entirely different reason.

*<I take it you had no idea we can talk to each other telepathically?>*

Slowly, he shook his head.

*<Then we have a literal shit-ton to update you on. This is megaimportant: You've gotta pretend everything's normal till we can get someplace private. Clyde is bugged, probably with cameras too.>*

His stare shot to my naked boobs.

I shrugged. *<It's either let them see or not get to share this with you. I'd rather share this with you.>* I let him see how my eyes softened. *<I'd rather share everything with you.>*

Eyes still glazed with surprise, I could tell he didn't know what to think or do.

*<Let's just get to the others, then we'll talk.>*

His throat bobbed but he nodded.

"We'd better go or we're gonna be late for first period," I said aloud, certain I couldn't possibly care less about our pretend school.

"Okay," he croaked.

His hands were still wrapped around my breasts. My nipples hadn't gotten the memo that we had to play a part we had no interest in playing and continued to strain to reach his mouth.

With a mischievous smile, I ground along his hard-on for a few too-quick moments.

"You can't do that and expect me to go anywhere but inside you," Griff growled, all shock absent from his eyes, which were back to burning for me.

I groaned without meaning to. I ground along his dick again, and this time deposited a heavy boob in his mouth. Instantly he sucked on it.

My head fell back, my spine arched. I wanted to live in this moment for eternity.

Like a proper gentleman, he gave my other boob equal attention before asking me, "Which is it, baby? Tits or school? Making love or classes?"

"God, when you put it that way, is there even a question?"

"No. There isn't." He lowered his tongue to my breasts again, trailing his hands along my thighs.

"Fuck my life," I grunted angrily. "We gotta get to school. But know that this is, like, the hardest fucking decision of my life."

He pumped his erection up against me. "Hardest, no doubt about that."

Cursing a furious string of expletives the entire time, I tucked away my tits—he groaned like it was one of the greatest losses of his life—and lifted off his lap. I slammed onto the passenger seat with a smack, as if it were its fault our parents and Magnum were the biggest dickwads in the entire universe. I crossed my arms over my chest, not bothering to smooth over my pout, and grumbled sullenly: "Drive."

Griffin stared at me for several beats before adjusting himself. His dick bulged against his zipper, the straining fit looking painful.

I was staring at the hard dick I was missing out on when he growled out: "Fine. But be forewarned, I might just set the whole place on fire for making me miss out on you."

"You and me both, buddy. I'm in a burn-it-all-down mood."

Fuck, was I ever.

# 4

# The Truman Show, Psycho Style, Baby

With his eyes darting toward me almost as often as to the road, Griffin zipped Clyde out of the Periwinkle Hill neighborhood without picking up Hunt. By the time the blaze of Griffin's desire ebbed, and the crotch of his jeans loosened, his right hand wasn't on the gearshift but was running through his hair, leaving the dark strands messy and mussed, a clear sign of his agitation—and an indication I was going to struggle to keep my hands off him. His hair standing up in all different directions was sexy as fuck, like we'd been pressed to the bed together all night.

A slight frown tugged at his mouth. He probably had a million questions but was heeding my warning, too confused, stunned, and cautious to ask any.

I should use the time to update him. I mean, obviously. There was so much to tell him! But all of it was as unpleasant as a surprise sucker punch to the gut on a full stomach. He'd startled so hard when he heard me speak into his mind.

But Griff was chill under pressure. He'd roll with things until he understood—and then he'd probably want to course correct and speed over to "Uncle Magnum's" to murder the fucker while he sat at the breakfast table.

My stare hadn't left Griffin since he'd rocketed up my driveway. I couldn't stop admiring his every perfect detail. There wasn't a single blemish on him that I could spot around his Thrasher t-shirt that exposed his arms. There was just smooth, tanned skin, sculpted by lean muscles and highlighted by the weaving bands and swirls of his tattoos.

The last time I'd seen that flesh it had been a charred crisp that flaked off the bone. Or perhaps worse, it had been covered in red boils and blisters, the meat beneath the skin not yet cooked. The smell . . . oh God, the smell. Too reminiscent of putrid barbecue when I knew I was smelling the burnt body of the man I loved.

His car—*this car*, sort of—had blown up like a cask of gunpowder. The explosion had brightened the night more than the plumpest moon. There'd been nothing to dampen the senses, to disguise the visceral signs that Griffin was burning with us mere feet away and unable to do a single damn thing to prevent it. The adrenaline that pumped through my veins had made the sizzling smell, the popping and crackling of the consuming fire, the taste of meat in the suddenly sweltering night air, and the sight of the Mustang reducing to its steel skeleton all the more vivid.

"Stop the car," I mumbled on a cresting wave of nausea.

Already slowing, Griffin's eyes were on me immediately. "What's going on? Are you okay?"

*Fuck no, I'm not okay. I'll probably never be okay again.*

With my hand hovering around my mouth, I said the first thing I could think of for our invisible audience's benefit. "A rock. In the tire. On my side."

Griffin's eyebrows arched at the glaring absence of the clicking against the pavement that signaled said stone lodged in the tread of a tire.

"Pulling over," he said.

The moment he drew to a complete stop on the shoulder—I'd never jump out of a moving vehicle again, thank you very much—I hopped out, bolting for the nearest bramble of bushes.

I puked, heaved, then puked again before I finally realized I was shaking, and that at some point Griffin had begun rubbing a soothing hand over my back, not saying anything, just being there for me like he always was.

When I couldn't bring up even bile anymore, I staggered away from the patch of vomit and collapsed onto my butt on the grass. Griffin lowered himself next to me, still rubbing my back, still waiting. When I swiveled to point my face away from the curious looks of passing drivers, he turned with me.

"You okay, baby?" he eventually asked, his voice deep as always, but as calming as a swaddling blanket. I could wrap myself up in the sexy lull of his voice and remain there forever.

I shook my head, tucking some of my loose strands behind my ears. "I must've eaten something that didn't sit well." My voice was a croak, inconsistent with my first story of a stone in the tire.

"Don't worry. I'll remember to check the tire before we get back on the road," Griffin said.

He'd always been sharp. Didn't matter that he'd essentially been thrown into the deep end without knowing how to swim. He was treading water like a champ regardless.

"I'm only worried about you right now."

"I'll be fine," I lied. "Just need to catch my breath for a few, that's all."

I leaned my head on his shoulder, breathing in his fragrance: his usual soap that reminded me of fresh, crisp mountain air, and today the faint scent of sawdust and leather, as if he'd been working on cars, not coming back from the dead. I willed this smell—of him so wonderfully alive—to overwrite the memory of his burning flesh.

I shuddered.

"Hey," he soothed, rubbing a hand along my thigh. "I need to get you home."

"No," I said, too fast, too forcefully. *Home* was the place our not-parents lived, though it seemed he wouldn't know that.

"I'll stay with you."

I was shaking my head again but had to stop when another wave of nausea rolled through me.

"I don't have to stay with you if you don't want," Griffin offered.

I squeezed his hand. "Of course I want you to stay with me. It's not that."

"Then what is it?" He bit his lip, probably remembering how I told him our conversations weren't our own.

"Like I said, just something I ate."

I sucked in a fortifying breath, rubbed my tongue along my teeth—no longer minty fresh, yuck.

<*You died,*> I told him.

He stiffened but didn't say anything. Whether that was because he didn't know how to or because of the gravity of the news he likely wasn't expecting, I didn't know.

<*It was . . . God, Griff, it was so fucking awful. Like, the worst thing ever, by a long shot.*>

He let out a long, shaky exhale, but never stopped rubbing my thigh, comforting me.

<*I didn't know . . .* we *didn't know if you'd be able to come back from that. You died once before—*>

He jerked his body back so he could look at me. "What?"

<*Remember, not out loud. Try talking to me through our thoughts like this. It's actually really easy once you know you can do it. Just . . . think at me.*>

He nodded, cleared his throat as if preparing to speak aloud, then, hesitantly, <*Is it working?*>

I smiled, easier now that the side of his body was pressed against mine. The grass was wet enough to dampen the seat of my jeans. I'd care in a bit, but I couldn't bring myself to care just yet.

<*Yeah, it's working.*>

<*Oh.*> He gave me a *Hmmph, whaddya know, that was easy* arch of his mouth and brows.

<*You've died twice*,> I told him.

His eyes grew wide, their hazel churning, troubled.

I gulped as my memory assaulted me with the acerbic sounds of sliding gravel, next the crunching, creaking, and straining of steel as Griffin went over the cliff in Clyde. Then, that awful, disturbing, terrifying silence.

Fuck, a decade of therapy might not make a dent in my trauma. Swallowing again, I winced.

"Think you could hand me my water? It's in my bag. My mouth tastes like something died up in it." I winced again. What a fucking poor choice of words.

He disengaged from me gently. "Yeah, of course. Sorry, should have thought of that."

I *tsk*ed. "Nothing to be sorry for. You're being wonderful." I received the bottle with a smile of thanks.

As composed as I was going to get, I told him, <*Both times you died, you died in Clyde.*>

His brow drew low, shadowing the trouble that wasn't leaving his eyes now. <*What? How?*> He looked at Clyde with open suspicion.

<*First time, Magnum cut the brake line. Well, I'm sure he didn't do it himself, just had one of his minions—*>

<*Uncle Magnum?*> His brows couldn't furrow any more deeply. Lines bunched between them.

I chortled darkly. <*Yeah,* Uncle fucking Magnum. *You're gonna hate his guts like nobody's business, trust me. You're gonna wanna slit him from balls to throat and rip out his insides.*>

<*Fuck.*> He ran his free hand through his hair some more.

<*There's so much to update you on, it ain't funny, dude. They've fucked with us so much and for so long. Get ready for your mind to be blown.*>

<*My mind is already blown.*>

<*Well, it's gonna blow sky-high. For real. The second time you died . . .*> I swallowed, drank more water, nibbled on my lip. <*. . . Magnum planted explosives in Clyde.*>

He gaped at me.

<*Even though we checked Clyde over, and we were real thorough after the tampering with the brake line from before, we missed it. They packed C-4 into the cushion of the back seat. Closed it up like pros. Our asses were over it the whole ride over to the crossroads, and we had no clue.*>

<*What? But . . . how? We built Clyde from the bones up . . .*> But he trailed off, glancing once more at his baby. <*So that's not my Clyde?*>

<*Nope. Sorry to say, not sure how many Clydes you've gone through without even knowing it.*>

<*That's not possible.*> Only the hand raking through his hair told me he was already accepting that it was. He'd never doubt me.

<*Do you remember the drag race? Against Rich in the Aston Martin Valkyrie?*>

He shook his head slowly.

<*Yeah,*> I said with a scowl of disgust. <*News flash: They can erase our memories and plant whatever they want.*>

His mouth dropped open. <*No.*>

<*I only wish I could tell you it ain't true.*>

<*So . . . Uncle Magnum's . . . doing all this to us?*>

<*He's the head honcho. But our parents are in league with him.*>

He barked an incredulous laugh. <*Our parents? No way. They're fucking lame-ass nerds.*>

<*I'm serious.*>

His mouth dropped open again and took a few seconds to close.

<*There's so much, seriously. Maybe we do skip after all. I'm sure the others won't mind. They're as desperate to see you as I was. And we need to get you up to speed.*> I scowled. <*Really, it might be a matter of our survival.*>

I slid my phone from my back pocket. <*You good with missing classes?*>

<*Is that even a question?*>

I smiled but it fell quickly. Our lives were so royally fucked.

All too aware that our text messages were being monitored, my thumbs flew across the screen of my iPhone.

**Me:** U guys up for playing hooky? Just had a puke fest on the side of the road. Griff's with me.

Twenty seconds later, my phone lit up with the first of several messages.

**Layla:** Yas, bitch! Skool can suck it!

**Layla:** We'll stop by the front office on our way out. Tell em U R puking.

*Great.*

**Layla:** We're loading up in Bonnie now. Where we goin?

**Me:** Treehouse?

Griffin was reading over my shoulder.

<*You sure you're up for that? You were just hurling.*>

My phone buzzed in my hand, but I smiled at him sadly instead of checking it. <*My stomach's fine. I haven't even eaten yet today. Seeing you, it all just caught up to me.*>

He only continued to regard me.

<*Last time I saw you, you were . . .*> My eyes misted, and he tugged me closer, rubbing his thumb back and forth across my shoulder. I swallowed thickly, certain I'd never get over the terror of losing him—motherfucking *twice*—so long as I lived. <*You were inside Clyde, and Clyde was a fireball. For real, a raging inferno. Total nightmare material. Your body . . .*> Tears slipped free without my permission, rolling down my cheeks. Good thing I wore waterproof mascara and eyeliner. <*It was so awful, Griff.*>

<*Aw, baby.*> He pressed a kiss to the crown of my head, and I wanted to freeze time to remember that kiss forever, instead of all the tragedy, all the fucking torment, all the injustice we had no idea how to escape.

<*The shock probably would've hit me sooner, but before I could process, your tongue was in my mouth.*> And I was thinking of other body parts of his I wanted to get inside me as quickly as possible.

He chuckled. <*I can't keep my hands to myself when it comes to you.*>

<*And I don't want you to.*>

We gazed at each other, our eyes softening, until my phone buzzed again.

**Layla:** Treehouse it is.

**Layla:** And hurry the F up. I wanna C U guys.

Meaning, she wanted to see Griffin. The guys too.

**Me:** On the way.

<*They've been as freaked as me,*> I explained. <*We even had to attend your funeral.*>

<*My funeral?*> Griff shook his head in stunned disbelief as he reached his hand to help me up—slowly.

Once I was on my feet, not as steady as I'd like, he asked again, <*You sure you're all right?*>

I leaned into his chest. <*Even if I were still puking my guts out, I'd be all right. You're here. In one beautiful piece. So yeah, I'm fucking all right. So long as you're with me, I'm all right.*>

I wobbled a bit on the way to the passenger side, but I felt steadier once tucked into Clyde's bucket seat. Griff closed my door and circled the front to his side.

As he merged into traffic, I said, <*We're gonna have to start at the beginning to make sure we don't forget to fill you in on anything, but wanna hear something wild we just found out last night?*>

<*Definitely.*>

<*I'd ask you to guess first, but no way could you guess it. I'm still struggling to believe it, and I've already had my mind blown so hard there's no piecing it back together to what it used to be, not ever.*>

<*Okay. I'm super curious.*>

<*Hunt hacked into our parents' computer network last night. Oh, by the way, our parents aren't our parents at all, in case I didn't make that clear already. We all had surrogates. We checked out their names but we didn't recognize any of them.*>

Griffin was looking from me to the road and back again, his mouth slightly ajar. <*Our parents . . . aren't our parents?*>

<*Nope. They're fucking* liars. *Every single one of them. Actually, I'm gonna start calling them lie-rents, that'll be easier.*>

<*Wow.*>

<*So much wow, dude. You're seriously not gonna believe this shit.*>

<*So what's the thing?*>

<*You know how we all just turned eighteen a little bit ago?*>

<*Yeah . . .*>

<*Well, turns out we're not eighteen.*>

<*Whaddya mean, we're not eighteen? How the hell not?*>

<*They lied to us about our birth years. Probably so they could reboot us who knows how many times. Lied to us about pretty much everything. You know that old Jim Carrey movie* The Truman Show*?*>

<*Mm-hmm. We saw it ages ago, right? It was randomly on TV in the middle of the night when we were all toked out. Don't remember all that much of it.*>

<*Yeah, that one. Picture Ridgemore as* The Truman Show, *only way more psycho. Like, waaaaaaaaay more psycho.* Majorly *more psycho. With killers on the loose, trying to kill us all the damn time, Magnum's goons with a hard-on for the lot of us, just so they can lap up his praise like good little pets. It's so messed up I still haven't wrapped my mind around it all the way. I keep forgetting. Keep thinking our lie-rents are our parents, that our classmates are real people, not just assholes on Magnum's payroll, or however he's getting them to do all this.*>

<*Shit. I guess I really do need you to start from the beginning. You don't mean . . . everyone in town is in on . . . whatever this is you're telling me about, right?*>

<*Yeah, bro, I absolutely do. Told ya. It's bonkers squared.*>

"Holy shit," he said, accidentally whispering it aloud. "That's a sweet car," he added quickly, covering beautifully.

<*So how old are we, actually?*>

<*Twenty fucking two.*>

<*Twenty-two,*> he repeated, his deep voice pitched with incredulity, as if trying the new number out. <*Damn, dude.*>

<*Mm-hmm. They stole four years of our lives and don't feel bad about it a fucking bit. All we are is experiments to them, to do with as they please. None of them really give a fuck about us, though our lie-rents tell us they love us every chance they get.*>

<*Why? Why are they doing this?*>

<*We'll get there. Let's wait for the others.*>

<*Not sure I can wait.*>

<*I know the feeling. But better to wait so we can cover it all. Together.*>

He clasped my hand, squeezed my fingers on the straight stretch of road when he didn't need to shift. <*Always together, baby.*>

<*Love the sound of that.*> I chuffed. <*Guess that explains why Brade's been a fuckin' horndog for so long.*>

Griffin chuckled. <*That, or it's just the way he is.*>

<*Well, there is that. Maybe it just runs in the twins.*> I chuckled as well, then referenced aloud a passing car to cover for us.

I hated the constant lies everyone fed us. All the fakeness, the ruses, the fact that we couldn't believe a single thing anyone ever told us.

But even more than that, I hated that *we* had to lie, to pretend, to hide when we'd never wanted to be anything but ourselves.

Ridgemore was a typical small town. Some might claim it was boring here, but we'd carved out a place for ourselves. We'd adventured, had fun, found peace in the woods and the natural beauty of these misty mountains.

I'd never before felt the urge to escape Ridgemore. To travel elsewhere, sure, maybe even to see the world. But now I wanted to load up our cars with our crew and drive off into the sunset, pedals to the metal, putting Ridgemore and everyone in it permanently in our rearview.

Gazing out the window, I leaned my forehead against it and sighed. <*At least this time around we're allowed to be together, if that's what you remember.*>

Griffin stiffened. <*We weren't before?*>

<*Nope. They've been messing with everything about our lives. They kept us apart for a long time. I think, anyway. It's hard to be sure about anything, really.*>

<*They kept us apart?*> Griffin growled into our bond as he took the turn back into the Periwinkle Hill neighborhood. The vein along his neck bulged, making him look angrier than he'd been when I told him we'd been robbed of four entire years of our lives.

<*Yeah*,> I said sadly. <*Earlier, you made it sound like we've made love before. If we really have, I have no memory of it.*>

Griffin huffed angrily, that vein popping more. <*Oh, I'm so gonna murder some assholes.*>

<*I think we're all gonna have to before this is over. They aren't leaving us any other choice.*>

<*Griff!*> Layla's voice popped into our conversation. <*Ohmyfuckinggawd, it's really you!*>

Griffin startled at the sound of her in his head, glancing sharply at me.

<*Oh yeah*,> I said. <*Didn't have a chance to tell you. When we're close enough to each other, we can all talk together. We can't do private. If we're close, we're all gonna hear.*>

<*Bro!*> Brady chimed in. <*Hurry up and get here already! We'll wait for you at the parking spot.*>

<*We're almost there*,> Griffin said, rounding a turn fast enough to squeal tires a little.

<*Man, is it good to hear your voice*,> Hunt said, his relief palpable through my mind.

Griffin looked at me and smiled. Our private time was over, but at least in moments our crew would be together again.

It was exactly how we were meant to be.

And we'd kill every single motherfucker who ever tried to tear us apart.

It was time to get to the murdering part of our plan. *The Truman Show*, psycho style, baby. It was time to weapon up.

# 5

## To Carpe Our Fucking Diem

Layla scrounged some toothpaste for me in her purse, which was an otherwise unremarkable marvel that reminded me of Mary Poppins's handbag. Girl almost always had the random thing I needed, having my back. Probably the only time she'd needed tampons and didn't have any stashed in there led me to discover that our lie-rents had a secret superspy lair, and that our entire lives were a carefully orchestrated deception. It was almost as if Layla's Mary Poppins purse had our backs too.

If only it were actually possible to have a team of animated objects watching out for our interests, we wouldn't feel so alone. We sure as fuck could use some allies. It truly was us against the world. No matter how vast the globe was, there was nowhere for us to hide that Magnum wouldn't find us eventually, most likely sooner rather than later.

Even so, now that I'd scrubbed my mouth, every sign of my earlier nausea was gone.

The five of us were together again, that was what mattered most.

*My crew.*

*My family.*

Here with me.

I kept finding myself caressing the hairline scar that sliced my palm, similar to the scars my four friends also had, a faded sign of one of our very first friendship pacts. I caught Brady circling his friendship bracelet around his wrist over and over. We'd all started with handwoven bracelets of our own, but his was the only one that remained. Frayed and worn, his had outlasted all of ours.

I noticed the twins, Hunt, and I staring at Griffin often, as if we were quietly afraid he would disappear on us somehow, his presence some ploy or artifice that might still be ripped away from us. I recognized the haunting of my own face in theirs. All but Griffin, who didn't remember the horrors with which we were burdened. What a very different thing it was to hear of another's death than to be there to witness it firsthand. This Griffin had no recollection of the Fischer House party or the downward spiral of awful discoveries that had ensued since then.

Fall was slowly settling into the mountains of Ridgemore in veils of nightly mystical-looking mists that didn't dissipate until late morning. The ground was cool, too chilled to lie on for extended periods of time. Regardless, the five of us lay sprawled out in the clearing in front of our treehouse, our heads huddled together and our bodies spread out like five spokes of a wheel. Better yet, like a star. As a whole, we weren't usually ones to hold hands, especially not Brady, who was quick to make known his opinion that hand-holding was for wusses. Today, though, he didn't complain, and when Griffin laced his fingers with mine, Brady snatched my other hand. Layla and Hunt were quick to complete our starry circle.

Initially, we'd headed outside to avoid the many bugs we knew to be concealed in our treehouse. But once we escaped them, Hunt's warning rang loudly: We wanted to believe no one had violated our bodies and wills and planted chips inside us, but we weren't willing to risk our minuscule advantage on the hope that they hadn't. At every turn, our lie-rents had abused our trust. Magnum had never had it and contentedly leaned into his *devil you know* persona.

So we'd put on a brief performance within range of the listening devices, claiming to want to meditate like the Shaolin monks do to improve our ninja skills. While we *meditated*, we didn't need to concern ourselves with carrying on aloud with frivolous chatter to cover for the telepathic conversations we were silently having—in case we were secretly chipped. Under the guise of meditating, in an hour that had flown by—Layla, for once, focused on our goal—we'd updated Griffin on everything substantial he'd been forced to forget.

<*I'm still having trouble believing it, guys,*> he said. <*It's just not absorbing well.*>

<*Totally know the feeling, dude,*> Brady said. <*Half the time I think of our mom as Mom, but then sometimes it's Celia, sometimes it's Jackie. It's a jumbled mess, man.*>

Layla scoffed through our link. <*Looks like my dumbass brother forgot Ms. Gail's counting lessons.*>

<*The fuck you talkin' about?*>

<*You said half, then listed three parts.*>

Annnnd apparently Layla's focus time had drawn to an abrupt end.

<*So what are we figuring happened, then?*> I interjected quickly. <*The four of us went to sleep last night at Hunt's house. We wake up, we're all in our own beds, and Griff's alive and back in his bed too.*>

I paused for several moments just to enjoy that fact. Griff squeezed my hand; I squeezed back, the heat of his palm such a welcome sign he was here, part of our starry circle, his heart beating once more.

<*My arm hurt this morning, like they shot me up.*>

<*Me and Brady too,*> Layla said in a grumble. <*The motherfuckers.*>

<*Hunt?*> I asked.

<*Yup.*>

<*And you, Griff?*>

<*Nope. I didn't hurt anywhere. No new scars that I could see either. Though maybe you'll help me out later, Joss, and make sure I'm right.*>

<*Mmmreow,*> Layla purred. <*Joss is gonna get some.*>

<*According to whatever hypno stuff Griff was fed,*> I said, <*he and I've already been getting some. Only, obvi, I don't remember that, if we even have at all. For all we know, that might just be an implanted memory for Griff.*>

<*Or it coulda happened,*> Layla countered, <*and then they wiped it away for you.*>

<*Could be.*> My mouth settled into a severe line. Seriously, if they erased my first time with my best friend slash lover, I was gonna kill Magnum and the lie-rents twice.

<*So Griff remembers you and him together,*> Brady said, <*but what else? 'Cause I'm assuming they prob subjected us to the same hypno shit, right? And it just didn't take with the rest of us for some reason. Hunt?*>

<*I've been thinking about that,*> Hunt answered. <*If they did try to hypnotize us, which it seems very likely they did since Jackie said it's been their MO—*>

<*Which one's Jackie again?*> Griffin asked.

<*Our mom,*> Brady offered.

<*Our* not-mom,> Layla corrected. <*Joss, dude, totally diggin' the* lie-rents *term. I'm gonna totes use that shit. I've been so over wanting to call them our parents in my head.*>

<*Legit,*> Brady said.

<*Maybe the hypno didn't take,*> Hunt continued, <*'cause our brains are resistant to it now.*>

<*How so?*> Layla asked.

<*Like, remember how Jackie said she hadn't erased our memories, she just created a bypass around them with the new implanted memories? It sounds like she didn't even overlay our old, real memories with the new ones, just diverted their path. So if our memory's supposed to go in a straight line, instead, after her bypass, it shoots off—*>

<*Shoots off,*> Brady said on a boyish chuckle.

I could feel Layla rolling her eyes. <*You're such a boy.*>

<*What? Tell me you didn't think the same thing, and I won't believe you.*>

Layla was silent. She totally thought the same thing. The twins were cut from the same cloth in more ways than just genetics.

Hunt, used to their constant interruptions and detours, rolled on as if they hadn't spoken.

<*Our memories now veer off in a loop, like a . . . like a looping ramp onto the interstate, and then merge back with our true memories. Though, it gets a shit-ton more complicated 'cause it sounds like they've rebooted us who knows how many times.*>

<*The fucking bastards,*> Layla bit out.

<*Hear, hear,*> grumbled Brady.

<*If our true memories are a straight line,*> Hunt went on, <*it's possible we have hundreds of these bypass loops that keep circling around to meet with the original line.*>

<*Okay,*> I said. <*And how's that explain why the hypno didn't take this time?*>

<*I'm guessing the fact that we know about the bypasses somehow prevents them from forming. Like, now that our conscious minds are aware of the fucked-up shit she's been doing to our subconsciouses, our conscious minds are preventing her from creating any more of her fucking bypasses.*>

<*And she doesn't know this . . .*> I said, feeling a slight tingle of excitement sweep through me. Could this finally be another

advantage? I was ready to start collecting the fuck out of the bitches!

<*She doesn't,*> Hunt said, <*since she doesn't know that one hypno sesh when the recording cut out didn't work on us. We all heard what she was saying, all the thoughts she was trying to implant into our minds.*>

<*It's like the curtain in Oz falling to reveal the wizard pulling the levers,*> I offered. <*Now that we've seen the wizard, there's no putting the curtain back up.*>

<*Exactly. At least, that's my working theory.*>

Any of Hunt's "working theories" was always based on tons of research the brainiac did. Dude loved reading even more than I did.

<*So what about Griff?*> Brady asked. <*This new hypno stuck for him.*>

<*There's one difference between Griff and us right now.*>

<*I died after the curtain dropped,*> Griffin said softly, as if still struggling to believe it.

From beside me, I felt Brady shudder. <*You did, dude, and I don't want you to ever do that shit again. It was fuckin' awful.*>

<*The worst ever,*> Layla agreed, <*and that's taking into account that Brade had a pole the size of my arm straight through his chest.*>

<*If we could sue for emotional damage, we'd come out rich as fuck,*> Brady said.

<*Anyone else been having nightmares about it all?*> Layla asked.

<*Maybe,*> I said. <*I wake up feeling uneasy but then don't remember why.*>

<*Could just be our lives,*> Brady said on a bitter snort. <*We're living out some dark-ass shit.*>

<*And dying too,*> I said with another hard squeeze of Griffin's hand.

*He's here. He's real. He's not going anywhere.*

But that was willful denial, now wasn't it? If Magnum and the lie-rents had proven anything, it was that they could take from us, whatever they wanted, whenever they wanted, and there was fuck all we could do to stop them in the end.

My friends were quiet for long enough for me to realize the ground's cold was seeping into my bones.

<*If we accept Hunt's theory as our working one for now . . .*> I said.

<*'Course we do,*> Layla said. <*What else we gonna do?*>

<*Right. Well, if so, then it seems that our, ah, dying somehow wipes out the conscious awareness that prevents Jackie from erecting the bypasses.*>

<*Erecting,*> Brady said.

Layla was already chuckling.

I snorted at their antics but continued. <*Obvi, we try not to die as much as possible. But . . .*>

<*But them bitches got a ragin' hard-on for killing us,*> Layla said, eloquent as always.

<*Exactly. We should maybe write ourselves letters explaining some of this, just in case.*>

Just in case we all die again.

<*Great idea,*> Hunt said. <*But no clue where we'd stash them that we'd be sure to find.*>

<*We can't just hide them in our rooms?*> Griffin asked.

<*No,*> I said. <*They snoop. Remember that lone pearl earring we found in my room that one time?*>

<*No, sorry.*>

<*It doesn't matter. Just that it was Monica's, or Lynne's, or what the fuck ever. They're up in our business all the time, sniffing around.*>

<*We have no idea how far up our asses their noses go,*> Layla elaborated.

<*Ewwww,*> Brady said.

<*Always such colorful descriptions,*> Hunt said. I couldn't decide if he might actually mean it as a compliment or not.

<*Okay. But we find a place to hide the notes,*> Griff said. <*And then what?*>

Then what, indeed.

<*We kill Magnum and go on the run,*> I said, <*possibly to the Aquoia res, going off what Hunt's dad said to us and assuming they even want us there.*>

<*He seemed legit,*> Brady said.

<*So did the lie-rents,*> Layla quipped.

<*Touché,*> Brady granted.

<*Or we run first,*> I went on, <*to the res or not, and hope Magnum doesn't find us.*>

<*Without adequate funds or resources,*> Layla pointed out.

<*Mm-hmm,*> I agreed grimly.

<*We'd need Jason Bourne–level skills to hide from Magnum, and we saw how that went for Bourne. His boo was murdered.*>

<*It was a movie,*> Brady said.

<*But no crazier than our lives have been recently. Less crazy, actually. He was a spy. We're teenagers. Or twentysomethings anyway. Still not used to being twenty-two. It's so fucked.*>

<*Can't argue with that,*> said the man who was prone to argue with his twin about practically everything. <*Our lives have been weirder than Jason Bourne shit. That's saying something.*>

<*No doubt, bro, no doubt.*>

<*If we don't run,*> I said, <*our only other option is to stay and fight.*>

<*And he's got all them G.I. Joes,*> Layla said. <*Which leads us right back to needing to be Jason Bourne, which we're not, no matter how much Brade parades his junk around in his Ninjas R Us costume.*>

<*Hey!*> he protested. <*Enough already with this shit. You're just jealous.*>

<*Ha. What might I possibly be jealous of when it comes to you?*>

<*That kind of lengthy list'll take time to put together. And I did too look like a ninja.*>

<*Ninjas don't wear wetsuits.*>

<*It wasn't a wetsuit, ya dolt!*>

<*It wasn't ninja-wear either.*>

<*How—?*>

<*Guys,*> I stepped in.

Self-awareness wasn't either of their strong suits, yet they silenced instantly for once, as if feeling the weight of the dangers pressing in on us.

<*When I stop giving Brady shit,*> Layla whispered down our link, <*then you'll know I'm really dead.*>

<*Let's find a way where there's no more dead,*> I said.

<*But how?*> Griffin asked. <*We run or we fight. Okay. But how do we fight an enemy so much stronger than us?*>

<*Maybe we get lucky and find some allies.*>

Layla scoffed.

<*The lie-rents did write us little secret notes saying they wanted to help us.*>

<*And they lied to us from forever,*> Layla said. <*They'd sell us out for a pretty Nobel in a hot second.*>

<*She's got a point,*> Hunt said.

<*There's gotta be* some *good in them though.*> When none of my friends begrudged me even that faith, I added, <*Right?*>

<*Like I said,*> Layla answered. <*The Nobel Prize.*>

<*Okay, so then maybe one of the new students at the institute.*>

<*Like the one we saw running for his life and being taken down like a bitch? They've got* heavy weaponry. *Artillery kinda shit.*>

But Hunt jumped in. <*We don't know who they've recruited. Maybe there's a chance there. We'd just have to infiltrate the place.*>

<*And not get taken down ourselves,*> Layla said.

<*How about our ninja instructors?*> I persisted. <*I caught Armando giving us thoughtful looks.*>

<*He's hot,*> Layla said.

<*Yolanda seemed potentially sympathetic too.*>

<*She's hot,*> now Brady said. <*I'd take her sweet, tight ass out for a spin.*>

Layla barked a laugh. <*Yolanda would crush you between those muscled thighs of hers. You'd be dust.*>

<*Might still be worth it.*>

Griffin chuckled, and the rolling sound was like a balm to the pulpy, healing mess that was my heart.

<*You're both idiots,*> he said, somehow making the insult sound loving.

Layla and Brady laughed, too, and my heart grew a fraction more buoyant. We had no plan and too few answers, but having one another had always been enough before. Why couldn't it be now?

*Because there's a murderous psycho after you all?* suggested a pesky and annoying voice of reason.

<*We also need to consider these "other powers" our lie-rents say we have. Griff, we forgot to mention it, but when Hunt hacked the lie-rents' files, there was only mention of our paranormal healing abilities and how we can come back from, ya know, the dead.*>

<*Oh, that minor detail,*> Griff said, as if we were still fighting to accept what he hadn't confirmed with his own two eyes as we had.

Layla snorted.

<*No mention of our telepathy.*>

<*We were probably always smart enough to keep that shit to ourselves,*> Hunt said. <*We've always been sus of others.*>

<*Not sus enough, apparently,*> Brady groused.

<*How could we ever be sus enough to doubt everything about our entire lives? Our parents? Anyone would fall for that,*> Hunt said.

<*They counted on it,*> Brady growled.

<*Still can't believe my mom's made up,*> Griffin said. <*I mean . . . fuck.*>

<*I don't mind that one as much,*> Brady said. <*Tracy, that's the woman Mitzi's based on, Griff. Tracy's a straight-up hottie in her sexy little white lab coat.*>

<*Hey,*> Layla snapped. <*Dick for brains. Don't be insensitive. Griff's still adjusting and you just said you're glad his mom's made up so you can bone the chick who played her.*>

Even though I couldn't see Brady's face, I knew it was scrunching up. <*Sorry, bro. Didn't think that one through.*>

<*Ya never do.*>

Layla never did concern herself with insignificant things such as blatant, glaring hypocrisy.

<*You guys are both boneheads,*> I said on a friendly chuff. <*We didn't see any mention of the weird thing that happened with Bobo becoming a tat on my body either. I worried we'd slipped up on that one, talking in the mansion when it first happened, but maybe they didn't get what we were talking about.*>

Hunt pushed up to his elbows, drawing me to do the same. Shortly after, the others did as well.

<*What about what my dad said?*> Hunt said. <*About Joss being special.*>

<*I don't think he put it quite like that,*> I muttered, but to be fair, shortly afterward I had the living daylights shocked out of me—no less than twice.

<*He said you were walking his dreams.*>

Shit, he *had* said something like that!

My heartbeat sped up a bit. <*You think that's an ability we could get to work for us?*>

Layla sat up, bouncing excitedly on her bottom. <*One way to find out, girl. Give it a try!*>

<*What? Like, right now?*>

<*You got something better to do than figure out how the hell we're gonna survive the day, the week, the month, the—*>

<*I get it. But . . . how would I even do something like that? I don't know how to* dreamwalk. *That's like something from fantasy books.*>

One by one, slowly we all ended up looking at Hunt, who understood exactly why. After all these years—more than we'd realized—we knew one another nearly as well as we did our own selves.

He nodded as if we'd spoken. <*Yep. I'll get right on the research.*>

<*But you're gonna have to be real careful,*> Griffin warned. <*They'll for sure be tracking your search history with how insane they are.*>

<*Thanks, bro. I set up reroutes all over the place, bouncing from one IP to another, plus I've got a proxy server. But I'd be happy for the help to make sure there's nothing else I can do.*>

<*Maybe a new, secret computer,*> I suggested. <*We could buy a cheap basic one in cash. Or better yet, we could buy a refurbished one at a repair shop. I don't think they even log those sales like a big retailer would.*>

<*Smart,*> Hunt said. <*Yeah, that'd be good.*>

<*'Cause if they happened to catch us hacking into their files last night, then they'll think it's all taken care of with the latest reboot. But if it happens again . . .*>

<*They'll figure out we're on to them,*> Brady said. <*And that would be* no bueno.>

I exchanged looks with each of my best friends. <*So we wait till Hunt figures out how I can try to dreamwalk, and until then we hang tight?*>

Hunt was nodding, but Brady added, <*Find out how we see if we're chipped too. Like, can we use an RF detector for that? 'Cause if so, we gotta get one. They totally stole the one we had in one of the reboots. I can't ask about it.*>

<*Good idea,*> Griffin said then shook his head in an uneasy shudder. <*If they've chipped us . . .*>

Brady reached over me to palm him on the back. <*We'll get our revenge, bro. One way or another. They might have all the money and science on their side, but we're the only fucking immortals in Ridgemore. We can kill them and they can't kill us. Not permanently, anyhow.*>

As far as pep talks went, I couldn't help but find ours severely lacking. But hey, it wasn't Brady's fault he had fuck all to work with.

<*We research,*> Layla said. <*We think. We pay attention and see if we can figure out more abilities or whatever. We train. We watch our backs. And we have fun in the meantime. 'Cause, y'all, we ain't never gonna get more proof of how much we need to* carpe *our fucking* diem.>

I glanced at Griffin.

He was already looking at me.

I allowed my relief at having him at my side to spread into a huge smile.

He smiled back. When he winked at me, sexy as all get out, it sent tingles rushing up and down my spine.

I was looking straight at the kind of fun I wanted to have.

<*Wanna go for a run first?*> Hunt asked. <*We don't have training till tomorrow.*>

Layla threw back her head and groaned. <*No way, dude. We just lazed. I'm not in the mood to move now. Move, then laze. But not laze, then move. That shit don't work for me.*>

<*We didn't laze,*> Hunt said around a chuckle. <*We brainstormed.*>

<*Yeah, yeah. You have a huge brain. We remember.*> She rolled her eyes, but the playful spark in her eyes I hadn't seen since Griff died was back.

Hunt chortled. <*Like your brain's not just as awesome.*>

She preened, fluffing her chin-length hair, currently sporting wildly colored feathers nestled among its strands. <*I am pretty awesome. Thanks for noticing.*>

A chuckle that felt like a warm, beachy breeze swept around our circle, and my heart felt even a little lighter.

Hunt's phone buzzed in his pocket. Frowning, he pulled it out. Everyone he wanted to receive messages from was right here. He studied the screen, the toasted brown tint to his skin paling rapidly.

"What is it?" Layla asked aloud.

In answer, he turned the screen toward us.

**Zozo:** Hey babe. We need 2 talk. It's really important. Like life-changing important. Pick me up?

Next followed a string of emojis that had me blinking at it while Hunt asked Griffin, <*In your hypno, am I supposed to be dating Zoe?*>

Griffin gulped. <*Yeah, bro. You're totally in love with her.*>

Hunt's lips thinned until they all but disappeared.

<*Guess I shoulda figured that was a lie,*> Griffin said.

But to do that he would have had to be open to considering all our lives were a lie, and who would even think that?

I demanded of no one in particular: <*What kind of life-changing important shit is she talking about?*>

<*I have no idea, but I'm finding out,*> Hunt said while he texted back.

**Me:** C U soon then

Zoe's reply arrived immediately, followed by more emojis.

**Zozo:** K, boo. Can't wait to C U

Hunt grimaced and stood. <*Just what I want, more life-changing important shit.*> He groaned. <*The sooner I get this over with, the better. Wish me luck, guys.*>

None of us did. Luck was unlikely to have much sway over Zoe's big news. Magnum had almost certainly provided her with a detailed script already.

# 6

## A Wet and Wild Ride to Pound Town

My girl Layla was a lot of incredible things—most of them brash, brazen, loud, and wholly obnoxious. After we were gunned down in the high school gymnasium, and Griffin outed our love to our friends, I would have never guessed that she'd be the one to look for ways to be considerate of our budding relationship. But when Hunt borrowed Bonnie and stomped off for his talk with Zoe, Layla convinced Brady to join her in chilling at their house while Griffin and I took "a wet and wild ride to Pound Town."

Even while revealing unexpected thoughtfulness, subtle she was not, and never would be.

While I'd blushed, wondering since when the fuck blushing was a regular activity for me, Griffin hadn't. He'd taken me by the hand, led me to Clyde, and driven us to his place. He hung a Do Not Disturb sign on his bedroom door he made when he was eight, locked the handle, and drew the blinds—as if that would afford us actual privacy. But there was no preventing the superspy, pervy lie-rents from getting an earful, and possibly an eyeful too.

Abstaining from whatever wonders I'd experience with Griffin, when I'd believed I might have truly lost him, wasn't an option.

My crew was fighting on the daily to survive the mother of all perilous shitstorms. He was one of the reasons fighting so hard was worth it. If we had an invisible audience to whatever would come next, so be it. I'd do my best to forget we weren't as alone as we should be.

We lay sprawled on his queen bed, relaxed, as if we were still just friends. Our socked feet touched, our fingers laced together like we used to do about the time he created his door sign, when friendship truly was all that was on our minds—when Ridgemore was a safe haven, our parents were supportive, and our houses were homes.

<*I don't know what I'm allowed to say out loud and what's gotta stay in our heads anymore,*> I told him silently. <*With you rebooted and us not, it's all gotten so damn confusing.*>

He rubbed his thumb along my hand. <*Seems like it's always been confusing.*>

<*Well, there is that.*> I slid my head closer, until our temples dipped together.

He hummed contentedly. <*At least we're allowed to be together this time around. That's something.*>

<*Oh, that's something all right. That's something huge.*>

He chuckled softly.

I snorted. <*Tell me you didn't think of a dick joke.*>

<*Okay, I won't, then.*>

A laugh rumbled through me. <*Since when do you hold back with me?*>

<*Since my dick's no longer interested in being only friends and he's got about ten thousand ideas of what he wants to do to you, and that's just for today.*>

It wasn't all that outrageous of a thing to say, especially when Brady and Layla practically lived for dick jokes and sex talk. But my stomach warmed. My skin became suddenly hyperaware of how close Griffin lay to me, the few places our bodies already touched . . .

I swallowed. <*Yeah. I guess it is different.*>

<*It's kinda strange, actually. It doesn't really feel all that different.*>

Atop the pillow, I turned my head toward him.

<*I mean, yeah, okay, it is different,*> he went on. <*Obviously it is. But I guess what I'm saying is, it's not as different as I thought it'd be. To want you, I mean, want you like that.*>

<*Like what?*> I prodded, though I damn well understood what he was talking about. How could I not, when I'd been drooling over his body for longer than I should have?

<*Like you're my reason for breathing. For starting every day. For going to sleep just so I can hurry up and see you again the next morning. Like you make everything make sense, even when it really shouldn't, 'cause shit's totally fucking bonkers right now.*>

My breathing sounded loud to my own ears, wishing for him to continue, greedy for more.

<*You're my everything, Joss.*>

Griffin didn't open up very often, but the rare times he did, it wasn't like this. He was cleaving himself down the middle and exposing all his insides for me.

I'd never been so glad we had these secret telepathic abilities. His confession belonged to me and me alone. I would have set the lie-rents on fucking fire if they'd been able to eavesdrop on this conversation. Instead, I tucked his precious words away near to my heart for safekeeping, where I could revisit them later—when I'd allow myself to simmer in the feeling of how very much they meant to me, when I'd let myself squeal and giggle and celebrate how the boy I'd loved since forever had fallen in love with me too.

<*And why isn't that different from before, when we were just friends?*> I asked in a whisper, unwilling to disrupt whatever

magic held us in its thrall and wanting him to explain every last thing he'd mentioned.

He rolled onto his side, wrapping his leg around my thigh and sliding me closer. He lowered his face to mine, stopping just far enough away that our vision wouldn't blur.

<*You've always been my everything. Even when we were just friends, I'd always be thinking about you. I dunno. You've just always been . . . it . . . for me, I guess. Special.*>

He lowered his forehead to mine. I scooted closer atop the comforter, nestling my body into his. Automatically, his arm draped around my waist.

<*You're not usually this quiet,*> he said. <*Shit, am I saying something you don't like? Don't want me to be saying? Have I read this—us—all wrong?*>

<*No!*> I answered right away, too loud. I softened my inner voice. <*No, Griff, absolutely not. I was just letting myself gobble up every beautiful thing you're telling me. I love what you're saying.*>

I loved a hell of a lot more than that. Did he remember that we'd already swapped *I love you*s, or was that wiped out in his most recent reboot?

I could be chickenshit and wait to find out, or I could—

<*I love you, Griff. I've loved you for a long, long time. Maybe always.*>

I discovered my eyes closed when I realized I was feeling—not seeing—the warmth of his smile. More like a grin, probably, but I didn't want to look yet. Didn't want to pull my forehead from his.

<*I love you, baby. I maybe woulda never believed in fate, kismet, destiny, all that crap, whatever we wanna call it, if not for you. I think we were always meant to be together. To find our way here, to this.*>

"Yes," I whispered aloud while my heart fluttered excitedly. I inched my lips closer to his. <*I don't ever want to have to live without you.*>

Memories of Clyde erupting into a ball of fire that climbed toward the night sky. Then, of the slide of gravel and the groan of metal knowing Clyde was catapulting over the cliff.

Both times, Griffin had been snatched away from me without warning, without a chance to protect him, to fight for him.

As if Griffin understood where my thoughts had veered, he drew me closer, until my breasts brushed his chest and our hips were lined up.

<*Wanna make a deal with me?*>

<*Yes,*> again I whispered into our minds. <*Wait, does it have something to do with your dick?*>

He laughed. <*Would it change things if it did?*>

<*Probably not.*>

He laughed again. <*Let's make a deal. Whenever we're together like this, when it's just you and me, and we're in each other's arms, we make it all about us. No lying scum parents who aren't really parents. No psycho rich dudes out to murder us. No legends of Sky People, whatever they are, or other supes trapped back at the institute, or Bobo appearing on your sexy skin to eat your tats.*>

<*I can't believe you don't remember that happening. That's, like, the top third strangest thing that's ever happened to me. I'd say number one, but we died and came back, almost like zombies, except not undead, ya know, so . . . my standards are skewed.*>

<*What's number two, then?*>

<*Hmmm, gotta think about that one. There are a lot of contenders, like overhearing Celia slash Jackie talking about how she thinks it ain't no thang to rewrite our memories over and over. Or maybe . . . maybe Bobo should be number two. My boy does* not *belong all up on my skin, yo.*>

Griffin tipped me onto my back and rolled on top of me, propping himself up on his elbows to keep some of his weight off me, the rest of him pressed along the length of me—*mmmmm.*

<*He doesn't, but I'm thinking I do,*> Griffin rumbled in that deep, sexy-as-fuck voice of his. It sounded the same inside my mind as it did aloud.

My breathing and heartbeat were stuttering, or maybe they were coming too fast, I couldn't tell. My legs melted open, carving out room for his body as if all on their own, drawing him closer to my center. The outline of his dick was hard against me. I clenched with anticipation.

Griffin's lips lowered to mine, and instantly my mind went blank. At first they were a light touch, as if it were the first time we'd ever kissed and his mouth were still a stranger to mine. But I kissed him back with the pent-up ferocity of someone who'd seen the love of her life murdered in front of her very eyes and had been given a second chance—a miraculous, wondrous second chance—at loving him.

With the phantom fear of believing I'd lost him battering at the edges of my awareness, I kissed him with everything I had.

With every bit of love I hadn't yet expressed to him.

With the force of every fantasy I'd ever had about him, with every wish and hope and dream and fucking desire I'd ever conjured around wanting—so desperately wanting—a moment with him exactly like this one.

He matched the intensity of my kiss with a savage wildness of his own that suggested some of the things he hadn't uttered. His lips, his tongue, the way our teeth were sometimes bared almost ferally . . . they told me he loved me beyond words. Just as he said: like we were meant to be together. Like every sick, twisted, and mega-fucked-up thing that had ever happened to us had been steering us toward this.

Toward *us*.

A love powerful enough to move mountains and create worlds.

Or maybe that was just how it felt.

My hands were running through his hair, scratching at his neck, shoulders, and back. They tugged on his waist, holding him against me. Squeezed his ass through jeans that were entirely in the way.

I tried to pull from his kiss to speak and couldn't. He wouldn't let me get away. I didn't want to anyway.

Even through our thoughts I panted. <*I want you—*>

<*God, baby, I want you like I've never wanted anything else in my entire life. You feel . . .*> His tongue swirled along mine, consuming me with heat I never wanted to escape. <*You feel . . . so fucking amazing.*>

I nipped at his lower lip and he startled, then let loose a rumbling laugh that was one of the sexiest things I'd ever heard.

<*I bet I'll feel way more amazing once we get our stupid clothes off,*> I said.

He panted and jerked his hips against mine as if on instinct alone.

<*Once you sink your hard . . .*>

He groaned.

<*Stiff . . .*>

He rolled his hips against mine.

<*Beautiful cock into . . .*>

He pulled his lips from mine to murmur, <*Are ya tryin' to fucking kill me here?*>

Poor choice of words, sure, but who cared? Definitely not I as I chuckled a rolling, seductive purr. <*What I'm trying to do, in case it wasn't obvious, is get your hard cock*>—he sucked in a breath—<*deep inside me, already.*>

At normal times, Griffin moved fast, I knew that. Dude was agile and honed like an athlete. We'd been training together and tearing across these woods for as long as we remembered. I'd seen him move lightning-fast more times than I could count.

But apparently, he'd never been more motivated.

His t-shirt was torn from his body when I was scarcely starting to register that he was yanking it off. His belt was similarly gone in a whip of leather and clank of metal buckle landing somewhere on his carpeted floor. His fingers had already undone the button on his jeans and were reaching for his zipper when I halted them with my own.

"Uh-uh," I said aloud. "I get to undress you the rest of the way."

He stared at me, his eyes molten, their colors like an entire forest ablaze with the light from the sun nearing the horizon and shining its final glow of the day in a warming blast.

His entire body went completely still as he watched, barely seeming to breathe as I dragged down his zipper, spread it wide, and dipped my hand inside the fly of his boxers. With him as hard as he was, I'd have to tug his dick down to finesse him through the front, so I tugged on his jeans and boxers. They slid down his hips.

Griffin's breath left him in a hiss, as I sucked in through my teeth in a sibilant gasp.

Griffin knelt between my legs. His strong thighs were like twin pillars holding up my prize.

His dick . . . by God, it was the most beautiful dick I'd ever seen. Granted, I'd only seen a few, but those other ones were veiny, crooked, ugly things surging from even uglier, saggy, hairy balls when compared to this one. Griff's dick was a splendid, sculpted piece of art, smooth, thick, and standing proud. I found myself literally salivating.

Whereas I'd blushed when Layla teased about all the naked playtime Griffin and I would indulge in, now there was no hint of my former out-of-character timidity. With his dick inches from my face, I openly admired him . . . and admired him . . . and then just kept on looking.

He rasped out, "Now it's my turn," and reached for me.

I was faster. I lunged for him and wrapped my fingers around his cock.

He froze.

When I stroked the length of him, a shudder traveled up and down his spine before he pierced me with a stare so hot I felt ready to combust under its regard.

Incensed, I stroked him again. He wobbled atop the bed, then threw his head back.

I ran my hand up the hard length of him again, and again, and again, and again, all the while greedily eating up the sight of all his tight muscles, smooth tanned skin, and the fierce ink accentuating the sexiest body ever created.

He snapped his head forward, his mouth a fierce scowl. He flung himself off the bed, was out of his jeans, boxers, and socks in an instant, and then crawling back over the bed like a predator—with me in his sights.

I dragged my teeth along my lower lip without noticing I was doing it until his eyes followed their trail.

"I'm gonna getcha," he growled, and fuck me, never had I wanted to be gotten more. "Now it's my turn."

I licked my lips, imagined them and my tongue on his cock. "But I'm not finished with you yet."

He grinned wickedly but only repeated, "It's my turn now, baby."

"Griff, you home?" traveled up the stairwell, through the door, and into the bedroom.

I jerked back along the bed, eyes darting to the door. Griff kept his predatory eyes fixed on me and shouted, "Yep, I'm home. But I'm really busy right now. Catch ya later."

On all fours, he prowled toward me even as Orson mumbled some *Yeah, sure*s, and other platitudes I couldn't have cared less about.

Griffin was fierce and sexy and strong and gorgeous . . . and he was coming for me. After all these years of fantasizing about him, I'd finally get to feel him inside me. Where my own hands had been the only ones to warm my skin before, now they'd be his.

He pounced, catching my legs and tugging me down the bed until I was almost under him again. A giggle that sounded entirely unlike me escaped, and once it was out, I didn't want to stuff it back wherever it came. Griffin was the one lover I could be my authentic self with. We were besties.

Besties who'd get to fuck. What could be better than that?

With extreme efficiency, he removed my jeans and socks but left me in my panties. "This little scrap of lace . . . this I'm gonna take my time with." He circled a finger on either side beneath the waistband of my thong, pulling it out a couple of inches before letting it snap back against my skin.

A gush of warmth surged between my thighs and I bit my lip, leaning back onto my elbows.

On his knees between my thighs, and with his proud, beautiful dick at eye level, he reached for my shirt. I helped him slide it off, but when I was left in a camisole, and his fingers were reaching for the straps, I asked, "What about condoms? You have some? I don't carry any in my bag."

He blinked at me as if coming out of a trance before answering. "Uh, yeah . . . I should have some somewhere."

He bounded off the bed with a bounce of his erection, dashed into his walk-in closet while I openly admired every inch of him on display, then came out with a small box of them, examining its contents with a frown.

"Expired." He tossed them back into the closet without care to where they landed.

"Expired?" I asked aloud, before switching to telepathy. I wasn't risking our stories being out of sync with the latest brainwashing. *<You don't use 'em with all the girls you're with?>*

He arched a brow at me as he sat on the bed. <*Um, who are all these girls you think I'm going around banging?*>

I sat up. <*You've had sex before.*>

<*Yeah, you know I have. But it's been . . . a while.*>

<*Why?*>

<*You already know why.*>

He caught me. I sure did.

<*Once I figured out how I was feeling about you,*> he offered anyway, <*no one else was worth it.*>

<*It's been, uh, years for me,*> I admitted, then flicked my gaze downward to pick at a seam on his comforter.

<*For me too.*>

I glanced up, allowed my hand to roam his bare knee, then to travel along his thigh as I slid closer. <*Years?*>

<*Mm-hmm. Joss, I'm not messing around with you. I've been nuts for you for ages. Just didn't want to risk our friendship by saying anything sooner. It apparently took dying to put things in perspective.*>

<*Or fucking hypnosis,*> I said with a scowl.

<*Uh-uh. Remember our deal. None of that.*>

<*Okay, yeah, you're right. So . . . we're both clean.*>

<*Squeaky.*>

I licked my lips, allowed my attention to travel from his face to his hard-on, twirled one of my minibraids.

<*Wanna raw dog it?*>

He barked out a laugh. <*Joss Bryson, Miss Romance herself.*>

I laughed, too, before turning serious eyes on him and scooting closer so that our bare thighs touched. I cupped his balls, tugging them upward, then ran my fingers along the underside of his dick until the breath hissed from between those pillowy lips of his.

<*Jokes aside, I want you bare inside me,*> I told him boldly.

He hissed another inhale through clenched teeth.

<*Fuck that rubber shit. I want to feel you the way we're meant to be together.*>

His hot stare trailed from my face, down my body, pausing on my tits and then the lacy bit of thong between my legs, before landing on the way I teased his dick.

Admiring how I stroked him, he asked, <*What about pregnancy risk?*>

<*My period's scheduled to come in a couple days. I'm not fertile right now.*>

<*You sure?*> His stare was still on my hands, on his dick.

<*Totally sure.*>

He breathed in, then out. A shudder raced along his body before he jumped into motion so swiftly it startled me.

Suddenly, I was flat on my back, my legs opening automatically for him as if they'd been doing it for eons. My camisole was hiked above my tits so that they were right in his face, and his fingers were sinking under the band of my thong.

<*I wanna take it slow,*> he grumbled, though his actions suggested the exact opposite. <*Especially since this is maybe our first time.*>

<*I know. Me too.*> I tugged his hips against mine and ground against him, a scrap of insignificant lace against smooth shaft.

The veins in his neck bulged. His shoulder muscles strained as he seemed to use all his self-restraint to hold back.

<*But next time,*> I finished. <*We'll go slow next time. Right now . . . fuck, right now, Griff, there's only one thing I want, and I want it right the fuck now. You gonna make me wait when I want it this bad?*>

<*No, baby. I'll give you absolutely everything you want, whenever you want it.*>

We probably should have waited. I maybe should have agreed and let us take it slow. There was no repeating our first time—unless we were rebooted by lying assholes, of fucking course.

But my body was shouting at me to get what I wanted, and so much had been out of my control lately that waiting felt somehow like a loss. Living wild and free felt like the only kind of win I could get.

This was *us*. What *we* wanted. Nothing to do with anyone else.

His hips were already lined up with mine. I guided his dick between my thighs, slid the scrap of red lace to one side, and notched his tip at my throbbing, hot entrance.

His eyes leapt to mine, a question obviously forming on his lips.

I didn't give him the chance to voice it.

I brought a hand to either of his hips . . . and pushed him inside me.

Together, we groaned at the sensation.

Finally, the man I loved, my best friend, was filling me the way I was always meant to be filled.

His mouth opened and closed, but he said nothing, not even in our mindspace. His eyes mirrored everything I was feeling.

We felt so . . . so . . . so very right.

Eventually, his lips lowered to mine, pressing the tenderest of kisses upon them. His forehead touched my own for a heartbeat before the hot skin of his chest flattened against my breasts.

With our faces mere inches apart, he breathed, "I love you. Man, do I fucking love you."

"I love you too."

Then he began to roll his hips, pushing farther inside me, filling me to completion, and I understood right then I'd never experience anything better.

This, this right here, this alone was worth fighting for. This was worth clawing our way back from death for, and murdering anyone who tried to come at us.

He angled his next thrust upward, somehow hitting my fucking G-spot, and my eyes rolled upward as I moaned.

"I'm never leaving your bed," I grunted.

"Promise?" he whispered over my lips, then kissed me again, rolling in and out of me.

And then, *of course* fucking then, our phones buzzed from our pant pockets, wherever our jeans had landed.

Griffin stilled for a second, then thrust up into me again. I grew impossibly wetter.

Our phones buzzed again, at the same time, which meant it was our group text message.

He hesitated again.

"Don't stop," I said, but a third buzz caused the two of us to groan, and not in the good way.

"Dammit," I exclaimed. "It could be Hunt."

"Prob'ly is," Griffin said while balls deep inside me and appearing unwilling to go anywhere else.

He sighed heavily, his eyelids fluttering closed for a moment of evident regret, then pulled out of me.

Immediately I missed his warmth like I didn't know how to live without it. I stared at his erection with feral possessiveness while he fished his phone from his pants. The screen lit up his face, highlighting how his eyes widened and his mouth tightened.

"Fuck," he snarled.

I leapt from the bed and sidled up next to him.

**Hunt:** SOS

**Hunt:** Treehouse, now

**Hunt:** Already on my way

A minute ago, I would have thought there was nothing that would have gotten me to walk away from naked playtime with Griffin. But when our crew needed us, we dropped everything—even beautiful, glistening erections—and were there for one another.

That's what family fucking did.

We barely spared each other a single look of regret before hurriedly tossing each other our clothes.

Griffin's thumbs skimmed his screen, and my phone lit up seconds later.

**Griff:** Joss n I'll be there in 5

With his dick still hard and shoved into his jeans, Griffin and I raced out the door.

# 7

# The Irony Was Tremendous, the Role-Playing, Less So

Our treehouse was nestled deep in the woods of our lie-rents' combined properties. Though neither Griff nor I were dressed for a run, we both leaned into the movement, whipping along the well-worn trail. At first, the exercise was a good way to work off the lingering rush of our lovemaking, the excruciating frustration at our first time being cut far too short. But the more we moved, the more concern for Hunt shadowed what intimacy Griff and I were missing out on.

Hunt had never texted an SOS before. None of our crew had, though if we'd been in a position to do so during our dying and resurrecting, we probably would have.

Something was wrong. Very wrong. Hunt wasn't prone to exaggeration or false alarms. But it wasn't just that. Something *felt* wrong. The sensation prickled along my body, urging my legs and arms to pump faster, faster. With how insane our lives had become, I didn't want to guess at what could be causing Hunt to call us to such an urgent meeting.

When Griffin and I charged up the porch steps and barreled through the door, we were breathing heavily, our bodies slick with sweat, our clothing sticking to us. We were the last to arrive, and if we reeked of sex, our friends either didn't notice or didn't care enough to comment. With both Layla and Brady in the room, the fact that neither of them followed up on Griff's and my "ride to Pound Town" told us as much as Hunt's SOS.

That Hunt's face was drawn, his eyes heavy, his mouth a strained line, told us even more. When Griff shut the door behind us, Hunt turned from where he'd apparently been pacing to simply . . . stare. His chest heaved as he appeared to try to catch his breath, or maybe it was to corral his thoughts.

I rushed over and threw my arms around him, pulling him tightly to me. Only when the sweat on my arms stuck to his shirt did I consider my state of dress.

"Fuck, I'm sorry." I tried to pull away.

He only pulled me closer, crooking his head so his cheek rested on my head.

"I'm sweaty and gross." I tried again to disengage.

He shook his head atop mine and whispered, "Not yet."

I settled into our embrace, his shirt slowly growing damp. After long moments of hugging, his breathing slowed, and finally he released a long, laden exhale.

I pulled back, searching his face. Griffin, Brady, and Layla were on their feet, surrounding us.

"What happened?" I asked.

Hunt opened his mouth, closed it. Rubbed at his jaw, his nape, the tatted skin along his collarbone peeking out from the crew neck of his shirt, before stalking toward the weight rack against one wall, spinning, and returning with hard, swift steps.

His eyes blazed as he looked around at us. His jaw clenched, his nostrils flared. Next, his nose bunched. After pressing his lips together for several moments, long enough that I wondered if I'd die right then and there from the suspense and save Magnum the trouble, he spoke.

"Zoe's pregnant."

The air whooshed from my lungs.

"Say what, now?" Layla said.

Hunt scowled while his brows drew low, accentuating the storm that brewed in his eyes. "Yep. She even showed me the pregnancy test. Actually, several of them." His scowl deepened. "They even smelled like piss." He scrunched up his nose again. "Convincing."

"And she says you're the father?" Brady asked.

Hunt's jaw was so tight, so chiseled, it was as if a sculptor had just finished hammering it out.

"That's what she says."

"Fuck, bro," Griffin exclaimed before running both hands through his hair.

<*I have no memory of fucking her,*> Hunt said, switching to our telepathic connection now that we were veering off the path Magnum and the lie-rents had so purposefully and so fucking intrusively orchestrated.

<*As far as I remember, I've never even really kissed her. Nothing more than the kissing I was forced to do, like, in the school halls, all for show.*>

Now Brady was the one breathing heavily, his anger growing until he physically bunched his fists at his sides, the muscles in his forearms bulging in long, visible cords.

<*That's beyond fucked-up, man,*> he seethed into our minds. <*They can't do that!*>

<*Apparently they can,*> I muttered.

Brady's head whipped toward me. <*No. That's too much. Too far. Fuck,* no.>

I tutted. <*Surely you don't think I'm agreeing with this. All I'm saying is they're doing it.*>

<*It's fucking* wrong,> Brady insisted.

<*It's totally fucking wrong. If I didn't already wanna kill Magnum, I'd want to murder the shit out of him right now, for this alone.*>

<*I'll flay him alive,*> Brady said, a bit too matter-of-factly. Enough so that I couldn't help but wonder if Magnum and his cronies had broken us beyond repair. Was there a chance we'd ever recover from the trauma they'd already inflicted when it *just kept coming*?

<*Killing him now won't change Zoe being knocked up,*> Layla said.

Brady gave her a savage grin, teeth on display. <*But it'll stop him from doing anything else to any of us ever again.*>

Layla shrugged. <*So let's kill him already. We keep circling back to the same thing. Killing Magnum's the only thing that'll get us our freedom from all this crap.*>

She stepped closer to Hunt, looking up into his face. <*You're probably not the father of the kid, if she even really is pregnant. It could all be an act.*>

<*Would they do something like that when we'd be able to tell if it's a lie?*> I asked. <*I mean, Zoe's either gonna balloon up or she's not.*>

<*Unless the ploy is to have her pretend to be pregnant and then pretend to have a miscarriage . . .*>

<*What'd be the point of that?*> Brady asked.

Layla shrugged. <*Get Hunt involved for real. We all know Hunt's a good egg. He'd care. Maybe get him to put some distance between him and us.*>

<*I'd never do that,*> Hunt protested. <*Not even if I really did have a . . . shit, have a . . . baby.*>

I patted him on the shoulder. <*We know that. But maybe they don't.*>

<*It's not yours, dude,*> Griffin told Hunt. <*Don't sweat that part of it.*>

Hunt's eyes were still burdened. <*But it* could be. *Maybe I did have sex with her before in one of the many reboots and now I don't remember. Or maybe they*>—he blinked repeatedly, as if considering what he was about to say was bonkers—<*maybe they got my semen somehow and injected her with it.*>

Layla's breath hitched. <*That would be so incredibly messed up.*> She ran her tongue along her teeth. <*But I wouldn't put it past them. Past Magnum. I mean fuck, guys, they* killed us. *More than once. That's the standard we're working with here.*>

<*Right,*> Hunt said. <*That's what I was thinking. Who's to say they haven't . . . ?*> He shared loaded looks with Griffin and Brady. <*I know we'd never willingly shoot off into a cup for them, but it's possible they might've convinced us to do it in one of the reboots.*>

<*No, no way,*> Brady said right away.

Hunt gave him a *really think about it, dude* scrunch of his brows. <*With a gun to Lay's head, tell me you wouldn't do it.*>

<*That's too far. They wouldn't do something like that,*> Brady said, but his denial was weak, trailing at the end, as if even he knew that, as wackadoodle as this new theory was, it truly was possible.

Layla smacked him on the arm. <*If my life's ever in danger and all you gotta do to save me is jerk off into a cup, you'd damn well better do it.*>

Griff sank to the floor to lean his back against the couch, spreading his long legs out in front of him. <*It's just a crazy theory—*>

<*Still a plausible one,*> Hunt insisted.

<*Sure, but I'd really love to move on from it. Not in the mood to think about all the things they might've done to us that we've got no idea about. What they* have *done's bad enough.*>

<*I only bring it up 'cause my supposed girlfriend insists I'm her baby daddy,*> *Hunt said.* <*You shoulda seen her. She was crying, hiccuping, fanning her eyes with her hands. Red nose, mascara streaks. It was a whole production.*>

His eyes glistened, like he was either about to lose his ever-loving mind or maybe cry too. <*They all but grew us in test tubes.*

*Just 'cause we were carried by surrogates doesn't mean we weren't mixed up in a Petri dish or something. What if they're doing the same with me now? With Zoe? An eventual DNA test would say I'm the father.*>

<*If for no other reason than they'd fake the test results,*> I said.

<*Right,*> Griffin said, before extending his leg to nudge my foot with his.

I managed a somber smile and went over to sit beside him, telling Hunt, <*Whether there's even really a baby, and whether or not it's yours—genetically, I mean—it doesn't change that we know for a fact it's not a result of your free will choices. So either way, it's not your baby.*>

<*If there even is one,*> Layla pressed. <*Zoe's a hussy.*>

<*You didn't say that about her before,*> Hunt said miserably.

<*That's 'cause she wasn't trying to entrap my bestie into being a teen father.*>

<*We're in our twenties,*> Hunt corrected, just as miserably.

She frowned. <*Damn. Why do I keep forgetting about that?*>

<*'Cause our lives are literally the most insane thing ever,*> Brady said.

<*My question was rhetorical, Brade. Obviously. I can barely keep straight what I'm allowed to say and what I'm not, what I'm supposed to know, what I've gotta keep secret, and you guys know how hard that shit is for me. I'm not used to . . .*>

<*Having to think before you speak?*> Brady suggested.

Layla didn't bother denying it. Grimly, she just nodded.

Hunt gazed at us with wide, imploring eyes.

<*What do I do?*>

I plopped my head back onto the couch cushions, suddenly exhausted by it all. <*That's usually our question to you.*>

But Brady was already nodding to himself. <*We kill Magnum. Right now. Or tonight anyway. After dinner, when he's presumably finished for the day with the work of being a supervillain out to conquer the fucking world. It's the only way to make all this other shit go away.*>

For several long moments, we all seemed to consider the implications of finally following through on murder plans of our own.

Eventually, Layla said, <*I mean, my twin's not wrong. We all know it already. We've talked it through till we were blue in the face. It's our only real option, the only one likely to work. We can't run.*>

It truly was nothing we hadn't discussed already.

<*If we don't do it once and for all,*> Layla persisted, <*they're just gonna keep doing horrible shit to us. Now it's Hunt with a maybe baby. Who's to say what it'll be next time?*>

She rolled her neck, then asked, <*Do we really wanna keep playing their game to find out?*>

<*When you put it like that, hell no,*> Griffin said, taking my hand.

I studied our entwined fingers, wishing our lives could be easy again—I could simply be enjoying finding out that the boy I'd been in love with since forever loved me back, I was his *dream girl.* I should've been lapping up that juicy stuff, gorging on it. It was literally what dreams were made of.

But no.

There never had been any avoiding it. We'd never stand for what Magnum and our lie-rents had done. Or worse: what they intended to continue doing.

The irony was tremendous: In killing us, Magnum had created killers. The man we intended to murder had forged his very own murderers.

I drew in a steeling breath, squeezed Griffin's hand.

<*I'm in. Let's do it.*>

<*Me too,*> Griffin said. <*Soon as the lie-rents are lights out, let's roll.*>

<*I'll start getting stuff ready,*> Brady said.

<*No Ninjas R Us gear,*> Layla told him.

He ignored her, seeming to be composing mental to-do lists.

<*I mean it, Brade.*>

<*What's it to you if I'm invisible to the naked eye in the nighttime and you're not? If you choose to be lame, that's on you. But no one's gonna spot me tonight.*>

<*Oh, we'll be spotting your junk plenty, and trust me, that's a look no sister should have to see.*>

<*You just asked me to shoot off into a cup for you.*>

<*I did not! I—*>

<*Guys,*> Hunt interjected. <*I don't know if I can really kill him. I mean, I know I want to. Like, I really,* really *want to. But I'm not sure I'm gonna be able to do the deed when the time comes.*>

Brady sauntered over to tap his fist to his shoulder. <*Don't sweat it, bro. I got you. I can kill 'im. All I gotta do is picture his goons shooting you, Lay, and Joss in the gym, and I'll be down to go all Rambo on his ass.*>

His eyes on me, probably recalling the identical scene, Griff growled into our group chat, <*Me too.*>

Layla glanced at me, then to the others. <*I'm not a hundred percent, but I think in the moment I'll be down. I've wanted to murder the shit out of him lots of times. It just takes seeing his smug, has-it-all-and-still-wants-more creepy face, and then I'll be into it.*>

My friends' attention shifted to me.

I shrugged. <*You know me. I'll do whatever needs to be done.*>

How I'd feel about it later was an entirely different question, one I didn't intend to ponder. What difference would it make how I'd feel later? This entitled prick was threatening me and my crew—*my family*—and he would pay the price for our freedom. He was, after all, the one imprisoning us within invisible bars.

<*We've got a hella lot to talk through and set up before we go kill the motherfucker,*> Brady said, taking a seat opposite the coffee table from Griffin and me.

<*But before we get into it,*> Griffin said, <*we've been silent a long time talking all this through. Can't go making our spies suspicious. Time for a little role-playing first.*>

<*Good point,*> Layla said. <*I keep forgetting, I swear.*>

<*We believe you,*> I told her. <*All the more reason to kill Magnum before you blow our cover.*>

<*'Cause we all know I will.*>

<*Oh, we know.*>

So next, as if we didn't have one of the most significant and dangerous events of our entire lives to anticipate, we put on a performance about consoling our friend with an unexpected bun cooking in the Zoe oven.

# 8

## Ever a Ray of Sunshine, I Love Me a Good Underdog Story, Better Than a Sob Story, No Matter the Oscar

After a cumbersome half hour of role-playing for the invisible spies keeping tabs on us—we had a megalomaniac to kill and no time to waste!—we'd resorted to more meditating-cum-telepathic-communication. By the time we'd talked through our plans for attack, along with how to cover our tracks—there was no good way—and how to protect ourselves—again, there was no good way—we were twitchy. All of us, even Layla, yearned to go for a nice, long run to work off some of our pent-up energy. But it was dinnertime, and through all the many ruses, dinnertime remained a sacred event for the Rafferty household. The Celia Rafferty persona hadn't let up on her demand that her two children be present for a family meal every evening.

Unwilling to separate with tensions so high, and too dark out for a run through the woods anyway, Griffin, Hunt, and I crashed dinner. Ever the chipper, fake hostess, Celia appeared delighted, trilling as she claimed she'd fortuitously made enough for leftovers so she'd have plenty of her spaghetti Bolognese for all of us despite the lack of warning.

I couldn't help but wonder if she, one of the world's foremost brain function experts, had somehow listened in on our thoughts and what we believed was a private conversation to receive notice of our arrival. It was still possible we were chipped. We hadn't been able to research the science as planned. Hunt had been as careful as he knew how to be when he'd hacked into the lie-rents' computer system. Even so, that night while we slept, we'd been drugged and moved, and almost certainly a reboot had been attempted. Was it because Griffin was finally healed enough to rejoin us? Or was it because Hunt's hacking had been detected? Or perhaps both? Without any way to know, we had to be even more cautious, which meant no easy internet searches about chipping, dream-walking, or anything else we might need to learn about. And if they were monitoring everything about us, they were surely tracking any visits we might make to Ridgemore's library. It also ruled out our idea of finding a used computer at an off-the-beaten-path electronics repair shop. It was becoming frighteningly apparent that, somehow, Magnum and his peons were staying several steps ahead of us at all times.

We clung to the few advantages we did have like they were lifelines, a rope thrown to us on the open sea, able to lead us back to safety—whatever the concept would look like to us after this was all over.

I needed it to be over. I needed my crew to make it out of this alive, healthy and whole at my side.

In the hours after dinner while we waited for the lie-rents to go to sleep, we built a blanket fort in Hunt's sleepover room, much as we used to do when we were children. Inside, hidden from cameras, we wrote ourselves warnings, in the tiniest scrawl possible, that life wasn't at all as it seemed—in case we died tonight and the next reboot took.

Even though every one of us had died and returned to life, the thought of any of us dying again remained terrifying. The idea of having our memories wiped was almost as awful. It was bad enough to be knowing pawns of a psycho with too many resources and lacking a moral compass; it was another to be unwitting. At least now we could fight. We could look our lie-rents in their phony-ass faces and know they were lying fucks.

There were no absolutes in life—or in death either, it turned out. I'd learned that already. Death meant at least a chance that one of us wouldn't come back. The label of *immortal* didn't come with any guarantees.

My note was rolled into a tight scroll half the size of a cigarette and shoved through a double seam of my panty's waistband. Every time we'd been rebooted that I could recall, when I'd woken to find myself in PJs I hadn't dressed in myself, my underwear had remained the same. Now, if I were murdered and my memories overridden, I was hoping the unfamiliar bump in the elastic would be enough to draw my curiosity. But my note could also just end up in the wash. It was far from foolproof, but it was the best I could come up with so the note would remain on my person.

Layla concealed her note inside a tampon applicator. There was as much a chance that she'd find it as there was that it'd end up shoved up her vajayjay. Brady buried his in plastic in the woods behind the treehouse in a spot he claimed was special, though I'd never heard him mention it. Griffin sliced open the tongue on one of his Vans and slid the note inside. And Hunt laid his note flat beneath the endpaper of his favorite edition of Douglas Adams's *Dirk Gently's Holistic Detective Agency*.

The risk that we'd never come across our cautions was as significant as that of a lie-rent finding them instead. And if what we knew were to be discovered . . . well, we were majorly fucked. We all knew it. The odds weren't particularly in our favor.

Not that it would stop us from fighting. We'd always fight for one another.

<*I love me a good underdog story,*> Layla said into our group chat as, just past midnight, we rolled up to the manned gate of Magnum's newly constructed mansion. Even though he was, as far as we knew, single and without dependents, his new house was as big as the one he'd built us on campus that was for five people. Big money sure could buy a lot.

<*We've so got this,*> Layla added with a nervous bite of her lip, glancing out the passenger-side window of the back seat. She sat next to me and Griffin.

No one responded. We were all piled inside Bonnie. We'd deliberated about the benefit of driving Clyde as well to give us two getaway options, but in the end, if we were forced to separate and we didn't all escape together, we would have failed anyway.

The tension inside the Mustang's cabin was tangible enough to slice with a knife—which we didn't have. This had been another point of contention, with Brady arguing that we needed weapons, of course we did, to kill a mofo who used rent-a-soldiers for his security. But if we didn't arrive laden with knives Rambo-style and shit went sideways, we could maybe still talk our way out of it. We'd also left Bobo behind, and Brady's Ninjas R Us getup. Brady had straight-up pouted about having to dress in plain ol' jeans and a hoodie when he could "kill it, ninja style."

We had our story worked out and we had to stick to it.

Bonnie's headlights lit up a tall black gate crowned in spikes as a man in black paramilitary gear stepped out from the gatehouse. He wore a severe buzz cut, a sidearm, a tactical baton, and a Taser. Plus, the pockets of his cargo-style pants bulged with who knew what other goodies. I was jelly.

I could sense Brady's grimace from the back seat as he muttered, <*We shoulda brought weapons, dammit.*>

But then the guard was at the driver's-side door. Brady plastered an amicable smile on his face and rolled down his window.

"Hey there," he said while the guard's brow furrowed in glaring disapproval.

With open suspicion, the soldier dipped his head to peer into the car. Layla waved at him.

"What are you doing here at this hour?" he demanded, without acknowledging either of the twins' greetings.

<*He recognizes us,*> Hunt said into our chat.

*Everyone in Ridgemore does. They're in Magnum's pocket and out to get us*, I wanted to say. But Brady needed to focus.

"Yeah, sorry, I know it's late. But we've got a bit of an emergency on our hands."

"Is Mr. Chase expecting you?"

As we'd rehearsed, Brady ran his hand through his hair and cast heavy eyes in Hunt's direction.

"No, man. We probably shoulda texted first though. We were too overwhelmed to think of it. Hunt here . . ." Brady shook his head in theatrical lamentation. "He just found out he knocked up his girl. He's pretty shook about it."

Layla slid forward on the bench seat and leaned over me so her head popped between the front seats. "We're *all* shook about it. A baby's gonna totally change his life. It's so messed up."

Hunt didn't have to fake the anguish etched across his face as he fiddled nervously with his earring. It was the same silver hoop with a dangling turquoise gemstone he'd believed belonged to his dead dad and had worn to feel closer to him. Now, he wore it to best play a part.

"We can't talk to our parents about it," Brady continued. "They're totally lame."

"So lame," Layla echoed.

"But we really need some help, ya know? And Uncle Magnum's always been so cool with us." Brady sailed smoothly over the *uncle* endearment that made me want to gag. "And he always tells us he's here for us if we need him, anytime."

The guard's scowl didn't so much as waver at our sob story.

"Damn, we really shoulda texted him first," Layla said. "And now I forgot my phone."

We'd all "forgotten" our phones. A lie-rent or another of Magnum's minions had probably placed a tracker in Bonnie. But we knew for a fact our phones were being tracked. No point making things any easier for them than they already were.

The guard arched a single brow, likely wondering how many groups of supposed teenagers would willingly leave their phones behind.

I leaned forward next to Layla: "We like taking regular tech breaks. Staring at screens too long'll mess with your head. They've proven it leads to addictive behavior and can even affect intelligence levels."

The guard's one brow remained arched.

"Can't you just call him?" Brady asked. "Tell him his nieces and nephews are here to see him?"

At the "nieces and nephews," the guard's lone brow lowered to join its companion.

Hunt leaned across Brady. "We'd really appreciate it, man. I'm just . . . I'm real out of sorts. I mean, what would you do? Do I suggest an abortion to her? Is that a total douchebag move? Or do I quit school to support both of them?" Hunt gulped, his Adam's apple bobbing. "Do I marry her?" His voice caught at the suggestion.

Hunt was as likely to ask someone like this guard for advice as I was, which was to say, not even a little bit. But Hunt was rocking his part.

The guard winced at the prospect of dispensing life-altering advice to strangers, or maybe it was that he knew Magnum would rip his ass to shreds if he advised the wrong path that didn't line up with this week's scripted narrative. Regardless of the reason, the guard said, "Give me a sec," and stepped back into the guardhouse.

<*You know the one thing we haven't talked about,*> Hunt said, <*is* why *Magnum wants me to think Zoe's pregnant. And if she really is, why does he want her pregnant? What's he up to?*>

<*My guess . . .*> Griffin said. <*He wants us to pass our immortality on to a new generation.*>

<*Yup,*> I said, having already considered the topic. <*More malleable test subjects, plus backup options, in case we don't do what he wants us to.*>

<*Or he kills us one too many times,*> Layla said.

<*Wow,*> Brady said. <*Ever the ray of sunshine, aren'tcha?*>

<*Fuck off, Brade. I'm nervous, all right? Premeditation ain't my thing. I don't like having time to think.*>

<*I can't believe I'm going to say this, but neither do I,*> Hunt said, before clarifying. <*In this one specific instance of murder. Otherwise, I love thinking.*>

<*We know,*> Layla and I said together.

Ordinarily, saying the same thing would have made at least one of us squeal out a laughing, "Twinsies!" As it was, neither of us cracked a smile.

<*My ass cheeks itch when I'm nervous,*> Layla added. <*New discovery.*>

<*Well, thanks so much for sharing,*> Brady muttered as the soldier exited the guardhouse.

Brady tilted his head up toward him as he stood, legs hip-width apart, in front of his window.

"I can't reach Mr. Chase. He's probably sleeping. However, you are on his preapproved visitor list."

<*How about that?*> Layla chimed in with a delighted half sneer.

"I've alerted the guards stationed at the house. Drive on up and they'll let you in. But if Mr. Chase is asleep, don't disturb him. He needs his rest."

"Of course," Brady said. "We wouldn't want to *disturb* his rest."

<*Watch it,*> Griffin warned. <*You're starting to sound mildly murderous.*>

A hand on the steering wheel, Hunt leaned over Brady again. "Thanks for the assist, man. Uncle Magnum always knows just what to do, no matter how rough the situation. He's the best."

<*And the Oscar goes to fan favorite Hunt Fletcher,*> Layla said into our silent chat.

Girl just wouldn't shut up. It was how she was made.

The guard smiled for the first time since our arrival. "It's been a privilege working with him. The man does such important work."

The man's smile froze, as if he was only then realizing *we* were Magnum's "important work."

We hadn't been able to tell if everyone in Ridgemore was in on Magnum's murdery plans, or if there were varying tiers informed on a need-to-know basis. Based on the guard's deer-in-the-headlights look, he knew Magnum liked us slow roasted to a crisp over a spit.

<*Dude doesn't work* with *Magnum,*> Layla said. <*He works* for *him. He's Magnum's bitch.*>

No doubt he was.

I hated that Magnum had made us his bitches too.

The soldier ducked into the guardhouse, and the gate started to open on oiled hinges. As its halves swung slowly inward, the guard called out, "Good luck with the baby."

Hunt gave a burdened, "Yeah, man, thanks," to seal his Oscar-worthy performance, and finally Brady guided Bonnie down the long drive.

<*Why do all bajillionaires need the longest driveways in history?*> Layla asked. <*Is it like a dick thing?*>

<*Everything's a dick thing to you,*> Brady said.

<*True, true. But ya think they, like, compare driveway lengths? Instead of dick inches, they do feet?*>

<*Who cares? Magnum's gonna be dead soon.*> Brady's comment swiftly returned the solemnity to our group.

<*I thought the guard would never shut up,*> Layla said, though she'd talked as much as he had. <*Why'd he have to be so sus about us? Us being innocent kids is part of their narrative about us.*>

Brady snorted. <*Yeah, right, we're all* so *innocent. Especially you.*>

<*You know what I mean.*>

<*We're not supposed to know they kill us all the time, but they all probably do. That's gotta be weird, right?*> I said as Bonnie wound through stretches of dense forest on either side.

<*Def less weird than being the ones doin' the dying,*> Layla said.

<*True dat,*> I said on a heavy sigh. <*I'm so freaking ready for our lives to get less weird.*>

Layla nudged me in the ribs with a pointy elbow and a fleeting grin. <*A girl can hope.*>

Brady parked in front of the main entrance to the house, a massive double door that was as tall as several humans. No guards rushed out to question us or lead us to their master.

We tried the door, but it was locked. After circling the house, we discovered the sliding glass door from the pool unlocked, however. We slipped inside, still without anyone popping up to escort us.

Elegantly dim recessed lights illuminated just enough of the house to keep us from bumping into furniture.

"Hello? Uncle Magnum?" Layla called out softly.

Brady whirled on her. <*Why are you calling for him?*>

<*'Cause that's our cover?*>

<*You're gonna blow our cover. If no one's here, then finally we get a fucking break. Let's murder him while he sleeps, easy-peasy.*>

Somehow I doubted we were going to get quite that lucky. *Easy-peasy* hadn't exactly featured prominently in our vocabulary lately.

<*But the gate dude told us he notified the other guards . . .*> Layla said.

<*And maybe they're on a piss break or didn't see their phones or however they get their notifications. I dunno.*>

<*I don't like* I dunnos,> Griffin said before purposefully bumping his arm against mine.

I reached out to squeeze his, but then we parted around a massive leather couch that looked comfy enough to sleep on. I wanted one. Our potentially resting gazillionaire, however, was not in it.

<*It's too quiet,*> Hunt said.

<*Not if Magnum's sleeping,*> Brady insisted. <*We'll be in and out in no time. Before they even realize he's dead.*>

My fingers twitched as we tiptoed across the mansion that was definitely too quiet. Unease crawled along my skin like tiny ants as we passed room after room—a parlor and a den, a secondary kitchen, powder rooms and a library, an exercise room that made me want to pause and admire it, though we didn't. Every room was empty. We even checked behind closed doors. No one; some spaces hadn't even been decorated yet and were vacant without furniture.

We were about to creep up the main set of stairs when, with a foot on the first step, I stilled. Around me, my friends stopped too.

I perked my ears and listened for several seconds before blinking in surprise. <*Is that . . . ?*>

<*Someone getting it* on*?*> Layla completed. <*Hell yeah it is. Someone's gettin'* boned *and loving it.*>

<*You sound entirely too pleased at the prospect,*> Hunt said.

<*Well, yeah.*>

I glanced up at her on the step ahead of me.

She shrugged. <*Fun's fun. We can still kill him. Easier with his pants down, am I right? Dude can't run from us with a boner.*>

<*Men can run with a boner,*> Brady corrected. <*Just not as easily.*>

<*Nothing like brotherly fact-checking.*>

But then even Layla silenced to listen.

As we padded up the carpeted steps, the moaning became louder, the grunts of pleasure more pronounced.

I couldn't resist a quick glance at Griffin, only to find him already looking at me. Mere hours ago, I'd been learning his happy sexed-up sounds.

He winked at me, clasped my hand, and led me into a wide hallway—and stopped midstep, his foot in the air for a moment, piling us up behind Brady and Layla. Hunt peeked his head above mine.

The groaning grew louder as I gaped and blinked and actually rubbed my eyes, cartoon-style, at the sight I simply could *not* make sense of.

Seconds passed, or damn, it could have been whole minutes.

My mouth hung agape. Griffin's hand was limp around mine as if he was struggling just as much as I was to comprehend the scene before our very eyes.

Layla let out a long, quiet exhale. <*What was that you said about our lives getting less weird, Joss?*>

<*I have no idea,*> I breathed into our group chat, amazed I could form words. <*I can't think of a single thing right now. I just . . . I can't . . .*>

<*What the holy fucking* fuck *am I looking at right now?*> Brady barked into our minds, expressing what I probably really wanted to say.

I rubbed my eyes again as Griffin guided us to better hide behind one of the massive pillars that supported the open room . . . filled with . . . filled with . . .

<*I think my mind's melting,*> Hunt said.

Now *that*, that was exactly what I was thinking, if I was thinking anything at all.

# 9

# How, Oh How, Do We Get Back to Logical World?

The pleasured moans boomed at full volume in the otherwise silent night as my crew and I gaped from behind marble columns. Perhaps entire minutes slipped by as my shock pressed heavily upon me, as if I were at the bottom of a deep pool.

The pillars framed the entrance to the large room I could only describe as a . . . playroom?—like if cats were people and enjoyed cushy luxury for their climbing gyms, scratching posts, and napping recliners. A couple of divans occupied either side of the space, but the rest of it was furnished with staggered, plush surfaces in varying sizes and set at differing heights and angles. I probably would have been perplexed about the purpose of the room if not for the fact that a couple of men were draped across two of the peculiar pieces of furniture, which provided knee and elbow support for one, a perch for the ass of the other. Both were buck naked, sporting raging hard-ons, and one man was giving the other head. The receiver had both hands tangled in the other's hair, setting the dicksucker's rhythm, his moans arriving faster now, louder as they colored our stunned silence with broad, shocking strokes.

It was, by all appearances, a made-to-order sex room.

Though unexpected, that on its own wasn't particularly shocking. What did men like Magnum do with more money than they could ever possibly need? Build fancy, velvet-sheathed sex rooms, apparently.

He'd done stranger. Gunning us down in a high school gymnasium with a whole school of kids just outside was one such example.

No surprise, Layla recovered her usual snark first. She'd been working her snark muscle consistently since kindergarten, at least.

<*This brings a whole new meaning to self-pleasure, don'tcha think?*>

<*I can't think*,> Hunt said, almost certainly for the first time in his entire life. <*Did one of you slip me shrooms again? 'Cause that's all I can come up with to explain this.*>

<*Nope, no shrooms*,> Brady said in a flat monotone I didn't think I'd ever heard from him. His mind had to be melting too.

<*Then just to make sure I'm seeing what I think I'm seeing . . .*> Hunt said. <*You all* are *seeing Magnum . . . sucking off another Magnum?*>

<*Yup*,> Layla answered, sounding downright chipper all of a fucking sudden.

<*So this is actually happening*,> Hunt said.

<*Uh-huh. He's, like, inventing a new kink, all on his own. Think of it, guys, we're witnesses to a whole new fetish being born right here, right now. To think, if we'd brought our phones, we coulda filmed this. We'd be millionaires by the end of the week. This beats out any porn in existence.*>

<*I can't deal with your bullshit right now*,> Brady told Layla. <*Keep the crazy nonsense to yourself.*>

Layla turned toward him, her eyes alight with the insults she was about to hurl at him.

<*I mean it*,> Brady cut her off before she uttered a word and without looking away from the next-level kink we had front

row seats to. <*I'm not in the mood. We can't just . . . This isn't . . . normal.*>

Griffin's fingers finally tightened around mine again. <*This isn't possible.*>

<*Only, clearly it is,*> Brady said. <*I just don't know . . .*>

<*How?*> Hunt supplied.

<*Yeah, I don't know how.*>

<*Guys,*> I said, <*we're fucking* immortals. *This isn't any weirder than finding out we can come back to life if we die.*>

<*I feel your point, Joss,*> Brady said, <*but this def feels weirder.*>

I didn't even bother denying it.

<*It does,*> Griffin said. <*I mean . . . the fuck? Are they . . . twins?*>

At once, Layla and Brady's faces screwed up in mutual disgust.

<*Maybe clones,*> Hunt suggested. <*He's obviously into the science shit.*>

<*For all we know, our lie-rents did this,*> Layla said.

<*They're too young,*> I pointed out.

<*Unless there's a way to speed up growth rates,*> Griffin countered. <*They could be keeping that shit secret, no doubt.*>

<*Possible, I'm sure,*> I said. <*I mean, dudes, if* this *is possible . . .*>

<*Anything is,*> Griffin completed.

The man standing threw his head back, his ass clenching, and tugged the kneeler's mouth around his dick over and over to a chorus of wet slurps.

<*Which one of 'em do we kill?*> Layla asked.

I started, all at once recalling why we were there in the first place.

<*Maybe we should kill him later . . .*> Brady said.

<*Why? You were all kill, kill, kill before we got here.*>

<*I was. And now I can't decide whether I'm grossed out or turned on, and I just wanna go. Only I'm not sure I can stop looking.*>

<*I keep trying to look away,*> Griffin said, his eyes glued right where the rest of ours were.

Standing-Magnum's moans shifted, becoming guttural and deep.

<*Oh shit,*> Brady said. <*He's gonna blow.*>

<*I think it's the other guy who's blow—*> Layla stopped abruptly, her eyes bulging as wide as mine suddenly were, and mine felt so big they might pop out of my eye sockets and roll away.

A third Magnum sauntered through the other entrance to the room—on the opposite side from us, thank fuck. He was just as naked as the others, just as openly aroused. He shook a bottle of lube before squirting some onto his cupped palm.

"Don't you dare come without me," he scolded. "We're coming together."

Standing-Magnum groaned—in frustration this time. "But I'm so close," he whined.

Lube-Magnum stalked toward him. He tossed the bottle onto one of the many open, padded surfaces, rubbed the lube along his erection, then smacked a hand to either of Standing-Magnum's hips. He lined himself up behind him while Sucking-Magnum kept right on sucking.

<*Oh my . . .* dudes,> was all Layla managed to sputter.

I was incapable of even that level of coherence.

<*I really wanna look away,*> Hunt said.

Luber began kissing Stander's neck.

Hunt added, <*You sure about those shrooms?*>

<*I'm not sure about anything right now,*> Griffin said. <*I'm kinda hoping this is shrooms.*>

Stander leaned his head on Lube's shoulder, pulling one hand free of Sucker's hair to tangle it into the other man's.

Or were they the same man?

*Fuuuuuck.* This was so messed up!

I had to remain mindful to keep myself from exclaiming aloud or from breathing too loudly. <*Maybe we're in some kind of hypnosis right now.*>

When none of my friends answered, I did. <*Yeah, I don't believe that either.*>

Sucker came up for breath, peered up at the scene between the other two men, and rose, pulling Stander into a deep, hot kiss.

<*We shouldn't keep watching*,> I said.

<*Why not?*> Layla asked. <*This is gold.*>

<*Feels pervy*,> I said.

<*Why?*>

<*Uh, we wanna kill the guy? Guys? Fuck, I dunno. But what if he—they—catch us? Then not only did we come to kill him—them . . . this is too strange . . . but first we watched them fuck. It looks bad.*>

<*Worse than killing a mofo?*> Layla said. <*Nah. We're good.*>

<*That's insane, Lay*,> Brady said.

<*Uh-uh. What we're* seeing *is insane, not me, bro.*>

None of us argued with that.

<*Must be clones*,> Griffin said. <*Odds of them being real, natural triplets seem low.*>

Hunt gasped softly, but it was loud enough to make my heart thunder until the three Magnums kept kissing—and now also groping—each other without pause.

<*What if* we're *clones?*> Hunt asked.

Before I could properly freak out about that possibility, someone *tsk*ed at our backs.

We whirled around, Griffin gripping my hand more tightly as if preparing to run with me.

My mouth dropped open, when I didn't think I had more shock left in me. Surely, I should have been completely numb by now.

But a fourth Magnum stood on the other side of the pillars. He wore a dark mask around his eyes, a cowboy hat and boots, and booty shorts—with an open fly in the front, through which his stiffy was poking.

There was no shortage of Magnums or erections in this joint.

*<At least his dick isn't wearing a mask, too, or a little cowboy hat,>* Layla said when my brain was legit broken.

"What are you lot doing here?" Bootyshorts announced aloud.

Which caused the other three Magnums to immediately cease their kissing and fondling—and trail surprised stares along the length of the room to eventually land—and remain—on us.

Oh, their surprise had nothing on ours . . .

"We came to see Uncle Magnum," Layla said. As the only one among us capable of speech, she was our perfect spokesperson. "We needed him. But now we don't know which one of you to come to for our heart-to-heart." She barked a brief laugh. "No pun intended on the coming bit."

She canted her head to one side and examined Bootyshorts up and down, not shying away from his dick, on full display and not losing any of its rigor.

"Who are you supposed to be, dressed up like that? Are you . . . Zorro?"

Zorro? I couldn't even spell Zorro right now, let alone carry on like we weren't surrounded by no fewer than four naked Magnums—when there was only supposed to be one of them in Logical World. How, oh how, do we get back to Logical World?

*Hey, destiny, fate, the universe, whatever, wasn't one rich asshole out to murder us enough?*

I received no answer, though Layla did.

Bootyshorts smiled triumphantly. "Why yes, I am Zorro. Thanks so much for noticing. These assholes never can figure it out."

Based on personality alone, Zorro was not our usual Magnum.

Zorro looked over at the others. "Do we have to erase all of them? I like this one. She gets me."

Stander disengaged from the two Magnums at his front and back and stalked toward us. His brows were drawn low over stormy eyes. His stiffy bounced at first, but it was rapidly deflating to half-mast.

"Yeah, we have to erase them. All of them." He frowned. "Which means we have to start over again, dammit."

"Then you shouldn't have excused the guards for the night."

Stander huffed. "Yeah, right. And have them ogling us like the kids are?"

Zorro scanned us before sighing in defeat. "Fair. They do look surprised."

I barked a laugh, drawing everyone's eye.

"Surprised . . ." I muttered incredulously. It was all I had.

Stander slammed his hands to his hips and yelled, "Fanny!"

I crowded closer to Griffin and Hunt. Brady pulled Layla to his side.

Fanny took less than a minute to arrive, and when she did, the eyes of Magnum's executive assistant and all-around kissass grew round—not at seeing four of her precious, naked Magnums. Oh no, it was the five of us who had her boggled.

"What are *they* doing here?" she demanded. "This is your private time."

"I'd go more with kinky time," Layla snorted, drawing a glare from Fanny. "What? It's true. This is some real kinky shit."

When Fanny advanced on her, Layla held up her hands. "Hey, no judgment. I'm a straight hottie. If there were four of me, I'd be doing me too. Though without a dick to get all up in there, it probably wouldn't be quite as fun. But hey, I'm sure I'd make the most of it."

"What are you doing here?" Fanny asked. "And at this late hour?"

Hunt took half a step forward. "I just found out my girl's pregnant. We wanted to talk it through with Uncle Magnum. He always tells us he's here for us, so we figured we'd get his help."

"Our parents are too lame to talk something like this through," Brady added, amazing me that any of them could get their shit together after the crazy fest that hadn't even ended yet.

"The guard at the gate told us he warned the guards at the house," Griffin said.

"So we came on up," Hunt elaborated.

Fanny's hands were akimbo, her mouth a savage line of disapproval. "And you thought to just stand around and watch such private, sacred time?"

"Sacred?" Layla asked with another snort, and I wanted to slap a hand to her mouth. "That didn't look sacred to me. Looked more like—"

To stem whatever damage was about to slip free of her mouth, I hastened to say, "We didn't mean to intrude." Thoughts were rapidly shooting through my mind, finally assembling into something helpful. "We really didn't. We're confused . . ."

Was that the understatement of the millennium or what?

"Why are there four Uncle Magnums?"

"Because Magnum Chase is a *god*," Fanny snarled like she was a big-clawed, big-toothed, big cat defending her helpless cub. "And you're lucky he wants anything to do with you."

Her hands rose and she flicked a pair of fingers in signal at someone now at our backs.

We spun toward this new danger.

But all I managed to make out was a blur of black, a pop, and a sting as something sharp shot into my neck.

*A tranq dart*, I guessed before everything went dark.

# 10

## We Know Jack on a First-Name Basis

It was *Groundhog Day*—again—or as I was now coming to think of it: Reboot Day.

My dad, aka Reece Bryson, aka Jude Corlett, aka Judas—and a big, fat, fucking liar—woke me up for school again with a gentle nudge and with nearly the same script he'd used before: If I didn't get my butt up and moving, I'd be late for school. Plus, I wanted to especially be there for my boyfriend, Griffin, today since it was the anniversary of Mitzi's leaving him and Orson. He just knew Griffin appreciated my compassion and understanding so much.

Who came up with this shit? Who even marked the anniversary of spousal and parental abandonment—over and over again?

In the long list of questions I had about my life and that of my crew, those didn't even rate more than a passing thought. They did, however, make me want to clobber my lie-dad over the head with my bedside lamp. Here he was, right on schedule, pretending to love me and care for me. I'd believed him for most of my life, when he hadn't given a damn beyond how I could secure his coveted Nobel Prize.

I used to like his smile. It had been one of my favorite parts about him, always making things a little lighter, a little bit better. Now it felt smarmy and wheedling even though it didn't look it. Everything about his performance, as usual, was spot-on, down to the flushed cheeks and damp hair, confirming he'd recently returned from his morning, care-fucking-free run.

Waking to Bobo beside me on my bed was possibly the only thing that kept me from blowing the whole damn ruse wide open. His warm, furry body and happy, goofy grin were proof that there were indeed good things in this world, even if so much of it was revealing itself to be screwed up beyond measure.

Bobo was real. His love for me was real. Same for my friends. For them, too, I resisted the urge to hiss at my lie-dad whom I knew—*I damn well knew*—was stabbing me in the back every freaking day—after he recovered from the blow from my lamp to the head, of course.

Our lie-rents deserved punishment, and with each passing day of this bullshit, I was growing more and more in the mood to be the one to deliver it.

Thanks largely to Bobo's sweet morning greeting, I managed to keep my cool until my lie-dad left to do whatever his superspy self actually had lined up for the day. According to his script, he and Porter were treating Orson to lunch and beers to soothe their friend's feelings on the whatever anniversary of being dumped.

*Yeah, right.*

I left my note concealed in my panties' waistband in my dirty clothes basket. I'd been doing my own laundry since I was tall enough to reach the buttons on the washing machine, so it was probably safe from discovery there. Of course, if I died today and was successfully hypnotized, I'd almost certainly never find it. The note would dissolve in the wash and that would be that.

My already slim options were growing slimmer by the day. Coincidentally, so was my emotional stability. If I hadn't been ready to snap before, I sure as shit was now. This, all that had been happening to us, was the stuff of mental breakdowns. I was one more naked Magnum away from snapping.

On the way out, I snatched a small tray of fluffy, buttery, supposedly homemade croissants from the kitchen for me and my friends. A chef was *so* coming into the house and cooking when I wasn't here. No way was Monica slash Lynne responsible for this deliciousness. What was one more lie in a sea of thousands of them?

I managed to slip the house with a quick, barely there peck to Monica's cheek that I despised giving, but within minutes I was sitting in Clyde—or at least a version of him—my eyes feasting on the sight of the man I loved.

The tightness in my chest, which had been there since I first woke, finally loosened. And when he kissed me, the heat of his mouth and tongue swept me away and, for just those beautiful, wonderful moments, very nearly made me forget what we'd witnessed the night before.

Alas, not even the frisson of Griffin's kisses was enough to accomplish that. A nuclear blast, sure. Short of total annihilation, there was no forgetting.

For as long as I lived and wasn't successfully rebooted, I'd never forget.

My friends and I were a twisted anthropomorphic bundle of nerves. But it seemed only we noticed the outward signs: the jumpy stares, the bunched shoulders, the twitchy fingers, the way our smiles were brittle. All too aware we swam in a fishbowl with a whole town of observers, we made it through our prelunch classes unusually broody and quiet, but without incident. My friends were also struggling to recover from last night's mind-melt.

Only once we were settled at a booth in one of our regular haunts, Hughie's Hoagies, with a sandwich each, did the dam come crashing down all the way.

Hunt fiddled with his Italian sub, not taking a bite yet. <*Did you see Zoe? When I told her she couldn't join us for lunch?*>

Layla huffed out a breath and took a ferocious bite out of a Reuben. <*Yeah. Like you punched her in her cute, little kitten face.*>

My brows arched in question.

She chewed and rolled her eyes. <*As in, if she were a cute kitten, and Hunt punched her in the face. Like, how dare he? When all he did was tell her we needed alone time. He even used Mitzi as an excuse, and if I have to hear that story about Mitzi leaving, blah, blah, blah, one more fucking time, I'm gonna pop,* The Matrix *style.*>

<*The whole Mitzi story has me worried,*> I said. <*Like, are they adjusting the date, too, all the time? The whole calendar? How else can it keep being the same day? After a while, logistically, it'd mess them up if they didn't adjust the date. Plus, they had to compensate for four years of our lives they erased on us.*>

I tore some lettuce that peeked out of my sandwich and ripped it into tiny pieces, just to have something to do with my hands. <*This is, like, deep fake territory. How far do their cover-ups go? And if they go as far as it seems they might, then who else is in on it?*>

Brady took a loud sip of an energy drink and frowned. <*Good questions with, I'm sure, bad fucking answers we're gonna hate.*>

<*That's not what I meant,*> Hunt said. <*Did you see how Zoe kept placing a hand on her stomach?*>

I sighed, feeling like I was actually deflating. <*Like she's still pregnant.*>

<*Exactly.*>

<*Damn, bro,*> Griffin said. <*That really sucks. But try not to worry if you can. We'll figure something out. We always do.*>

Brady's eyes were uncommonly vulnerable when they pinned on Griff across the table. <*How are we gonna figure* this *out? You saw what I saw last night.*>

<*I know,*> Griffin said, crunching a salt and vinegar potato chip. <*It's totally fucked. But Hunt won't be going through it alone.*>

<*Fuck no, he won't,*> Brady said.

I swiped a chip from Griffin's plate and tossed it into my mouth. Advantage of speaking telepathically: I could talk while I chewed.

<*We're extra in the dark this time around. They def woulda tried to hypnotize us again, only this time none of us know what changes they made.*>

<*If they made any,*> Layla said, taking another feral bite of her Reuben. Girl was pissed.

<*With how our luck's been going,*> Brady said, <*they totally did.*>

<*No being a downer, Brade,*> Layla said. <*I gotta keep some pep in my step or I'm gonna fuckin' lose it big-time. So pretend for me, will ya?*>

She smiled at him viciously around a mouthful.

<*At least we already know how the whole Zoe story's playing out,*> I offered by way of pep talk. I had scant material to choose from.

<*Not the whole story,*> Hunt corrected.

I sighed. <*True.*>

We all ate in silence for a while, lost to our own freaked-out thoughts. Griffin pressed his thigh to mine, rubbed his hand along my leg a few times.

Finally, I said, <*We can't fight whatever it is we saw last night. We gotta run.*>

<*What* did *we see last night?*> Griffin asked. <*I keep replaying the scene—*>

Layla bubbled with a laugh that sounded slightly unhinged. <*Perv. Told ya it'd make for a rockin' porno. It'd totally go viral. If only we'd had our phones . . .*>

Griffin scowled at her. <*I can assure you, Magnum on Magnum is so not my thing. And in case your pervy mind needs to hear me say it, neither is Magnum on Magnum on Magnum* on Magnum. *Man, that's such an insane thing to say.*>

He turned his face toward mine. <*Joss is my thing. Just Joss.*>

I smiled, the first real, happy one of the day. At least we knew we were allowed to openly be together in this reboot too.

<*While you two lovebirds moon over each other,*> Layla said, <*I might cry. Joss is right. How the fuck do we fight* that*? What even is that? How do we kill a man who isn't a man? I mean, that's what we're all thinking, isn't it? That he's not a man? Maybe not even . . . human? Though, then, what the fuck is he if he's not human?*>

No immediate answer came.

<*He's not a fucking quadruplet,*> Layla continued. <*That'd be ridiculous. I don't even think quadruplets happen naturally, do they? And since we can't search up anything online anymore, or even at the library, we're stuck with what we already know.*>

<*He could be an experiment, just like us,*> Hunt said.

<*He's way older,*> Layla said.

<*Science has been doin' sus shit since way back. Long before they tell the public about it, they're doing it.*>

<*I don't doubt that. So okay, maybe he is quadruplets. I guess that doesn't change much, except we'd have to kill all four of them to be sure.*>

<*If he's cloned himself,*> I said, <*then who knows how many of him there might be.*>

<*He's got the funds to do that kind of crazy shit,*> Brady said.

<*For sure he does,*> Griffin said with another crunch of a chip. <*Question is, why would he want to? To have more of him to test on? To try to get our immortality and whatever other powers he can foist on us?*>

<*Maybe,*> Brady said. <*That could explain it.*>

<*And what about Fanny saying he's a* god*?*> Layla said. <*She didn't actually mean that? Right? Like, pretty please with cherries and whipped cream on top, tell me that's not what we're dealing with, 'cause I'll for real lose my shit right into the last bites of my Reuben, right the hell now. I won't even care that it's a waste of fucking deliciousness.*>

<*He doesn't seem like a god . . .*> I ventured. <*But what do we really know?*>

<*Oh. Wait. I actually have the answer to this question,*> Layla said. <*And I know I'm actually for sure right about this one.*>

She waited for us all to stare at her.

<*What do we really know? We know* jack fucking squat, *that's what. We know Jack on a first-name basis. We know nothing. Absolutely nothing. More than nothing, when it's more important than ever that we know. Oh. Yeah. And we also know that we're so majorly screwed,* we *may as well be getting boned by four Magnums, 'cause that's what he's already doing. He's giving it to us up the ass, and we have no fucking say whether or not we take it.*>

More silence settled in while we chewed, sighed, and generally brooded.

Eventually, Brady grumbled, <*Always such a way with words, my baby sister.*>

She elbowed him hard. <*Shut up, you old fat fart.*>

<*Hey,*> Brady snapped. <*That's uncalled for.*>

Softly, I inserted myself between them. <*We can't fight what we don't understand. We have to run.*>

When no one said otherwise, I added, <*We have to at least try.*>

<*And if they catch us and kill us and then wipe our memories?*> Griffin asked, rubbing his hand nervously along my thigh. <*Then we won't have any of this anymore. We won't even remember we're into each other. Already, I don't remember the first time we swapped* I love you*s.*>

<*For all we know,* I *don't remember it either. We're dealing with an unknown number of reboots.*>

I grabbed his hand, squeezed it. <*Regardless, whether we're dating or just friends, you'll always have me.*> I included the others with a sweeping look. <*We'll always have each other. Family forever.*>

I held up my palm, the skin at its center marred by a paper-thin scar every one of us still wore. Our superior healing, it seemed, didn't erase marks from when we were ten, long before we were ever shocked back to life, our immortality kicking in.

Griffin, Hunt, Layla, and Brady also held up their palms, faces out. Layla's was smeared with Russian dressing, Brady's with marinara sauce from his meatball sub. They were similar in more ways than they liked to admit.

<*Family forever,*> the four of them repeated.

Then Layla reached for our hands. <*We gotta do a friendsies forever team thing, hands together in the middle.*>

<*Then you gotta wipe all that shit off your hand first,*> Brady said. <*You're gross.*>

Layla examined her hand, wiped it clean, then smirked when she noticed the streak of marinara on his.

<*You've got something on your nose,*> she told him.

<*Where?*> he asked.

<*Here. Rub like this, and you'll get it.*> She demonstrated by running her palm across the tip of her nose.

When he copied her, she busted out laughing.

It was almost possible to believe the Fischer House party had never happened, that we were normal high school seniors with higher-than-average intelligence and an uncommonly close friendship.

After Brady cleaned his hand and his face, and smacked Layla on the arm, and after she smacked him back, we piled our hands together in the center of the table.

<*It's the five of us against the world,*> Brady said.

<*Always and forever,*> Griffin said.

<*Not even four Magnums have anything on us,*> Layla tried, but then winced.

Yeah, I didn't believe it either.

<*We've got this,*> Griffin insisted anyway.

<*Yeah, we do,*> I said.

Now was not the time to be concerned with hows or likelihoods. Now was the time to gather whatever pep in our steps we could, just as Layla said. Without believing in ourselves, we were doomed already.

<*All right. Enough with the hands,*> Layla said. <*Mine's getting hot at the bottom. Plus, you guys are all idiots.*>

I smiled at seeing more of my usual friend shining through the nonsense. <*Idiots you love.*>

<*Fuck yeah. I love you morons so hard, I'm gonna puke in my mouth if I keep thinking about how we're gonna get through this.*> She popped the final bite of Reuben into her mouth and proceeded to lick her fingers, the feathers in her hair bouncing as she did so. <*So I'm gonna embrace Denial like she's my main bitch, and we're gonna do this thing.*>

<*And, to be clear,*> I said, <*"this thing" is running, yes?*>

<*Mm-hmm. Best next step.*>

But was it really?

I swallowed the lump in my throat that was interfering with my appetite and slid my half-eaten chicken salad sandwich to Brady. Without comment or question, he accepted it like he always did and dove in.

<*We gotta get Bobo before we go,*> I said.

<*Obviously,*> Hunt said. <*We'd never leave him behind. But other than that, take nothing but any cash you've got stashed. We got lucky last night.*>

Griffin and I arched our brows at him. *Lucky* wasn't the word I would have chosen.

Hunt answered our unasked question. <*They don't know we went there to kill Magnum. They bought our story.*>

My brows lowered. <*True. Some more pep for Lay.*>

Hunt nodded, the turquoise of his sole earring swinging with the movement. <*So when we run, let's leave ourselves a way out of it if, ya know, we get caught.*>

<*We come up with another convincing story,*> Griffin said. <*That should be easy enough. We can say we wanna take Clyde or Bonnie on a nice, long drive, feel 'em out.*>

<*Or we could say we're feeling stressed and not sure why,*> Layla said. <*They'd probably think it was our subconsciouses dealing with all the reboots.*>

<*I am feeling mighty stressed,*> I said.

Griffin leaned his lips to my ear and whispered in a deep, husky drawl, "We need to find time for me to help you . . . release that from your system."

My core clenched at the implication, and Layla rolled her eyes.

"I'm totally jelly, not gonna lie," she offered aloud, before adding into our private chat, <*If they shoot us up with who knows what crap just one more time, I'm gonna stab Fanny in the eyeball with a damn tranq dart.*>

I rubbed the sore spot at the back of my neck where last night's dart got me. Around the table, the others worried at their puncture sites too.

<*If we didn't have awesome healing powers now,*> Brady said, <*we'd probably be fucked-up from all the drugs they keep pumping into us.*>

<*Our stellar parents and* uncle,> I muttered bitterly. <*Most family encourages their kids not to do drugs. Ours force them on us against our will.*>

With a matter-of-fact grimace, Layla nodded, curled her hand around an imaginary dart, and pretended to stab the air over and again.

<*Fanny's eyeball.*>

She raised a second similarly curled hand, jabbing upward with it. <*Magnum's ball sac. I'm stabbin' bitches.*>

<*If it comes to that,*> I said, <*we'll stab bitches together. But now, we run.*>

I scanned the faces of my friends, searching for unanimous agreement.

I found it in their resolved yet uncertain stares. In their determined nods.

In more courage than we should need to have.

Brady polished off my sandwich, then the rest of Hunt's, and soon we were piled back in Clyde.

Why wait when you had a highly dangerous plan with very low odds of success? Better to rip off the Band-Aid quickly from that sucker.

We ditched our bags in our school lockers since it would support our stories of an impromptu joyride, and Griffin pointed Clyde toward the Periwinkle Hill neighborhood and my sweet boy Bobo.

Afternoon classes were gonna suck it. And maybe, just maybe, so were Magnum, Fanny, the lie-rents, and Magnum's murder squad with the happy trigger fingers.

When Griffin's hand wasn't on the gearshift, it was on my leg. We drove home in complete silence, feeling the weight of the world on our shoulders. Feeling the razor-fine line between life and death chomping at Clyde's back bumper.

We were going to run. But could we really outrun our deaths?

# 11

## We Hope You Enjoyed Your Visit to Ridgemore, Where Strangers Become Prisoners—Oops, I Mean Friends

Bobo was ecstatic at the unexpected ride with all his favorite people. I managed to sneak him out without encountering my lie-rents, and I now occupied the passenger seat of Clyde so he could stick his head out the window, which he did, as far as I'd allow him. His cute boxy face was split into a wide grin, his eyes narrowed to slits against the wind, his jowls quivering comically as they caught air. A slim stream of his drool trailed behind us like a banner.

If only the rest of us could be that excited to be nearing Ridgemore's town boundary . . . We'd set the scene for our "joyride," explaining aloud for our listeners that we needed a break from the stressors of school and general life demands. And what better way to ease some of that tension than to feel out how Clyde was running after his latest tune-up? To really let him loose on the open road?

After that, Griffin turned the radio to the classic rock station to cover up how we'd settled into a burdened silence. I kept tasting what I had eaten of my chicken salad sandwich as a nervous nausea swirled through my gut. Were we foolish to risk escaping?

If Magnum or any of his lackeys discovered that we were on to them, that we knew way more than we should given we were rebooted just the night before, they'd kill us for sure. And chances were they'd succeed in wiping out what limited understanding we did have of the situation and our adversaries.

But continuing to play dumb in their lethal game wasn't reasonable either. How could we continue to allow them to do what they'd done to us? To *murder* us, to erase entire years of our lives? To toy with us and our futures as if we truly were Magnum's chattel?

Whatever choice we made, one certainty remained: The stakes were too damn high, the people at risk far too fucking important to be risking.

Clutching Bobo around the hips so he wouldn't fall out the window, I leaned my head against the headrest and closed my eyes. The opening notes of "Bad to the Bone" burst forth from Clyde's speakers, and Layla yelled loudly enough to be heard over the music and the rush of air from the open windows, "Fuck to the yeah! Perfect song for a joyride!"

Griffin's hand landed on my knee. When he squeezed, I opened my eyes to find him glancing from me to the road and back again. His eyes were troubled. They seemed to ask, *Are you okay?*

I offered him what smile I could. It was flimsy, betraying too much of the fear I was working hard to hold at bay, the visceral memories of death and the terror of losing my loved ones forever that I was trying hard to forget.

His responding smile was part grimace. It appeared to say, *Yeah, I know. We're not okay at all.*

We really weren't. I didn't know if we'd ever be all right again. This was the kind of recurring trauma that was featured in psychiatry journals.

When the song drew to a close, Griffin turned down the volume and leaned forward over the steering wheel.

"We're almost at the edge of town," he announced.

Living in a town as small as Ridgemore, we were never more than twenty or so minutes away from its limits, no matter where we were. There was no more drawing out our escape plan. The moment of truth was upon us. Would Magnum's forces swarm us the moment he realized we were trying to leave? Would they wait until we put enough miles between us and town that it became evident we didn't intend to return? When we bailed on our scheduled training session with our ninja instructors later that afternoon?

"I'm so glad we decided to do this today," Layla said for our audience. "It's a perfect day for a joyride. Warm enough but not hot. Fall crisp but not yet cold. Clear skies. No traffic since it's the middle of the day."

My girl was doing her best to sound normal, but she'd never been one to list out the mundane. Still, her performance was so much better than anything I could manage.

"It was about time for a nice, long drive," Brady added. "We were majorly overdue for one."

We were overdue for a lot of stuff. A reprieve from being hunted like beasts would have been nice, for starters.

Griffin dipped his head lower, studying the quaint, eagerly happy sign announcing the departure from town. The words were painted in a bright, scrawling flourish.

*We hope you enjoyed your visit to Ridgemore, where strangers become friends. Come back to see us soon!*

I scoffed under my breath. More like, *where strangers become prisoners—oops, I mean friends*.

Griffin turned off the radio entirely. <*Here we go, guys*,> he said into our minds.

I gripped Bobo tighter and held my breath.

Clyde zoomed by the sign, blurring its absurdly fake message . . . without incident.

Layla laughed loudly. I exhaled shakily into Bobo's fur.

<*Nothing happened,*> Griffin told us with a happy slap to the wheel, his relief stark. <*We're totally fine.*>

<*Well, what did we think was gonna happen?*> Brady asked. <*Did we think we were gonna combust when we crossed the line? That Clyde was rigged to blow if we left the allowed perimeter? We checked him over today, but we did when Griff raced, too, and we know how that went. Or maybe that Magnum had drones lined up to shoot us down the moment we exited town? That the chips inside us were gonna explode and blow up our brain stems or some shit?*>

"Fuck me," I muttered. I hadn't even considered those possibilities! So much for my relief. Any of those things could still happen!

<*I've been thinking about the chips,*> Hunt said. <*If we had them, they would've probably fried when we were defibrillated.*>

<*Good point,*> Griffin said as he continued to drive the empty stretch of road, his shoulders relaxing against his seat back, his hand loose atop my knee since he didn't have to shift gears. <*Unless they put new ones in us after that.*>

<*I thought of that, but I think we'd notice. They'd leave behind a bump, or if they implanted them into our brains like Brade just suggested, we'd have at least a tiny incision scar.*>

<*Not necessarily,*> Brady said. <*Not with our superhealing.*>

<*Maybe we need to strip down and check each other out,*> Layla said, for once serious despite her suggestion involving nudity. <*See if we spot anything. It'd be smart to put them on our backsides somewhere, where we can't easily see them ourselves.*>

<*We should do that,*> Hunt said.

<*I'll do Joss,*> Griffin said with a wink to me and one of his true, natural smiles.

I waggled my brows at him. <*And I'll do Griff.*>

His smile widened while Layla groaned and then whined, <*You guys suck. I need to get me some, stat, or else I'll get way too jelly. I . . .*>

My stare was eating up how fucking hot Griffin was, and how amazing it was that I could openly ogle him. I didn't immediately register that Layla had trailed off for good reason, until Griffin's stare hardened on the road up ahead.

His throat bobbed as he asked aloud, "Uh, guys . . . what the hell is that?"

Layla was already perched on the edge of the back seat, peering between the front seats. Hunt and Brady also scooted forward to better see while I bobbed my head around Bobo's rump and tail.

Griffin pointed at a sign that was fast coming into view.

None of us uttered a word until we read it.

*Welcome to Ridgemore, where strangers become friends. Make yourselves at home and stay a while!*

Griffin slowed Clyde to crawl past it. There was no mistaking the upbeat scrawl—an identical stylistic match to the farewell signage—or what it said. As to what it meant . . . fuck if I knew.

When the sign was far enough behind us that it was the size of a postage stamp, Layla broke our stunned silence.

"How the *fuck* can we be entering Ridgemore when we just freaking left it?"

I didn't answer. Neither did the others.

"Huh?" she insisted, a hysterical edge creeping into that single-worded demand. "*The fuck*, guys? Whatthefuckwhatthefuck*whatthefuck*! Fuck, fuck, fuck, fuck, *fuuuuuck*!"

Though surely we were all thinking something along those lines—I certainly was—an entire additional minute passed, during which Layla's breathing grew heavy, like she was maybe about to hyperventilate, something she'd never done before.

"Guys, I think I'm . . . I think I'm losing my ever-loving shit," she panted. "Right now. Right the hell now."

After the Magnum times four sexcapades we'd witnessed the night before, I didn't think my mind could be blown open any wider. But *damn*, if the universe didn't love to tell me to hold its beer and *watch me top that shit, motherfucker*.

All I kept thinking was, *We just left town and now we're being welcomed back into it*. That was it. No deductions or conclusions. No brilliant hypotheses as to what that implied. No if A leads to B, then C must be true. Nothing but a numb repetition of that one glaring fact.

*We just left. And now we're . . . back?* That, and chicken salad. I might actually puke it back up if I didn't calm down real fast.

"Guys, I mean it," Layla said. "I need . . ."

"What do you need, babe?" I asked, surprised to hear my voice sounding level, in control. Layla threw her hands up, then brought them down with a smack against my seat and Griffin's. "I don't know what I need," she yelled, too loudly in the confined space, even with the windows open. "I just know I don't need *this*, whatever the holy motherfucking fuck *this* is."

Layla had been dropping F-bombs since we were, like, nine. Even then, how many she fit into a sentence was a pretty accurate gauge of either how upset or how excited she was. The needle was tipping toward red now, the zone where she lost control entirely.

<*Maybe we should bring the convo back into our mindspace*,> I suggested.

<*Don't think that's necessary*,> Hunt said. <*It's normal for us to freak out about something like this.*>

I turned in my seat to face all of them, keeping a firm grip on Bobo, who'd pulled his head inside the cabin at the panic in Layla's voice. He was looking everywhere, attempting to locate the source of her distress so he could attack it. I ran a soothing hand down his back, and I wished someone would do that for me.

Griffin gripped the steering wheel with both hands, continuing straight on the road that was supposed to lead us out of town—not the fuck back into it.

"Okay then, Brainiac," I told Hunt even when I normally wouldn't. He wasn't overly fond of the term.

"You all are as smart as I am and you damn well know it," he said automatically, like he usually did whenever one of us was an idiot and called him that.

"Yeah, I know. Sorry. So . . ." I peppered Bobo with more pets. His tail was tucked though his ears were perked. My sweet boy didn't know what he was supposed to be doing. "This ain't normal, obvi. What are we thinking? A mistake in the signs? Maybe a prank? Wouldn't put it past one of our moronic classmates to move it. Pike Bills would totally do something like this."

Layla's heavy breathing slowed some. "I could absolutely see him doing this."

"He probably took a hard tackle in practice yesterday or something," Brady added. "Got drunk with the guys, wanted a break from doing drive-bys on mailboxes or whatever the fuck they do for fun these days, and came up with this brilliant plan." Brady laughed. "That's gotta be it."

But every one of us knew we were grasping at straws and clutching them for dear life. If everything else in our lives were ordinary, sure, then maybe it was Pike Bills and whatever crew of buffoons. But our lives weren't ordinary. Not even close.

"So what do we do?" I asked. "Just keep driving?" I looked at Griffin.

"Yeah, let's just keep going. If the signs were switched up, then nothing changes. We're still out for a nice joyride."

Griffin kept driving, and indeed nothing changed, just not in the way he meant.

Before long, we passed the road that led to Raven's Lagoon, and soon after, the location of Magnum's institute, concealed behind dense trees. Next, we drove by the turnoff for the Fischer House.

The closer we drew to the center of town, the more familiar and irrefutable landmarks rolled by, and the more that chicken salad insisted I wasn't finished with it yet.

When we breezed past the high school, Layla whispered, "You guys . . ." And that was it.

I preferred it when she was laying down a long streak of F-bombs. A quiet Layla who couldn't find the words, when to her most would do in a pinch, was unfamiliar territory. We already had enough of that to choke on.

Brady patted her on the leg before starting to rub comforting circles across her knee, a behavior just as unlikely as Layla's trailing off yet again.

"I know," Brady cooed to her. "It's wack."

I chortled darkly. "Wack? No, man, this is . . . dammit, this is next-level . . ."

Tears suddenly stung my eyes. I hid my face along Bobo's neck. He craned his head back so he could kiss me, no doubt feeling my turmoil, but couldn't reach.

"Maybe there's a logical explanation that we're missing," Griffin offered, sounding wholly unconvinced.

His eyes flicked to the rearview mirror. <*Brade, you're sure you didn't slip us shrooms again? We won't even be mad.*>

<*Actually, I'll be fucking grateful,*> I said. <*After Magnum Four, shrooms would be a fucking fantastic explanation.*>

Brady only pursed his lips. <*Sorry, dudes. No shrooms. Though I wish that were the reason too. Way more fun than whatever hellhole we're stuck in.*>

"Let's just get to the end of town . . . uh, again," Hunt said aloud, "before we freak out any more."

"Easy for you to say," Layla muttered. "I'm already freakin'. I'm majorly freakin'. I'm freaking out so hard I don't even have a dick joke in me at that perfect setup."

Brady's brow pinched in concern for his twin. If Lay was out of dick jokes, we really were in trouble. Dick jokes were like her factory default setting.

The fifteen or so minutes it took to traverse Ridgemore along its main road passed swiftly. Before I was ready to confront any more upheaval of our already disturbing lives, Clyde whipped past the farewell sign again.

We held our collective breaths until the outline of the next sign popped into view. Immediately after, Layla started her quasi-hyperventilating again.

There it was, bright and indisputable beneath the afternoon sunshine: the welcome to Ridgemore sign.

Alternating between cursing vehemently, worrying silently, and Layla doing her heavy breathing, Griffin drove us through town a third time, just to be sure.

When we passed the farewell sign again, and then the welcome sign loomed within sight, he guided Clyde to the shoulder and parked. He turned off the car, threw his head against the headrest, and closed his eyes.

I watched him. His chest heaved. His lips pursed. His nostrils fluttered as he fought to calm himself. He clutched the steering wheel with a white-knuckled grip even though we were stopped.

He and Hunt were the most levelheaded of the five of us. I sought out Hunt.

He'd leaned his forehead against the window, his jaw as tight as I'd ever seen it, and flicked the dangling turquoise of his earring—over and over and over again. Harder and harder, the blueberry-size turquoise swung. He must have felt my stare on him, but he didn't turn to meet it.

When Layla began another continuous chant of *fuckfuckfuckfuckfuck*, my fingers fumbled for the door handle. Pushed it open.

Bobo jumped out. I stumbled after him. Lowered myself to my knees on the grass.

Before I realized it would happen, the chicken salad rushed up my throat. I bolted upward, staggered to a clump of bushes, and threw up behind them.

After I was sure no more was coming up, I turned. My friends were all out of the car, and along with Bobo, they looked at me with big, worried eyes.

"I'm fine, guys," I mumbled, though I was shaking, and *fine* was probably one of the very last words I should be using to describe any of us. "Can I use that toothpaste again, Lay?"

She ducked into the back seat and dug through her Mary Poppins purse. She rarely was without her bag, whereas I'd left mine at school. While she handed over the travel-size tube and a bottle of water, Brady spoke just for the five of us.

<*Okay. So we . . . somehow . . . ended up in some crazy-ass science-fantasy story, with immortals and other peeps with supernatural powers locked up in an institute and a villain who's four of him and a hell-loop of a town we can't leave . . .*>

I snorted. <*I mean, I hate to agree with such an outlandish theory, but shit if it ain't the best one out of all of them. 'Cause what's the alternative?*>

Whining, Bobo rubbed against my legs. I scratched behind his ears while I brushed my teeth with my finger with the other.

<*That we're living out a reality stranger than fiction,*> Griffin offered before drawing closer, waiting for me to finish brushing.

<*Or as strange as, certainly,*> Hunt added, crossing his arms and leaning back against Clyde's hood. <*I think it's time for us to stop looking for answers in the mundane and start stretching that box.*>

<*Whaddya mean?*> Layla asked.

He crossed his legs at the ankle. Brady reclined against the hood next to him.

Hunt said, <*It’s time to consider that Magnum might be more like us than he lets on.*>

<*How?*> Layla asked.

<*He’s not immortal or he wouldn’t be gunning for our ability to return from death. But there are apparently others like us out there, or close to it. Which means, paranormal abilities, as absolutely fucking nuts as it sounds, are real.*>

I finished brushing, returned everything to Layla, and sank to the ground to love on Bobo, who rushed onto my lap with a relieved whimper. Griffin lowered down next to me.

<*It’s not just the Aquoians with legends of Sky People and the like,*> Hunt said. <*Across practically every culture and every time period, there are stories of people and creatures that defy the laws of logic, science, and societal understanding. For example, legends of vampires and shape-shifters and even immortals can be found all around the world. I don’t know if vamps and shifters are real, and I woulda guessed they’re not if not for, you know, the fact that we’re apparently immortals.*>

<*No matter how times we say it, no matter how many times I hear it,*> Layla said, <*it doesn’t stop making my mind go* pooooooooooooosh.>

With both hands, she mimed her brain exploding, before settling onto the grass beside me and letting her legs plop out in front of her.

<*That’s how I feel too,*> Brady said. <*I keep wondering, when’s it gonna stop feeling so insane? Maybe never, huh?*>

<*Maybe never,*> Griffin muttered, picking at a blade of grass and leaning his head on my shoulder.

Hunt stuffed his hands into his pockets. <*We don’t know much, that’s undeniably true. But we do know for sure that immortals are real. So if immortals are real . . .*>

<*What else might be?*> I said.

<*Exactly. The Aquoians have got lots of legends. Besides the Sky People, they’ve got skinwalkers, and they’re not the only tribe that*

*does, maybe not by that same name though. Skinwalkers can take on the appearance of another person. Some tribes even say they can imitate animals, creatures, whatever. Magnum's not a skinwalker, I don't think, but what if it's not science, not cloning? What if he can duplicate himself some other way?*>

<*Shut up,*> Layla said. <*That's impossible.*> She winced. <*Isn't it?*>

Hunt just gave her a look that reminded her: *Immortals, dude.*

She flung herself theatrically to the grass. Bobo bounced over to lick her face. She laughed, which was far better than her earlier panicked wheezing.

<*So Magnum's got superpowers too,*> Brady hedged. <*The greedy fucker just wants more.*>

Hunt shrugged. <*Yeah, maybe. Maybe not. Maybe it's something else we don't know of. There are a lot of insane theories about magical creatures out there. Who's to say what's real and what isn't? When our baseline is that we can come back from the dead, and heal from major shit like it was nothing, then we have to reevaluate everything we thought we knew.*>

Layla groaned. <*I don't want to.*>

<*Tough cookies, Lay,*> Brady said. <*We ain't got a choice.*>

<*What's up with the looping?*> I asked. <*'Cause that's what it is, right? We try to leave and immediately we're brought back right to the start. It's like a . . . like a video game. Every time we leave, we trigger the same response. It kicks us to the beginning. A loop we can't escape.*>

<*Sounds about right,*> Hunt said. <*Though I can't explain it. There's no science that can do that. None that I know of. You guys?*> He looked at us. We shook our heads.

I tapped my foot against Griffin's just to touch him more. <*If it's not science, none that we know of, 'cause it's not a hologram or anything like that, then what does that leave? Magic?*> I barked a laugh. <*That sounded more absurd saying it than I even thought it would.*>

My friends all wore serious expressions though.

My brows shot skyward. <*Are we really talking* magic *here?*>

Hunt frowned. <*I don't know, I really don't. But we can't rule it out. My dad said he saw you in his dreams, and that his ancestors said we'd protect the Sky People's legacy now. I mean,* Sky People. *'Nough said, no? What's that if not magical?*>

I chuffed. <*Bonkers?*>

That got a laugh out of all of them.

Layla was hugging Bobo to her chest, much as I had earlier, like he was a source of comfort when everything we believed to be true was rapidly unraveling.

<*And we can't escape Ridgemore,*> Layla said grimly.

<*Doesn't seem like it,*> Hunt said.

<*You know,*> Griffin said, <*I've been trying to remember . . . are we even sure we've ever been anywhere else? I have what I feel are memories of other towns, but every time I reach for them, it's like they dissolve before I can grab on to them.*>

<*That sounds like reboot hypno stuff to me,*> Brady said.

<*That's what I was thinking,*> Griffin said. <*What if we've never actually left Ridgemore before?*>

His question hung in the air like a stench we couldn't escape.

<*What if it's more like* The Truman Show *than we guessed?*> he added.

This time, instead of her recent litany of *fuck*s, Layla brought a hand to her mouth and nibbled on a nail.

Softly, so that it was a whisper into our minds, I asked, <*Guys, what the hell are we gonna do?*>

Hunt sighed heavily and frowned. Brady kicked at the grass. Layla chewed her nail more savagely. And Griffin linked his fingers through mine, automatically rubbing his thumb soothingly over the back of my hand.

<*There's gotta be something,*> I added miserably. <*Some way to save ourselves that doesn't involve killing Magnum, now Magnum Four, and hoping for the best.*>

I was still hoping for an influx of unforeseen brilliance when Bobo wriggled out of Layla's embrace, stiffened, and ran to Clyde's bumper. He listened for a moment, then barked a sharp warning.

Immediately, we all stood and lined up beside each other.

Bobo kept barking until a convoy of cars crested the horizon, then he stopped, drawing to stand in front of us.

With my stare pinned on the approaching vehicles, I told him, "Good boy, Bobo."

<*Maybe they'll drive on by,*> Layla offered emptily. <*Or pull over just to ask if we need a jump or something.*>

But when the cars came closer, they revealed themselves to be a line of black Cadillac Escalades. Almost certainly, *Magnum's* black Escalades.

And we were sitting ducks, without any way to defend ourselves and even less of a way to escape.

<*We can run into the woods,*> Brady said, but then added, <*but they'll only chase us down.*>

<*And probably shoot us,*> Griffin growled, drawing closer to me.

As one, we closed the gaps between us, as if that would help a damn thing.

<*Let's just pretend to be baffled that we couldn't leave,*> Hunt said. <*But that's it. We know nothing else. They'll probably just tranq us and reboot us. As long as we don't die, we'll be okay. And if we do die, we've got our notes.*>

<*That* maybe *we'll think to find,*> Layla said somberly.

<*So we don't die,*> Brady said.

<*If only it were that easy,*> I said, rubbing with my free hand at the ring of five scars on my chest, now barely visible, the only physical sign that Magnum gunned me down.

<*Play it cool, guys,*> Griffin said. <*For all they know, the hypnos worked and we're clueless. We just don't understand why we can't leave town.*>

But when the Escalades pulled up behind Clyde, Fanny was the first one out—and she pointed a pistol at us without bothering with an *I'm your cool, fun aunt* fake smile or even a single *hello.*

# 12

# Why You Been Actin' So Messed Up Toward Us?

Palms facing forward, Griffin's hands shot up while he sidled in front of me, blocking most of my body from Fanny's line of sight—or rather, the sight line of her revolver.

"Whoa, there, Fanny," he called to her. "What the hell's going on? What do you think you're doing, pointing a gun at us?"

"Yeah, what the hell?" Layla asked, her voice rising in pitch, convincingly conveying befuddled terror. She was either in full actress mode or genuinely panicking, I couldn't even tell anymore.

While Fanny cocked a hip in her standard floral maxi skirt and Birkenstocks, with socks this time, and so incredibly at odds with the unwavering grip she held on the gun, Griffin spoke urgently into our secret chat.

<*At all costs, protect Joss. Remember we don't know why she's not coming back as fast as the rest of us. No risks when it comes to Joss.*>

<*For sure,*> Brady said, while a mean smile spread across Fanny's face, erasing my earlier comparisons between her and Judi Dench or Helen Mirren.

She stalked closer, three mercenaries dressed for a showdown shadowing her. Jaggar and Raynar weren't among them, though that provided no relief, given the resolved, unfeeling look in their eyes. They were killers who didn't see a bunch of inoffensive young adults, but rather *targets*.

Brady had moved immediately beside Griffin. From behind a wall of their muscled backs, I could barely see Fanny. Hunt stood in front of Layla. Even before all this dying and resurrecting, our guys had always been especially protective of us, no matter how many times we insisted we could defend ourselves.

"What are you doing out here?" Fanny demanded of us, ignoring Griffin's and Layla's questions.

She and her three goons came within a dozen feet of us when Bobo barked then growled, low in his chest.

She pointed the gun at him. From the other two Escalades, another eight mercenaries, also decked out in full paramilitary gear, emerged but remained beside the cars. The threat they posed was clear, however.

I rose to my tiptoes and glared at her over Griffin's shoulder. "Don't point a gun at my dog."

Griffin reached behind himself to hook his arm around my hip in a steadying touch.

"I asked you a question," Fanny said, keeping the barrel pointed right where it was.

Bobo bunched his shoulders and dipped his head into them. His lips pulled back to bare sharp teeth. His tail was pointed, stiff as an arrow.

"And I told you not to threaten my dog," I said.

Bobo's growls were vibrating through his barrel chest.

"He's threatening me," Fanny said.

"Because *you're* threatening us," I said. *Like, duh?*

"Drop the gun and he'll calm down," Griffin said.

Fanny tipped her head as if in consideration, taking in the lot of us, all huddled together.

"No."

"Whaddya mean, *no*?" Brady asked. "What the fuck are you pointing that thing at any of us for anyway? What the fuck did we ever do to you?"

Fanny chuckled brightly, as if she found real humor in his questions—or maybe it was in our predicament. Being such a fan of Magnum—and of Magnum Four, even—I didn't doubt her gauge of normal behavior was skewed.

"*What did you do to me*, he asks," she muttered. "You ungrateful little shits!"

She waved her revolver in the air before settling it back on Bobo, whose rolling growls came without ceasing.

Brady crossed his arms over his chest. "Does Uncle Magnum know you're here, being all crazy with us like this?"

Fanny snorted before her features pinched back into cruel angles. "*Does Uncle Magnum know . . . ?* Of course he knows! Everything I do is for him. Everything I've ever done is for him."

Her tone was strident, as if she were as close to a mental breakdown as the rest of us, which seemed ridiculous, given that we were the ones under constant threat of death and not her.

*Fuck. Her.*

Layla sidestepped Hunt and also raised her hands in a silent, *Don't hurt me, you crazy bitch.*

"So, I'm megaconfused right now. What happened to you? You've always been so nice to us. Why you been actin' so messed up toward us right now?"

I suspected the *Zoolander* reference was lost on our audience.

"We just wanted to go for a nice drive. But . . . something's wrong." Layla shook her head artfully, and now I was sure it was all theatrics. My girl was aces.

Her face scrunched up into dumb-bimbo levels of confusion. "For some reason, it's like we can't . . . leave. I dunno. Do you know what's going on?"

<*Way to deescalate, Lay,*> I said privately.

Fanny no longer considered Bobo from along the pistol's barrel, but she still pointed it at my sweet boy. Her eyes on Layla, she sneered openly.

"Of course I know what's happening. I know everything. And you are idiots for making Magnum work so hard for everything he's fighting to accomplish."

"What . . . ?" Layla looked from her to us as if flummoxed by this change of direction. "What are you even talking about?"

Fanny chortled darkly. "Magnum is the greatest gift ever sent to humanity. The Aquoians and their stupid Sky People . . . They don't recognize a god when he walks among them!"

"Wait," Layla said. "What? Uncle Magnum's a *god*?"

Fanny rolled her eyes. "Magnum is as close to a god as anyone who walks this Earth is going to get. Closer than the bunch of you, that's for sure."

"Well, duh," Layla said. "We're not gods." She snorted. "Obviously."

Fanny threw up both hands, including the one with the gun. Her index finger remained alarmingly close to the trigger. "That's what I keep telling everyone! Just because you can do some things Magnum can't doesn't make you any better than he is. He's . . . he's humanity's salvation. All he ever tries to do is help humans. Help, help, help. He gives, gives, gives, and gives some more. And you selfish bastards defy him at every turn. You're selfish spoiled brats, and one of these times we get to kill you, you're going to stay dead."

It wasn't part of our act when the five of us took a big step backward. Hunt grabbed Bobo by the collar and shuffled him back with us. Bobo didn't so much as pause in his snarls, his fierce stare pinned on the crazy lady in Birks with socks.

Layla made a show of looking at the rest of us. "Uh, guys . . . do you have any clue what the fuck she's talking about? I'm so lost."

"That's 'cause you're the biggest idiots this Earth has ever seen," Fanny shouted. "Your powers are wasted on you. Magnum should have *all of them*."

Her eyes glittered with avarice. Or maybe that was insanity. How had we ever believed she might be an ally, however brief that hope had lasted?

"I don't know what she's talking 'bout," Brady snapped, "but I do hear her saying, loud and clear, that she wants us all dead. So, Fanny, get the fuck away from all of us. Right the hell now."

Fanny stared at us for a good ten seconds before laughing.

The five of us, and Hunt still pulling Bobo, took another big step back. There wasn't much retreat left before we hit bushes at our backs, and a puddle of my upchucked chicken salad behind them.

Finally, Fanny said, "You all really are dim-witted, aren't you?"

"Hey," Layla protested. "Watch it."

"Or what?" Fanny gave a little twisted smile that made a shudder run through me and—fina-fucking-lly—brought the gun to her side.

I breathed a little easier.

Without turning to look at them, Fanny barked at the soldiers, "All of you. In the cars with the doors shut and windows up. Now."

Without so much as a squeak of protest, the goons obeyed. When the last door pulled closed, Fanny turned to verify their compliance. With a flaring swirl of her skirt, she studied us.

"Maybe I've been going about this wrong," she said.

"Oh? What makes you say so?" Layla said, slathering on snark thick as goopy icing.

"Ha, ha. You always think you're *so* funny."

"Actually, not really. I'm just confused. I thought you liked us. But you just said you want us dead, and we can't seem to leave town, so yeah, I'm actually freaking the fuck out. I'd really like it if you'd just let us go."

"I'm not letting you go anywhere."

"Then take us to Uncle Magnum," Hunt said, releasing his grip on Bobo's collar.

Fanny's smile shifted to adoration. The hard glint in her eyes softened to dreamy. "I can see why you'd believe he'll help you. He's incredibly magnanimous. And that's why I'm not going to kill you today."

"Gee, thanks a bunch," Layla said, with more of that snark icing dripping from her words.

"Watch your mouth, young lady, or I'll watch it for you."

"I don't even know what that means."

"Because you don't know much. And part of that's not your fault. Much of it is, but your lack of understanding isn't entirely thanks to your mind-boggling inability to see the bigger picture."

<*She's so fucking generous,*> Layla said into our bond.

<*And so fucking insane,*> Griffin said. <*Protect Joss, remember. The woman's unhinged. Who knows what she'll try to do.*>

Fanny changed tack yet again. Her smile transformed. Had I not known we were dealing with a crazy lady, I would have believed it was genuine. Apparently our lie-rents weren't the only one who could win Oscars around here.

She crossed her arms, the hand with the gun hanging loose.

<*No one go for the gun,*> Griffin warned us. <*The guards in the car'll be on us in seconds, and we're totally outnumbered.*>

We so were. What I wouldn't do to get a little advantage around here . . .

Fanny's gaze bounced around each of us, her smile growing wider. When she pointed that smile at Bobo, his growling quieted to a wary whine before silencing.

"Great," she said. "We're friends, aren't we?"

My true friends and I didn't utter a word. If she believed she could wave a gun at us and tell us she wanted us dead, and then waltz in talking all buddy-buddy, she was nuttier than a rabid squirrel.

"Good," Fanny continued, unfazed by reality. "I'll make you a deal. We come to a satisfactory arrangement today, and I'll let you leave and go about your day. Though you won't be able to leave town no matter what. You just have to accept that."

"And why is it that we can't leave town?" Layla asked.

"You just can't. Magnum needs you here."

"So Uncle Magnum made it so we can't leave town? But how?"

"Oh, I see. You still haven't gotten even the basics. Magnum Chase isn't from this world any more than you are. He can do things you would only dream of."

"So then what's he need us for?" Layla asked.

Fanny's smile tightened in place. "Because for as magnificent as he is, he isn't immortal. And you are."

My mouth dropped—part performance, part shock that she was telling us this out in the open. If she was being this transparent, that didn't bode well for us.

"I see you're surprised, of course you are. Magnum is brilliant. You'd have no memory of your powers or where you come from."

"Where do we come from?" Hunt asked.

*Please, please tell us.*

"Where do you think?" she said.

"Um, Ridgemore?" Layla said.

Fanny had a good laugh at our expense.

"You're from another world. So is Magnum."

My mouth fell open again before I whispered a strangled, "Say what, now?"

Another chuckle from Fanny; I wanted to reach into her throat and rip out her vocal cords.

"Do you really think you'd be immortal and from *here*? From Earth? Where humans are so puny?"

"We didn't think we were immortal at all," Griffin said. "Why do you think that?"

"Oh, because we've killed you three hundred sixty-nine times so far."

My eyes bulged. My knees weakened for a few stunned moments.

Not even Layla had a ready quip for that fun fact.

"You always come back to life," Fanny said with a grimace that suggested she wasn't nearly as pleased by that little detail as I wanted her to be.

*Us alive* was a very good thing.

I stepped out from behind Griffin. Immediately his arm shot out to hold on to me. I leaned into his grip so he wouldn't fear for my safety any more than necessary.

"You say 'humans' like we maybe . . . aren't human?"

Had I ever asked such an outrageously unbelievable question in my entire life, over however many reboots? I doubted it.

"Of course you're not. How could you be?"

"Right," Layla said in a deadpan. "How could we be?" She blinked as if in a daze.

I was in one too. There had to be a reason for our immortality that I'd known. But surely we were human . . .

Fanny seemed to lose herself to her own thoughts for several moments.

So I pressed, "Uh, if we're not human, then what the ever-loving fuck do you think we are?"

Fanny *tsk*ed in annoyance, whipping up a hand that silently said, *Stop*. At least it wasn't her gun hand.

"Stand down," she said, but not to us. "I've got it under control."

*The chip in her head.*

"I said, I've got it, Todd. Now be silent until I say otherwise."

Her stare narrowed back on me. Greed, or perhaps disapproval, swam in it once more.

"Joss Bryson." She chuckled, probably at her inside joke that my family name was invented along with the rest of my supposed past. "Just because you look human doesn't mean you are human. Or at least, not entirely human. In some ways, you're as human as any Joe Schmo. In other ways, you're so much more extraordinary. You aren't *just* human. Appearances can be deceiving."

<*No shit,*> Layla grumbled only for us. <*I wanna murder this* cool, fun aunt *bitch like I've never wanted to murder anyone before.*>

"Fanny," Hunt said, his tone level, serious. It was his *let's get down to business and get answers* tone. "Please, we're understandably confused. Give it to us straight. If you're certain we aren't fully human, please, what are we, then? And where do we come from if not from Ridgemore? Also, what is Uncle Magnum, and where's he from?"

Fanny uncrossed her arms, dropping the gun back to her side. Sunlight glinted across its shiny metal.

"That's where our little deal comes in. You want me to give you answers that explain your existence?" She spread both arms like a showman, the gun pointing off to the side for moments. "I can do that for you. I have those answers."

"And in exchange?" Hunt asked.

"Besides letting you go today? You want me to be even more generous?" She tutted. "Of course you do. You always want more."

<*Fuck, she's beyond delusional!*> Layla commented privately.

"Fine," Fanny went on. "I'll tell you whatever you want to know about yourselves *and* I'll let you live today—"

"So generous of you, indeed," Layla grumbled. My girl really couldn't help herself.

Fanny glowered at her. "All you have to do is tell me how you transfer your immortality to someone else."

It took me a second to register that she was talking only to me right now.

"And how you steal powers from others."

"Oh, is that all?" Layla quipped.

Fanny whirled toward her. "Shut it, young lady. Or I'll be very happy to make you." She tapped her gun against her thigh a few times.

Layla, wisely, for once shut the fuck up.

"You're talking to me?" I asked, despite the obvious signs.

Fanny's brows arched in a pained, *Why am I stuck dealing with dimwits?* "Yes, you. Of course I'm talking to you. You're the one who gave the others immortality. If you can do it for them, you can do it for Magnum."

"I-I can't," I said, without pausing to think. "What you're suggesting's absurd."

"Are you saying you won't cooperate? You don't want the deal I'm offering you? I assure you, it's a good one."

<*Suuuuuuure it is, lady*,> Layla said, at least only for us this time.

"How can I tell you what I don't know? I didn't give"—I laughed nervously—"*immortality* to anyone. And I certainly didn't take *powers* from anyone else, either. I-I . . . I mean, that's not possible."

Fanny studied me for long beats, during which my heartbeat thundered. Eventually, on a heavy sigh, she said, "That's one thing you'll never have that Magnum does. He doesn't allow believing something is *impossible* to stop him. He decides on a result and then moves entire worlds to achieve it. That's why he'll always win over you, every time. You have never stood a chance against him. No matter how many times we do this, he'll always come out on top."

I had no idea what to say to that.

"Fanny, be reasonable," Hunt said. "How can we provide you with information we don't have? That Joss doesn't have?"

"Because you know it. Even if it's somewhere deep inside you, you must know it. Your kind simply aren't this stupid."

"Our . . . *kind*?" Griffin repeated.

Fanny smiled, sadly now. "Yes, your kind. Not all the way human, remember?" She *tsk*ed again. "How am I expected to do anything with this level of idiocy? Really?"

"If you share what you know," Hunt countered, "maybe then we'll understand. And once we do, we can give you the answers you want."

"We've tried that before. You don't remember, but we have, many times. You always hold back on me in the end. You cheat. No, it's time to change the dynamic. This clearly isn't working. We've made it too easy for you. Too nice. Too many comforts."

She scowled and spoke to the chip in her head, "*Shut up*, Todd. I told you to leave me alone, so *obey*."

When her attention landed back on us, something indeed had changed, and I didn't like it one bit. Her face was . . . blank, as if the woman felt absolutely nothing at all.

"Todd, stay out of this. We'll tranq them in a second. They won't remember anything I'm saying. I have an idea."

Her features grew animated just to hiss at him, "If you utter a single other word, I'll rip your dick off—from the inside—drag it up through your intestines to your throat, and make you choke on it. You hear me?"

My friends and I exchanged wide-eyed looks. Griffin guided me behind him once more. Hunt resumed his stance in front of Layla. And Brady cracked his neck to either side, preparing for a fight.

One we had little chance of winning.

But hey, we still had our notes, right? It wasn't a total loss. We'd learned new material, however difficult it was to wrap our minds around at present.

Todd, apparently, recognized a psycho when he heard one and opted to remain completely silent.

Fanny brought the gun up in front of her, patted it on one of her palms. Then, as if arriving at a decision, she muttered under her breath, "Screw it."

In whip-fast movements, she flung her empty hand at the Escalades behind her. Some sort of shimmering shield rose around them . . . completely blocking them from sight.

I gasped. Next, with the speed of a lifelong soldier, she disassembled her gun with a series of fast clicks and slides, flinging all the separate parts, including the loaded magazine, in separate directions. They sailed into the woods at inhuman velocity, reaching no doubt inhuman distances.

Another gasp slipped from my lips, joined by sounds of my friends' surprise.

Then, oh then . . . fucking then, Fanny gripped either side of her head—and motherfucking tugged.

Her scalp . . . split open . . .

"Oh fuck," I breathed while my legs wobbled. My insides churned in utter, stark disbelief.

Fanny yanked the skin of her head and face down to pool around her neck, as if it were a fucking snood, as if her face were nothing more complex than a mask discarded.

A harsh exhale escaped Griffin. I melted against his back as I spied over his shoulder.

Beneath the mask . . . *Fuck me*, beneath the mask . . . was something without a single doubt *not human*.

She was a pasty, grayish, uh, *creature* with shiny skin and more teeth than a freaking prehistoric shark. They spread to occupy the space where her nose, mouth, and chin were on her "Fanny" face. A tongue, long as a giraffe's but pointy, slithered out. Above her mouth were two eyes that reminded me again of a shark's, mostly for their unfeeling look.

With a bone-chilling creak, she unhinged her jaw like a snake's and stretched her maw until that's all her head was. Even her eyes disappeared somewhere behind it, and terrifying, sharp teeth was all there was to see. A goopy, gray slime slid down to gather at the base of her teeth, along what perhaps passed for gums.

As if the sight weren't paralyzing enough, she *screeched*. It was the sound I imagined a fox made when being slaughtered.

"Fuckfuckfuckfuckfuckfuck," Layla was back to chanting without end.

The five of us huddled together. I trembled.

Monster-Fanny sprinted forward on her Birks with a flourish of flowered fabric.

"Run!" Brady shouted. "Fucking *run*!"

We pivoted and bolted, as agile as deer bounding away from the predator who had them pinned in its hungry sights.

We put hundreds of feet between us and her—*it*—before I realized my mistake. Before it hit me like a big-rig truck going twenty over the speed limit.

"Bobo," I said on a panicked wheeze as I whirled around while Hunt and Griffin zipped past.

Brady and Layla sailed by.

I sprinted in the opposite direction.

My sweet boy was hunched over his strong haunches, his muscles coiled for attack.

He was covering our retreat.

I hadn't ordered him to run, dammit, and I should have. He always obeyed my commands.

I ran faster than I ever had before.

And still I could already tell I'd be too slow.

Griffin shouted my name. So did the others.

Their footfalls pounded after me.

I stumbled and lunged forward, doing what I could to eat up the distance that separated me from my dog.

I had to watch as Bobo launched himself at Fanny.

She backhanded him across the head so hard that he flew against Clyde, slammed hard against steel, and slumped to the ground without so much as a pained whimper.

As I screamed at her to stop, Monster-Fanny spun toward him, grabbed for Bobo with normal-woman hands, and tossed him up into the air as if he didn't weigh sixty pounds.

Her head was all nasty teeth and nastier tongue.

Bobo slid through her teeth as if through a welcoming tunnel.

They snapped shut behind him.

The cunt swallowed my dog whole.

# 13

## A Swan Dive over the Edge

When Brady first died, impaled on rebar at the Fischer House party, I was devastated. We didn't yet know his death was temporary.

When Griffin sailed over the cliff in Clyde on the way to Raven's Lagoon, I was equal parts terrified and hopeful. At least then I knew there was a chance he'd come back.

When I had to watch while Magnum's hired guns shot Layla and Hunt, and then pointed a pistol at my head, I was both furious and horrified. What if one of us didn't come back? What if *I* didn't, and that was the last I'd ever see of the people I loved?

When Griffin exploded into charred bits inside Clyde, that especially shook me. The damage to his body was so extensive, the likelihood he'd resurrect was slight despite our history.

Through all that, and through the endless reboots, threats, lies, and deceptions, I'd more or less kept my cool. Sure, I'd puked from the trauma, and I no longer enjoyed pleasant dreams but nightmares I fought to escape.

But now? This time? When Fanny revealed herself to be a literal monster from some . . . some *hell realm*, only to *eat* my *sweet, wonderful* dog? The only being I loved on this entire fucking planet that wasn't immortal . . . ?

I'd been on the edge before. Now, I took a swan dive over that edge and I was in free fall.

Whatever composure I'd still possessed vanished so suddenly I didn't even note its passing. One moment I was gaping at the nastiest, most hideous cunt I'd ever had the displeasure of seeing, the next I finally *snapped.*

I lost my motherfucking, ever-loving shit.

My scream morphed from a keen of loss to a violent, assaulting battle cry.

Distantly, I registered my friends at my back, calling to me, both aloud and via our secret bond. I didn't process a single one of their words. I'd plummeted beyond the reach of measured reason. The entirety of my focus homed in on a single mission: Get Bobo out of the monster as fast as possible.

Fanny's head was still mostly teeth—*so many awful teeth*, long like fangs, crowded and overlapping each other. Like a macabre circlet, her jaws crowned her head, which continued to point upward as she appeared to relish in the meal she'd just consumed. Her gullet bobbed as if she were swallowing. With how many teeth she had, I worried she might have them on the inside, too, coating her throat. But I didn't notice any movement that indicated chewing.

Her eyes were closed as she seemed to savor her prey, as she trusted that she was the apex predator here, and we were her and Magnum's playthings, to do with as they pleased, just as they'd always done.

I launched myself at her, tackling her to the ground.

She uttered a surprised gasp, with a whoosh of foul-smelling breath when I landed on top of her—which meant I also landed atop Bobo. But I couldn't worry about what damage my weight might be causing him.

He was *inside a monster*. I had more immediate problems than my crushing weight.

From her neck down to her hips, her chest was engorged. Beneath the skin suit she apparently wore, maybe she didn't have an actual rib cage. Again, like a snake, the outline of Bobo's body pressed against hers, the ridges and bumps of his form deforming hers.

I straddled her hips, and when she shot her arms forward to restrain me, I gripped them—and realized my error. Bobo gave her a massive potbelly—and was in my way.

She bucked her hips to throw me, and *fuck* was she strong. She almost managed it, but I held on, snarling as I fought to keep my balance.

Beyond her disgorged torso, I eyed her head. Its teeth gnashed, snapping at the air. She screeched—more foxes being slaughtered.

Without a blade or gun—any handy weapon would do—and unable to damage her chest for Bobo's sake, my best bet was to break her neck.

I sensed my friends crowding around us by the shadows they cast. I kept my attention on the monster beneath me, on keeping astride it.

Someone delivered a brutal kick to its head. Fanny screeched some more. Then another of my friends joined in, and they kicked her head from both sides. Constant blows rained down. Her cries became a continuous wail pitched to make the ears of mere mortals bleed.

I yanked one of her arms down to the ground and stepped on it, leaning my weight onto it, pinning it in place. I squatted onto my other leg, gripped her other arm with both hands, and slammed it down against my knee. The bone snapped as if it were a branch, tearing through her human-looking flesh to poke through in two jagged pieces. She whined and bucked, arching her laden back upward.

With her pushing her chest upward, the outline of Bobo's body was prominent.

I clutched the wrist of her broken arm to either side of it and brought it, too, down hard across my knee. The wrist snapped, though no bone poked through this time.

I'd have to try harder with her second arm.

I repeated the process on the other side and did manage to push her bone through her wrist.

The monster squealed and gnashed its teeth in the breaks between the kicks to its head.

Monster-Fanny was still strong, still fighting so that I struggled to stay atop her.

I knelt over her, pressing a knee against the arteries along both of her inner thighs, and did what I never once, in my entire life, so much as imagined myself ever—*ever*—doing.

I hooked my curled fingers around the fleshy snood that hung loosely around her neck like a scarf . . . and tugged it down.

It was a little bit like peeling a banana. Enough that I might never eat the fruit again.

I stripped her of her flesh suit down to her hips, revealing more of that slimy, shiny, pasty, gray flesh.

And more Bobo. Bare of her borrowed skin, the outline of my dog pressed against her upper body, clear as if he were simply covered by a blanket.

Seeing him more clearly, trapped inside her, drew another savage cry from me. As if he'd been buried alive, I began digging at the barrier between him and me.

I rended and ripped at the gray flesh—strangely cool to the touch.

The monster's screams, as disturbing as they were, faded into the background while I zoned onto my singular task.

*Save Bobo. Get him out of there.*

I yanked and tugged and shredded flesh until I hit the black of Bobo's fur, wet and slimy, slick instead of fluffy and soft like it usually was. At some point, other hands joined mine in excavating as I continued to unearth my sweet boy.

Until all of him was exposed, curled into a tight ball within a large, gaping body cavity. Indeed, the monster had no ribs, and there was nothing to indicate whether Fanny, in her true form, was actually a female or male.

Finally, I rose from where I'd knelt my weight onto the monster's legs, keeping the beast immobilized while I dug Bobo out. With the kind of care I'd taken with him when he was just a tiny puppy, entirely vulnerable and dependent on me to meet his every need, I slid my arms under his body. I couldn't fully ignore the squelching that accompanied the action, or the way I was reaching into a *body*, dammit.

Slowly, the reality of what I'd done, what I was still doing, began returning. Sounds, which had been muted and dull, started sharpening. My pulse, a constant whooshing that had acted as a buffer between me and my surroundings, began to slow, to hush.

Bobo slid from inside the monster with a pop like a calf bursting free of its mother's womb.

His weight flung against me, knocking me onto my ass. I fell awkwardly, half seated, half sprawled across the monster's legs, the bunched-up human suit, which felt, incongruously, just like flesh, even though it had pulled off like a costume.

Bobo's weight was heavy across my lap, pressed to my chest.

"Is he alive?"

The question floated toward me as if from a great distance. But it arrived now. It touched me.

"I don't know," I mumbled, sounding foreign to my own ears.

"Fanny's dead," another of my friends told me, though my senses were still emerging from the haze, not yet capable of identifying which of my friends had spoken.

I bent over Bobo. His chest was unmoving. His eyes were closed. His body entirely limp when I moved him.

Someone's arms tugged me and my precious cargo back off the monster's body. Ah, not someone. *Griffin.* I always did recognize his touch before anyone else's . . .

His legs slid around mine, bracketing me. His arms rested gently on my thighs beneath Bobo. His head rested softly on my shoulder in silent support.

"Is he breathing?"

This time I looked up and was met with Hunt's stare. The dark chocolate of his eyes was bright amid the blood and gore that had splattered his face.

For the first time, I noticed that I was covered in it. I'd be getting it on Griffin. My fingers and arms were coated in gore.

I bent my head over Bobo's, examining his nose, his mouth, then his chest. No movement whatsoever.

I shook my head. Hunt's eyes darkened.

*My sweet, sweet boy.* All Bobo had ever done was be a good dog. All he was to blame for was loving me, loving my friends too. His goodness was met with evil, with a terrible darkness. With greed and a power-hungry need for more, more, and ever more.

It took me several moments to realize I'd begun speaking.

"No. No. No," spilled from me, over and over.

"Joss. Baby," Griffin whispered soothingly at my ear.

"No!" I only said it louder. I only meant it more.

"Everyone, get away from me. Don't touch me."

I didn't bother couching my request in politeness.

Griffin, being the awesome bestie-boyfriend that he was, slid back and away from me without comment or question.

Around a monster's body and the blood and gore of its insides—gray like the rest of it—my friends knelt and crouched on the ground. They circled Bobo and me but didn't touch us.

"What are you gonna do?" Brady asked, his words sad as a dejected trombone.

Bobo might have been my dog in name, but he was all of ours. We all loved him.

And we'd already lost enough.

I closed my eyes and cradled Bobo's heavy, limp body. I ignored the goop that coated him and felt beyond it to what was only him.

My pittie. My baby boy.

And then I recalled that, somehow, in some inexplicable way, I contained power beyond this world's understanding. I had, apparently, gifted my friends with immortality. I'd presumably taken lightning or something from one of the institute's students. According to Hunt's father, I even walked his dreams. I could speak telepathically to my friends.

And I could love them and Bobo so freaking much that it practically felt like a superpower.

I had no knowledge of the extent of my abilities. I had even less of a comprehension of where exactly they came from, or why they were mine before anyone else's.

But, however it had happened . . . whyever it had . . . magic had found me. Whether it was from this world or another entirely, it was, I allowed myself to believe, *mine.*

And so was Bobo.

In a ferocious pulse, I released into Bobo's body *my will*, my determination that, despite all appearances, *he shall live.*

I heard crisp crackling but didn't see it.

I smelled the electricity, mingling with the scent of blood and remains.

I pulsed and pulsed and pulsed what was feeling more and more like my magic with every passing breath.

I pressed and pushed my magic into Bobo.

Until I felt him move his legs.

The motion was subtle, hardly there, but my eyes flung open.

The pale blue of lightning arced across his body, jumping from mine to his and back again, so that he practically glowed.

I stared at him—willing, willing, willing him to be alive, not to have imagined his weak movement—until his eyes fluttered open.

I exhaled a disbelieving laugh, a sound incongruous in our surroundings.

Beyond the bright light that still encompassed his body and mine, I glanced up.

My friends' expressions were all varied in their details, but uniformly awed.

I laughed again, and finally smiles dared to inch across their stunned faces, all splattered and smeared with dull gray blood.

"He's alive," I breathed, nearly afraid I was imagining this result as much as my magic.

Bobo blinked rapidly as if to dispel the gunk that covered his eyelids. When his tongue emerged and started to lick his face clean, he grimaced with a spread of jowls, pulling his head back into his neck until his skin wrinkled and he gagged. Then he stuck out his tongue and gacked, his eyes going wide.

I laughed again, as did my friends.

<*Bisthcuiths, that dithguthting*,> a voice with a lisp, sweet and innocent like a child's, said into my mind.

It took me an entire minute to process that it came from my dog.

# 14

## Beast Mode with the Best Sidekick Ever

I was on absolute overload. Shit, my overload was on overload.

Our wannabe overlord Magnum was four people, and his right-hand gal was a . . . a . . . I had no fucking clue what Fanny was beyond definitely *not human*, and definitely not pretty to look at, or to taste, based on Bobo's continued reactions to her bodily fluids coating his tongue.

He hadn't stopped grimacing, hacking, and scrunching up his face. My dog was being dramatic, but damn if he hadn't earned the right to his theatrics.

To think all we'd set out to do was leave Ridgemore . . . Not only could we not escape the quaint mountainous town that was feeling less and less quaint by the second, but we were stuck inside its boundaries with *not-humans*.

Not.

Humans.

My chest heaved from the effort of taking on a monster to save Bobo, but more from the dismay of achieving it. Shock vibrated along the length of my body, making me numb all over. If I started shaking from the adrenaline dump, I might never stop.

I stared down at Bobo until my eyes blurred.

Eventually, Hunt murmured, <*Tell me I'm not the only one who heard that.*>

<*Heard what, exactly?*> Layla asked. <*I'm gonna need you to specify.*>

I glanced up to find her collapsed on the ground, too near a seeping pool of gray goop, leaning heavily against her twin.

<*'Cause I think I heard a* newly resurrected dog *talk. And now I'm worried it's not everything else that's straight-up crazy, but that it's me.*>

We delayed in answering only a beat, but it was long enough for Layla to sit up and whine, <*Oh no. Ohno, ohno, ohno. I made that shit up, didn't I? I've completely lost my noodles. I mean, I guess it was bound to happen eventually, no?*>

Bobo's hacking ceased. His head jerked upward and off my arm. His ears perked.

<*Bobo find. Bobo fetch.*>

Griffin scooted next to me. Hunt leaned low over Bobo. And Layla and Brady slid so close Brady pressed his arm along the length of mine.

<*I'm not making it up, am I?*> Layla asked in an awed whisper.

<*If you are, then we're all just as nuts,*> Brady said, almost reverently.

Bobo's head jerked again. <*Bobo play?*>

When none of us were quick to reply, he added, <*Bobo fetch noodleth? Lothst?*>

With his toddler-like inflections and the lisp, his esses sounded like *th*es. *Noodles* became *noodleth*. *Lost* became *lothst.*

It was ridiculously adorable. It probably would have been even cuter if he hadn't been coated in a monster's intestinal juices, or whatever all the wet slimy stuff was.

<*Bobo can talk,*> Griffin said, as if needing to hear the statement aloud to believe it. <*Our dog can talk.*>

Brady whistled. <*Dayum. Appears so.*>

Bobo's ears drooped. <*No Bobo play?*>

I blinked rapidly and shook my head to clear it. <*You can play later, Bobo. Not yet.*>

Bobo whined, but when I narrowed my eyes at him, he ceased.

<*Good boy. No whining. We're in trouble.*>

His ears stood up another time. He scrambled to rise in the cradle of my lap, then slid off to stand beside me.

<*Danger?*> he asked.

<*Yes, danger. Quiet.*>

Bobo nodded. He stood strong, ears and tail at attention. Aside from the glistening evidence of the dunk he took inside Monster-Fanny, he appeared to be his usual self.

<*We can figure out Bobo later,*> Hunt said, his words taking on a sharp edge. <*We've got bigger problems right now.*>

He glanced at the very nonhuman corpse lying mere inches from us. The stench of its open body cavity was beginning to push through my numb shock. The monster smelled as rank as it looked, like rotten-egg stink bombs and doo-doo all at once.

I quickly took stock of the situation as my friends appeared to do the same. Monster-Fanny's shield, or whatever exactly it was, was holding strong. If the three Escalades remained on the other side of it, I still couldn't see any signs of them or the soldiers waiting with them. I could, however, make out the welcome-to-Ridgemore greeting beyond where the vehicles should be, taunting me with its semblance of normalcy.

<*I don't think they can see us,*> Griffin said in a conspiratorial whisper even though he didn't speak aloud. <*Which means they probably didn't see that Bobo died or that Joss brought him back to life.*>

He said it so matter-of-factly, like the idea of me bringing someone—anyone—back to life wasn't absolutely mind-blowing.

<*We should be careful not to let on,*> Griffin continued. <*We don't need anyone finding out all of what Joss can do, and especially we don't want them to know that Bobo can talk. Maybe we can teach him to be our version of notes. Maybe he can be the one to warn us something's wrong if they ever manage to kill and hypno us again.*>

I was hearing every word Griffin was saying in that deep voice of his that sent excited tingles rushing through me more often than not lately, but they weren't fully registering.

The shakes had started, so mild at first that I wasn't sure they were really happening. But now there was no denying them. My teeth chattered as if we were on the Arctic tundra with whipping winds and not in Ridgemore on a balmy fall day.

Griffin didn't hesitate to wrap me up in his arms and pull my body back against his.

"It's okay, baby," he cooed aloud. "It's okay. You're just in shock."

"Ho-how are you n-not?"

"I've always known you're amazing." He said it again so matter-of-factly. "I've always believed in you."

"Me too," Layla said, before glancing at Brady and Hunt. "All of us."

My eyes moistened. My head bobbed as the intensity of my shivering ramped up.

Like he was readying for a piggyback ride, Griffin wrapped his legs around me as well, enveloping my body in his heat as much as he could.

It took a minute, but finally my shivering began to diminish.

<*We're sure Bobo was . . .*> A final tremble rolled through me. <*. . . dead, though?*>

<*Girl,*> Layla said, eyes bright and made brighter by the contrasting gray sprayed across her face. <*Yeah, he was dead. You're just gonna have to own it. You're a motherfucking badass, and I can't even be jelly 'cause I love ya like a sister.*>

I sniffed and breathed in a bit of Monster-Fanny. I winced. <*Are you guys trying to make me cry?*>

<*No, we aren't,*> Griffin said, his face nuzzling my back.

<*I kinda can't believe you went at Fanny like that,*> Brady said, and my eyes snapped to his.

Like Layla, his eyes were made lighter by the gray smeared around them.

<*You went beast mode on the bitch.*> Then he grinned. <*Didn't know you had that level of feral in you, dude, but it was good to see. We might need lots more of that before this is all over.*>

<*Yeah,*> Hunt said. <*You kicked some major ass.*>

For the first time, I allowed myself a glance at the monster's head—or what remained of it. It was a deformed heap of gray flesh, ooze, and teeth.

<*I'd say you guys were the ones doing the kicking,*> I commented, unsure how I felt about the damage we'd caused, or how unfazed I'd felt about it while I'd been inflicting it.

<*We did what had to be done,*> Griffin said, as if reading my mind. <*We've got each other's backs, no matter what.*>

<*That's right,*> Brady said. <*Family forever.*>

<*And Bobo's family too,*> Hunt insisted ferociously.

Bobo smiled and wagged his tail. <*Bobo! Famwy!*>

A laugh burst free of my chest, relieving much of the weight I was carrying. My friends were laughing too. There was no helping it despite the morbid setting.

Seeming to realize his words had caused our reaction, Bobo repeated it exactly as he'd said it before.

Again, we laughed.

<*Furry dude just* had *to go and sound like a little kid,*> Layla said, chuckling. <*He's, like, the best sidekick ever.*>

Bobo's brow furrowed. His smile faltered. <*Bobo famwy?*>

I chortled. <*Yes, Bobo family.*> I glared at Layla but was unable to put much oomph into it. <*Not sidekick.*>

<*Aw, come on,*> she griped. <*I've always wanted to have a cute, funny sidekick! If we're superheroes, we need a sidekick.*>

I pointed a meaningful look at what had once been our fake fun-cool-aunt and was now a pile of body parts. <*Don't think we're heroes, Lay.*>

<*'Course we are. It's us against the world. Nasty-ass alien bitch eats one of us, what else are we supposed to do? I mean, was it macabre and dark as fuck? Yeah, for sure. Was it necessary? I'd argue, fuck yes. We're dealing with* aliens *here. Aliens who are* attacking *us. Who have us trapped like rats in a maze, who're running experiments on us. Experiments that, in case you missed it, are of the killin' kind. So do I think you had to go at Fanny like a lioness protecting her cub? Fuck yeah, I do.*>

<*Is that what we think we're dealing with?*> I asked. <*Aliens? That seems like . . . a lot . . . but . . .*>

Layla grimaced grimly. <*But . . . not sure what else she could be. That's some Hollywood special effects shit right there.*>

I gulped. <*Only real.*>

We sat with that for a few moments.

<*You didn't do anything wrong,*> Griffin told me. <*I'd've done that and then some if Fanny had hurt you. Or any of the others, for that matter.*>

<*Yup,*> Brady chimed in. <*It's the least I woulda done. Cunt had it coming.*>

<*I lost it, too, when I saw Fanny gobble Bobo up,*> Hunt admitted. <*You just beat me to it. Not that I could've brought him back to life. But I would've gotten him out.*>

I sniffled, nodded, and offered my friends who knew me so well a watery smile.

Bobo suddenly barked, and we all spun toward the direction he pointed.

<*Danger,*> Bobo told us unnecessarily.

The shield was down. Eleven mercenaries stood together with the three cars at their backs. They each gripped a pistol, and I couldn't tell if they were loaded with tranquilizer darts or bullets. Their eyes grazed us, then Fanny's remains—and stuck there.

"Weapons live," one of the men said to the others. "Circle them."

With a jangle of weapons and a rustle of fabric, Magnum's muscle jogged over, fencing us in.

"Eyes on them only," the apparent leader of the bunch commanded.

But a woman and two men, those who stood closest to the monster, appeared unable to stop their eyes from drifting downward.

A guy with a tight buzz cut and a meticulous goatee goggled at the sight, blinking repeatedly.

"I said, eyes on them only," repeated the commander, this time with bite.

The woman and man beside him snapped their stares upward, but Goatee gawped.

I tried to view the scene from his perspective, assuming he'd been kept in the dark about the true nature of the people he worked for as we'd been.

Beyond the grotesque sight of a pulverized head and an abdomen ripped apart with the brutality of bare hands, he'd be seeing inexplicably slippery gray flesh, gray blood, and gore. He'd be spotting sufficient teeth to fill the mouths of a dozen humans. And he'd be seeing how the body of the woman we'd believed to be Fanny pooled limply around her hips and hands—how I'd shattered her arm and wrist bones. The skin suit was bunched up in an accordion of pale-colored skin, gray alien flesh, and blue shirt. The rest of her was unnervingly human-looking. Her flowered maxi skirt had barely been disturbed, save for the gray gore that spattered it. Her feet were still stuffed into matching blue socks and her ever-present Birks.

Goatee gulped, visibly shaken, and dragged his stare across me, my friends, and my dog. The guys' sneaks were covered in alien gray, and the monster's blood spattered up the legs of their jeans. Gray blood was on their shirts, arms, hands, faces, and hair too.

Layla and I were also covered in it. Her and my hands and arms were so thick with gray blood, it was as if we'd dunked them.

The commander sighed, and before I could decide what that signaled, he opened fire.

*Pop.*

Blood blossomed in the center of Goatee's forehead.

Before he dropped: *pop, pop, pop, pop*.

The leader caught the woman in midturn, preparing to flee, and he caught the man as he was raising his revolver to shoot back.

A scarlet crimson bloomed through the back of the woman's head as she plummeted forward. The man's knees gave out as blood dripped from an eye socket. He slammed to his knees before pitching forward.

Their bulletproof vests had been useless.

My crew and I leapt to our feet.

<*Bobo, stay*,> I commanded. If he charged the commander, I had no doubt he'd aim that gun at my sweet boy. <*Quiet*,> I added for good measure, so Bobo would do nothing to provoke the trigger-happy fucker.

Griffin, Hunt, and Brady lined up in front of Layla and me. She and I quickly sidled up beside our guys.

The commander trained his gun on me.

Griffin and Brady dove in front of me. Hunt darted around to shield my exposed side.

But the commander didn't shoot. He only glared at us while he spoke to his soldiers: "Anyone else unwilling to follow orders?"

In unison, the seven surviving mercenaries barked, "No, sir!"

The commander scowled. "Good."

To us, he sneered, "It's naptime, assholes."

From the others' guns, much softer *pop*s rang out into the afternoon. They hit Griffin, Brady, and Hunt first. When my guys wobbled, they shot Layla and me.

A dart pegged me in the neck, spearing my throat. They were probably all sharpshooters, which meant the extra fuckery was intentional.

I growled at them, yanked out the dart, but wasn't even able to keep myself from sliding into my friends and the monster's gunk before the world went dark on me—yet again.

# 15

# A Freaking Whopper of a Ten-Tiered Violation Layer Cake, or Pounding the Dreamwalking Nail on the Head with an Overkill Hammer

As if it had its very own pulse, my throat throbbed rhythmically. It was the first thing to demand my attention as awareness nudged at the heavy mantle that enveloped me in its darkness. My head also hurt, as if I'd boozed too hard and was now suffering from a hangover. I was lying down, warm and sluggish. I didn't possess the strength to open my eyes.

A constant background lull began to define itself into a vibration that rose and fell, rose and fell. It took a while before I realized they were words being whispered into both ears. It took quite a while for the events of the day, and then of the last several weeks, to click into place.

The voice was that of the woman I'd long known as Celia, Layla and Brady's mother, though she was neither of those things.

My overpowering listlessness, then, was due to the tranquilizer I was shot with, a drug to make me more susceptible to their hypnosis, or a combination of both. My *hangover* was no such thing, and I hadn't earned the punishment after some wild fun worth the price. My throat felt as if it had been stabbed with a knife instead of a dart.

Not-Celia's voice streamed through headphones that wrapped my ears tightly, and as I tried to focus on her words, I was careful not to so much as twitch a finger until I figured out more of what was going on.

<*Guys?*> I asked groggily into our private chat. <*Are you here too? Can you hear me?*>

If they were either, they weren't able to say.

I was eventually able to process that Celia was talking about our early days in Ridgemore, just as she did during the previous hypnotherapy session, when her recording glitched and we finally got our big break—and yet still nothing greater than a minor advantage in the game Magnum was making us play.

Celia was mentioning Ms. Gail, our kindergarten teacher. I had no way to know whether there had ever been a Ms. Gail—the kind, happy teacher who gave the best hugs—and also picked her nose—or if she, too, was yet another fabrication.

By now, there had to be hundreds of them, maybe even thousands.

While I listened to Celia prattle on about our childhood, the sluggishness faded, though only enough for me to guess that I was strapped down to what was likely a medical bed. A soft blanket draped over my hands. Any movement at all would ripple its fabric.

<*Guys?*> I tried again. <*Can you hear me?*>

Still no response.

I was tempted to call out to Bobo as well, now that we had a handy-dandy telepathic channel between us, but if he happened to be there, he wouldn't be able to control his reactions and he'd give us away.

I wanted desperately to clear my throat, to try something, anything to ease the ache where the dart had pegged me. It was torturous to suppress my natural urge to clear or cough.

Celia was steadily making her way through our formative years. Nothing was new. There were even the identical encouragements to exercise and eat my veggies. Evidently, Celia reused the same material over and again.

At least she was nearing the end of her spiel . . .

And then the information abruptly departed from what she said last time. Celia probably used the same front material and mixed up the end bits.

"I've never heard of anyone by the name Frances 'Fanny' Leeman, or Kitty Blanche, or Bryce Reynard, or Cameron 'Cam' Bradbourne, or Caroline Dinley."

I didn't recognize those final names. Did that mean Magnum ordered them killed like he did Kitty?

Celia proceeded to mention many more names I had no recollection of, with the imperative that I shouldn't remember the people ever existed.

Her previous programming sessions had worked all too well, it seemed. Whoever those people were, I had no clue if they'd been important to me or not, whether they'd been good or bad, human or not-human. Like so much about our lives, Celia had simply stolen them away.

"I am very excited to get to study at Uncle Magnum's Ridgemore's International Institute for the Advancement of the Gifted, Unique, and Extraordinary."

When my crew and I were last there, the school was called Ridgemore's Institute for the Advancement of Immortals. Finally I understood why the campus was so oddly devoid of branding. There were no placards announcing so much as the name of the institution, of which "Uncle Magnum" was presumably so damn proud.

Celia's voice droned on: "My friends and I are so brilliant that there's no reason to wait to attend the institute. We want to take advantage of the opportunities offered us by Uncle Magnum and to advance as much as possible, as soon as possible. When he suggests we transfer from Ridgemore High to the institute, we are all extremely happy to do so. We're very grateful to him and show him our gratitude at every turn. We do our best to please him."

I fought to keep my face from revealing its instinctual disgusted grimace.

*We do our best to please him—a total predator? Yuuuuuck.*

"My friends and I jump eagerly at every opportunity Uncle Magnum presents us with. We trust him implicitly to know what is best for us and to put our needs first. We trust him without question. Uncle Magnum is a wonderful genius of a man tasked with changing the future and saving humanity."

*Double yuck.*

Maybe it was Magnum and not-Celia writing the script.

"My friends and I understand Uncle Magnum's great value. He is more important than we are. He can better the lives of every creature on this planet, and for endless generations to come. We are willing to make any and all sacrifices for him. If it would help for us to die for him, it's the least we can do."

Though I was being careful not to betray my alertness, my already unnaturally still body stiffened at the blatant evidence of our disadvantage.

We had paranormal powers, that much was now indisputable. I was beginning to believe we might even have magic of some sort, or something very much like it, perhaps with another name. Regardless, despite our abilities, which Magnum so desperately desired, he still pulled every one of our strings.

We were marionettes dancing dim-wittedly in the shadow of our unseen puppeteer.

Celia continued elaborating on how much we admired Uncle Magnum, how much we liked him, how much we *blah, blah, blah,* all of it distilling into us wanting to kiss his royal ass, so much so that we'd think nothing of *dying* at his mere suggestion.

The ache in my throat and head spread to my stomach. Nausea and disgust churned deep in my gut. The vulnerability they'd forced on us, the overriding of our own free wills, the abuse of our bodies—injured, killed, hurt, drugged—all of it amounted to a violation so immense that tears pricked behind my closed eyelids. I clamped down on my will so they wouldn't keep coming.

It wasn't just me they were abusing. It was the people who mattered most. They even hurt my dog, dammit.

My previous discomfort with how violently we ended Fanny vanished. She was Magnum's mouthpiece, his biggest supporter, his right-hand cunt. She deserved every single hit we landed.

Magnum deserved more—*so much more.*

"I have no interest in dreamwalking," Celia's voice told me.

I listened closely.

"I do not believe I have the ability to dreamwalk. I do not believe I ever had the skill. If anyone were to mention dreamwalking, or if I ever hear it spoken of, I have no interest in learning about it. Dreamwalking is nonsense, an unfounded legend of the Aquoian people, a baseless superstition."

Even after all that, Celia added, "I cannot dreamwalk. I do not dreamwalk. I have no knowledge of dreamwalking. I have no desire to gain any. Dreamwalking is a myth and a lie. If any mention of it were to appear in media of any kind, be it books, movies, TV shows, an internet search, or anything else, I immediately find a reason to discontinue consuming that form of entertainment without voicing the reason to any of my friends."

Celia was pounding the dreamwalking nail on the head with an overkill hammer. She might as well be using Thor's Mjölnir.

"I am *not* a dreamwalker," Celia insisted once more, before saying, "I have never before seen or heard of a skinsnatcher. If I think I'm remembering an incident where someone peeled their skin off their body to reveal another creature beneath it, I am mistaken. I must be recalling a scene from a book or a movie. Skinsnatchers do *not* exist. No one can remove their skin as if it were an article of clothing."

So skin*snatchers*, not skinwalkers . . .

"I have never seen an unfamiliar creature with gray skin and a great deal of teeth. There is no such thing as aliens, extraterrestrial creatures, or monsters. Anyone suggesting otherwise is stupid and ill-informed. There is no such thing as life on other planets. Humans are the only intelligent life in the universe. I have no thoughts or suspicions otherwise.

"There is no such thing as a person who can split into several copies of themselves. Any such notion is ludicrous. Skinsnatchers are not real, and neither are the rumors that they can steal another person's body as well as replicate themselves. Those ideas are completely false."

My heart thudded. My ears were perked so as not to miss a single word.

"There is no such thing as immortals. My friends and I are certainly *not* immortal. We die just like everyone else. No person can return from death.

"Sheriff Xander Jones is not trustworthy. I have no desire to speak with him or to answer any of his questions. If he approaches me or any of my friends, I will immediately notify Uncle Magnum. Sheriff Xander Jones is an idiot with insane ideas with no basis in truth.

"I can, however, trust the sheriff's deputy, Kyle Carter. If Sheriff Xander Jones is being persistent and my friends and I cannot reach Uncle Magnum right away, we can confide in Kyle Carter about the sheriff's unlawful behavior."

The relatively mild ache of my head had transformed into a full-blown headache. I fought to cling to every morsel of information.

"My mother, Monica, has no interest in Xander Jones. She doesn't even like him. There is no romantic past between them.

"My mother, Monica, and my father, Reece, are deeply in love. They are a happy couple in a happy marriage. I am so grateful to have them both as my parents. I treat them with kindness and respect, as I do the parents of my friends.

"Big changes are coming for me and my friends."

I tensed, then immediately fought to relax my body, hoping the slight shift was unnoticeable. With the constant stream of hypnosis coming through my headphones, I had no way to tell if I was alone or if someone observed me.

"My friend Hunt Fletcher is very happy that his girlfriend Zoe Wills is pregnant. I am very excited for him. It's fun to have a baby! Babies are cute!

"I will encourage Hunt not to ask Zoe to marry him. He will be happier raising his baby without her. If Zoe were to die in childbirth, I will offer to help him raise his baby.

"Babies are so wonderful, I want to have a baby too."

I tried to prevent the hitch in my breath, I really did, but it happened nonetheless. Even so, it was slight, and unless someone was watching me very closely, they wouldn't notice.

*Get your shit together, Joss. Do not react to anything you hear.*

"Griffin Conway is my boyfriend and he wants to have a baby with me. Griffin and I love each other. We are the perfect match for each other. There is no reason to wait to start a family with him. The sooner we begin having babies, the sooner we can all be happy together.

"My friends will be a fabulous aunt and uncles. I tell Griffin I want to have sex with him. I also tell him I am not fertile and cannot get pregnant even when I can. I enjoy sex with him and want to engage in sexual intercourse with him often."

I had to bite my tongue to keep from reacting.

Celia just kept piling violation upon violation. It was a freaking whopper of a ten-tiered violation layer cake. What despicable bastards!

"I encourage my friend Layla Rafferty to get pregnant too. I tell her she will make a great mother and that it will be incredibly fun to all have babies together. I encourage her to have sex with Hunt Fletcher and to have a baby with him. Layla and Hunt can raise his baby and their baby together.

"Brady Rafferty will want to have a baby too. He will fall in love with Gwyneth Stradbrook and they will have sex together without using protection. Gwyneth will soon conceive."

Gwyn was a senior at Ridgemore High and the captain of the cheerleading squad. She was also, apparently, a breeder—not an exclusive club.

Fuck Celia and her brainwashing.

I could no longer control the disgust roiling through my body, but I held perfectly still.

Celia was still waxing on about how our lives and our bodies weren't our own when cold suddenly rushed through the vein of my left arm—an IV drip inserted into the crook of my elbow, the motherfuckers.

Whatever fluid they'd just injected traveled swiftly throughout my system, chilling me from the inside out. Before I had a chance to do more than experience an initial frisson of terror at descending into unconsciousness once more—entirely at the mercy of those so clearly out to hurt us—my awareness of Celia's voice faded. I struggled to hold on to the words as they kept coming, but I couldn't.

Next, the throbbing in my head and the tenderness in my throat dissipated. After that, I felt myself sinking deep within myself. Lower and lower, deeper and deeper, I went, until I no longer heard Celia at all.

My last conscious thought was of my friends, the family I *did* trust, beyond my reach.

We were all on our own.

I was alone.

# 16

## A Ceremony and an Occasion and a Freaking Celebration

It was reboot day number . . . who knew.

Again.

With Bobo at my side, I'd been lying awake in my bed, pretending to be asleep while I waited for my usual sharpness to return. Whatever they dosed us with to knock us out was powerful. I had no doubt that if I didn't possess some sort of advanced preternatural healing I'd scarcely be able to function today. Magnum and his team were doing their damnedest to cause severe damage to our bodies—when they weren't outright killing us, of course.

*How very delightful it was to be the puppets of raging psychopaths.*

By the time my not-dad, not-Reece, arrived to wake me, I was fully alert. I put on a drowsy act, however, even though I wanted to scream, to cuss him out at the top of my lungs. In truth, I wanted to do more than that—much more.

I'd gotten a taste of what it felt like to make one of our captor-tormentor-abusers pay for their crimes. Tearing into Fanny's monstrous body had been visceral, bloody, and violent. It had been beastly and brutal. I'd completely lost myself to the instinct of defending what was mine to protect. I'd become a primal version of myself beyond the dictates of contemporary society.

And I'd fucking *liked* it.

Killing Fanny had been gross, no doubt about it. But it had also been *righteous*—motherfucking righteous, and that was a beautiful thing. It had been just and empowering when so much of our power and knowledge had been stripped from us.

Magnum and minions had done their ruthless best to make my crew victims.

What we'd collectively done to Fanny proved we were victims no longer.

When not-Dad began his usual shtick—*Get up, sleepyhead, or you'll be late for school. It's the anniversary of Mitzi's abandoning Orson and Griffin*—I buried my face in my pillow and claimed to be woozy and sick to my stomach. I left out the part where I was woozy because the assholes kept drugging me without my consent, and how my stomach was churning because every last one of them were evil scum, and on top of that now I had to come to terms with wanting to murder them.

I was no longer certain killing Magnum—all four of him—would be sufficient. It was possible our lie-rents, eager-beaver scientists with hard-ons for the Nobel Prize, would in his absence continue the work of murdering us, industriously noting the results on their clipboards, no matter their claims that they wanted to help us. All we knew for sure was that they lied at every turn.

When not-Dad tried to turn my face toward him, I clenched my eyes shut against his observation. I worried he'd recognize that all the unrelenting torment had finally transformed me into a killer.

At first, he was hesitant about my staying home from school, but then he capitulated, probably since he knew exactly how many times my body had been forced to recover from their reboots. He left to go call the school so my absence would be excused.

I wondered if he'd actually place a call to the high school's front office or if there was some sort of app or notification system that updated my crew's whereabouts in real time for every citizen of Ridgemore—except for us, obvi.

Once my newfound murderous instincts began to extend to our classmates, who all must be aware of the plot against us, I grabbed my phone from the bedside table and texted Griffin, Layla, Hunt, and Brady in our usual group thread, which our lie-rents would see.

**Me:** Feeling like 💩. Staying home. I already told my dad. Wanna meet up at the 🌳🏠 after school? Not sure if I'll be up for training today.

My friends' responses arrived quickly.

**Layla:** If U R skipping, so am I

**Brady:** Ditto

**Hunt:** Meet up at the treehouse soon?

**Me:** Def but in a bit. I wanna spend some time with Griff alone first. It's the anniversary of Mitzi's leaving, remember?

**Layla:** How could we forget?

Even through text messaging, Layla's sarcasm was thick enough to choke.

**Layla:** U gonna comfort 😉🍆😽 him?

Chuckling, I rolled my eyes at her antics, entirely expected.

**Me:** Yup

**Griff:** Be there in 10. Catch up with the rest of you later?

**Layla:** Git some of that hot monkey sex & C U after. Hunt and Brade, dudes, we just got sexiled.

My phone continued vibrating with notifications, but once I saw the incoming messages were all from Layla, almost certainly making additional remarks about what Griffin and I might get up to, I abandoned my phone and rushed off to brush my teeth and take a quick shower.

Someone—I had no idea who—had cleaned me of the Monster-Fanny yuck after the mercenaries tranq'd us. Someone had scrubbed my nude body and hair while I was unconscious. But hey, what was one more violation in an infinite tally of them, right? Now I needed to scrub off the touch of this anonymous *pervert*—I mean *person*.

Man, did I ever want to kill some bitches . . .

When I walked back into my bedroom wrapped in a towel, running a comb through my wet hair, Griffin was already sitting on my bed, petting Bobo.

He brazenly trawled his stare along my bare flesh, immediately heating it, evaporating any water droplets that still clung to my skin.

"Good morning, baby," he grumbled in that deep voice that lit me on fire as he stood to greet me. "You're looking fucking beautiful, as always. And damn if it doesn't feel good to be able to tell you that instead of having to keep the thoughts to myself."

He wove his arms around me and pulled me against him for a slow, languorous kiss. It was by far the least murderous I'd felt since waking.

I pulled back in his embrace just enough to really look into his eyes. There, intertwined with the brown, green, and blue of their hazel, I identified a dark, hard resolve.

Not only was Griffin Conway angry, he was fucking furious.

<*So you heard the hypno too, then?*> I asked him silently.

<*I did.*>

<*You look like you feel as murderous as I do.*>

<*Probably more so.*>

<*You heard her saying they wanted you to knock me up?*>

A sudden, thrilling rush zipped along my body, making me frown. *The fuck?* Was it some sort of primal, reproduce-to-save-the-species instinct?

I was twenty-two. Just, like, a week ago I'd believed I was eighteen. Motherhood wasn't exactly a current aspiration.

Griffin was studying me closely. <*You know we won't let that happen, right? Just 'cause they want that, fuck them.*>

<*Yeah, I know. It's just, I realized I told you the other day that it was safe, that I wasn't fertile. But with them rebooting us all the time like this, they've gotta be switching up the days on us. I mean, every fucking day, according to them, is the anniversary of Mitzi leaving.*>

He shook his head. <*It's ridiculous. Why'd they even choose that day of all made-up days to bring us back on each time? Like, what's up with that?*>

<*Who knows? Lazy script writers? It's got me confused too.*>

<*All these years you thought your period was irregular,*> he said, <*it's probably been right on all along. It's just been them messing with our heads. Your body is perfect, so makes total sense.*>

<*You noticed that? I mean, that I was irregular? Or that I thought I was, I guess?*>

<*Of course. I notice everything about you.*>

I cracked a smile. <*You're not squeamish about it like Brady.*>

He chuckled. <*No one's grossed out by it like Brade is.*>

<*I'll bet morons like Pike Bills are.*>

Griffin's brows waggled. <*You'd be surprised. I heard him bragging about sailing the Red Sea the other day, with Nina Waits, I think it was.*>

<*She's done with Rich, then?*>

<*Who knows? Were they even together this reboot?*>

I scowled. <*Right. Who knows? They've got us by the balls and they don't wanna let go.*>

Griffin pressed another kiss to my lips, teasing his tongue across the tip of mine. <*How 'bout we let go of all that shit for now? Remember our deal?*>

<*Of course I do. I don't forget anything about you.*> I scowled. <*Well, unless they make me. How much stuff do you guess they've made us forget?*> I grimaced. <*Right. Never mind. Our deal. We forget all the bad shit when we're together.*>

<*That's right, baby. Right now, it's just you and me.*> He glanced over his shoulder. <*And Bobo.*>

I followed his line of sight to my pittie. He was sprawled out on my bed on his back, his legs in the air, the tip of his pink tongue hanging out of his mouth. He gave no indication he'd so recently survived a monster-eating. Even his fur was soft and shiny once more. Someone had obviously also given him a good scrubbing.

<*It's not quite the same now that he can talk,*> Griff added.

<*No, it isn't. I haven't been awake long enough for it to feel weird yet.*>

<*We'll have to talk to him, see if there's more to him and the situation.*>

<*For sure.*>

<*But later.*> He faced me again. <*Much.*> He kissed me. <*Much.*> Another kiss. <*Later.*> A third one that lingered and stoked the fire rapidly growing inside me.

When his lips finally pulled away from mine, I leaned forward, instantly wanting more. <*Not sure if Lay's got the patience in her to give us that much time.*>

He gave me a sly smile. <*No shit. We'd better make the most of it.*>

His hands tightened around my waist. He was already leaning in to kiss me again, when I said, <*Hold up a sec.*>

I looked around him to my bed. <*Bobo,*> I said, directing the thought to my dog.

It worked. He snorted awake. His legs cycled a couple of rounds. Then his head swiveled in my direction.

I couldn't help but smile at him. <*He's so fucking cute and goofy,*> I told Griffin before addressing Bobo: <*Go outside. Wait for me. I'll come find you soon. Do you understand?*>

Speaking to my *dog* was perhaps one of the least shocking revelations of the last several days, considering we'd seen four Magnums lined up for a fuckfest, and a full-on alien . . . or something.

Bobo rolled onto his stomach, tucking his legs under him. <*Bobo underthtandth.*>

I tried to keep a straight face, but his kiddy lisp was just too endearing.

<*Good boy. Now, go.*>

Bobo leapt from the bed with his usual grace—being gobbled by Monster-Fanny hadn't harmed him, *whew*—and padded toward the door.

Griffin opened it for him, closed it behind him, and locked the handle. When he turned back toward me and leaned against the door, his stare was molten, his hunger for me written all over his face.

God, *could he get any fucking sexier*?

He wore low-slung jeans, Vans, a belt with a silver skull for a buckle, and a short-sleeved Thrasher t-shirt that was tight enough across his chest and arms to outline his lean muscles. Ink peeked out from under his sleeves, accentuating his tanned, olive skin.

He ran his hand through his dark hair, mussing it, and licked his lips, like I was a creamy cake, dripping in icing, that he craved and was about to plow into.

*Day-um.*

He grinned wolfishly, showing straight, bright teeth. <*Like what you see?*>

<*Uh-uh. I* love *what I see.*>

The rogue vanished. His smile softened. <*I love you.*>

He sauntered toward me with a swagger that was natural, all sexy Griffin.

When he was a few feet from me, I said, <*I love you too.*>

<*My dream girl,*> he said, dragging me into his arms so fast I stumbled.

He caught me. He always caught me.

<*What about my parents? My* lie-*rents?*> I frowned for a beat before remembering our deal, hurrying to wipe the indignation from my face. <*Did you see them?*>

<*Sure did. The "lovebirds" were sharing coffee and chocolate croissants. They offered me one, but I passed. I've got something much more delicious to eat . . .*>

My insides simmered. My core clenched.

<*Then they said they were so sorry about my mom and told me to come on up. You were waiting for me.*>

I stiffened. <*I didn't tell them you were coming over.*>

He shrugged, making even that *couldn't care less* tip of his shoulders hot. <*They assumed, I guess. Remember, you're my girl in this reboot.*>

<*Thank fuck.*>

*<My thoughts exactly.>*

I was going to say something more. Maybe they probably thought he was here to check in on me since I said I wasn't feeling well, or how lucky it was that my room was on the second floor and on the opposite end of the house from the kitchen and outdoor deck, the main two places they ever breakfasted. What exactly I was intent on saying, though, I no longer recalled.

His plush lips caught mine and kissed me—softly, lovingly, enchantingly.

It didn't take long before I wanted more—more, more, more, and still fucking *more*.

I wanted all of Griffin Conway.

I escalated the kiss and he followed my lead, devouring my mouth, caressing my tongue, sucking on my lips. Consuming me. Enrapturing me.

My hands roved along his shoulders, back, and chest. Across his arms and waist. I clutched and rubbed and scratched.

I was reaching for his ass while he was reaching for my towel. I squeezed through his jeans, gorgeously molded to his even more gorgeous body, as the bath towel cascaded to the floor, leaving me completely naked—and him completely dressed.

He stepped back to admire the view. Instantly, my body missed the heat of him. My skin pebbled. More so, my nipples hardened to stiff, tender peaks.

Another time, he licked his lips; I didn't think he realized he was doing it. My breath caught. Never had a man looked at me like this.

Like I was everything he'd ever wanted.

Like he was instants away from feasting on me.

Like he'd die happy if he could just devour . . . and devour . . . and devour me.

My arousal was hot and wet between my thighs. His pressed proudly and eagerly against the fly of his jeans.

I could think of nothing beyond my desire to be consumed by this man. He smoldered, making it blessedly easy to forget everything but him.

And fuck, did I ever *need* to forget everything else.

To lose myself to him.

Allow him to lose himself in me.

As if we were of one mind, we suddenly and swiftly stalked toward each other, eradicating those few steps that separated us.

Griffin yanked off his t-shirt while I unclasped his belt, then his jeans. He was stepping out of his shoes and socks when, without ceremony, I tugged down his boxers.

No preamble was needed when his dick was this beautiful. As it sprang proud and free, his cock was a ceremony and an occasion and a freaking celebration all on its own.

In a frenzied tangle of fevered kisses and roving hands, we shuffled over to my bed. The energy between us was frantic. Even so, he slowed down to guide me reverently onto my comforter.

He was still lowering himself onto the bed when my legs parted for him all on their own. My body was a hussy ready for action, and shit if I didn't mind it one bit.

Propped on his elbows to either side of me, he held much of his weight off me as he settled between my legs. His erection pressed stiffly against my inner thigh when his eyes met mine.

I swallowed.

<*I didn't have a chance to get rubbers.*>

I chortled darkly. <*How come? You mean it wasn't a priority when we were digging Bobo out of a motherfucking alien?*>

I offered a grimace in apology at breaking our pact.

<You *are* always *my priority*,> Griffin said. <*No matter what. Condoms, not so much.*>

<*You've already been inside me bare*,> I breathed, realizing we could be speaking aloud as this kind of talk would be expected. But then, what we said to each other wouldn't be private.

He hissed in a sharp breath through his teeth. <*And I'll never forget it.*>

<*I don't know exactly where I'm at with my cycle, but I can tell I'm not ovulating.*>

He stared deep into my eyes. <*You saying you want me inside you bare again, baby?*>

My core clenched sharply, and I swallowed. <*Uh, Griff, is that even a real fucking question? Of course I do.*>

He dragged his gaze from my eyes to my mouth, across my collarbones, to my tits. He flicked his tongue over one nipple, then the other. My back arched, pushing my boobs into his face, wanting so much more of that tongue action.

Licking them again—and drawing a moan from me—he spoke to my tits. <*I can pull out before I come.*>

I discovered myself frowning. No, pouting—*jeez.*

Even with his stare on my breasts, he noticed and laughed. <*You want me to come inside you, baby? Is that it?*>

Another pulse of my core. <*More than seems reasonable. The fuck's up with me?*>

He growled possessively, a deep rumble that vibrated his chest. His eyes blazed as they pierced mine.

<*We'll get there. I promise we'll get there. I'll shoot all up inside you and make you* mine.> The declaration was raw and rough as gravel.

My insides tightened. My inner slut was apparently conspiring to get me pregnant. She was gonna have to cool her fucking jets, stat.

<*How about for now I come all over your fucking gorgeous titties?*>

The question was out before he suddenly flicked his stare up to my face. <*Shit, was that too much? Too fast? Too blunt? Revealing too much of my secret fantasies?*>

<*Was that too real, you mean? It's how you really feel, isn't it?*>

He nodded, eyes big and earnest. <*I want to have all you. I want to claim every single bit of you. You're my forever, though, baby, so we have plenty of time to get there.*>

Did we really, though? There was a very high probability that we might die tomorrow. Hell, we might die later today.

<*We'll have time to go slow.*> I hoped. <*We'll have time to go fast. We'll have time to explore everything about each other.*>

I gulped, surprised this wasn't easy to say, that it felt too vulnerable.

<*You're my forever, too, Griff. I want all of you. And I'm ready to give you all of me.*>

His eyes glistened, making the bright hues in the hazel pop.

<*So we take it day by day, baby. Every chance we get, we make the most of it.*>

<*Promise?*> I asked.

<*I promise you that and the world. I just hope I get the chance to give it to you.*>

His lips lowered to mine in a soft, gentle kiss that touched my heart.

He lifted his hips, notched his swollen tip in my hot, supple entrance . . . and pushed inside with a single thrust.

My eyelids fluttering closed, I gasped.

Never had anyone—fuck, any*thing* in my entire life—felt so right.

So. Right.

He lowered his chest to mine and whispered in my ear, over and over again, loud enough for only me to hear, while he thrust deliciously in and out of me.

"I love you. I love you. I love you, my dream girl."

I almost came from his declarations alone.

# 17

## Well, I'll Be Damned, Time to Play Their Game and Fucking Win It

Hours later, when it was nearing lunchtime, hand in hand, Griffin and I strode into the treehouse, with Bobo on our heels. Hunt, Brady, and Layla were inside and looked up at our entrance.

The voice of a breathy narrator drifted from Layla's iPhone, filling the space.

" . . . *stole her breath. His waist-long, ebony hair curved around his face like the velvet curtains of the local theater, framing the striking beauty of his visage. His skin was smooth, pale alabaster, as light and alluring as the face of a full moon, the same one that controlled Rafael. Much as she'd been by Rafael, Hanita was enraptured by Guillaume. Never had* . . ."

"Oh my God, Lay," Brady griped from where he sat on the floor, surrounded by metal parts, his box of tools, and what appeared to be a small engine he was in the process of building. For what, I didn't know. It wasn't large or powerful enough for any of our Mustangs.

"Shut that shit off, already," he said loudly enough to be heard over the audiobook.

Layla was bent over her sketchbook at the table, mischief dancing across her face. She tucked some hair punctuated with colorful feathers behind her ear, smudging a streak of charcoal along her cheek.

"Don't even pretend you aren't loving it, Brade, 'cause I won't believe you."

". . . *his hair tickled the pert, pink rosebuds of her nipples, striking a chord of ecstasy deep within her sex. She gazed upon his bareness, drinking in the vision, dragging her hungry perusal down his physique until it swept across the engorged shaft of his manhood.*"

I chuckled, released Griffin's hand, and sauntered over to the couch, plopping down beside Hunt, whose face was buried between the covers of a large tome. He appeared engrossed and entirely unbothered by the background noise.

Bobo's claws clicked across the floor. He jumped onto the couch, claiming the open spot between Hunt and me. Hunt's hand automatically dropped to Bobo's back to pet him. Griffin sank into the open space between me and the armrest, leaning his body against me.

The heat of his body and his closeness only fueled our afterglow. I rested my head on his shoulder and waited for the twins to finish. It was often easier and faster that way.

With a long-suffering droop of his eyes and mouth, Brady looked at me and Griffin. "She's been tormenting us the entire time."

". . . *his arousal glistened enticingly along the head of his sex, a bead of moisture she wanted to drown in* . . ."

I laughed. "It doesn't sound that bad to me."

"That's 'cause you just got some. She claims it's not erotica—"

"It's not!" Layla interjected. "It's paranormal fantasy. Sure, it's spicy, maybe even smutty, you judger. But it's not erotica. I'd know."

"I'm sure you would," Brady muttered with a shake of his head as he tightened a bolt before setting down his wrench.

"Hey," Layla complained, speaking over the narrator, whose voice was only getting breathier as the scene heated up more. "There's nothing wrong with reading about sex, you prude."

Though I agreed, I knew Layla well enough to believe she'd chosen this particular book to torture Brady, just as he claimed. Tormenting him was her catnip.

Brady shook his head some more as he rose, wiping his hands on a rag. "Don't be ridiculous. As if I could ever be a prude . . . I just don't wanna have to hear about some wolf shifter going down on *Haaaa-ni-taaah*." He punctuated the female main character's name not only with the frilly pronunciation, but also with a head wag.

"Guillaume isn't a wolf shifter," Layla corrected. "That was Rafael. Guillaume is a vamp. And a superhot one."

"All the dudes are hot," Brady complained.

"Well, duh. Of course they are. It's *fantasy*. May as well fantasize right."

"I don't think fantasy's supposed to be about actual fantasizing. It's about imagination. It's—"

"Shhh," Layla interjected. "Let me listen. It's getting to the good parts."

"It's pretty much all been 'good parts.'"

"Shhhh," Layla hissed, and Brady finally quieted as he sauntered over to us.

" . . . *she thought, perhaps, she should have been frightened of his fangs. They were long, curved, and wicked like the swords worn by her father's soldiers. The nearest candle shone across them, making them gleam while also bathing them in shadows. Guillaume lowered his mouth to her neck, whisking away her breath. He bit her in the precise instant his sex glided inside hers. Her surprise thundered through her body, her climax fast on its heels as she crested. She screamed so that all in the palace would hear her ecstasy, her cries spiraling down all the way to the dungeons, where Rafael festered, his wolf*—"

Abruptly, the narrator's voice cut off.

Brady was holding Layla's phone. She lunged for it, but he was half a foot taller and held it easily out of reach.

"Give. It. Back," she growled.

"I will once you calm the fuck down. Don't you think we've got better things to do than listen to your smutty books?"

"Of course we do. That's exactly why I was trying to distract myself."

<*Guys,*> Griffin cut in urgently. <*Remember not to say anything that'll give us away. They're listening.*>

<*They're always listening,*> Layla said in a panicked whine. <*I'm losing my mind. I need my smut to get me through it. I can't keep thinking about everything they're doing to us.*>

She jumped for the phone. Brady whisked it away.

They'd been playing this particular game for as long as I could remember. Those memories had to be real.

<*So you all remember everything still?*> I asked.

Hunt set down his book on the table, giving me my first good view of the cover: *An Argument for the Purposeful and Controlled Modification of the Human Genome in the Twenty-First Century*.

Noticing my attention, he said, <*I can't research all that I really want to online or at the library, so I'm making do with our lie-rents' resources. I told Alexis, whoever, that I'm considering following in their footsteps at the university level.*>

Layla sank into the L of the couch, chortling, her phone and argument with Brady forgotten. <*I'll bet she just about creamed herself.*>

Hunt shrugged. <*It was all I could think of to say that would explain my sudden fascination with all things genetics and their mutations.*>

<*They'll probably think nothing of it,*> I said. <*They know how much you love to study just about everything under the sun.*>

<*I hope so. I've gotta find out as much as I can. We can't keep doing what we've been doing.*>

With both hands now free, he scratched behind each of Bobo's ears. My dog's eyes closed. His smile stretched the width of his face.

My afterglow ebbed a little, much of the tension Griffin had so effectively erased returning in a rush of nerves.

<*I take it you all remember everything? Did you all hear the latest hypno they tried to brainwash us with?*>

Even before they replied, I knew their answers. Their eyes went hard and unforgiving. Their mouths set in furious, determined lines.

<*Yeah, we know,*> Layla bit out. <*Hence, my need for smut.*>

I'd been thinking about it while Griffin, Bobo, and I walked over here.

<*We've gotta change things up. Gotta find a way to turn the advantage our way. We can't let them keep playing us. One of these days, I'm worried we're gonna lose, and lose big.*>

I hadn't allowed myself to dwell on the fear of our failure, what it might entail or what all it might mean, but there it was anyway.

<*When they tranq'd us,*> I continued, <*a part of me wondered if we'd ever wake up. They can do whatever they want to us while we're out.*>

<*We can always come back if they kill us,*> Brady said.

<*But can we really?*> I pressed.

Hunt glanced over me to Griffin. <*He came back after being blown to bits. That's encouraging.*>

<*Not what I'd call it, but I get your point. They were probably trying to get him to come back, though. What if part of their experiments are to also find a way to kill us forever?*>

Beyond Bobo's happy rumbles, my friends were silent.

<*What if Magnum plans on killing us off for good once he gets what he wants?*> Still, they didn't reply. <*It's possible.*>

Hunt nodded thoughtfully. <*It is. And we surely can't trust them.*>

<*Fuck no, we can't,*> Brady said as he deposited Layla's phone on the table by her now abandoned sketchbook and sat next to her on the couch, kicking his feet up onto the coffee table. <*What I wanna know is who's bathing us while we're out? Anybody else majorly weirded out by that?*>

<*Uh, yeah, obvi,*> Layla said. <*What kinda perv's lathering up my gross brother's junk?*> She shuddered for effect. <*Whoever it is, they'd better not get anywhere near me after that. I don't need the cooties.*>

<*If I've got cooties,*> Brady said, <*then you've got a hundred times more than I do.*>

<*Bro, your dick's been in, like, half the senior girls.*>

<*Exaggerate much? But sure, why not? So?*>

<*So,*> I swooped in, <*as disturbing as it is that someone's getting us naked while we're knocked out and then doing who knows what to us, let's remember we were all but dipped in monster goo—*>

Layla winced in distaste. <*Let's not and say we did.*>

<*I'm a tad more pissed about the fact that they're trying to get us all pregnant.*> I glanced at the guys. <*You know what I mean. They want you to do the knocking up.*>

<*Me and Hunt,*> Layla said, her usual playfulness absent. <*That's really wrong, man. So wrong. Hunt's like my brother.*> She looked at Griffin and me, the way his hand linked with mine and rested on my thigh. <*Just 'cause you two are boning—*>

<*It's a lot more than that,*> Griffin inserted.

<*Yeah, yeah,*> she dismissed with a wave. <*I know. I'd have to be blind not to see how in love you two are with each other. You're close to spiking my insulin, you're so sweet.*>

Brady interlaced both hands behind his head. <*Really happy for you both. You deserve each other.*>

<*I second that,*> said Hunt while Bobo spun in the tight space between him and me and finally settled on his back, his belly up for rubs.

Hunt laughed softly and indulged the silent request.

<*Appreciate that, bros,*> Griffin told Hunt and Brady.

I already had my mouth open to say something else when Layla continued.

<*True love and all that crap aside, it's majorly messed up that they want Hunt to put a bun in my oven.*>

Brady scowled. <*And I'm supposed to . . . what? Get Gwyn pregnant and raise a kid with her for-fucking-ever? I don't even really like her.*>

<*You fucked her,*> Layla pointed out.

<*I did, but that was months ago, and maybe they made up that memory—who really knows anymore? She's cute with a tight ass, and she gives a mean BJ. But that doesn't mean I wanna have a kid with her, for fuck's sake. What do they expect? For me to* marry *her?*>

<*Probably,*> Layla said. <*I mean, if it's to their benefit.*>

<*Everything's always to their benefit,*> I said. <*They've been playing us like fiddles our entire lives.*>

<*Seems like it,*> Hunt admitted on a despondent sigh that caused Bobo to jerk his head to the side to look at him.

Hunt rewarded his concern with more belly rubs.

I slid forward a few inches, struggling to remain still. <*Well, I don't want to keep being at their total mercy. I'm not willing to waste a single other day of my life waiting around to see what they decide to do with us next time. Guys, seriously, we only just found out we're* four years *older than we thought we were. They've been making us lead the lives* they *want from us for* twenty-two years. *That's enough. It's too fucking much. I'm done. I won't throw away another day, if I can help it.*>

<*I'm done too,*> Griffin and Hunt said at the same time.

<*So toast,*> Layla said.

Brady nodded, sliding forward along the couch. <*So what do we do? How do we take control?*>

<*We can't leave town,*> Layla said.

<*And we can't take on practically an entire battalion of Magnum's armed soldiers,*> Griffin said. <*They'll just kill us, and then the hypno will probably stick. Plus, we're not risking Joss. Not when she took longer than any of us to come back last time.*>

<*Did you guys hear what Fanny said?*> Layla asked. <*You know, before Joss gutted her, like a fucking boss? By the way, girl, that shit was hawt.*>

<*You're so weird,*> Brady said. <*You know that, right?*>

Layla shrugged. <*That's why I'm upping my paranormal reading. Gotta prep for whichever sexy-as-fuck shifter or vampie or whatever supe is waiting to make me swoon at the institute.*>

My stare glued to my leg, I ran my nails along the knee of my jeans. <*I . . . I don't know what to make of it, but I think I . . . I kinda liked tearing her to pieces. It felt . . .*> I drew in a steeling breath, clawed at my jeans some more, then spit it out: <*It felt good. Like, empowering.*>

<*Fuck yeah it did,*> Layla said right away, and I snapped my head up to look at her. <*I've had enough of being their little bitches. Besides, uh, guys . . .* what the ever-loving fuckballs are we dealing with here? *Are we really thinking aliens? Like,* alien *aliens?*>

<*What else could Fanny have been?*> Brady asked. <*Looked alien to me. I wouldn't've even blinked if she'd shown up in some alien flick.*>

I glanced at Hunt, then Griffin, whose eyes were already on me.

<*Maybe not alien,*> Hunt ventured. <*Maybe just monstrous.*>

<*Fanny said even* we *aren't fully human,*> Layla said.

<*There are lots of creatures on this planet that aren't human,*> Hunt said with a pointed look at Bobo. <*He's just one of millions of them.*>

<*Yeah, okay. Maybe.*> Layla's mouth screwed up into her *I'm busy thinking* expression.

<*But when you take into account my dad's Sky People comments . . . sounds more like alien, then.*>

Griffin's eyes bored into mine.

<*What do you think?*> I asked him.

He blinked, as if lost to some other thoughts. <*I think we'll find out eventually. But we don't need to know what Magnum is to kill him. We just need to know how to kill him.*>

His fingers squeezed mine. His eyes were steady. <*I'm ready to kill anyone and everyone that's a threat to us. I need to keep you all safe.*>

His eyes continued to take in only mine.

<*I'm ready to kill some motherfuckers too,*> Brady said. <*They've left us no choice but to go on the offensive. And after Fanny, now we know we've all got what it takes to get the job done.*>

I was nodding. <*To go on the offensive, we need the element of surprise—*>

<*Which we've got,*> Layla said.

<*And allies would be helpful.*>

<*Those, we def don't have,*> she again commented.

<*And we should probably be at the institute. It's where we'll find others like us. I'd bet they all want out and would be willing to help us to escape.*>

<*Plus, the hypno suggested we wanted to go to the institute now, so that tracks,*> Brady said.

<*It sure would help to know more about this whole dreamwalker deal,*> I said.

<*And the skinsnatchers.*> Layla shivered. <*They sound awful.*>

<*They sound like maybe what Fanny was,*> Brady said.

Layla shivered again. <*That's one sight I'd give a lot to unsee. Talk about nightmare material.*>

We were racking up a whole lot of nightmare material lately . . .

<*Maybe we could reach out to the lie-rents,*> I suggested hesitantly.

<*No,*> Brady said immediately.

<*They did write us notes saying they wanted to help.*>

<*They also lied to us our whole lives and are working with Magnum now, knowing all he pretty much wants to do is kill the fuck out of us.*>

I tipped my head. <*Fair point.*>

<*What about the sheriff?*> Griffin said. <*Jackie went on about how untrustworthy he was, how we shouldn't believe anything he says.*>

<*How would we do that without drawing their attention, though?*> Layla asked. <*It's not like the sheriff's office is a regular haunt. We never run into him or anything. I wonder if Lynne's still boning him?*>

<*We could maybe figure something out,*> Hunt said.

<*Okay, so that might be an option,*> I said. <*Maybe. There's also our ninja instructors.*>

<*They work for Magnum,*> Layla objected.

<*Armando had a look about him. Like he felt uneasy about how things've been going down.*>

<*Not uneasy enough to stop shit,*> Brady grumbled. <*Fuck him. If he's informed and working for Magnum, he's in on it.*>

<*Also fair,*> I conceded.

<*If only we could get to the Aquoia res,*> Hunt said. <*If we could find my dad . . .*>

<*For all we know,*> Layla said, <*they've got him locked up at the institute next to Earthquake Boy.*>

<*Sounds like we're back to trusting only ourselves,*> Griffin said. <*Which I'm down with. But we really do need help.*>

<*There's one final ally we haven't mentioned yet.*> I glanced down at Bobo.

<*What's he said since you woke up?*> Hunt asked.

<*I haven't talked to him much yet.*> I smiled at Griffin. <*I was kinda busy—*>

<*Gettin'* boned, *baby. Bangin' it out,*> Layla started. <*Gettin' tickets to Pound Town.*>

Before she could offer more opinions on the matter. I turned toward Bobo and grabbed a paw, directing my thoughts at him in a way my friends would also hear. <*Bobo?*>

His eyes popped open and he turned his head to look at me. An exhale I didn't realize I was holding burst free of me.

<*You can hear me,*> I said with a smile.

<*Bobo hearth.*>

<*We should hide a note to ourselves somewhere he can find, and then teach him to lead us to it if we, ya know, get killed and forget,*> Layla said.

<*Mine's already buried out here,*> Brady said. <*We can do that today before training.*>

<*Great,*> Hunt said.

<*Bobo . . .*> I didn't know exactly how to go about this. He was still an animal . . . <*How is it that you can talk?*>

<*Bobo Thky People.*>

As one, my friends and I sat up straighter.

<*What do you mean, Bobo is Sky People?*> I asked, heart pounding.

<*Bobo not people. Bobo keeper.*>

<*Keeper?*> I asked, glancing at my friends, all of whom wore similar perplexed expressions as my own.

Bobo panted eagerly. <*Bobo keeper.*>

<*Keeper . . . of what?*>

He spun around to lie on his tummy. <*Bobo keep you.*>

My brow furrowed. <*Keep . . . me?*>

Bobo smiled and panted some more.

<*What do you mean, you keep me?*>

Hunt leaned over him. <*Bobo, do you mean you keep Joss from getting into danger?*>

<*Bobo keep dream danger.*>

My heart thudded and I barely breathed as I asked, <*Do you mean you keep me from being in danger when I . . . dreamwalk?*>

Bobo nodded and smiled broadly. <*Bobo keep danger. Go dream.*>

I sank with a thump against the couch. <*Well, I'll be damned.*>

<*No damn. Thave. Bobo thave.*>

I beamed at him, rubbing my palm along his head. <*You're here to save me?*>

<*Bobo thave. Go dream. Bobo keep. Thky People compan.*>

<*Compan?*> Layla asked with a scrunched brow.

<*Companion,*> Griffin said. <*Bobo, are you a Sky People companion meant to protect Joss as she dreamwalks?*>

<*Yeth. Bobo yeth.*>

Brady was nodding appreciatively. <*I'd say that's big advantage number two to us. Fuck yeah. Time to play their game and fucking win it.*>

# 18

## An Unwitting Siren and an Unwitting Sailor Beholden to Its Power

The afternoon was eventful. We successfully taught Bobo to lead us to Brady's buried explanation of our true natures, should we die or otherwise forget. And we helped one another search for the infamous chips we didn't know if we actually had.

Although it was Griffin's hands that roved my bare skin, feeling for any unexplained bumps or scars, and though I'd scarcely stopped daydreaming about our earlier lovemaking, nothing sexy came of his touch—or of my later examination along his skin. Layla made sure of it with her constant heckling and obnoxious inquiries that demanded to know if Griffin and I'd reached Pound Town or if the rocket-in-your-pocket train hadn't yet left the station. It was fortunate I loved the crap out of her, or I'd have been tempted to strangle her.

The good news was that we found no disturbances to suggest buried chips in any of us. The bad news was that Hunt suggested the chips might have been laparoscopically implanted inside our heads, the resultant tiny incisions concealed by our universally thick hair. The embedded chips could possibly be kill switches, Hunt further theorized. If that was the case, and we were really running around with tech in our heads that could blow at their command, we were so beyond screwed that there was no point fretting about it. At least the end would arrive swiftly and without warning so we wouldn't dread it.

After all that, we trained with Homer, Yolanda, and Armando for several hours. If my not-dad informed them I supposedly wasn't feeling well, they didn't let on. As usual, they kicked our ever-loving asses, pushing and pushing us until Layla whined nonstop into our secret chat, and we collapsed to the forest floor, our chests heaving, muscles quivering.

While we completed their exercises and sparred, we carefully observed our instructors. We searched for any sign whatsoever that at least one of them might be a willing ally in our fight for our freedom, that even one of them had a conscience that was worth a damn. There were a couple of lingering, pensive looks from Armando, and a prolonged perusal by Yolanda, which Brady insisted was her checking out his "hot ass"—though he was the only one to think so.

In the end, it wasn't enough to risk revealing we were in the know. Their loyalty probably aligned with their no-doubt generous paychecks.

Between the full-body-melt orgasms Griffin gave me that morning, the giddy high from knowing that the boy I loved very much loved me back, and the pummeling of our ninja training, my body was totally spent and ready for sleep when I finally slumped into bed that night. My mind, however, was wired.

After Bobo's shocking revelations, I was going to try to dreamwalk tonight while he kept me safe from his position next to me on the bed. Allowing an animal *companion*, who couldn't even pronounce the word but who seemed to know more about me than I did, to protect me as I ventured into the unknown, where my friends wouldn't be able to reach me, and which was probably populated by creepy aliens à la Fanny . . . wasn't exactly reassuring.

At first, my friends camped out on the floor of my bedroom and kept guard as much as they could while I presumably dreamwalked. In practice, I couldn't settle into slumber with all their eyes on me.

If I managed to dreamwalk—some-fucking-how—and to travel somewhere useful—where, who knew—and to return with helpful information—a fucking tall order since I had absolutely no clue what I was doing—we might secure another significant advantage. How absolutely wonderful that would be. Perhaps even lifesaving. It might be the answer to our freedom.

No pressure at all.

When all I did was toss, turn, and sigh—and *not* sleep a wink—my friends eventually capitulated and prepared to leave. But not before Griffin slid a hunting knife under my pillow as he kissed me good night. I couldn't imagine how a physical blade would serve me as I walked through *dreams*, but it was always better to have a weapon than not, that was a given.

When they began hemming and hawing, wondering if they should sleep over, just in another room, I shooed them away with a promise that I'd text if I needed them so they could dash right over. We didn't want the lie-rents curious about why they were reluctant to leave me alone, especially during nighttime. They were very well aware that I could dreamwalk.

If only I was as well . . .

Even after my crew was gone, nerves kept me awake for a while longer. But eventually, the scent of Griffin on my sheets, of our joined bodies, of the love we shared, lulled me into that peaceful space between waking and sleeping. I was no longer alert, barely aware of my surroundings. Sleep was only moments away—or perhaps I was asleep already, I couldn't tell, and was careful not to wrangle my thoughts into something coherent.

However this dreamwalking worked, it made sense that I'd have to be asleep for it.

At first, I sensed only Griffin, his warmth, the comfort of his embrace. I felt his kisses dragging along my skin, his hands caressing me. When I could all too easily conjure the sensation of him plunging inside me, loving me, I drifted toward it. Asleep or awake, Griffin had long been my tether to everything good in this world. My entire body heated and grew supple as I drifted without notion of time or reality. My body pulsed, its reactions visceral, but without becoming too aware, it was impossible to tell whether or not this was indeed sleep. It didn't feel like dreamwalking. It barely felt like dreaming when it was what I'd experienced mere hours earlier.

At some point, Bobo stretched his body lengthwise along mine. At another, I lost the ability to retain awareness of my dream, even though I always wanted to hold on to Griffin.

Sometime later, awareness returned, as if it were purposeful, attempting to snag my attention. By then, I didn't remember what it was I was supposed to be doing, and, groggy, I resisted.

Slowly, gradually, lights like elongated, blurry stars began to appear behind my closed eyes. There was one, then two, then suddenly five. A warm, coral hue, they overlapped, like a series of afterimages after staring at too-bright lights the color of the sun.

More long, glowing figures appeared around them, intertwined with them. The new lights were of varying colors. Some were a cool blue, others a deep indigo, some brilliant white.

Their whispers swam through my sleeping mind next. They sounded like the murmuring of waves, cresting and crashing to the shore. They were soft, then insistent. Soft and insistent again. The undulating whispers morphed into a song I instinctively understood didn't belong to this world but refused to coalesce into words.

The starry lights stretched longer until I could almost believe they were people. It was as if I were seeing auras without the physical bodies at their centers. Their colors thrummed in tune to a melody that was so harmonic, so balanced, so utterly perfect, that it couldn't be human.

*Am I dreamwalking? If so, where am I? More importantly, who are they? And what do they want from me?*

I tried to formulate questions for them, but the lure of their song was too great. Every time I tried, I succumbed to its beauty. They were sirens, and I an unwitting sailor beholden to the song's power.

I tried to think harder, to formulate words, to engage them in some way, to do anything but just lie there listening, taking in the striking melody they offered me.

Time passed—a little or a lot, I had no way of determining—and I knew peace, I knew safety. I knew completion and contentment.

But then . . . it changed. Their combined voices grew frantic, their song chaotic and disturbing.

Their starry lights swarmed at me, converging. What felt like hands but didn't look like them reached for me—

Darkness filled my vision. Within me, there was only a quiet but pervasive thrumming that seemed to have its own looping beat after the consuming nature of their music.

Just as I began to feel the loss of . . . whatever that had been, Griffin was there again. As before, his fingers trailed my arms, my collarbones, the outline of my body through the comforter. He peppered feathered kisses across my cheeks, pressed the softest of them yet along my lips.

I moaned softly, unsure whether aloud or only in my dream.

His kisses continued, his touch, too, before he lifted the covers and slid in next to me. When his body pressed against mine, I felt only skin—and his arousal, hard and incredibly erotic against my hip.

If this was a dream, let me not wake from it.

Unsure whether I was asleep and dreaming or slowly waking, I didn't open my eyes.

<*Bobo,*> I thought sluggishly, pointing the thought at my dog. <*Go, and be quiet. Wait for me downstairs. I'll come find you in a while.*>

Now that he could talk, it felt wrong to have sex in front of him.

Griffin's hand was under my camisole, palming my breasts. His lips dragged along my bare shoulder.

<*Griff,*> I murmured silently to him. <*Let Bobo out first.*>

Neither Bobo nor Griffin answered, but Griffin's hand was trailing down from my breasts, across my abdomen, and slipping beneath the waistband of my sleepshorts. I wasn't wearing panties.

He ground his erection against my hip. I decided I no longer cared if Bobo stayed. We were under the covers anyway, and Bobo wasn't even moving. He was probably fast asleep on the job. He was, after all, a *dog*, not a person. And didn't dogs go at it, humping away without care of their audience?

Griffin's fingers slipped between my rapidly slickening folds.

I moaned, and this time, I heard my pleasure aloud.

"That's it, baby," Griffin encouraged, dipping a finger inside me, then dragging my wetness up to circle around my clit.

I moaned some more, my hips circling in an echo of his movement.

"Get nice and wet for me," he said.

Couldn't he tell I was plenty wet for him already?

"Then I'll plow into that pretty cunt of yours and fill you up with my cum." His words were hot as he growled them against the shell of my ear.

My core pulsed at the imagery they evoked. He rubbed my clit faster, harder. My breathing came faster and harder too.

"That's it, baby," he said against my ear. "Come for me. Come, hard as you can."

He flicked my clit—hard—and my eyes popped open.

Not dreaming, then.

My blinds were closed. The faintest of moonlight struggled to stream through. It was too dark to make out much of Griffin beyond his silhouette. But I knew the feel of his body intimately. Every hard plane and provocative bulge, every one of his gestures and movements.

His usual scent.

He flicked my clit again—harder this time.

I gasped.

"You like that, don't you?"

I wasn't sure I did. It kind of hurt.

But his fingers were back to rubbing. Pressing harder, harder, faster, faster.

"Come for me now," he commanded, and fuck me if I didn't obey.

My eyes clenched shut to a flash of light as a wave of nearly painful pleasure raced through me, fast as flames, singeing every part of me.

Still clouded with sleep and whatever had occurred in my dreams, and hazy from the force of my orgasm, I wasn't prepared for Griffin climbing over my body and shoving his dick in my face.

"Suck my cock," he demanded. "Then I'll rail your pussy till you milk my dick. I'm leaving a full load inside you."

My body, soft as melted butter, stiffened. I blinked at the hard-on inches from my mouth.

"What are you waiting for?" he asked.

He brought the tip of his dick to my bottom lip, using it to drag my lip out.

"The fuck, Griff?" I said, muffled around the penis in the way of easy speech. "Why are you being so aggressive? You know I'm into it. Into you."

Griffin's demeanor changed abruptly. He seemed to smile, though I couldn't see the gesture behind the dick still at attention and all up in my business.

Finally, he pulled back, lowered himself back under the covers with me.

"Sorry, baby. I just want your pretty cunt so bad. You're so fucking hot."

His lips smeared along my arm while he lifted my thin camisole and hooked it above my boobs.

He pinched a nipple—again, too hard.

I sucked a sharp inhale through my teeth.

"Gentle! That hurt."

"Sorry, sorry," he said with his head dangling above my chest. "Just so fucking eager to be inside you."

He straddled my hips, his legs fitting easily to either side of me—when Bobo was supposed to still be right next to me.

"Where's Bobo?" I asked.

His only response was to suck a nipple into his mouth. On instinct, my back arched, shoving my nipple farther into his mouth. He rewarded me by sucking on it with so much fervor that it ached.

I pulled it from his mouth with a wet *pop* of his lips. Immediately, he lowered his head to chase it again.

I wove my fingers into his hair and held. He fought me, trying to lunge downward. I tightened my grip and held him in place.

"Easy, Griff. I'm not going anywhere. We have all night. Why the big rush?"

With my hands tugging on either side of his head, he said, "I've been thinking of doing this for a long time. I'm really horny. For you, I mean."

"Griff? What the fuck's going on?"

I didn't even manage to get my whole question out before he was speaking over me.

"If I could just get inside you, I'll calm down."

"Griff?" I tried again.

"You're my girlfriend," he said as if he wasn't hearing me at all. "We've already had sex. What's the big deal?"

Though his head remained in my clasp, he slid one of the leg openings of my sleepshorts to one side, dragged his dick across my thigh so that it sprang into place, sliding easily along my folds to rest at my entrance.

"Stop," I said.

"Why would we stop, baby? This is what you want too. Don't deny it. You're all wet for me."

Either hand dug into each of my thighs, pinning me down. And he started to slide into me.

I yanked his head back as far as my arms would reach, but his weight was on me, his arms keeping me open for him.

"I said fucking *stop*."

He did, but only just. The tip of him was in place. All it would take was a single thrust of his hips, and he'd be sheathed inside me.

His demeanor changed again.

"Sorry, yeah. You're right. Let's take it slow. I'm just so excited. You feel so amazing. Just like I always knew you would."

The head of his dick remained right where it was.

So did my hands, tugging his face away from mine.

I lowered my hold to his shoulders, pushing him to the full length of my arms.

"Get off me."

A stillness came over him that felt too much like deliberation. Like he was actually considering forcing me against my will.

"Griff, get the fuck off me right this fucking second or I swear to you I'm gonna fucking rip your dick off, even if it'll make me cry as much as you. There's something wrong with you."

Griffin slid his dick inside me the tiniest bit.

"I'll be fast, I promise."

"Pull out. Right. Now."

He slid farther inside me, if only by a slight fraction.

I didn't give him a chance to thrust fully into me.

I dropped my grip on his shoulders so suddenly that he fell forward and scrambled to move his hands from where they pinned me to the bed to catch himself. He broke his fall only partially, the rest of his weight smacking into my chest, his head crashing into my nose.

But at least his dick pulled out of me.

While he fell, I slid the blade out from under my pillow.

And when he yanked his head back off mine, hissing something that sounded like it was meant to be "You stupid cunt," and he left his neck exposed—

With a double-fisted grip, as if my hands were clasped for prayer, I slid the knife behind his chin bone.

And I didn't stop until it sank up to the hilt.

# 19

## A-Hunting We Will Go

My hands shook around my phone as I sent my crew a text message.

**Me:** Sad Over Something

If only our telepathic connection spanned a greater distance, I wouldn't have to disguise the true nature of my message: *SOS*.

My friends would read my message and see it for the distress call it was, while hopefully our lie-rents wouldn't once they reviewed the logs of our messages.

My phone informed me that it was 3:23 a.m., plenty of time for my friends to get here before my lie-rents woke, even my not-dad for his morning jog.

I wasn't sure, however, that it would be enough time to deal with the . . . situation.

My friends arrived all together, all at once, at 3:33 a.m. Only ten minutes had elapsed. It felt like a thousand while I waited to see *who* would walk through my door.

I was mostly certain I was right, but only mostly. The small chance that I was wrong was . . . terrifying.

What happened when the person who'd supposedly gifted someone with immortality was the one to . . . kill him? What happened if I'd actually ended Griffin? And if I hadn't, was Griffin all right?

Griffin was the first to barrel across my threshold, breathing heavy, his eyes roving around my now-dimly-lit room. They bulged when they skimmed across the bodies:

A very dead man who looked *exactly* like him.

And Bobo, unmoving but with a heartbeat—thank fuck—limp at the foot of my bed.

Brady, Hunt, and Layla, who gripped an open jackknife, piled up behind Griffin.

<*Is he dead?*> Layla asked while considering the corpse on my carpet, inching toward it with the open blade. She shook her head as if to clear it. <*And who the fuck* is *he?*>

<*Please tell me Bobo's not dead,*> Hunt said before I could answer, shutting the door quietly behind him.

<*Bobo's not dead.*>

All four of my friends exhaled loudly in relief.

<*I think he*>—I pointed at the dead man who looked so very much like the last man I'd ever want to hurt—<*drugged him.*>

<*And* he *is?*> Layla asked again.

Hunt squatted beside the body. <*Magnum, I'm guessing.*>

Brady kicked the body in the leg. No movement, not even by reflex.

Griffin lowered himself onto the bed next to me, his thigh pressed against mine, and draped an arm around my shoulders.

I flinched.

He'd been leaning toward me. Now his body straightened like an arrow.

<*Did he fucking hurt you?*> he accused silently, glaring at the body on the floor—a reflection of himself.

Hunt, Brady, and Layla yanked their stares toward me.

Brady stalked to the bed, sinking down on my other side, a snoring Bobo beside him. Anger radiated off him already, like heat waves.

<Did *he fucking hurt you?*>

I swallowed, forced myself to relax and lean into Griffin—the *real* Griffin.

Hunt crouched in front of me, tension corded along his neck while he, too, anticipated my answer.

Finally, I shook my head and looked down. My loose hair curtained my face to hide how close he'd come to really hurting me.

<*It's gotta be Magnum, right?*> I asked.

<*I think so,*> Hunt said. <*It feels like it's gotta be him. Maybe he's wearing a Griffin skin suit like the alien did with Fanny. Or maybe he can mimic someone else, like those skinsnatchers from the hypno. If there are already multiple copies of him, and he's actively trying to add new powers to his arsenal, who's to say what else the asshole's capable of?*>

<*This is leagues better than mimicking, dude,*> Layla said.

<*It is. And we can't even be all the way sure it* is *Magnum. But we'll figure that out after.*>

*After* I answered their questions.

Four sets of eyes darted between my strands of hair to blaze along my face.

<*He tried to have sex with me.*>

I didn't think my guys could tense any more. They did. Griffin and Brady actually vibrated beside me.

<*Tell me he didn't,*> Layla begged.

<*He didn't.*>

<*Thank fucking fuck.*>

<*Not really.*>

<*What do you mean, "not really"? His dick—or Griff's dick but not Griff's dick—was either inside you or it wasn't. Can't be both.*>

I breathed in deeply. It wasn't enough, so I inhaled again.

<*He pushed in the tip while I was telling him to stop.*>

My friends—not one of them—breathed. Bobo's soft deep-drugged-sleep snore was the only sound for several seconds.

<*That's when I killed him.*>

Layla shot to her knees. Leaned over the corpse. And stabbed it through the heart. Once.

Twice.

Thrice.

With her knife still lodged in its chest, her hand wrapped around the hilt, her ribs heaved.

When she pulled out the blade, very little blood trickled from the wounds. His heart had already stopped pumping.

I'd left my blade buried to the hilt under his chin.

Layla sank onto her butt. Glanced from me to Griffin. <*I woulda preferred to stab him in the dick, but I couldn't do that to you, man. It looks too much like you.*>

Griffin didn't say a word.

<*He tried to rape you?*> Brady asked, each word crackling like a live wire.

I took a few moments. After another deep breath, I nodded slowly.

Griffin became so rigid he bounced on the bed.

<*Not at first,*> I said. <*I was sleeping. Or dreaming, maybe even dreamwalking, I don't know. Next thing I knew, he was in bed with me. At first I thought it was really Griff, and I was so out of it that I didn't ask questions.*

<*But then he kept saying he wanted to . . . finish inside me. And then he started getting aggressive. Started sounding not at all like Griff. Maybe he never did, but I was asleep when he got here, and then he's probably listened in on how we talk to each other. It was enough to convince me at first.*>

Brady was shaking his head angrily. Hunt was staring hard at a blank patch of carpet. And Layla was glowering at the face of the dead man on my floor—likely Magnum, but who the fuck knew anymore?

Griffin . . . Griffin barely breathed, barely blinked.

I turned to face him. <*Griff?*> I said softly, still in our private chat. We didn't need anyone else knowing about this.

His nostrils flared then unflared. Flared, unflared. His jaw clenched and unclenched. His nostrils flared anew.

<*If that's Magnum, then there are at least three more of him for me to kill.*>

<*Sharing is caring, bro,*> Brady said. <*I'll take one.*>

<*I want one too,*> Hunt said.

We all looked at Layla. She leaned forward, yanked out the hunting knife. A spurt of blood erupted from the wound, getting on her hand, on the body's neck and chest.

<*That's okay. I'll do without. But I'll piss on his steaming, ugly meat suits once you're done with them.*> She grinned evilly. <*Triple the fun.*>

She wiped her blade on the body's thigh, flicked the jackknife closed, shoved it in her pocket, and stood. <*Let's deal with this mess so we can get to what's next.*>

<*What's next, Lay?*> I asked.

She looked from the Griffin lookalike staining my carpet to me. Her evil grin spread.

<*Why, we're gonna go hunting, of course.*>

# 20

## Tangled in an Inescapable Conundrum

In the scant hours until daybreak, my friends and I put aside our shock and outrage to dispose of the body and clean up all traces that the man who so precisely resembled Griffin, but definitely wasn't him, had been here at all.

However, we quickly found ourselves tangled in an inescapable conundrum. We were trapped in a town we couldn't escape. Furthermore, everyone who shared Ridgemore with us was likely in on the plot against us. Maybe there were some outliers, some who resisted Magnum's insane orders, but we couldn't guess at who they were, or if they'd actually help us. After all, they presumably agreed to dupe us, *The Truman Show* style, in the first place. That choice didn't exactly imply any of them had hearts of gold, just waiting for us to give them an opportunity to rescue us.

Since Brady and Layla's not-mom had warned us so intently in her latest hypno not to trust Sheriff Xander Jones, we considered going to him. But on his own, he didn't seem force enough to stand up to Magnum's might. And our only reason to trust him was not-Celia telling us *not* to. Too risky.

We debated driving out toward Raven's Lagoon and dumping the body off the side of a cliff. A poetic option, truly, since Magnum had surely ordered Clyde's brake line be cut, sending Griffin to his first death. But then we'd have all sorts of biological material up in one of our Mustangs, ripe for a forensics team to find—assuming any would come looking for evidence of a crime in this inescapable town. It wasn't as if we had large plastic sheets lying around tagged for future corpse disposal, or flesh-dissolving acid and its attendant accoutrements, for that matter, which Layla suggested.

Plus, there was no cleaning the blood from the carpet. After I stabbed the impersonator, I shoved him off me and the bed before I could consider the importance of containing a crime scene. The blood on me, my sheets, and the knife, not a big problem. But the richly dark blood had soaked deep into the carpet fibers. There was no point in even attempting to scrub it out. The best we could come up with was to use Bobo's bed, which he rarely used in favor of mine, to conceal the spot, and then arrange for fresh carpet in my room—while somehow avoiding all the informants who would tattle the very instant we strolled into a flooring store casually inquiring about new carpet.

Besides, *my* DNA would be all up on the body. As much as I wished I could deny it, the Griffin impostor had been a little bit inside me. He'd kissed me, touched me, licked me, rubbed all up on me. Even hacking the body up into little pieces—another of Layla's suggestions—wouldn't help if they ever were to be found and analyzed by real professionals who weren't Magnum's lackeys. And where exactly were we supposed to do something like that, anyway? How would we contain such a gruesome scene?

After the more violent disposal methods, which held a punishing appeal, we also considered the obvious option of simply burying the body somewhere in the woods out back behind our houses. Between all our lie-rents, they owned all the property.

Unless someone went looking for a cadaver, it would probably never be found.

But that was when we landed on the most limiting predicament of them all: We were being surveilled. Constantly.

No matter where we went or when, the lie-rents—possibly even Tracy, aka *not*-Mitzi, and the rest of the team of scientists Magnum employed to analyze every little thing about us—would know. When we'd hacked their system, we'd discovered camera feeds with vantage points every-fucking-where, stopping just short of aiming for a good view up our rectums.

If we moved a body, no matter what precautions we took, the lie-rents would know it come morning.

We were still grasping at better alternatives—and failing to find them—when the dead man on my bedroom floor shifted from an identical image of the man I loved to the one I most despised.

The complete transition took only a minute at most, but all five of us caught it, staring, mesmerized, as Griffin's familiar features stretched, strained, and morphed, until a bare-naked Magnum was what remained.

Seeing him, we made our decision.

Hunt, Brady, and Layla kept eagle eyes on the corpse—not that it was going anywhere—and on a still-snoring Bobo while I cleaned up. Griffin insisted on following me into the shower to help scrub off the blood and Magnum's touch. The memories, regrettably, wouldn't be quite so easy to erase.

I brushed my teeth aggressively three times while Griffin, naked under the spray with me, washed my hair and body with such tender care I couldn't believe it had taken me as long as it had to figure out the man who'd entered my bedroom without my invitation wasn't him.

As scoured clean as I was going to get, Griffin hesitated before eventually wrapping his arms around my waist and pulling my back against his chest. He rested his chin on the top of my head, kissing me there over and over while the hot water streamed down on us.

<*Can you still bear my touch?*> he asked into our private chat, which our friends in the other room would be able to hear plainly. It was either that or have the lie-rents later listen to a recording of us instead.

I leaned my head back onto his shoulder. <*Of course I can. I know it wasn't you. I just don't know how I didn't realize it sooner. Before . . . I could've stopped it from going as far as it did.*>

<*If you blame yourself for any of it, I'll get you to resurrect his ass just so I can murder him a few extra times. None of what he did's on you.*>

I smiled sadly and tilted my closed eyes up to the water, allowing the rainfall showerhead to pitter-patter upon my face. <*I know. I really do know it's not my fault. Deep down, I do get it. At least, I think I do. I mean, how was I supposed to guess he could do that? Maybe the lady we thought was Fanny was actually somebody else, and the alien just stole her appearance.*>

I sensed that comment drew my friends' rapt attention, so I changed tack, swiveling in Griffin's arms to look up at him.

<*None of what he did is on you either.*>

Griffin tensed, his slick muscles corded under my touch. <*He used my body to hurt you.*>

In my mind, his words trembled.

<*He used* my body to violate *you. He tried to* rape *you. I just . . .*> He shook his head; it deflected the rainfall. <*I can't . . . That's so fucking* wrong. *So majorly fucked-up.*>

<*I know,*> I whispered into our shared bond.

<*It was bad enough, all the other stuff he's done to us. You can't get much worse than outright killing us.*> He chortled darkly. <*Or at least, that's what I thought.*>

<*I know,*> I repeated, resting my face on his chest, tilting my head to the side so the water would sluice down my back.

"I'm so sorry, baby," Griffin murmured aloud against my hair. "So, so sorry I wasn't here to stop him."

I pulled back to look him in the eyes, pivoting so the spray no longer reached our faces. <*You did nothing wrong.* Nothing, *Griff, you hear me?*>

<*I shoulda stayed with you. You were exposed, trying to dream-walk for all of us.*>

<*I asked you all to leave, remember? That was my choice. Besides, Bobo was with me. He was gonna keep me safe.*> I grimaced. <*Until the asshole drugged him. Guys, is he awake yet?*> I asked the others.

<*No,*> Hunt replied, the one word vibrating with his fury.

<*If I hadn't left you with that knife . . .*> Griffin said, shuddering.

<*But you did. And nothing happened that I won't be able to recover from.*> I wove my arms around his neck. <*That you won't be able to help me get over.*>

I pulled his mouth down to mine and pressed my lips to his.

For the first awful moment, all I could think of was how those lips had felt when they'd been Magnum's. Their touch delivered me instantly back to Magnum's body on top of me, forcing its way inside me.

But then Griffin kissed me back with so much gentleness, his hands caressing long lines down my back with such precious care, that he overrode those memories.

Eager for him to replace more of them, I pulled him down harder into my kiss.

He didn't make me ask, seemed to know what I wanted, what I *needed.*

His tongue was hot and wonderful as it slid along mine. A moan slipped from between our pressed mouths.

He pulled my hips into his, where I discovered him already hard and straining to be inside me.

I hitched a leg around his thigh, opening myself up for him, and angled myself so that his dick slid easily into place.

I was about to sink down onto him when his hands gripped me around the waist.

<*Fuck. Joss. Wait*,> he panted into my mind. Into that of our friends just outside.

Shaking my head, I began lowering myself onto him.

But he jerked his pelvis away so that, once more, only the tip remained notched inside me.

<*It's too soon*,> he insisted. <*There's*—>

<*I know there's a dead body right outside. Doesn't matter. Changes nothing.*>

His eyes studied me, but he didn't argue. He lowered his lips to my ear. "Let's wait, baby. Give you—hell, us—time to recover first. So that it's just us again. I don't want . . . him," he spat, "between us."

"He isn't," I whispered back. "I promise." There was, however, a tiny chance that I was lying, as much to myself as to him. I realized it even then.

Wrapping both arms around his shoulders, I gave a little hop, and wound my legs around his hips. He, of course, caught me, with both hands under my ass.

As if he couldn't help himself, he squeezed my butt cheeks and moaned deeply.

When I lifted myself up and lined us up again, he stilled me with those strong hands that massaged my cheeks, spreading them.

"Joss, baby, I love you. We've got time. No need to hurr—"

In a single stroke, I sank down onto him, sheathing the hard length of him entirely inside me.

Together, we threw our heads back and groaned.

<*Yo*,> Layla's voice cut in sharply. <*I know you two aren't bangin' it out right now while the three of us sit here in the dark with a doped-up, snoring dog and the motherfucking dead body of our archnemesis.*>

Griffin and I stilled for a beat before he ground up inside me again. My eyes fluttered shut at the sensation of being so gloriously filled by him. Layla wasn't wrong, obvi she wasn't. But fuck if I couldn't help myself.

<*Right?*> Layla pressed. <*I get that Griff's got one fine dick on 'im, and good on you, bro. Your equipment looks nice and thick, primed for fucking. Didn't wanna say anything 'bout it earlier 'cause it didn't seem appropriate since your naked dick was staring back at me from a dead body n' all.*>

<*And you think* now's *the time to say that?*> Brady asked. <*Really? It's* never *a good time to say that kind of shit.*>

<*You told Joss she's got a rockin' bod when you saw her naked at the mansion. Do I remember you also commenting on her titties? Was there even something about motorboating?*>

<*You know damn well there wasn't. You're too fuckin' much sometimes, Lay. No joke. Too fucking much.*>

<*Knock it off. You know you love me.*>

<*'Course I love you. I'm your twin, for fuck's sake. I've got no damn choice. Doesn't mean I don't think you're a total dipshit sometimes. The crap that comes outta your mouth, I swear . . .*>

<*Now* is *the time, Brady,*> Layla went on, unperturbed, <*'cause Reece the fuckin' liar's gonna be up soon for his little peppy morning jog, and Joss still hasn't told us what happened with the whole dreamwalking part. Plus, don't you think she shouldn't have Griff's dick—though a fine one, as we've established—all up inside her vajayjay when the lie-rents get here? We gotta hope they wanna help us and that their top-secret notes weren't just another ploy. Better not push our luck by making them jelly of all the pounding going on in the shower right now with us* right here *within listening distance.*>

Layla's point fully taken, I sighed, enjoyed the crap out of Griffin gliding me up and down his cock a few more times, before I unwound my legs from his hips and brought my feet gingerly to the tiled floor, without dislodging him.

He thrust inside me again, causing me to claw at his back with my nails, before growling against my ear.

"Rain check. It's only a brief rain check. I'll be back inside you first chance we get."

"Promise?" I breathed.

He nodded his nose up and down my neck. "Never's a promise been so easy to make."

The water temperature began to turn tepid as he withdrew. I didn't realize I was staring at his dick, wearing my feelings all on the outside, until his rolling chuckle yanked me from my daze.

He lowered his lips to the shell of my ear again. Dragged his tongue along my earlobe, sucked it into his mouth, then said, "You're looking at my dick like I'm breakin' your heart by putting him away."

Eyes wide and earnest, I glanced up at him before admiring his proud, beautiful dick some more. "You absolutely are."

This time, his laugh was hearty. "Come 'ere." He opened his arms for me.

I stepped into them, but not before ducking down to drag a long lick up the length of his shaft.

His head hit the tiled wall before he wrapped me in his arms.

A soft knock rapped on the bathroom door. <*Hurry up, lovebirds. Time to hitch a ride back from Pound Town. I hear noises in the house. Guessing Reece saw Bonnie and Clyde out front and is wondering where we all are. And I wanna scrub down the murder weapon before they show. Talk of dreamwalking's gonna have to wait, and I don't want it to.*>

As I allowed Griffin to dry me off and then wrap me in a fluffy towel, I smiled at him. <*Believe me now when I say I know it wasn't you? That all of me knows it wasn't you?*>

Down on a knee to dry my legs, he gazed up at me. <*Yeah, baby, I do.*>

Then he slid open the two halves of my towel, parted my folds, and trailed his tongue up the entirety of my slickness.

I bucked and gasped.

He licked his lips.

"Fair's fair," he murmured in that deep rumble of his as he rose, a wolfish gleam twinkling in his eyes.

I stared deeply into them.

I saw him and only him.

There was no one else.

# 21

## Time for a Motherfucking Reckoning, I Tell Ya

Even though our lovemaking was—justly—interrupted, Griffin's reverent kisses and touch were sufficient to erase much of the night's earlier traumas. I emerged from the shower emboldened, my courage replenished, ready to face the dead body stinking up my bedroom.

Or so I thought.

So fully was I convinced that *I had this* that I didn't even take a moment to steel myself for the sight before striding confidently from the en suite bathroom while towel-drying my hair.

The sight of Magnum's corpse, though sprawled precisely where I expected it to be, proved to be like a slap to the face, a crack hard enough to make my ears ring and my eyes sting with pricking tears.

There, mere feet away from me, beside the bed where I let go of all my defenses to be vulnerable and sleep, lay incontrovertible evidence that a literal psychopath had come here to exert his will over me, one way or another. His flaccid dick resting against his thigh was disturbing proof of all that he'd meant to steal from me: not just my consent and the sacredness of my body, but also my decision whether or not to grow life within my womb. If he'd gotten his desire, to him I would have become no more significant than an incubator for his latest science experiment. The fetus wouldn't have been my *child*; he wouldn't have viewed him or her as precious at all. I wouldn't have become a *mother*, ready or not for the role. I would have become an unwilling perpetrator of a jillionaire's terrors. I would have contributed to an awful cycle, subjecting another life to what my friends and I had so far endured, if not much worse.

Layla's hand landed on my bare shoulder above the towel at the same time as Griffin's.

Her eyes were big as they studied me. <*You okay there, girl?*>

That she didn't rib me or Griff for getting it on, and made no additional mention of Pound Town, could only mean that I was wearing my shock on the outside.

My eyes smarting, I smiled shakily. <*Yeah, I'm all right.*>

Griffin rubbed reassuring circles along one shoulder while Layla chuffed in disbelief.

<*Right. You don't need to pretend with us.*>

I sucked in a deep, nurturing inhale. <*I know.*> My eyes, all on their own, roved away from my best friend to Magnum, my thoughts once again careening along the course he'd tried to set for me.

<*Come on,*> she said with a glance over me at Griffin. <*I'll keep you company while you get dressed.*>

When she steered me toward my walk-in closet, I let her.

<*Don't worry,*> she said. <*You don't need to get your shit together before we confront the lie-rents. Probably better if they really see how rattled you are, actually.*>

<*We're all fucking rattled,*> Brady added.

Layla nodded. <*For sure. Better they see the effect their fucked-up shit's having on us.*>

<*Well, that'll be easy,*> I muttered.

Layla chirruped. <*No kidding. It's time for a motherfucking* reckoning, *I tell ya.*>

<*You think that's what we'll get?*> I asked while I reached for a crop top with a built-in shelf bra.

<*I dunno what we'll actually get today, dude, but I don't plan on stopping till we* get *our reckoning.*>

<*Same,*> Brady said.

<*One way or another, they're gonna pay.*>

<*Oh, they're gonna pay all right,*> Griffin said with a growl.

<*Guys,*> Hunt announced. <*Bobo's starting to stir.*>

My heart thudded. I hurried to yank on curve-hugging, tight jeans with tears in the knees and thighs and grabbed a slouchy long-sleeve that hung off a shoulder.

I felt Griffin's stare following my movements when I lowered myself to the bed beside Bobo, Brady and Hunt purposefully facing my back to the corpse. I joined the guys in running a hand along Bobo's fur, soothing him awake.

While Bobo snuffled and turned his head, his eyes still shut, Layla opened my bedroom door to peek out and give a listen.

<*Still quiet,*> she told us. <*But I think not-Reece is out on his run. He'll be back soon. Slacker never runs more than three miles.*> She snorted with a superiority that wasn't necessarily earned when she was consistently the first to protest when our jogs ran long.

Bobo's pink tongue pushed adorably in and out of his mouth, until finally his eyes popped open with a loud snort.

<*Hey there, my sweet boy,*> I said while my friends spoke over one another to greet him as well.

<*Nice to see you awake, buddy,*> Hunt was saying while Griffin and Layla settled to either side of me on the bed.

Sprawled on his back—his favorite sleeping position—Bobo cycled his legs a few times before trying to flip over onto his stomach. Midturn, he wobbled, and crashed onto Brady's folded leg.

Brady's hands shot out to steady him. "Whoa."

Bobo sank half on top of him, half on the bed. Griffin's and Layla's bodies formed a wall that blocked my pittie's view of the dead man.

Bobo licked his lips, opened and closed his mouth a few times, before coughing.

Hunt jumped up. <*I'll get him water,*> he said and quickly placed the bowl I kept for Bobo beside his doggie bed on the floor on my own bed, something that was definitely against my rules.

But damn if I didn't understand exactly how awful it felt to wake up after being drugged. I was always parched.

Bobo lapped up the water until he licked the bottom of the bowl, making a sloppy, wet mess of my comforter at the center of our impromptu circle. None of us cared. As for my bedding, I planned to burn it all, including the mattress.

At last satiated, Bobo circled his tongue around his snout and looked at me. <*Bobo keep?*>

My worry for him softened into a smile. <*Yeah, my good boy. You did a great job keeping me safe.*>

I looked at my friends before breaking the news. <*You kept me safe. But then a bad man came, and he made you go to sleep.*>

Bobo's ears perked in alarm. <*Danger?*>

<*Yeah. Danger.*>

Bobo stood, though his legs shook.

Hunt ran hands along his body, trying to settle him.

I kissed him on the forehead. <*There's no danger anymore. Look.*> I pointed toward the floor behind me.

Griffin and Layla leaned in opposite directions so he could see around me.

Bobo's ears stood straighter, his tail pointed menacingly, and a growl rumbled deep in his chest.

<*Is he . . . Sky People?*> Hunt asked of Magnum.

<*No Thky People.*> Bobo growled harder. <*Danger Thky People.*>

Layla's brow scrunched. <*Sky People are dangerous?*>

<*No. Danger. Bad Thky People.*>

I lowered my face for another kiss to his head. <*Are you saying he's the enemy of Sky People?*>

<*Yeth. Bobo thay. Bad.*>

<*Well, on that we can easily agree,*> Hunt said.

<*Bad man,*> Bobo emphasized with incessant growling. He looked at me. <*Keep.*>

<*You did a good job keeping me safe, Bobo. It wasn't your fault he made you sleep.*>

Bobo whined. <*Bad man. Hurt Thky People?*>

My friends glanced from him to me.

<*I think he's saying you're Sky People,*> Layla said.

I barely breathed. <*Yeah, I got that. Bobo, boy, is that . . . what you're saying? That I'm a . . . Sky People?*>

<*Yeth. Bobo thay.*>

<*But . . .*> My thought fizzled out.

<*What about the rest of us?*> Brady asked, pointing at each of them. <*Me, Hunt, Griff, and Layla? Are we Sky People too?*>

<*Thky People,*> Bobo answered, affixing an accusatory glower on the body on the floor and growling some more.

<*We're all . . . Sky People?*> Layla asked.

<*All Thky People. Bobo compan.*>

I sat back, leaning into my hands while Brady whistled.

<*Well, ain't that something,*> he said.

<*That . . . can't be,*> I finally murmured.

<*Why not?*> Brady asked. <*Makes sense. I mean,* dude, *we can come back to life when we're dead. According to the crazy alien lady, you're the one giving us life. So yeah, makes total sense.*>

<*But . . .*> Again, that was all I had. <*How can we be* Sky People*? Wouldn't that, like, make us from, ya know, outer space or something?*>

<*Fuck,*> Layla breathed, twirling the colorful feathers in her hair. <*I didn't think of it that way.*> She sucked in a gasp.

<*What?*> the rest of us demanded at the same time.

<*Are we fucking* aliens*? Like, Fanny aliens? What if . . .*>—she pinched the flesh of her arm around the outline of a tattoo in progress—<*this is a flesh suit?*>

Appropriately horrified at the prospect, she gaped at us. <*Can we, like, pull our skin off?*> She grimaced. <*Not gonna lie, that'd be totally fucking gross, and if that's the case, being a Sky People can shove it.*>

I wanted to know. In truth, I really, really *needed* to know. But I didn't want to be the one to ask the damn question.

Eventually, Hunt did.

<*Bobo, are Sky People what we call aliens? Like what Fanny was?*>

Bobo tipped his head to one side in question.

<*You remember when that woman . . . uh, ate you?*>

Bobo sucked in a horrified breath, yanked his chin into his neck, and winced like he was sucking on the sourest of all lemons. <*Bobo 'member. Yuck. Tatht terrible.*>

<*That's right. She tasted terrible. Was she . . . Sky People? Are we . . . like that too?*>

<*Thee no Thky People. Thee bad. Danger Thky People.*>

Layla tossed back her head and let out a loud whoosh of an exhale. <*Oh, thank holy fucking fuck. That woulda been too fucking much. Hating myself wouldn't've been a good look on me.*>

<*On any of us,*> Brady said with a rocking shudder.

Griffin scooted closer, his hand resting on my thigh.

<*Bobo,*> he asked. <*Was she, the one who ate you, was she like him?*> He pointed at dead Magnum.

Bobo shook his head. <*Not thame. Thee compan.*>

<*So . . . she, the one who ate you, was a companion to him,*> Griffin said. <*Like you are to Joss?*>

<*Yeth. Bobo compan. Thky People.*>

<*Okaaay,*> Hunt commented, flicking the dangling turquoise of his silver earring. <*So Fanny is to Magnum as Bobo is to Joss.*

*Maybe even to all of us too. So maybe Magnum doesn't have a nasty alien underneath.*>

<*Well . . .*> Brady arched his brow before glancing at his sister. <*There* is *one easy way to find out for sure. Messy, but easy.*>

<*We should totally do it,*> Layla said right away, popping up from my bed just to kick Magnum's foot with her sneaker.

I, however, never again wanted to touch another part of that man's body—not any of his bodies. Not even to slice him open for answers.

<*I think an autopsy can wait for now,*> Griffin told them with a meaningful and pointed look at me. <*Anyway, we're getting somewhere. Bobo, how are we Sky People?*>

Bobo tipped his head in the opposite direction from before.

<*Right,*> Griffin mumbled to himself. <*Simpler questions. Bobo, we are Sky People, yes? And if we're—*>

<*Yeth. No,*> Bobo interrupted.

Bobo pointed his snout toward the ceiling. <*Thky People.*> Then he looked at us, next me specifically. <*Thky People. Yeth. But no.*>

<*What?*> Layla asked.

Hunt leaned forward with another swinging flick of his earring. <*Are you saying . . .*> He sat up straighter. <*Bobo, are you saying that the true Sky People are somewhere up there, in the sky or something? And that we're, hmmm, part Sky People? As in, we're not all the way Sky People, just a bit Sky People?*>

<*Dude, that's way too much for him,*> Brady said.

<*That's way too much for* me *to absorb,*> Layla mumbled.

Bobo was tilting his head back and forth to either side.

Hunt asked, <*Are we part Sky People?*>

<*Yeth.*>

<*Are we Sky People in human bodies?*>

Bobo's head dipped again.

Hunt adjusted. <*Do Sky People look different from us?*>

<*Yeth. Difren.*>

<*Do* you *usually look different than you do now?*>

<*Yeth. Difren.*>

I sucked in a sharp breath. Griffin massaged my leg, his fingers rubbing the bare spots through my ripped jeans.

<*Holy shit,*> Layla interjected excitedly. <*Keep going, Hunt.*>

<*Are we*>—he gestured with both hands to include all of our crew—<*Sky People in new bodies that work on this, uh, world?*>

Layla bounced on the bed. <*Ohmyfuckingfuck. Keep going.*>

Brady snorted. <*Then don't interrupt him.*>

Thanks to said interruptions, Hunt had to repeat his question, simplifying it further. <*Are we Sky People in Earth bodies?*>

Bobo barked, his tail wagging. <*Bobo compan.*>

<*What do you usually look like, Bobo?*> Layla asked.

But Bobo only dipped his head again.

<*Are you a person, Bobo?*> Layla asked. <*Like us?*>

Bobo barked but shook his head. <*Bobo compan.*>

<*Duuuuudes,*> Layla said. <*I think we might be freaking aliens. Just not ugly, gross ones. What. The. Actual. Fuck?*>

<*In theory,*> Hunt said, <*not sure any of this, what we're understanding so far, makes us all that different from regular people.*>

Layla snorted. <*Uh, did ya miss the alien part?*>

<*We don't really understand anything about how souls, or whatever you want to call them, enter human bodies. All over the world, different religions, cultures, traditions, and spiritual practices have varying views on where and how we get our souls—whatever makes us tick while we're alive. We have these bodies, and there's this something intangible that no one can properly quantify, that makes us who we are. Obviously I can't be sure, but based on what we're gathering from Bobo, what if we essentially just have Sky People souls? Instead of whatever souls humans have, our bodies are just animated by Sky People souls, whatever? Could be, right? It'd explain how Bobo says*

*we are and we aren't Sky People. We don't have Sky People bodies, but we've got their souls, like their essences.*>

Griffin was rubbing my leg with one hand, the sexy scruff on his chin with the other. <*I mean, why not? That could actually explain it.*>

Hunt shrugged. <*It's a theory, anyway. We'd need someone with more concise information than a companion*>—he cast an adoring smile at Bobo—<*to be certain about it.*>

<*I like the theory, though,*> Griffin continued. <*It'd mean we aren't all that different from regular people. We wouldn't be aliens in the way Lay means.*>

<*No.*> Layla chuckled grimly. <*We just can come* back from the dead. *Like freaking zombies, yo, just without the yuck factor and the craving for flesh. That shit ain't normal, no matter how we wanna spin it.*>

She twirled her feathers some more. <*Though I ain't complainin'. The theory works for me. Didn't wanna unzip this bod*>—she ran her hands along her waist to her hips—<*to find gray alien goop underneath all my hotness. I'd never recover from that shit, for real.*>

I grimaced. <*Who would?*> Then, <*Bobo, before the bad man, enemy to the Sky People, made you go to sleep, I was dreaming. Do you know if I was actually dreamwalking? Did I do it?*>

Bobo nodded, his ears, relaxed now, flopping with the movement. <*Joth thream.*>

<*But did I* dreamwalk?>

<*Yeth. Bobo keep.*> He whined. <*Bobo no keep. Joth danger.*>

I scratched under his chin. Finally, he sank to the bed again, in the middle of the five of us.

<*It's not your fault, boy,*> I said. <*The bad man hurt you. You were doing a good job. A great job.*>

<*Bobo keep.*>

<*So what happened?*> Griffin asked me. <*You were actually doing it?*>

<*Maybe? I dunno for sure, since I don't know what it's supposed to be like. But I saw a bunch of lights, like maybe they were, not sure, but coulda been souls or something? Like what Hunt said. Just a guess, but it coulda been that. And there was music. Beautiful singing. And then they started to freak out.*> I glanced over my shoulder, allowing my gaze to graze Magnum's bare feet and nothing more. <*That's when he came in.*>

Griffin scooted closer, as if he couldn't stand recalling that he wasn't here to protect me. His second hand wrapped around my waist, tugging me nearer still.

<*So they were looking out for you,*> he said in a rumble that left unsaid a pained, *And I wasn't.*

<*Felt like it, yeah. But I can't be sure about any of it, really. I was asleep. I think I was, anyway. And I don't know what dreamwalking's supposed to be like, what I'm supposed to be able to do.*>

Griffin leaned his chin on my shoulder. <*Bobo, when Joss was dreamwalking, was she connecting with the Sky People?*>

Bobo only stared back at him.

Griff rephrased. <*Were the Sky People in Joss's dreamwalk?*>

<*Yeth. Thky People.*>

My friends and I exchanged long looks.

Eventually, Brady whistled through his teeth. <*Well, dayum. We're finally getting answers.*>

<*Hell yeah we are,*> Layla said with a grin and another jounce atop the bed.

Being singled out as the source of everyone's immortality, and the one who was supposed to dreamwalk to connect the dots between our earthly existence and who knew what, I didn't share Layla's enthusiasm. Anxiety mingled with trepidation as it coated my skin.

Squeeing, Layla bounced some more, softly clapping her hands together. <*Holy shit, girl. You made alien contact!*>

I tried to smile.

Layla frowned. <*Damn. Don't look so excited or anything.*>

<*Maybe not* alien, *Lay*,> Hunt said. <*We're not sure about a lot of the basics right now.*>

Layla waved a hand dismissively. <*Basics shmasics. We're talking* contact *with something so mega beyond our common understanding.*>

<*Yeah. No pressure on me*,> I said around another grimace.

Griffin began rubbing my shoulders. <*There isn't any pressure, Joss. We're all in this together. Always are. It's not all on you to figure out.*>

<*Def not*,> Layla said. <*Family forever, remember?*>

<*Only I'm the only one who can dreamwalk . . .*>

<*Doesn't change that we're all in this together*,> Layla said with a shrug. <*You're never alone, dude. Not ever.*>

I cycled through a few breaths, leaning into Griffin's massage before asking Bobo, <*Are the Sky People trying to reach me? Are the Sky People trying to talk to me?*>

<*Thky People talk. Yeth.*>

<*Do I need to dreamwalk again?*>

<*Bobo keep.*>

<*We'll* all *keep you safe next time*,> Griffin said, with a vicious growl and a glance of disgust over my shoulder at the body rapidly cooling behind us.

Shit had gotten so majorly messed up.

<*I can't do it yet*,> I said. <*I need more time.*> *To recover*, is what I didn't say.

<*No one's asking you to*,> Hunt said right away. <*We've got time.*>

Only, we didn't. Not really. Not at all, actually.

The enemy was circling us as rapaciously as a kettle of eager vultures zeroing in on the scent of decaying carcasses.

<*May as well see what else Bobo might know*,> Brady was saying. <*Maybe he can tell us what . . .*>

A knock I recognized from years of hearing it—*tap, tap, tap, tap*, in quick succession, always the four soft raps—rattled my bedroom door.

"Joss, honey?" It was my not-dad, Judas himself. "You awake, sleepyhead?"

When I didn't answer, he swung open the door. With his hand still on the handle, his eyes boggled as they trailed along the naked body with its obvious stab wounds. His jaw waggled open, closed, open, then closed again.

"Oh shit," he eventually muttered under his breath with a panicked look that skirted once more across the dead body of his boss, then the five of us.

"That about sums it up," Layla said, a little too peppily.

"Let me . . ." Judas mumbled while he fumbled for his phone in his back pocket. His hair was damp from his postrun shower, a few wet strands tumbling onto his forehead.

His thumbs flew across his screen before he looked up at us again. "Uh, I'll . . . I'll be back."

"I'll just bet you will, Mr. Bryson," Layla said with an unsettling smile that was part predatory, part jaunty.

*Mr. Bryson* scurried away like the seat of his pants was on fire and he was trying to stay ahead of the flames.

In less than ten minutes flat, as fast as my friends had responded to my SOS in the middle of the night, every single one of our traitorous lie-rents was crowded into my bedroom.

# 22

## Jig's Up, Mofos

Seeing our combined lie-rents flustered to the point of speechlessness had an oddly calming effect on me. Maybe it was simply nice not to be the only group of friends losing its shit. And the lie-rents were plainly losing their shit, even if some of them were working very hard to hide just how much of their shit they were losing.

Celia and Porter huddled together against the wall farthest from the body. Perhaps they actually liked each other beyond the facade, but really, who knew. Genuine, the 'rents were not. The two of them kept sliding their glasses up the bridges of their noses, when their glasses surely couldn't be sliding that often. Porter was also shifting his weight from foot to foot a little too regularly.

My mom and dad stood separately, bookending their group. Monica's face was eerily blank, and she scarcely blinked, while Reece, fresh from his shower, blotted with the back of a hand at a sheen of sweat rapidly beading along his brow and upper lip. He flicked jumpy glances at everyone else in the room, barely remaining on Magnum's dead body for more than a second at a time.

Orson leaned against the closed door, looking between the body and his supposed son, who was pressed protectively to my side. My crew and I remained on the bed surrounding Bobo, all of us tense despite our seated positions.

The 'rents might not be the worst of our enemies. That didn't make them, by extension, trustworthy chums. It didn't even make them decent people.

Alexis, the self-proclaimed seductress who admitted to using her wiles to get her way, folded her arms tightly over her chest. Her posture was precise and perfect as ever, but the crease of her lips twitched to one side. I caught the slight movement three times before deciding that the normally stoic woman was as ruffled as the rest of them.

When they first rushed into my room after my dad's summons, it was with what felt like rehearsed exclamations of shock and dismay at the dead body spread-eagled at their feet. There were lots of gasps, stuttered cries, *ohmyGods*, and *what the hell happened heres*. There were even a few belated *Are you all okays*.

Orson, Porter, and my dad especially goggled at the spectacle of their dead naked boss, his deep wounds with relatively little blood, and the pallor quickly settling into what had been a healthy complexion. I caught my mom and Celia staring specifically at the man's limp cock, almost as if they'd wondered what kind of heat the jillionaire was packing. His body was fit and toned, and my mom at least was definitely checking him out.

*Gross.* Something was seriously wrong with the woman.

My dad was the first to ask, specifically, why on earth *Uncle Magnum* was there, dead as a doorknob—and still not dead enough for me.

My response was a terse, "You tell me."

Betrayal stung extra sharp when my mom's eyes narrowed in accusation: "Did you hurt your uncle Magnum, Joss?"

At that point, Griffin and Brady rocketed up from the bed, Bobo barking at their sudden, jolting movements. Griffin told them I didn't owe them a single answer. They were the ones who needed to explain themselves to us.

Oh, but being forthright with us wasn't in their plans.

Possibly an entire minute eked by, during which nothing momentous happened beyond a ratcheting up of the already suffocating tension. With heavy, disappointed sighs, Griffin and Brady sat again. It was obvious: Our 'rents were total shits. We were better off without them.

When the 'rents merely fidgeted, Layla said, "What? You're caught with your pants down and you've got nothing to say for yourselves?" She scowled and shook her head. "Typical."

Typical of what, exactly, I didn't know. Nothing about our situation was normal, not by a long shot.

"You could start by apologizing, ya know," Layla added with a marked harrumph. "It's the very least you could do after all the majorly messed-up crap you've done to us."

Brady also *humph*ed. "If they start, there'll never be an end to it, that's how much apologizing they've got to do. Not that I'm in the mood to forgive them for any of it. No way. They went too far. Waaaaay too far. Besides, from the looks of them, not a one of them's got the guts to suck it up and even try to make things right."

"Hey," Porter and my dad protested at once.

Brady shrugged. "Just tellin' it like it is, *fake dads*. You don't like it, well, then ya damn well shouldn't've stabbed us in the back with a whole kitchen's worth of knives."

With a slight hitch, he added, "We trusted you."

"What do you mean, 'fake dads'?" Porter hedged, pushing his glasses up his nose.

Layla *tsk*ed. "He means, jig's up, motherfuckers."

"Layla," Celia automatically censured. "Watch your mouth, and your tone, too, while you're at it."

"I'll do no such thing, *Jackie*. You're all here, with a *dead fucking body* between us, still not wanting to say a damn word that matters 'cause you're waiting for us to talk so you can figure out what we know and what we don't know. 'Cause you're *still* planning on lying to us, straight to our faces."

As one, the 'rents exchanged telling looks. Even my mom and dad gazed at each other from across the room, sharing an entire conversation through their stares.

"We know *everything*, okay?" Layla said. "*Ev-er-y-thing.*"

She waited a long beat so that could really sink in.

"You've been found out. Caught with your arms in the cookie jar, up to the elbow. Caught with your dicks stuffed all up in the neighbor's wife, ya get me?"

"Layla," Celia breathed on an affronted wheeze.

If she'd been listening to endless recordings of our private conversations, surely she couldn't truly be surprised by how Layla spoke when she wasn't holding back. Not that dicks in neighbors' wives had anything to do with anything, but my girl had always been way better at bluffing than I was.

As much as we'd managed to learn thus far, it was more like a whole heap of diddly-squat than *everything*, considering how much life-altering shit we still didn't comprehend. I wasn't even sure we were in the ballpark of "everything."

But I wasn't about to split hairs, especially not when Layla was on a roll.

"I assure you, none of us"—she gestured to the five of us; Bobo perked his ears at the attention in his general direction—"are in any mood to play." She let her warning hang. "In case ya failed to notice, it's your disgusting boss lying dead on the floor. There's no talkin' your way out of this one." She harrumphed another time, glaring openly at all the liars crowded into my bedroom.

My mom looked around at her friends before taking a half step forward. "Not sure where all this anger toward us is coming from—"

Layla, Brady, Hunt, Griffin, and I all *huh*ed in disbelief at the same time.

A bit more timidly, my mom powered on. "Maybe you can start by telling us why Uncle Magnum is naked, and by all appearances dead, on Joss's bedroom floor."

I opened my mouth to answer but Layla was already muttering under her breath: "Uncle Magnum." She was only gathering steam. "Uncle Magnum, you say . . ."

I clamped my lips shut and got out of her way.

She jabbed a stiff, accusatory index finger at the air above the corpse. "That man's *not* our uncle anything. You didn't meet him in grad school. And he's no family friend. What he is, is a nasty-ass, revolting pervert who tried to *rape* Joss."

Half the lie-rents sucked in stunned gasps. The other half grew stonily silent. All their stares landed on me.

"That's right. He tried to *rape* her. Fucking lucky thing that my girl Joss here's a fucking badass who stabbed the shit out of him before he could take it too far."

Griffin grunted, his breaths coming harder, and I leaned my head on his shoulder to calm him.

"Not only do you owe us apologies, you owe us all the answers and explanations. More than that, you owe us *protection*." Her voice grew thick. "We believed you were our *parents*. We believed you'd keep us safe." She sniffed. "Instead, you conspired against us, lied to us, *murdered* us—"

"We didn't—" Porter started.

Layla snapped up a hand, instantly stopping him. "You spied on us. And as if all that weren't bad enough, 'cause did ya catch it, ya fucking *killed us*?"

Several of them started speaking at once. Layla flung up another hand. "Maybe you didn't pull the trigger, but what you did was just as bad. You knew it was happening."

"Honey, we didn't know," Celia managed to interject.

"Maybe at the beginning you didn't, but tell me you didn't guess at it."

This time, when Layla finally gave them an opening, none of them said a thing.

When she sniffled again, Brady rubbed her back, and Bobo rested his head on her thigh. Automatically, her hand dropped to pet behind Bobo's ears.

Looking at him instead of them, she added, "You allowed a predator to feel justified in preying on a friend I love like a sister."

My heart squeezed.

"Magnum came here and snuck into her room in the dead of night because he knew there'd be no consequences. 'Cause he knows you'll do whatever it takes to get the answers you want for your beloved *science*." She spat the word.

Celia opened her mouth but ended up saying nothing.

I reached over and grabbed Layla's free hand, holding it tightly.

She sniffled again. "Magnum knew none of you would stand in his way. He owns you all. Hell, he owns this entire town. He wanted to shoot his load inside Joss, so he came over here to do it, didn't matter one bit that she didn't want him to."

The 'rents as a whole, save for Alexis, squirmed.

"You know why?" Layla asked them.

They stared back at her.

"Of course you do. He wants a new generation of pets that's easier to control than we are. He wants his genes in the mix, so he can get one step closer to becoming the archvillain of all time with a full array of fucking superpowers."

Celia's brow furrowed. "Archvillain? Superpowers?"

"Yeah, yeah, whatever. I know we're not actually living in a comic book, but that's how it feels to us. Magnum's the villain, okay? And tonight he tried to get my girl pregnant so he could make it easier to combine his powers with hers."

"Powers?" Celia uttered with another scrunch of her forehead.

"Oh, knock it off already, Mom. Or, not-my-mom."

Celia's breath hitched, as if that were the worst of the things Layla had said.

"We know Magnum's not really human. We know this isn't even the only one of him walking around Ridgemore. Much to our disappointment . . ."

The 'rents shared yet another look among themselves. Did they not get how incredibly over their stupid, secret looks we were?

Layla had the situation plenty handled, but I found myself speaking anyway. "A lot of damage has been done. More than we can probably ever fully recover from."

"No kidding," Hunt murmured.

"But all that, everything that's happened to us, it all boils down to one question right now: Are you gonna keep lying to us and hurting us, or are you interested in finally doing the right thing?"

Again, the 'rents just looked at one another.

I sighed out my disappointment, though why I'd still hold hope they'd do right by us was beyond me.

"Look," I said, "in those notes you snuck to us, you said you wanted to help us. Was that all just another part of the story? Or do you really want to give us a hand? Be on our side? 'Cause if you do, we could really use some help right now."

Eyes wide, Celia glanced at Porter, asking him under her breath, "How do they remember the notes?"

Although the question was directed solely at him, Layla answered, "I told you. We know *everything*."

That's right, my bestie bluffed like a fucking *boss*.

"Well?" Griffin snapped. "Are you in or are you out? 'Cause you're probably not the only ones listening in on our so-called private conversations. Who else is lined up to listen to this chat?"

"Oh shit," Orson breathed.

"Yeah," Griffin said flatly. "Oh shit."

"Come *on*, guys," Hunt grumbled. "How can it be this hard to decide if you want to help your supposed kids not get raped and murdered? Are you really all just pieces of absolute shit?" His voice pitched high at the end, so unlike Hunt. I suspected it was the sound of his heart cracking.

<*Callous sonsofbitches,*> Brady commented into our telepathic link. <*I thought they cared at least a little. Behind all the lies and the plotting and the wet dreams of winning the Nobel Prize, I still thought they cared some.*>

<*So did I,*> Hunt said, his words, just for us, soft and crushed.

The five of us looked back at the six of them. Even Layla's previous blustery rage seemed to be deflating.

"Oh my God," Celia said. "Look at them. They're . . ."

Heartbroken. Devastated. Betrayed. Probably a little bit scared shitless, though I wouldn't admit to it. But what our 'rents didn't also see was that we wouldn't remain this way for long. Whatever awaited us, we'd face it head-on. We'd fight and we'd fight and we'd fucking *fight*—until there was no one left to stand against us.

Our 'rents had cut us deeply, there was no denying it. Regardless of their shit motivations, they'd still raised us since we were young children. It ached when those relationships crumbled. But those weren't the bonds that made my crew strong.

The lie-rents weren't our real family.

Griffin, Layla, Hunt, and Brady—they were my family. Bobo too. For them I'd fight to the death—and beyond. For them I'd resurrect and punish whoever was foolish enough to cause them harm.

"Be honest with us for once in your fucking lives," Brady said with a growl, but it felt forced, as if he didn't want them to see how difficult this was for us. "When you look at us, do you see your Nobel-Prize-winning research? Or do you see people you care about? That's really the question, and it's simple. If we're just research to you—"

"Or even if the research part is the most important," Hunt interjected.

Brady nodded. "Then do us a solid and actually admit it to us right here, right now. Be up-front with us. At the very least, the bare minimum, we deserve that."

Griffin added, "You owe us that. You *owe* us."

The 'rents didn't answer right away, consulting with each other with openly questioning looks.

<*The assholes might try to tranq us again,*> Layla said only to our crew. <*They're a bunch of sus motherfuckers. Can't believe we ever bought their lies.*>

Only, of course we did. They were supposed to be our *parents*, for fuck's sake. How were we supposed to know we were dealing with a gang of mad scientists out to leave their mark on their world, whatever the damn cost?

<*If they make moves for tranq guns,*> Brady added, <*I say we take 'em down. They don't wanna help us? Fine. Fuck 'em. But we don't need them around, causing problems for us.*>

<*You mean we kill 'em?*> Layla asked, sounding not entirely opposed to the idea.

<*Maybe we just tie 'em up,*> Hunt said. <*Wrap them in duct tape.*>

<*Then we'll have to take care of them,*> Brady said. <*Feed 'em, et cetera.*>

<*But not for long,*> I said. <*One way or another, we're gonna be ending this real soon.*>

<*That's right,*> Griffin said. <*Besides, I don't see any guns on them.*>

<*Sneaky fuckers,*> Layla said. <*Alexis might have one shoved up her tight ass. You see the pinched look on her face? Like she so doesn't approve of us.*>

<*Yeah, I do,*> Hunt said on a sigh that was loud enough to possibly draw our parents' attention.

I spoke aloud. "Wow, okay. So I guess we've got our answer. If it takes you this long just to decide whether to do the right thing and actually help your supposed *children*, well then, we see you."

"Oh, we see you, all right," said Layla, violence riding her words.

Alexis uncrossed her arms and tutted. "Enough with the theatrics."

I sucked in a gasp so loud I choked, while my friends universally went rigid around me. "The *theatrics*?" I asked. "Are you fucking kidding us right now, Alexis? Or wait, *Marisa*?"

Her shoulders jerked at hearing her true name and evidence that we did indeed know some things, if not the *everything* Layla kept claiming.

"I woke up in the middle of the night to that man"—I pointed at the cadaver—"trying to shove his dick inside me. How about we break into your supposedly safe bedroom while you're sleeping and shove a rod up your ass, see how you like it?"

I discovered myself standing beside the bed, fists balled at my sides. "You just don't get it, do you?" I looked from Alexis to the rest of them. "You don't know what it feels like to watch the people you love most in the world *die*."

"Of course we do," my mom snapped. "You can't actually believe we don't love you. We—"

"Yeah, that's exactly what we think," I jumped in. "You don't love us. How could you? How could it be such a difficult decision to help us not get killed? Not be trapped in this town without escape where every single fucking person's in on the plan? Everyone is trying to kill us. Or to hurt us. Or to . . . whatever."

I found Griffin and Layla on their feet beside me. I hadn't even realized they'd stood. Brady and Hunt shored up next to them, and Bobo, bless my pup, was circling us to stand protectively in front of me.

Griffin's hand wrapped around my fist until I relaxed it, then he wove his fingers through mine.

"You know what, forget it," I said. "Just forget it. We'll deal with it all on our own. Just stay out of our way."

"Yeah," Layla said, puffing out her chest, making her smaller frame appear larger. "Fuck y'all."

Brady added, "And don't mind the barbecue we're gonna be doing out back. You can explain that prick's bones away, assuming you even have to since the cops are bought and paid for."

"Especially since Monica's banging the sheriff," Layla said.

"Enough," Alexis barked with a slicing jerk of her hands.

My mouth dropped open to speak my mind while Layla's head was already wagging with mega 'tude beside me.

"We're going to help you," Alexis said.

"I can't believe—" Layla was already saying. "Wait, what?"

Alexis frowned at us for a long beat before turning to face her friends—or maybe they were just colleagues, dastardly scientists together at arms.

She looked at Orson. "Intercept the recordings before Tracy gets her hands on them." She glanced at her watch. "You've got minutes, Tobias, mere minutes before she strolls into the lab to get an early jump on things."

Orson didn't answer. He yanked out his phone, lowered his head over it, and got frantically to *doing*.

Next, she looked at my dad. "Coordinate the disposal team. Make sure they don't talk."

My dad frowned. "They all talk. Magnum will know."

"Magnum will already know. This one didn't come here all on his own. Silence the team after, however you need to. Even if it just seeds a little confusion, it'll buy us time."

"Right," my dad said, also drawing out his phone and getting to following orders.

<*Does 'silence the team after' sound like a kill order to anyone else?*> Griffin asked just our crew.

<*Sure does,*> Brady said.

<*Damn. Who* are *these people?*> Layla asked, presumably a rhetorical question.

They are fucktards, that is what they are. At least we know it now.

"It's time to take them to the institute," Alexis told the scientists before glancing at us. "I take it you know exactly what I'm talking about?"

"Sure do," Layla answered.

"How 'bout you disable our tracking chips before we go?" Hunt said. "Or are they kill switches?"

When Alexis tried to look away, he took a step closer so she couldn't easily avoid his stare.

"Mom," he said. "Are they kill switches?"

The woman who was ever so cool under pressure visibly swallowed. "Celia will disable them."

Brady whistled in disbelief. "Yo, you guys are some ice-cold fuckers. You put kill-switch chips *inside your kids*? I hope those Nobels are worth it to you, 'cause once we get through this, you'll never see us again."

"Truth," Layla said.

Celia had been looking at her phone, presumably to disable our kill switches—*yay*. Now she took a step away from Porter and toward us.

"You don't understand. It's not like all that."

"Well, *Mom*," Brady said. "I don't believe you, 'cause here I am wondering how I'll even trust you to actually disable the kill switches instead of lying to us about doing that too. It's pretty handy to be able to kill us at the touch of a fucking button, huh? What kind of psycho science mom would wanna give that up?"

I didn't have to look to sense the savagery peeking out from Brady's eyes; it vibrated in his voice.

Celia extended her hand toward him; the other gripped her phone. "Brade, honey, I would never—"

Brady crossed his arms defensively, as if that would do a thing to prevent the damage they'd so easily caused us. "Save it. I don't wanna hear it."

"Neither do I," Layla said curtly. "I think we're done here for now. Am I right, guys?"

"Definitely," Griffin said.

"We've had a long fucking night, actually helping the people we love." Layla's eyes grazed the side of my face. "We'll meet you at the gate to the institute in two hours sharp. Be there"—she shrugged—"or don't. Either way, we'll know what to do from there."

When Layla cut a swath around the dead body and through the stunned lie-rents, I scrambled to grab my nearest shoes—a pair of well-worn high-top Chucks—and jogged after her. Our guys and Bobo were on our heels.

Brady slammed the door shut behind us hard enough to rattle the hinges.

Whatever was coming next, things would never be the same again. That much was certain.

As far as I could tell, it was the only thing that was certain at this point.

Our fates surely weren't.

# 23

## Don't Bring a Knife to a Gunfight

Magnum's fancy institute—whatever the hell he might be calling it in this current iteration—was carefully concealed from view of the street. No sign indicated the turn, and the towering entrance gate didn't loom, grand and formidable, until beyond the first swooping bend in the drive, perhaps half a mile from the city road. Dotted with dense brush and old-growth trees, Ridgemore's lush foliage provided the perfect cover.

Magnum also had cameras everywhere—he must—monitoring the vast chunk of land that housed the institute, ensuring nothing happened outside of his control. And we couldn't forget his zealous band of ready guards and shooters, all with eager trigger fingers, twitchy with their need to obey his every unhinged command.

My crew and I had been ready for much of the previous hour. But we'd only just arrived, not wanting to ruin our element of surprise—if we even still had it.

We didn't know how far along the road the cameras watched, nor what other kind of alert systems Magnum might have in place. At the very least we were in danger of a vigilant busybody cruising by, spotting us along the road where we weren't expected, and tattling about our presence for Brownie points.

Parked fifty feet from the unmarked turn to the institute, I sat in the passenger seat of Clyde with Griffin at the wheel and Bobo on the back bench seat. Bonnie was parked directly behind us. Brady was driving, with Hunt up front and Layla in the back. With the Mustangs' bumpers almost kissing, we were plenty close enough to use our telepathic link across cars.

We'd debated whether or not to bring our cell phones since they were tracked, and we didn't have anyone trustworthy to call anyway. In the end, though we'd scoured our cars for anything amiss like trackers or explosives and found none, the Mustangs were still probably being tracked regardless—shit, we might have our own satellite at this point, thanks to psycho Magnum and his endless resources; and our phones were just one more tool with potential to help us out of a bind. After the doomed Raven's Lagoon outing, when we'd desperately needed to call the paramedics and didn't have our phones, we'd learned our lesson. The cells were off but in the cars with us.

Also in the vehicles was a pile of ambitious weapons. We'd ransacked my lie-rents' kitchen and garage, and then the treehouse. If it was pointy and stabby, or sharp and slicy, or hard and blunt enough to cause real damage, we'd brought it along. We had a chef's knife set, several jackknives and hunting blades, including the one that killed a Magnum, even a fully-charged, battery-operated saw and nail gun. We had nunchucks—a recent acquisition since we began working with the trio of ninja trainers—staffs, and wooden practice katanas. Sadly, we had no real swords, but the wooden ones could still knock someone out if we landed the blow just right.

Of course, if we weren't up against a minibattalion of professional mercenaries, killers by nature, our odds would look much better. We didn't have guns, though the paramilitary dudes most certainly would. We also didn't have tactical batons or Tasers. We didn't have armored vests or helmets, not even a foolproof plan.

We did, however, have immortality on our side. That was going to have to make up for every other disadvantage. The only other alternative was failure, and we weren't going there. Not now, and not when the fighting began.

<*Guys, I'm nervous,*> Layla said while we waited for the 'rents to arrive.

The two hours we'd given them would be up in ten minutes.

<*I'm trying really hard not to be nervous, but I fucking am, and when I'm nervous it makes me feel like I've gotta pee. Even though I don't think I really have to pee.*>

<*We know,*> Brady said, but he sounded distracted, as if he, just like me, couldn't quite stop thinking about what kind of crazy situation we might be about to charge into—and how many of us would survive it, without at least one resurrection.

<*Think I've got time to pop out and cop a squat?*>

<*Only if you want the lie-rents to roll up on your bare ass flashing them from the side of the road. They should be here any minute.*>

<*If they even show,*> Layla said bitterly.

<*My faith in them's lacking too,*> I said with a glance at Griffin and then Bobo.

I'd already made sure Bobo was set with a pee break and water.

Griffin was bouncing the leg closest to his door without ceasing. A hand roved up and down my thigh, then to tap on the steering wheel, then back to my thigh, my knee.

<*We give them till time, and that's it,*> Hunt said. <*Not a minute more. Someone'll spot us if we're out here too long, and my mom—not-mom—has never been late for a thing in her life. If they're coming at all, they'll be here when we said to.*>

The designated time at midmorning came and went . . . and no lying, scheming, traitorous lie-rents had shown.

Not even one.

<*What were we expecting, really?*> Layla asked, her disappointment loud despite how softly she muttered her question into our shared bond.

<*We def shoulda known,*> Brady said. <*I mean, I guess it's at least good we didn't bother getting our hopes up. Us against the world. That's it.*>

<*That's right, bro,*> Hunt said. <*Always us.*>

<*And that's all we need,*> Griffin said with a glance at me. <*Just us.*> His gaze lingered, heating my skin. <*We've got each other's backs big-time.*>

<*For sure,*> I said. <*Still, can't help but wish we were going in with a bit more than some carving knives and a saw. It's like breaking into an armed fortress with a lock pick and a slingshot.*>

Griffin's stare was still on me. He smiled. <*Even so, I like our odds.*>

I didn't.

I fucking didn't.

But I didn't dare say it.

<*I can't lose a single one of you,*> I said instead, and maybe that was just as bad of an admission.

<*Hey, we're immortals, remember?*> Brady said with feigned enthusiasm. <*They can't kill us. Or, well, they can. But we come back.*> His pep was fizzling fast.

<*Remember, we protect Joss,*> Griffin said. <*No matter what. If anyone's gotta die, let it be me first. Or if it's gotta be, then one of you before her.*>

His eyes blazed with emotions I hesitated to name. <*We need her . . .*>

He swallowed twice before eventually adding, <*We need her to bring any of the rest of us back.*>

His eyes seemed to vibrate as they continued to bore into mine.

<*Bro, we've all been coming back just fine now,*> Brady said.

<*Just 'cause that's how things went doesn't mean something different can't happen. This is us, after all.*>

<*And* thee crayzy sheete,> Layla said with an affected accent, <*happens to us all day long.*>

<*If that ain't ever true,*> Griffin muttered.

Griffin turned over Clyde; the Mustang rumbled to life, vibrating like a fine-tuned muscle car should. Moments later, Bonnie purred behind us.

<*Well. Guys,*> I said. <*I guess this is it, then.*>

<*Everyone remember what to do?*> Hunt asked.

<*Yup,*> Brady said.

Layla snorted. <*Not like there's much to forget. We're basically going in there fast and hard and wingin' it. Find Magnum, the fuck, as quickly as we can. End him first, figure out the rest later. Did I miss anything?*>

<*Nope,*> Hunt said. I could feel his frown from a car over. <*Still not feeling great about our plan. What if Magnum's not even there?*>

<*We keep our cool and lie up the wazoo,*> Layla said. <*Just like we did when we walked in on his sex-a-thon that took narcissism to a whole 'nother level. Then we go to the mansion. We hunt him till we get 'im.*>

None of this was news. We'd talked it all over already. It wasn't like there was all that much to talk about when we were flying in on a prayer—and had hoped to have a little helpful intel from the lie-rents.

Griffin squeezed my knee and offered me a reassuring smile that was so beautiful, I latched on to it hard. It would get me through.

<*Dudes, we've got this,*> he said to all of us while staring deep into my eyes. <*We do. I have faith in us. And remember, it's not just immortality we've got going for us. Joss has more skills too.*>

My saucy grin at a time like this surprised me. <*Don'tchou know it.*>

<*Oh, I do, baby.*> His voice, a sexy rasp, I latched on to as well.

Layla first gagged then whined into our link, undisturbed by her contradictory reactions. <*Don't make me all jelly before we head in. It's not a good look on me.*>

<*Hey, maybe we'll find a hottie shifter for you today, huh?*> I offered her.

An empty distraction. It was what I had.

<*Ohhhhhh yeahhhhh,*> Layla said, trying to sound like Barry White. <*I'm ready. Get me a fine-ass shifter hottie and I'll be all good. No more jelly episodes.*>

She laughed; it sounded strained. <*He'd better be one of them shifters who's gotta get full-on nekked to shift. Gotta check out the goods before I buy, ya know?*>

<*Yeah, Lay, we know,*> Brady said flatly. <*We ready, then? Or are we gonna keep stalling?*>

<*Keep stalling?*> Layla asked hopefully.

<*Lay, you know we can't—*> Brady started.

<*Okay, okay. Let's go before I think about how much I've gotta pee. Rip that Band-Aid right off. Let's go slice up some bitches.*>

I couldn't help but fret on the old adage, *Don't bring a knife to a gunfight.*

Seemed like sound advice.

Still looking at me, Griffin said, <*All right. Let's do this.*>

Then he mouthed, *I love you.*

As my smile bloomed, just for him, he told the others, too, <*I love you all. Now, let's kick some motherfucking nasty ass.*>

<*Fuuccckk, I love you guys,*> Layla said.

<*Love you all too,*> Brady chimed in.

<*Ditto,*> said Hunt.

Which all left me sniffling and blurry-eyed. <*Dammit, guys. I love you too fucking much.*>

<*No such thing, babe,*> Griffin said. <*Us forever. Family forever.*>

<*Forever,*> the rest of them chorused.

Then Griffin pulled out onto the road, with Bonnie lining up right behind us.

A breath before we reached the unmarked turn toward the institute, a horn tooted several quick, soft taps behind us.

I swiveled in my seat.

<*Ho. Ly. Shit,*> I breathed.

<*Ohmyfuckingfuck,*> Layla said. <*It's the fucking liars.*>

It was the fucking liars indeed.

They were driving an armored freaking truck.

# 24

## Keep Our Eye on the Prize, and Go Forth and Murder

We spared only a quick second for Griffin and I to goggle at each other before he and I hopped out of Clyde and ran to the armored truck that was now idling behind Bonnie.

Bobo barked in the back seat of Clyde until I sent him a telepathic, <*Quiet.*> My good boy silenced immediately.

We joined Brady, Hunt, and Layla between the passenger's side of the truck and the roadside foliage so we'd be somewhat concealed while we figured out how in the actual fuck it was that our lie-rents were in a freaking *armored truck*.

The passenger's-side window was already rolled down, anticipating our arrival. The man behind the wheel was strapped into a bulletproof vest and wearing polarized sunglasses that reflected our faces as he leaned across the seat so we could gawk up at him; the truck was tall enough to warrant a step bar.

"Dad?" I sputtered, momentarily overlooking how he wasn't my dad at all. He was a geeky nerd who loved science more than was reasonable, average in just about every way but his intelligence. And now he was playing soldier . . .

"Yes, honey," my dad said. "It's me."

As if I wouldn't recognize him. As if that's what I meant.

"Dayum, Reece," Layla said, also overlooking the lie-rents' long list of aliases. "Didn't know you had it in ya."

My mom's head peeked around my dad's. "No time for chatting."

She was similarly outfitted, her hair in a tight, severe bun against her nape, a style I'd never seen on her.

"Climb in the back," my mom barked at us. "And hurry."

"No, we're gonna take our own cars," Hunt said.

My mom frowned, lines creasing either side of her mouth. "Don't be stupid. This truck's armored. It's bulletproof."

"We know what 'armored' means," Hunt said. "We need our own means of getting the hell outta here once we're done."

My mom's frown deepened. "You still don't trust us? After we showed up like this for you all?"

Hunt shrugged. "Could be all a show."

Damn right it could. Some of my awe at the radical change in my lie-rents' demeanor drained.

"Be smart, son," my dad said to Hunt.

Of course, Hunt wasn't his *son* anything. But then, none of us were any of their actual children, so it made no difference.

Brady shored up next to Hunt and crossed his arms. "We are being smart."

Celia's head crowded behind my mom's. "Come on, Brady. We can talk it all through later. Right now, we need to move. Get in the truck."

"No," Brady said. "We'll be right on your tail."

"After you give us some guns," Griffin said. "We'll take two each."

"Who's to say we have that much firepower?" my mom asked.

The five of us merely stared back at her.

"Fine," she said with an irritated *tsk*. "Make your assumptions." Then, mumbling angrily under her breath, "And don't listen to us when we're trying to save your asses."

The back doors of the truck popped open to reveal Orson and Porter, also dressed in dark tactical gear, with guns strapped to vests, and holsters all over the damn place.

"Did you guys rob an armory or something?" I asked.

"Valid question," Layla said.

"We didn't rob anything," Porter answered. "We've known about the perils of the situation a lot longer than you have."

"Don't remind us," Brady said grumpily.

"We've been planning for contingencies."

"We just hoped it'd never come to this," Orson said, with a heavy look at all of us before sticking on Griffin.

Alexis was seated atop a bench that lined the wall of the truck, her sunglasses perched across a slim thigh. As outfitted for a fight as the rest of them, she sat with a straight spine and one leg femininely crossed over the other. She alone appeared implacable, like the whole bunch of us weren't about to charge headlong into a fight we definitely weren't prepared for, no matter how many guns they had.

The kind of money Magnum had? It could probably buy the entire world's armies and a nuclear arsenal all his own.

Porter and Orson began handing over a revolver for us each, along with a weapons holster that looped around our waists, and spare magazines of ammo. Griffin had demanded two guns for each of us; we got one. It was still more than we'd counted on.

"Where'd you hide all this?" Layla asked while she fastened her belt, patting the Velcro tabs to make sure it wasn't going anywhere.

"We have our ways," Porter said enigmatically.

Layla snorted. "You can't exactly hide a whole armored truck easily."

"There's no time for this," my mom snapped from up front.

There was no partition separating the driver's area from the back, suggesting the lie-rents had even had time to modify the vehicle.

"You really should get in the truck with us," my mom said. "It's the safest move."

"Safe?" I chortled. "Like anything about this is safe."

"She's got a point there," Orson muttered under his breath.

"We'll follow you," Brady said in a tone that also added, *End of discussion.*

Despite the hurry and danger, which mounted every second we were out on the road where anyone could spot us, there was a pregnant pause that invited someone to say something momentous before the farmload of shit really hit the industrial-size fan.

Brady said, "If you're expecting gushing thanks, you'll be disappointed. You've still got a whole hella lot of making up to do for all the lying and standing by while we got killed. You coulda at least told us we'd come back so we wouldn't think we'd lost each other for good, ya know."

Celia stood behind Porter, who was crouched, and smiled sadly. "We know. We really do. We want to make it up to you now."

"That's . . . new," I said, my thoughts tumbling unbidden from my mouth.

Celia's smile turned upside down. "Yes, well, we can't go back and change things. We can only do our best now."

I nodded with recognition. Our best is all any of us could ever do.

"We'll do all we can to help you," Orson said. "As much as we can."

"Are we sure Magnum's there?" Hunt asked.

"Confirmed," my mom said. "As of five minutes ago, he was in his office. But he knows we're coming."

"What? Why?" Layla said.

My mom's smile was taut and brittle as she lowered herself onto the bench seat beside Alexis. "Magnum knows everything. Things he shouldn't be able to know, he still finds out. You all need to be prepared. Things might not go as we hope."

I gulped.

She sought out my gaze from among all the others. "We really do love you. No matter what you think of us, please know that. Our love for you was never a lie."

Alexis uncrossed her legs, leaned her elbows onto her thighs to seek out Hunt's gaze. Her hair was tied back, an absolute first for the woman with the long, silky black hair that always cascaded around her shoulders. "Our caring for you is what made us go on the run with you in the first place, to move here, to Ridgemore."

"Where we thought he'd never find us," Porter said with a grunt that suggested, *How could we have ever been so naive?*

"We already knew Magnum was a formidable opponent then," Alexis continued. "We just didn't understand exactly how terrible he'd be to have as an enemy."

My mom and Alexis started strapping in to seat belts. The time we never had to begin with was up.

"Before we go," I said. "Show us how to use the guns."

We were no strangers to weapons, but only the kind that didn't require a license to own, which we couldn't get. It wasn't as if our lie-rents had ever taken us to the shooting range to prepare us for such a cataclysmic event, even though apparently they'd gone aplenty, all on their own.

Of all our 'rents, Orson was the one I would have pegged as the least inclined to violence. Yet it was he who leaned forward, drew his weapon, and ran us quickly through the basics with swift, sure slides and clicks. A total pro.

A minute later, Orson was joining Porter in rising, readying for our attack on the institute.

"Wait," I said urgently. "How many Magnums are there? Is it just the three left?"

"What?" Celia asked, while the others just looked at us, confusion all too clear upon their faces. Even my dad swiveled from the front seat to stare.

"What do you mean?" he asked.

Hunt's brow furrowed. "You really don't know there's more than one Magnum?"

"You're not just lying to us again?" Brady added.

"No, we don't know," Celia told him with angry, wounded eyes, though Brady's accusation was fair, obvi.

The 'rents exchanged exasperated looks.

"Maybe this isn't a good idea," Porter was saying. "If that wasn't Fanny in Joss's room, we need to rethink things."

"There's no time for that," Alexis said. "He knows we're here. And he knows why." She left the rest unsaid.

The ruse was up. We were exposed. There was no going back.

"So forward we go," I said.

Griffin's hand settled at the small of my back. "You do know about the others with powers locked up in some underground facility though, right?"

They exchanged another look before Orson, with pursed lips, finally nodded.

"We know."

"We get them out too," Griffin said.

"No," my mom said right away. "There's no time."

"We're not leaving them there," Hunt said.

"It's too risky," Celia insisted.

"Then *we*'ll get them out," Layla said, and then, just for us, *<Even if we have to do it after we murder the fucker. All of him.>*

My dad revved the engine a little. Hunt and Brady turned and started toward our Mustangs.

"I . . . I hope you all make it through this," I said, surprising everyone there, especially myself. "I'm really angry at all of you. Like, totally livid. But I don't want any of you to die."

I hadn't known it to be true until the words were out of my mouth.

"Yeah," Griffin added, but then said nothing else.

Layla just stared at the lie-rents. And Brady and Hunt, though surely they heard me, didn't return to the back of the truck.

From the front, my dad said, "Let's just get through this and then we'll have a chance to talk everything through after. We'll do right by you guys, you'll see."

Maybe they would, maybe they wouldn't.

"Just give us a chance to prove it to you," my dad said.

Layla tipped her chin up defiantly. "Earn that chance, and only then we'll give it to you. Years of lying to us straight to our faces, guys. *Years.* Oh, and by the way, we know we're actually twenty-two and not eighteen. A bit of a biggie, don'tcha think?"

My dad, who'd been looking at us with earnest, imploring eyes, suddenly glanced away. The others looked anywhere but at us, all but Alexis.

She shrugged, a graceful tilt of slim shoulders. "We did what we had to do. We aren't apologizing for that."

<*I thought that was exactly what they were doing,*> Layla said to our crew. <*The slippery fuckers.*>

<*Just what I was thinking,*> I responded.

"Look," Orson said, his expression dead serious. "We don't know as much as we should about Magnum, you proved that. But we do know he's the head of the snake. Lop it off, and the rest will die. You understand what I'm saying?"

<*They really think we're idiots, don't they?*> Hunt piped up into our private chat.

He and Brady were now lined up behind Griffin, Layla, and me.

"Yeah, we understand," Brady said aloud. "Of course we do. Keep our eye on the prize. Kill Magnum."

Orson's eyes drilled into us. "He's the priority. Everything else hinges on him going down. No matter what else happens, you go after him."

Porter bent at the hips to reach a hand down to Layla. She didn't take it.

He allowed it to drop with a sigh. "Magnum has power of some preternatural sort, something beyond our science, we just don't know what. He's always been tight-lipped about it. Even with our traditional weapons, we likely aren't equipped to end him. But you are. Or, at least, you are far more equipped than we are. You must be. Beyond your immortality, Magnum wants what you have. He wants it beyond reason. And to make extra-sure we're being really clear: There's no way out of this but for him to die."

"Precious. Our fake parents telling us to go forth and murder," Layla said. "Got it. After this is over, we should pick up a chisel. Modify those silly Ten Commandments."

"That's enough," Celia said to Layla, but also to the rest of us. "We've used up time we didn't have. Whatever else comes between us all will have to wait. Magnum's almost certainly gathering his troops right now. We have to go. *Right now.*"

I felt like there was still so much to say. And yet there wasn't. None of it would make a difference.

With the engine idling, my dad once more turned around. "Remember, your focus is on him and no one else. You get in. You kill him. And you all get out in one piece."

He wore his down-to-business, obey-me-or-else expression. I'd seen it only a few times in my life. Of my two lie-rents, my dad had always been the softy.

"And also, *please*, never forget, we love you all. Joss, honey, I love you the most."

The other lie-rents offered similar assurances, none of which I was certain we could believe. The only real thing we'd proven when it came to them was that they were superb liars.

"Now. Everyone. *Move*," my mom snapped.

With a burdened sigh and downturned lips, Orson pulled the doors closed with a clank that sounded of finality and doom and all the other things I didn't want to ponder.

Like how nothing stood in the way of my crew and imminent danger. Like, death-level danger.

Knowing that we were immortal, and likely to return from death, did little to dull the edge of my worry. *Likely* wasn't the same as one hundred percent *certainty*.

The only thing my life had proven thus far was that nothing ever went to plan.

All sorts of things could go wrong.

"Joss," Griffin said from beside me, dragging me from my worries. "You good?"

I looked at him—really looked at him. I memorized his gorgeous face, his beautiful lips, his amazing smile, even when it was worried.

I accepted the hand he offered me. "Yeah, I'm good."

His sad smile grew bigger, sadder. "Liar."

He kissed me on the lips, fast but hot and possessive, then led me to Clyde.

Before I could better ready myself for what was coming, my dad pulled the armored truck onto the road, and Brady, then Griffin, lined up behind him.

There were no more encouragements, and definitely no platitudes.

Shit was bad and about to get worse. Much worse.

And we all knew it.

*<Bobo, when Griffin and I get out of the car, you stay, okay?>* I told my dog without turning around to look at him. My stare was glued to the windshield and windows, sweeping both sides of the drive.

*<Bobo* go,> he said. *<Bobo keep Joth.>*

I glanced quickly back at him. <*I'm sorry, boy, but no.* Danger. Stay. Hide. Quiet.> I threw every relevant command I'd ever taught at him.

Sharp and piercing, he whined.

<*I'm really sorry, boy, but you've gotta do as I say. Promise?*>

Bobo whined some more.

I wouldn't have even brought him along—anywhere was safer than here—but Bobo was no normal dog, and neither were our circumstances. I didn't trust his fate to anyone else.

The bend in the drive was just up ahead. Beyond it was the gate to the institute.

Quickly, I turned in my seat toward my pittie. <*Promise me, Bobo.*>

He frowned, his jowls drooping more than usual. <*Bobo* keep.>

<*You're such a sweet boy. I love you so, so much. But you're gonna have to* keep *me safe from the car. You'll* stay. *Yes?*>

Bobo's jowls only sagged farther.

<*Bobo . . .*> I pressed as Griffin's breath hitched.

<*Bobo promithe.*> Then my dog lay down across the seat, chuffed dejectedly, and turned his face toward the back of it—and away from me. His tail tucked between his legs.

*Fuck.*

"Joss," Griffin said.

I faced forward just as Brady's voice came through our telepathic link.

<*Shit, guys. This ain't good. It's got my balls clenching.*>

<*Mine too,*> Hunt said.

A moment later, when Clyde sped around the curve, I understood why.

The tall, reinforced, intimidating gate that was designed to keep out intruders, to warn them that anyone who tried to pass uninvited would be gravely punished, hung wide open.

Brady and then Griffin slowed as we passed the guardhouse.
Empty. Unmanned.
When Magnum had to know we were coming.
<*I don't like this,*> Griffin said.
Neither fucking did I.

# 25

## A Psycho Jillionaire with Nothing Better to Do

Still in the lead in the armored truck they'd procured somehow, our lie-rents slowed. They had to be as unnerved as we were to be met with such a glaring lack of resistance.

<*This doesn't bode well,*> Layla said to our crew as Brady and Griffin matched the 'rents' speed. Her tone was understandably grim.

<*Doesn't matter,*> I said. <*We've totally got this. Magnum wants whatever powers we've got for good reason.*> My encouragement was as much for me as for them. <*No choice now but to move forward. We've got the momentum. Plus an armored truck and guns.*>

I nibbled at my lower lip. <*I hope we do, anyway. Still not convinced the 'rents aren't setting us up for something.*>

<*That's what I'm worried about too,*> Griffin said, his eyes tight while they continually scanned the road, the woods to either side of it, and the occasional building. Magnum had purchased some major acreage here, tucked away on the outskirts of Ridgemore. <*Their act always seems so convincing, even when they're bald-faced lying to us.*>

The institute's long, private drive wove through the campus. Since we'd last been here, mere weeks ago, more of the project's finishing touches had been completed. There were now sidewalks crisscrossing the quads, lampposts standing at regular intervals along them like spying sentinels. A grandiose fountain shot water from the centers of exotic-looking flowers grouped together in a ginormous bouquet up into the sky. Welcoming benches grouped around the display, inviting students and staff alike to stay awhile. More benches and picnic tables dotted the campus as if the setting were as innocuous and pretty as it appeared.

The idyllic scenery made me feel as taut as a freshly strung violin.

We drove past the mansion that Magnum had supposedly built for us, the dining hall, the campus store, the coed dorms, and then the lab where our parents worked at scrutinizing every facet of our lives like we were their good little docile lab rats.

<*Why're they taking the long way 'round?*> Brady asked.

<*They must have a good reason,*> Hunt said. <*Right? Or are they just parading us around till Magnum attacks us? Shit. That's prob'ly exactly what they're doing!*>

<*It'd be on brand,*> I muttered, sitting even straighter in my seat, my face practically pressed to the windows, searching for any threats to the people I loved too much to contemplate losing.

A significant stretch of forest lined either side of the drive before I noticed signs of another structure.

<*Look, it's their secret underground prison slash bunker slash messed-up torture chamber,*> Brady commented.

Griffin and I were already studying the place while we rolled by it. The grassy ground beyond its sloping, hidden entrance revealed no indication that we'd seen a guy around our age with some sort of earthshaking power battle here for his freedom, maybe even his life.

<*I really hope he made it,*> I said softly.

There was no need to clarify to whom I was referring. None of my friends were likely to have forgotten standing by helplessly watching while Fanny and her team had taken down a dude so outwardly similar to us.

<*I do too,*> Layla said. <*I think about him here and there. Maybe he's my hottie hookup.*> But her tone wasn't as light as her words.

The weight of our own fates was burden enough without considering how the outcome of today's confrontation held the potential to free others as well.

<*We'll get them o—*> Hunt started to say, then Clyde rocked so hard that the Mustang's tires lost contact with the asphalt for an instant.

Griffin slammed on the brakes while a concussive force so great that it sucked the breath from my lungs rattled the car's windows, dashboard, instrument panels, everything.

My breath returned to me in a gasp when the unmistakable sound of an explosion burst like a thunderclap. A fleeting moment later, I saw the flames.

Terror gripped me while the climbing fire up ahead—not Bonnie, thank fuck—whisked me momentarily back to the day of the drag race—to the explosion that claimed the man beside me in another version of Clyde and made my own heart burst into a pulpy, mushy mess.

Bonnie's doors pushed open. Brady, Hunt, and Layla were climbing out.

All I could do was stare at my friends, wishing to return from the nightmare that was remembering how Griffin's body had burned. How I'd smelled his charring flesh in the nighttime air. How indelibly I'd feared I'd never get to touch him again.

"Joss."

Griffin was calling me, I realized, possibly not for the first time.

"Baby, are you okay?"

I blinked as the rattling of Clyde diminished.

"Are you hurt?" he demanded—his own irrational fear of losing me, I knew.

I shook myself, cleared my head, turned toward him. “No, I’m fine.”

Of course, I wasn’t. Not really. Our trauma was the kind we’d need several lifetimes of immortality to overcome.

<*The whole truck’s on fire,*> Layla was exclaiming.

<*Got rocked by something,*> Hunt added. <*It’s on its side.*>

Suddenly, panic seized me. <*Get back in the car,*> I shouted at them through our mental connection. <*Right now. Run.*>

<*What is it?*> Griffin asked me while the others obeyed without question.

Even Layla and her big mouth didn’t complain, sprinting full-out back to Bonnie.

<*It’s a setup. It’s us they want, remember? It’s gotta be a trap.*>

Griffin was already reversing us back down the road at high velocity.

I extended a calming hand to Bobo in the back seat but kept my eyes glued up ahead. It took a few more seconds—doors slammed, brake lights illuminated—but then Bonnie was reversing too.

<*We’re just gonna leave ’em to burn?*> Layla asked flatly, like she couldn’t quite decide how to feel about that.

<*They’re behind armored plating,*> Hunt said. <*The fire might just be burning the tires, and that’s what all the smoke’s about.*>

Only . . . it was a whole lotta flames and smoke.

<*Magnum’s the head of the snake,*> I reminded them. <*We get him, all this ends. It’s what they asked us to do. They had to’ve known the risks.*>

It was all true, but I felt like a coldhearted bitch for saying it. Regardless of the countless times the lie-rents had betrayed us, there had been happy moments mixed in with all the deception.

<*I really don’t want them to die,*> I added softly.

<*They don’t deserve us caring,*> Layla said, but she sounded as conflicted as I was.

Griffin reversed onto the shoulder, and with a squeal of rubber, lurched us back in the same direction we'd just traveled. Brady pulled an identical move.

<*We go to the admin building,*> Griffin said, gunning Clyde's block engine to get us there faster. <*Magnum's our only focus.*>

<*That's right, bro,*> Brady said.

<*Seems like it was a very targeted attack,*> Hunt said. <*Like maybe a missile or something hit the truck.*>

<*Which means,*> Layla uttered, <*that they def meant to take them out and not us. Everyone recognizes our rides. Why? Why would they not try to take us down instead? Magnum tries to kill us every time we turn around, practically.*>

<*Way I see it, it's one of two things,*> Hunt said. <*Either Magnum's got something else planned for us that we really won't like, and that probably involves us dying. Or he believes he can get whatever he's wanted from us all this time without killing us.*>

<*Maybe he's figured out how to take our powers,*> I suggested glumly.

<*Yeah,*> Hunt answered. <*Though more likely, it's just your power he's after. You're the one who's the source of the immortality, and possibly whatever else he wants too.*>

<*We can't be sure of that,*> I objected right away, but only because we couldn't truly be certain about anything.

Quickly, I swiveled in my seat, finding an anxious Bobo, his tail no longer drooping but pointed in alertness, and behind us a dense plume of smoke clouding the otherwise clear sky.

We'd retraced our path and were nearly at the admin building and Magnum's last known location, when, around a curve, appeared a trio of black Cadillac Escalades. They were heading straight toward us.

<*Shit,*> Griffin hissed.

<*Triple fucking shit,*> Layla echoed in a concerned whine.

<*What do we do?*> I asked, working hard to subdue a rapidly mounting panic.

How could we have actually come here with no real plan beyond *charge the place and hope for the best*? Never had I felt more stupid.

Griffin's jaw was hard as stone. <*We shoot 'em up and take out as many of them as we can, then keep going till we get to the head fucker.*>

<*And then we decapitate the fuck out of him,*> Layla said. <*As many times as we need to till the job's done.*>

Griffin downshifted a gear and drew his double-action pistol in preparation. I pulled my own and pretended handling a weapon like this for the first time with so much at stake was no big deal.

I mentally reviewed Orson's quick instructions: *Gun pointed down, finger off the trigger till you're ready to shoot, then slide. Steady, take aim, and on an exhale, squeeze the trigger.*

My crew and I were capable. We so could handle this.

*Right?*

<*Dammit, I've so gotta pee,*> Layla complained. <*Maybe I can nervous-pee them to death.*>

I waited for Brady to make one of his usual remarks, something like: *Your smelly piss is so rank, everyone'll drop on the spot.*

But Brady was watching the three approaching SUVs as intently as we were.

<*Pull into the road and cut 'em off?*> Griffin asked hurriedly. <*Or let them do whatever they do?*>

<*Wait and see,*> Hunt said.

I had no better idea.

<*Ten. Nine. Eight,*> Griffin counted off.

<*Get down and stay down, Bobo,*> I ordered without looking back. <*Danger. Big danger.*>

<*Three.*>

I swallowed.

<*Two. One.*>

I held my breath.

<*Zero.*>

The first of the Escalades zoomed past us with a loud *hoosh* without slowing even by a mile. If anything, the SUV sped up.

*Hoosh*, zipped the second SUV in a sweeping flash.

*Hoosh*, went the third.

I sucked in a shaky breath. <*The fuck . . .?*>

<*Why wouldn't they try to stop us?*> Layla asked.

<*Dunno*,> Griffin replied before gunning Clyde. <*But it doesn't change where we're headed.*>

I heard a *tatta-tat-tat*. Then again, *tatta-tat-tat*. I rolled down the window.

Louder now, *ta-ta-ta-ta, ta-ta-ta-ta-ta*.

<*Machine-gun fire?*> I asked.

<*Sounds like it*,> Griffin said. Clyde surged forward faster, with Bonnie pacing us.

<*Man oh man, our parents are in a fucking shootout, an honest to fuck* machine-gun shootout, *and we gotta miss it?*> Layla protested, but her usual playful tone was starkly absent. Talking nonsense soothed her.

The trees whipped by in a blur of trunks and leaves.

<*I gotta see Dad playing Rambo*,> she continued. <*I mean,* say what*? Am I right?*> She laughed; the pitch was wrong: too high. <*Shit, I only just thought of it. Think their we're-cool-shits sunglasses are prescription? Or are they wearing contacts like true superspies? Hell, maybe they're violet contacts or something under the reflective lenses. Or some of those slit-eyed ones, like wolfy shifters.*>

Ordinarily too fast for a parking lot, Griffin traversed the one in front of the admin building in a sweeping arc. He stopped Clyde perpendicular to the lines, stretching across several of them. Brady parked Bonnie parallel to Clyde, right in the middle of the throughway.

There'd be no need to reverse for either car. Get in and race off straightaway.

Not that the getaway was our main concern. If we were having to escape, we'd have already failed, and there'd be nowhere within the boundaries of Ridgemore we could run where Magnum wouldn't find us.

Other than us, the lot was vacant. Possibly, there was staff parking behind the building that we couldn't see from here. From looks alone, the place looked empty.

Confident that Griffin was watching my back, I quickly turned to the back seat.

<*Bobo. Danger. Hide. Stay. Quiet. Wait for me to come get you.*>

My sweet boy whined in protest but climbed down into the footwell. He curled into a ball, where no one would notice him unless they knew to look.

<*Good boy,*> I cooed as I opened my door and hurried out, leaving the window rolled all the way down for him. Griffin's was halfway open as well; plus, the day was comfortably cool. Bobo would be fine.

Closing my door, I patted Clyde fondly, then leaned my head into the window and said aloud, "I love you, boy. Be good. I'll see you soon."

Fuck, did I ever hope I was telling him the truth.

I was already stalking toward the back of the Mustangs when Bobo spoke through our bond. <*Bobo wove Joth.*>

A whimper, most unbecoming of the courage I was feigning to feel down to my bones, tumbled free.

Layla drew to my side and sighed, plopping a hand on my shoulder. "He just had to go and say *love* like a sweet lil' chubby-cheeked toddler. Too damn cute." She sniffed.

I pretended not to.

More distant machine-gun fire chopped the noontime air, making me even jumpier while we popped the trunks and all dove for whatever weapons we could carry. I stuffed knives into every pocket of my jeans and tactical belt.

With guns in hand, eyes darting every which way, the five of us half jogged to the admin building's front entrance. Brady yanked open one of the double doors for us, but Hunt darted away.

Unwilling to lose sight of any of them, I spun to watch him next to a large planter, pillaging a sizable stone from its base.

Wielding the gun and stone, he rushed back to us, placing it on the ground against the mullion.

<*Ah. Good idea,*> Griffin said as I realized it was to keep the door from shutting.

Hunt nodded. <*In case they can activate autolocking or something. So we can get back out without having to take the time to break down the door.*>

<*Good call, you lovely brain,*> Layla said.

Without prearrangement, we aligned roughly into a star shape. Griffin and I were in the lead, scouting ahead. Brady and Layla walked behind and to the sides of us, scanning around desks, down halls, and into darkened offices. Hunt brought up the rear, walking half backward, half sideways, watching our backs.

Much like the last time we were here, the lights were recessed and dim, as if the place were shut down for the night, the bare-bones lighting left on for the nighttime security and cleaning staff.

When we arrived at the elevator bank, we hesitated, looking at one another.

Did we take the elevator and possibly trap ourselves in there like the proverbial sitting ducks? Or did we hunt for a stairwell we'd never used before and didn't know where it would lead us?

<*I say fuck it,*> Brady said into our link. <*If they kill us, we'll come back.*> My gut gurgled. <*At least this way we know we end up right in his private office.*>

My eyes bulged in realization. <*Fanny used a key card to access his office level, remember?*>

<*Motherfucker,*> Brady swore, running his free hand along the fade of his hair before rubbing the full top.

Hunt jabbed the call button. Immediately, the elevator doors dinged open. He glanced around before stepping inside, holding open the doors.

His head popped out again, his brows arched. <*It let me choose the penthouse floor.*>

<*It's a trap,*> Layla said, just as I was thinking it.

<*Pretty sure this whole thing's a setup,*> he said. <*It's been too easy. He wants us to come to him.*>

Griffin stood so close to me, I could feel his body heat. His eyes flicked in every direction. <*He's our goal. So we go to him, whatever. Doesn't matter that it's easy. He won't kill us till he gets whatever he wants from us.*>

Foreboding churned low in my belly. Magnum wouldn't hesitate to demand the ultimate of sacrifices from us.

From me.

<*Whatever we're gonna do, we gotta move,*> Brady said. <*Can't stand around here with our dicks out. It's just as dangerous as risking the elevator.*>

Certain only that there was no easy decision, no guaranteed right one, I strode into the elevator. The others followed, and Hunt pressed the close door button to expedite the process.

My heartbeat thumped while the elevator whisked us upward. In seconds, we arrived.

The doors slid apart with a hushed *swoosh*. My entire body felt like it was electrified.

Guns clutched in steady double-fisted grips, Hollywood 101 style, Brady and Griffin emerged first. They scoped each direction before waving the rest of us out.

Layla and I exited with Hunt close behind us, once again guarding our backs.

The overhead lights in Magnum's expansive office were off, but a long window wall bordered one side of it, illuminating plenty. We stalked past his hot tub. With the jets off, it was quiet, heat wafting off the water.

I clutched my gun and studied the door through which a masseuse had once exited. Pulled shut. No one behind the large, elegant desk either. I glanced down the empty wide hallway beyond the single exit door.

A *click* snicked behind me. I whirled toward it. Saw nothing. Stalked forward a few steps until I spotted an alcove over my right shoulder, farthest from the window wall, that was decorated as a reading nook.

From a free-standing lamp, shaded by a translucent wool shade, warm light pooled in a downward circle. Magnum sat beneath it in a sexy black leather Eames chair that I instantly wanted, architectural design tramp that I was. In the back corner of the vast room, the chair was partially obscured by a frond tree.

Magnum was relaxed, lounging, in tan pants with crisp, iron creases and a light, perfectly draping sweater with the sleeves pushed up. The ankle of one leg hooked over the knee of the other. A foot sheathed in a tan loafer casually tapped the air.

A psycho bajillionaire with nothing better to do than wait around for us to arrive.

My skin tingled in apprehension.

This was no ordinary psycho . . .

"Just the one of you today?" Griffin asked him.

Magnum smiled affably, like we were happy friends.

My whole body flushed, maybe with adrenaline, maybe with a sensation too akin to fear.

Magnum rapped the fingers of one hand sequentially along his upraised knee. *Truuuum. Truuuum. Truuuum. Truuuum.*

Beneath the glow of the lamp, he appeared handsome, perhaps a little bit wholesome, even.

Did appearances ever count for a whole lotta nothing . . .

His friendly smile widened. "It's just me for now." He chuckled as if to himself. "You're full of surprises, aren't you?"

"I'd say *you* are," Brady said.

*Truuuum, truuuum, truuuum* went his smooth, manicured fingers.

I wanted to snap them off, one by fucking one, before feeding them to him until he gagged.

He chuckled again. "Does that mean you remember walking in on me having a little fun with myself?"

"We saw everything," Layla said, her eyes glittering.

"Oh, I very much doubt that. You walked in on me when I was just getting started."

"Fuck. Then you're a total perv," Layla said, but she sounded morbidly curious, like she was wishing we'd stuck around to see the rest of the show.

"How many of you are there?" I asked.

A faraway explosion percussed against the wall of glass like thunder. I glanced outside but didn't see its source. Several moments later, the floor shook beneath us.

Magnum continued as if nothing were amiss. "That depends on my mood."

My smile was spiteful and mean to cover up its slight quaver. "Like if you're in the mood to *rape* me?"

I sensed my friends stiffening around me.

Magnum, however, continued perfectly at ease.

The more relaxed he was, the more I felt like I was moments away from jumping out of my skin.

"Awww, it wasn't rape, Joss. It was a little bit of fun."

"Fun?" I fumed. "Fun!"

Magnum *tsk*ed, frowned. "Now, let's not get distracted here. We have more pressing matters to attend to."

"Such as?" I seethed. "'Cause ripping your head off and stuffing it down your bleeding, open throat is top of my list."

"Then I'll pee on him," Layla added.

Magnum glanced at her, not with disgust, but abject intrigue.

"Total perv," she grumbled under her breath.

Sleek as a cat, Magnum unfolded himself and rose.

The five of us huddled closer together.

"Put those guns away, won't you?" he said. "I've always found them a bit . . . uncouth. Besides, they won't hurt me."

"I killed one of you," I said.

His head jerked toward me before his composure settled back into place. "Did you, now? I was wondering why he hadn't returned."

"So you can be killed," I insisted. It had to be true.

He looked me up and down, dragged his gaze across me, like insects slithering along my skin. Griffin growled.

"You really are special, aren't you?"

Without notice, Magnum's body began to vibrate.

At first I wondered if it was another explosion, another shudder of the earth. But no, I didn't feel any shaking.

His body began to expand, its edges stretching. The lines of his body vacillated, faster and faster and faster.

A faint *pop*, *pop* . . . and then three Magnums, identically dressed, stood where five seconds ago there'd only been one.

Then those three Magnums all began to oscillate in an identical way.

<*Fuckfuckfuck, whatdowedo?*> Layla asked into our private thread.

He had to be lying about our guns not hurting him. I'd killed him before, hadn't I?

I didn't bother answering Layla.

I racked the slide, gripped the gun in both hands, aimed at the center of his chest, exhaled steadily . . . and began shooting.

# 26

## A Damnable Frenzy of Magnums, and a Fading Pulse, a Weakening Heartbeat

My righteous anger thumped through my head, nearly as thunderous as the reverberations from my pistol as I shot at all three Magnums. Unnervingly, the identical men merely stood there, allowing me to target them point-blank while looking concerningly smug.

As they continued to vibrate, preparing—apparent-fucking-lly—to duplicate again, I shot them in the chest—thrice each for good measure—before the three Magnums burst into nine.

*Fuck. Me.*

Every handful of seconds, each one had the potential to transform into three more like him. As if a single one of them wasn't threat enough . . .

My bullets didn't do a damn thing to stop any of them, instead spearing straight through their bodies as if they were as insubstantial as smoke, leaving holes in their clothing but not in their flesh. The bullets embedded in the wall behind the Magnums with small puffs of plaster.

Immediately, each of the nine Magnums began to oscillate anew.

My friends opened fire as well, the booms of our revolvers stunningly loud in the space, which had before felt unreasonably cavernous for an office, and now was rapidly becoming snug with each addition to our nemeses' ranks.

I unloaded the entirety of my magazine into them—a full twenty bullets. In addition to the chest, I also hit them in the face, abdomen, groin, kneecaps, anywhere capable of severely incapacitating them.

The result was always the same: intact Magnums; shot-to-shit clothing and surroundings.

The reading nook no longer was welcoming; the sexy low-slung chair was battered.

The Magnums were at a twenty-seven count, and without so much as a single drop of blood shed between all of them.

There seemed little point to reloading. When my crew ran out of bullets, we switched out our magazines but allowed silence to settle, buzzing noticeably after so much racket.

"I don't understand," Layla murmured. "Joss killed you before."

Yes, I had. With a knife, not a gun!

I slid a blade from my back pocket and launched it at a Magnum. I repeated the action over and over and over.

My four knives pierced the wall, a book, and the stalk of a ficus. Four of the Magnums' fancy sweaters sported fresh slashes.

<*The motherfucking* fuck, *man?*> Brady muttered into our bond, sounding as disturbed as I felt.

<*Maybe he can only be killed hands-on?*> I suggested. <*He was on top of me when I stabbed him.*>

Despair trawled its icy tentacles up my hands and feet, spreading to my arms and legs. But hell, there had to be a way to kill him, there just had to!

The twenty-seven Magnums occupied so much space that some of them lined up in front of the window wall close to the large desk. They grinned, revealing bright, straight, attractive teeth I instantly wanted to bash in with the butt of the gun I gripped at my side. Seemed to be no reason to aim it.

"You can't kill us," the Magnums said, all together, all at once, in perfect synchrony.

A full-body shudder swept along the length of me.

"Well, that's creepy," Layla whispered.

*Creepy* times twenty-seven.

"I killed one of you," I insisted.

The Magnums' smiles held steady. "Only because he didn't anticipate it. You won't get the advantage over us again."

The words scraped, like rough cement against tender fingertips, sounding like they might contain truth. Still, I had to at least try, eliminate all possibilities.

Hands curled like claws, I launched myself at the nearest fucker. Surprise etched across the one's face, distinguishing him from the rest of them, before I jabbed him in the throat as hard as I could.

My friends, realizing it was all-out brawl time, ran at other Magnums.

When mine bent over, gasping and choking for breath, I slammed my hands to his shoulders, pushing him down. With a fast strike to my inner elbows I recognized as a standard self-defense move—which meant he actually knew how to fight, dammit, at least some—he attempted to dislodge them. But by then I was jerking my knee up into his balls with the totality of my might and fury.

It was considerable.

My knee squashed his scrotum far up where it never wanted to go. He wheezed and sputtered. His face reddened. His eyes watered. He pitched forward, cupping his junk tenderly, and landed with a *smack* half on an expensive-looking area rug, half on hardwood floor.

<*They're only immune to our attacks if they see 'em coming,*> Griffin told our crew. <*That's the key.*>

<*Shit, yeah,*> Brady exclaimed.

Sure, despite our aspirations, we were no true ninjas. But our fighting skills weren't too shabby either. We'd dedicated many thousands of hours to becoming stronger, faster, sharper, and more skilled.

The Magnums must have also realized we posed a real threat. The entire mass of them began to vibrate even while they fought back.

I snatched a Magnum, hooked an index finger in each of his ear canals, gripped the shell of his ears with my middle fingers, tugged, and jammed my thumbs into his eyeballs. He screamed and clutched my wrists, working to bend them the wrong way.

Without a single morsel of mercy, I pressed on his eyeballs with all my strength until the tissue gave way under the force. Like squishy pulp. *Yuck.*

He flung both hands blindly out at me, trying to grab me. I backed away, straight into the arms of another Magnum. A third came at me from one side, a fourth from the opposite. With more *pops*, less noticeable now with the noise of the scuffles, two new Magnums emerged from each one already standing.

Floor and walls rattled. Another thunderclap boomed outside the building. And more gunfire punctuated its rise and fall.

My braids bouncing, I thrashed, attacking savagely, not keeping still for a moment so they wouldn't latch on to me. If it was a Magnum body part entering my frame of view, I was striking or grabbing, scratching and clawing, twisting or breaking.

It was a damnable frenzy of Magnums, so much so that I lost sight of my friends—my family. The immediacy of danger was too great to use our telepathic link to keep tabs on one another.

I threw one of my last knives at a Magnum. Surprise widening his eyes, he twisted his torso with annoying agility, dodging at the last possible moment. The knife flew past him to nick the shoulder of another with his back turned.

A blow landed. *Great* and all, but far from serious enough to really even slow him down.

My final blade, at least, proved worthwhile. I faced a pair of Magnums. While they came at me, I leapt out of their way, slammed into another Magnum. When that one turned my way, I managed to drag my blade deep across his throat.

His eyes gawping, he clutched his throat uselessly while he dropped to his knees.

Even dying, with another *pop*, the fucker managed to expand into two more of him. They appeared on either side of him, on their knees, clutching their annoyingly intact throats. The lethal injury didn't cross over to the newbies.

A Magnum yanked my arms behind me, clamping them back like steel bands. He tugged so hard my shoulders screamed, the ligaments one wrong pull from tearing.

"Submit," he snarled beside an ear.

The office was now replete with Magnums, most of whom were vibrating, preparing to spawn even more nasty-ass copies. *Pop*s could be heard every few seconds. The mass of swarming, fighting bodies kept growing.

Shouts, grunts, and the smacking of flesh felt as loud as the gunfire still heard from outside. Every minute or so now, the floor and walls rumbled, rattling whatever fixtures still remained intact.

Ours wasn't the only battle raging at the institute.

I rammed the heel of my sneaker into the delicate bones of the guy's foot. He growled as his hold faltered, but only the slightest fraction before he tightened it again, pulling even more terribly on my straining shoulder muscles.

"I said, *submit*," he grunted from behind me.

Glass shattered like a crackling, tinkling rainstorm. One of the ample wall panels was largely missing, sharp, deadly shards lining what remained around the opening.

Charging at full speed, Griffin rammed a Magnum right through it, hastily grabbing onto a mullion to stop himself from catapulting after him.

The Magnum clutched at anything to halt his momentum, clasping a jagged piece of glass that rose thigh-high. It slashed his palm wide open and did nothing to keep him from falling backward, arms spinning, out the hole.

"Submit to me right now, or I'll kill every single one of your friends while you watch."

I stomped on his feet again. He grunted, absorbing the pain, but didn't loosen his grip even the fraction from before.

I slammed my butt into his groin, pushing him back a foot, but I didn't hurt him and his hold remained.

"Keep this up and I'll make it really painful for your friends before they die."

I stopped resisting, mostly because I had to come up with a better plan to get away.

"Believe me," he whispered into my ear with the familiarity of a lover.

His voice dragged along my skin, leaving smeared filth in its wake.

"I can make it really, really, *really* bad for your friends before they go."

<*Guys,*> I shouted into our link.

Magnums closed in around me, so tight all I could see was them. No flashes of those I loved.

I wasn't claustrophobic, but my chest tightened, making it hard to breathe. The Magnums crowded, denser and denser.

<*Guys,*> I yelled again, louder into our connection, trying to get them to hear me over the chaos.

<*Here,*> Hunt shouted back. <*How are we . . .*> He grunted with effort. <*. . . supposed to get an edge over them?*>

<*I'm hurt,*> Layla said, her admission faint over the nearly incessant *pops*, the rumbling and shaking of the building, and gunfire, much closer than before.

"Submit to me or you *will* regret it."

The Magnum holding me was too loud in my ear when I was straining to hear Layla.

<*How bad are you hurt, Lay?*> I asked.

<*Bad,*> was all she said.

<*What is it?*> Brady demanded. <*Where are you?*>

<*Doesn't matter,*> she said, softer still. <*Keep fighting. Keep going. Never give up.*> Then, more terrifying still, <*I love you all forever. Don't ever forget that.*>

<*Forget?*> Brady said. <*You'll be here to remind us.*> But panic rode his words. <*Lay?*>

Only *pops* and guttural grunts and the *tat-a-tat-tat* of nearing gunfire.

<*Lay!*> Brady yelled.

He waited. With my heart in my throat, I waited too.

Nothing.

<*Anybody got eyes on her?*> Brady asked.

<*Nope,*> Hunt said right away, the one word heavy before he yelped and groaned.

With my mouth open to ask, he said, <*I'm okay, I'm okay.*>

He didn't sound okay, though.

"You've made your decision, then," the Magnum holding me said. "It's a bad one. You won't be able to say I didn't warn you."

The circle of them was so tight around me I could make out the nose hairs of the Magnum directly in front of me. His eyes glittered with avarice, like he believed he was about to get to claim his prize.

*Me.*

"No!" I said. "No, no. Just gimme a sec to think it over."

"You don't have seconds. Your friends are already dying."

My heart thudded through its next beat.

*Fuck, were they?*

<*Griff,*> I called out.

I waited only a second before calling for him again.

<*I'm here. I'm here, baby.*>

His voice was thready.

<*What is it? What's wrong?*> I yelled.

The Magnum was shouting in my face to be heard above the din. I no longer cared what he said. I listened only for Griffin.

<*Dude, you're hurt.*> It was Hunt.

<*Yeah. I am. But it'll be all right. I just need you guys to be okay. Look out for Joss, remember?*>

He audibly groaned, something he'd be trying to prevent us from hearing.

<*Forget about me,*> I ordered. <*What's wrong, Griff?*>

<*I can never forget about you.*> He sighed into our bond. <*My dream girl,*> he mumbled, like he was fading.

<*Guys, guys,*> Brady shouted. <*The ninja teachers. They're here. They're fighting the Magnums. They're*—aaahhhgh . . .>

<*Brady,*> I shouted, my eyes smarting.

<*Your dad's here too, Griff,*> Hunt said. <*And*—>

He cut off abruptly.

"She refuses to submit," the Magnum facing me announced to the room.

Cutting through the cacophony, his pronouncement echoed as every other Magnum took a turn repeating the condemnation.

*She refuses to submit.*

*She refuses to submit.*

*She refuses to submit.*

"She'll never submit," Hunt cried above the momentary lull in the fighting. "To you or to anyone. Don't ever do it, Joss. No matter what. Never do it."

That sounded so . . . final.

Like Hunt thought he wouldn't make it.

"Kill him first," the same Magnum said, the others joining him, the death sentence ringing out all too clearly.

"Nonononono," I pled. "What do you want from me? What is it?"

The Magnum across from me smiled. This time, it was him alone.

"Nothing we need any of the others for." His smile turned pensive. "You won't be able to resurrect them this time, you know. Not anymore."

Could it be true? My heart, seized by fear for my crew, shrieked that this might be one of the few truths the man had ever told me.

"Please," I said, uncaring that the word tasted foul in my mouth. For my crew, whatever was necessary.

"Don't hurt them. I'll do whatever you want. Anyth . . ." But I trailed off.

Now I was lying.

I'd do *just about* anything to save those I loved more than I loved myself.

But I wouldn't do absolutely *anything*.

They wouldn't want me to either.

"It's moving to see you so concerned for them," the Magnum said. "Really, it is. I value loyalty greatly in my own people." He chortled. "Well, I use the term loosely, of course."

"What are you?" I asked.

This Magnum wasn't vibrating, though it wasn't that great of a relief when the gigantic office was already crammed with identical copies of the man. There were hundreds of him.

This one brushed plaster and glass shards off the shoulders of his sweater, a pointless exercise when the sweater was torn in several places; a single, bloodless bullet hole gaped from its front.

Magnum looked at me, really studied me. "The Aquoians call us . . ." His upper lip rolled with distaste. " . . . *skinsnatchers.*

"Such a crude term for our kind when we're capable of such great feats. We don't *snatch*. We *transform*. We're like stars, brilliant and astounding, like nothing else in the cosmos. But stars start out as dust."

"You're implying that humans are dust?" I said blandly, while silently calling out.

<*Griff? Lay?*>

A soft moan, I couldn't tell whose.

<*Brade? Hunt?*>

Nothing at all.

"Dust we make infinitely more impressive. More powerful. Mighty."

A general murmur swept through the Magnums. When the self-proclaimed orator turned toward the entrance, so did I.

Rich Connely, his grade-A prick of a nephew, waltzed in, along with Zoe Wills, Hunt's obligatory girlfriend.

The Magnums didn't exactly make way for them, but they didn't interfere as the two ambled through the maze of bodies.

When Rich and Zoe drew close enough that he didn't need to raise his voice to be heard, the orator cast a glare at our ninja instructors, before pointing at Homer.

"That one betrayed me."

Rich and Zoe exhibited no reaction beyond veering Homer's way. Their faces were calm and relaxed, as if they were just joshing around at Ridgemore High during recess. They drew to either side of our nimble and muscled instructor.

Homer punched Rich square in the nose, hard enough to crunch bone and cartilage, then spun a kick toward the smaller Zoe.

Our classmate with the pleasant face and demeanor, soft, brown curls, and a baby growing in her uterus, didn't so much as flinch. She struck Homer's leg so ferociously that his momentum jerked to a halt in midarc, jarring his hip out of socket. Then, she twisted the leg.

Homer cried out.

She'd dislocated his hip.

When she released him, he stumbled backward on his other leg and crumbled to the floor with another cry.

Apprehension was thick in my throat. Homer was a large, strong man. Zoe was petite. How much strength had it required for her to overpower him like that?

I'd only just begun to wonder if there might be more to her when she yanked down her face—her fucking face, yo—much like Fanny had done.

Her fingers clawed at the stripping flesh, digging under it, and yanked the rest of her skin down off her head. It came off clean, including her hair, as if her human skin wasn't all that different from a high-end costume mask. She left it pooling around her neck like a snood.

But I wasn't really looking at her neck.

I was staring at that now familiar shiny, glistening, gray flesh.

And the row upon row of vicious, predatory teeth that would be right at home in any good alien flick.

Homer's intelligent eyes goggled as he scooted back away from her—*it*, whatever the alien was—only to bump into a Magnum. Four others inched closer, cutting off any route of escape.

Monster-Zoe gnashed her teeth with an insectoid-like clicking. She stalked toward Homer.

His left leg dead weight, hanging loose from the dislodged joint, he scooted back onto a Magnum's loafer.

Zoe crouched down, scooped up Homer like he was a plaything that weighed a fraction of his densely muscled body, aligned his head with her mouth—and all those incredibly disturbing teeth. Her maw unhinged as it stretched wide enough to accommodate his bulk . . . and then she began chomping.

*Crunch, crunch. Chomp, chomp.*

Gore and blood, bone and spit flew.

She fed his body into her mouth with the ease—and grinding—of a pencil driving into a sharpener.

*Crunch, monch, monch, chomch.*

By the time his shoulders vanished into her throat—into a space physics suggested he wouldn't fit—his body had ceased its struggles.

I didn't even have a gulp in me. I gawked, an unsettling tremor starting in my extremities. I might never eat again.

<*Fam?*> I asked my crew weakly. <*Please tell me you're all right.*>

If they responded, I didn't make it out above Monster-Zoe's chewing. She was like a giant panda chomping down loudly on some bamboo—just as content but with absolutely none of the lovable cuteness.

When Monster-Fanny had swallowed Bobo, she hadn't chewed.

I didn't think Homer was coming back out of her in any recognizable form.

A sob, abruptly silenced, sounded over Zoe's chewing.

Yolanda, perhaps. Or maybe Armando. The sight was enough to bring anyone with a reasonable sense of right and wrong to their knees.

<*Griff?*> I tried again.

No answer.

I studied the chatty Magnum. Tested the hold on my arms. Still tight as a steel band, staying me in place, at his—their—mercy.

<*I'm still . . . here . . . my dream . . .*> Griffin's voice was softer than a faint breeze, too weak even to complete his sentiment.

Like a fading pulse. A weakening heartbeat.

The Magnum across from me smiled fondly at the sight of Zoe eating a grown man. A man I'd very much liked and admired, a wonderful specimen of human.

Now gone.

And for what?

"We are *drashneemooshta*," Magnum said fondly. "The pinnacle of creation."

He dragged his admiration from the meal still in progress over to me. The cacophony of ongoing struggles lessened.

"I am a special kind of *drashneemooshta*. Just as you are a special kind of *lushina*. The time has arrived for you to give me the rest of your power. I've been patient enough. I won't wait any longer."

The rest? That implied he had some of my power . . .

"You refuse to submit by choice, even to save your *lushina* friends. Then you will submit by force. The games are over."

He brought both hands to my shoulders.

I thrashed and flailed and slammed my forehead into his nose. It spurted blood, a bright crimson as if he were actually as human as he appeared.

He *tsk*ed while I slammed my head back into the face of the one holding me. He yelped, growled fiercely, and gripped me so hard that both my shoulders eased from their joints. A single millimeter more and both shoulders would be fully dislocated. I'd be at their complete mercy, even more than I was now.

I stilled completely.

With blood trailing from both nostrils down his lips, the Magnum in front of me gingerly patted his nose. He scowled angrily at me—like, how dare I?

He boxed my ears with a smack so intense it left my ears ringing, and he aggressively pushed his forehead against mine.

"I *will* take your *lushe*, *lushina*," he snarled.

An energy of some sort, which I'd never before known existed within me, stretched toward him through the point of contact. Like taffy being pulled, he sucked it from me.

I didn't even know how to resist this . . . this otherworldly shit.

*No*, I screamed inside.

And suddenly, *they* were there.

The Sky People. The *lushina*.

In my mind's eye, in a waking dream, whatever it actually was, light forms that vaguely resembled bodies filled my vision.

Their energy was manic, loud, and most importantly, motherfucking powerful.

# 27

## Dreamwalking, Ba-by!; I Made That Taffy My Bitch

My awareness divided. I remained only vaguely aware of my surroundings, as if they were the dreamspace instead of whatever bizarre shit was happening within my mind. The multitude of Magnums faded until I was cognizant only of two: the one who gripped my arms so unyieldingly that my shoulders were easing from their joints, and the one clasping my head with crushing force. His fingers squeezed my skull so brutally that I briefly considered it might be my end. With my skull shattered, bone splintering into my brain, and my crew already incapacitated, there'd be no one left to revive any of us—assuming that Magnum was lying and we actually could still return from the dead.

The pain—so acute, so devastatingly unbearable—nearly yanked me from the Sky People clamoring for my attention. But with my eyes squeezed shut, they were all I saw. I fought the agonizing touch of the two Magnums.

"Give it to me," Skullcrusher snarled, his breath hot and revolting near my mouth. "Give me your power. All of it. All you have left."

A sensation as of warm taffy stretching from my mind's eye and into Skullcrusher's was nauseating. I might not understand precisely who or what the Sky People were, or what all Magnum and his alien-looking bitches were, but I knew down to my bones that I shouldn't be surrendering a single iota of my *lushe*, as he called it.

It was my essence, my light, my life force, I suspected, perhaps even my actual soul. My *lushe* was whatever made me who and how I was. It was that part of me that marked me as a *lushina*—a Sky People.

Regardless of what it might cost me or my crew, I couldn't allow him to take any more than he already had.

I resisted. I *willed* myself to hold on to my *lushe*. The light bodies of the Sky People behind my eyelids shifted from the tall, thin outlines that suggested humanoid physiques to a smattering of light and color, blending together.

Pursing my lips, I battled to keep what belonged to me.

Not to him.

*To me.*

To fucking *me*.

First, I envisioned tugging my energy back into myself, and when that didn't work, severing the flow of it entirely.

But *dammit*, it turned out that wishing and willing weren't enough. Not even close.

More of my *lushe* snaked from me to this hideous creature sheathed inside a man.

The more I resisted, and the more it did no fucking good, the more I panicked. The more I nearly succumbed to the pain begging me to do something to protect my body from harm.

"Yes, that's it. That's it!" Skullcrusher said on a delighted, airy laugh. "Let it flow. Don't hold back. Empty yourself."

*Like hell I would.*

Though it seemed insurmountable, I pushed away my pain. I didn't exactly succeed in not feeling it, but it did dull just a little.

And that just a little turned out to be enough to once again hear the Sky People. Their light bodies again took more precise form.

They were fighting as hard as I was to stop the violation that was underway. The soothing, beautiful melody I heard from them the night before was replaced by jagged screeches. Calls to action, I realized—alarm too.

So then what Magnum was doing must be even worse than I guessed, with far-reaching implications beyond me as an individual.

My *lushe* was a flowing river. Its current was picking up speed, draining me all the faster.

At some point, despite the danger to my body, I couldn't help but sag into Shoulderwrencher's grip. It loosened. Eventually, I discovered myself on my knees, with Skullcrusher kneeling across from me, murmuring skin-crawling encouragements while softening his crushing hold on my head, just slightly—maybe to keep me from passing out.

"That's it. Just like that, yes, yes. Keep going." His voice was already gloating and celebratory.

My head lolled, held up only by Skullcrusher's forehead against mine. When had he removed his hands from my skull?

Vaguely, as if from whole oceans away, I heard screams, breaking glass, smashing furniture, and gunfire, pained cries, and those *pops* that had delivered our enemy right into our midst.

For many years I'd worked to learn how to defend myself and those I loved—with my body, with skills and weapons of this world. How was I to protect us from powers beyond this *world*?

My entire body went limp for long enough to startle me, to tug me fully back into it.

If I didn't do something now—like right the hell now—there would be no second chances for me—or for Griff, Lay, Hunt, or Brade. Everyone I loved would vanish from this world—Bobo, too, probably.

My breaths were coming in ragged wheezes I experienced only abstractly. Skullcrusher kept up his victorious commentary, but I barely heard it.

The Sky People's cries, however, grew louder.

With more determination than I'd ever had to employ, I homed in on their voices.

They were indiscernible squeaks, like a bunch of excitable chickadees.

My head rolled backward, only an inch before Skullcrusher clamped down on it with his bruising hold.

My energy whooshed into him with renewed vigor.

The Sky People's voices faded.

*No.*

No!

My eyes shutting out what was directly in front of me, I pursued the Sky People, chasing them farther inside myself.

Their birdlike squeaks became louder.

And then . . . oh fuck . . . oh fuck, yes . . . then they coalesced into familiar vowels and consonants, if drawn out slowly, spoken at a tenth of average speed.

As if they'd studied humanity from afar, learning all languages and accents at once, they communicated to me in an English that was part, well, everything.

In a hodgepodge of cultures and inflections, they spoke in a single voice. Despite its garbled slow distortion, its tone managed to be both urgent and commanding while also somehow compassionate and encouraging—a peppy cheerleader with a whip in hand, its end capped in feathers instead of flaying barbs, though a whip nonetheless.

<*Eeeennnnteeeeerrrrr* dddddrrrrraaaaaashhhhhh.>

Their voice was at once ethereal and homogenous, diverse yet unified. It pronounced *drash* to rhyme with "trash"—I approved—their own name for Magnum's kind, apparently.

<*Taaaaaake* lllluuuushhhhhheeeeee,> pronounced loo-sheh. <*Eeeeeennnnnndddddd* ddddddrrrrraaaaaaashhhhhh.>

Surely some prime details were being lost in translation. Like, how—precisely—did one go about taking *lushe* and ending a *drash*?

Even if the *lushina* were able to eventually give me more instruction, I didn't have time to wait for it. More connected to the *lushina* than my own body right then, I could still sense that my physical form was moments away from a point of no return.

Immortality or not, whether or not that power remained to me and my crew, I doubted there'd be any coming back once my essence—that which made me a *lushina*—was gone. After that I'd become merely human.

And humans weren't exactly known to resurrect.

A terrible choice was foisted upon me: wait for further details in that long-drawn-out voice and risk my end and, consequently, that of my friends, or fight now with all I had.

When Skullcrusher's giddy, triumphant giggles reached me, garbled as if from beneath water, my decision was made for me.

If he believed he'd already won, that I was at the very end, then there was no more time to wait. Not even a second to spare.

It seemed I was truly a *lushina* in human form, and as such, some part of me, somewhere, must know how to combat this terrible enemy. Beyond my rational mind and its reign of logic, I clutched my intuition . . .

Instead of resisting the final tugs of my *lushe* as it traveled into him, I dove after it.

My knees remained planted on the floor of Magnum's fancy office but I felt worlds away as I projected my consciousness into his.

Just as far away, I heard the *lushina*'s encouraging cheers. I was on the right track. I leaned harder into my instincts.

Inside Skullcrusher's mindspace, it was dark and cold, both all-encompassing, as if the light never shone there and never would. I could see nothing through the proverbial eyes of my awareness. I could, however, sense plenty.

The one Magnum's mindspace contained all the others. There were a total of one hundred forty-three Magnums still alive in the office. Within them lay the seeds for an infinite amount of our enemy. This *drash* could reproduce without ceasing. So long as one lived, he could multiply into two more, and then each of those into two more, and onward.

It was the quality that made Magnum special among the *drash*.

Skullcrusher began struggling—all in the mindspace or also in the physical, I couldn't determine. My own body felt beyond my reach.

He resisted my control. I fought back.

He hardened his will against me. I hardened mine more.

He attempted to pull free, to disrupt the flow of *lushe* that linked us. I didn't allow it. I reinforced the connection . . . and reversed the flow of energy.

This time, it worked.

Now his essence was streaming into me, mine that he stole returning with it.

When his fear first burgeoned, I believed it was mine. But before long I realized the terror I was experiencing was his.

He understood what I was only just beginning to sense: *This*, this that I was doing, it was *dreamwalking*.

There was no requirement for sleep or dreaming. I was traveling among his thoughts, *his mind*. Worse still for him, I suspected I could actually overpower them.

I could force my will upon his.

Abruptly, I discovered Skullcrusher's hands gone from my head. My skull pulsed, but only in recovery from his assault. Shoulderwrencher, too, had released me.

My thighs quivered as I struggled to keep myself upright. My shoulders tingled as if swarmed by fire ants.

It was a smart move on Magnum's part. My physical body was signaling, and loudly, that it required immediate attention.

I had to refuse it.

With an internal, guttural roar, I grabbed on to Skullcrusher's essence like I was in a tug-of-war—ferociously. I made that taffy my bitch.

Then . . . I *heaved.*

His essence pitched forward.

I felt more than heard him scream. I heaved and tugged and pulled more and more of his energy into me. All of mine finished returning.

Only then did I realize he was speaking aloud.

"Wait! Wait, wait, wait, wait," his voice pled, arriving as if from the opposite side of sprawling mountain ranges. "You can't kill me."

*Like hell I can't.*

"I took some of your power," he hastened to add.

My eyes remained tightly shut. My mind's eye was trained on his, on continuing to siphon his essence.

"It's true," he insisted in a whine. "You can't kill me."

"I . . . can." My voice sounded unfamiliar to my own ears. It was the same pitch and intonation as always, but it was as if someone far older and far wiser were speaking through me. The *lushina* within me, perhaps.

"No, no, you can't," Magnum said before yelping, then yipping again.

So my claiming his energy hurt him . . . *Good. May it hurt lots more.*

"I have enough of your . . . ow, ow, ow . . . power that if . . . you, ow, kill me . . ." He panted. Starkly gone was the composed archvillain who'd lorded over everyone else. "You won't be able to resurrect your friends. You'll die if you . . . ahhhhhh, ouch, ouch, ouch . . . if you try."

He paused just to pant some more. I pulled on that tug-o-war taffy rope with all my might, like I was a beauty queen and my winning grand prize would be global peace and harmony for all.

"You need the power I took from you," he said. "You need *me*."

"I . . . don't," I growled, a bear scaring a rival predator from her den.

Along the taffy thread connecting us, I felt Magnum shudder under my emerging fortitude.

"You do, you do," he said, unable to hide his desperation.

As deeply linked to him as I was, he couldn't conceal much.

"Look," he begged. "Look at what I'm trying . . . ah, ah, ow . . . to show . . . you."

In my own mindspace, images, cloudy like smoke, crispened in front of the *lushina*'s light bodies to form scenes—clips from Magnum's memories.

After Griffin went over the cliff on the way to Raven's Lagoon, Zoe's big sister, Hayden Wills, was one of the first responders at the scene. She was there when they defibrillated Griffin after my crew and I begged them not to give up on him despite the broken neck. Out of sight, later Hayden stepped out of her skin to reveal herself as a Magnum underneath the cute-girl facade.

Magnum was also Jaggar at the gymnasium, posing as the obedient soldier who offered up defibrillator paddles in anticipation of his murdering us.

At the drag race, when Clyde exploded into a raging fireball with Griffin inside, Magnum was again there, once more in the guise of Hayden Wills.

Save for the first occasion with Brady, since the press covering the "Miracle Kid" incident was what first garnered Magnum's attention, each time one of us died, Magnum was there. He eventually emerged from a cocoon of someone else.

Linked to his mindspace as I was, I understood that the confident, handsome billionaire was yet another shell. Like matryoshka dolls, the Magnum persona could nestle inside another. But within the Magnum hid a gray, creepy, toothy, alien-looking *drash* just like those within Fanny and Zoe.

This "special" *drash* far preferred his human disguise—and hell, who could blame him? So long as he didn't remove his Magnum skin suit, his body behaved exactly as his human counterpart's would.

When my crew or I were being revived, before Magnum shed his borrowed skin suit, as our essences returned to our physical vessels, he stole all he could, leaving sufficient to reanimate our bodies. Relatively, it was a minuscule amount, sure, but souls are meant always to be whole. Any part of it missing was a significant deficiency.

"You're the one who conferred immortality on them," Magnum explained, his voice steady and pedantic.

Distantly, alarm bells clanged. He was no longer suffering.

I tightened my mind's eye around his essence and gave a violent tug.

He winced and hissed. "Once you . . . gave them the immor . . . tality . . . they didn't need your pow . . . er. But only . . . because you were strong. That augmented the ability . . . you gave them."

I pulled as hard as I could. A spurt of his essence flowed into me.

He hissed again, louder this time, more drawn out. "They can't . . . do it now. You're not . . . whole. You"—*hsssssssss*—"need me to help you."

Even latched on to his mindspace as I was, I couldn't determine the veracity of his claim.

"If you try to bring them back . . ." he grunted, "it will kill you."

Perhaps I would die.

I knew one thing for certain: The creepy alien in the smooth-rich-dude skin would never, ever, help me or my family. Not unless it benefited him.

Magnum Chase would want all my abilities: immortality, dreamwalking, telepathy, *and* preternatural healing. With his own powers alone, he was scary enough.

And megalomaniacs never stopped.

*No.* There was no room for negotiation, or for error.

I could *not* allow him to escape.

No matter what it cost me.

Even if it cost me my *family*.

My crew.

My every-fucking-thing.

If they were in positions to advise me, my friends would tell me to do it. To risk them and myself to rid our world of someone as terrible as *him*. To spare countless people—with and without supernatural abilities—from his greed.

In a rush, he said, "You need me. You can't kill me. You'll die. They'll die. Most of them are dead already. You can't bring them . . . back without me."

*Hold my beer, motherfucker, and watch me.*

At the very least I was going to go out giving it absolutely everything I had.

Magnum Chase had to die. It was as simple as that.

He kept talking, but I was no longer listening. He tried to shove more images at me. I deflected them.

I strengthened my bond with the *lushina*. Within their light bodies, they crystallized into forms resembling humans at the center of their brightly shining auras.

<*Eeeeeennnnnnnddddddd drrrrrraaaaashhhhhh*,> they sang. Their imperative filled every part of my being, driving me with purpose.

Magnum was wriggling and screaming, struggling to free himself. But I wasn't crushing his skull against mine, as he'd done. I wasn't grabbing him at all. My hold on his mind allowed me to dominate his body. After all, what is the body but a vessel that carries out the commands of the mind?

He fought me. He even attempted to slip free of his Magnum skin suit, which he hadn't done since he killed and stole the body of a man in Ridgemore without family or friends to declare him missing.

My grip was a vise he wouldn't escape.

Magnum didn't like being a *drash*. He wanted to be a *lushina*—but a *lushina plus*. He wanted the advantages of his kind, those of mine, and any he could steal from other supes.

The man wanted it all and didn't care whom he hurt to get his way.

He was a true archvillain, Hollywood 101 style.

He screamed, his protest hazy as it reached me. As if it were second nature now, my instincts guided me. I molded his mindspace into believing it wanted to recall his duplicates.

Magnum stopped resisting. This was his idea—so he thought.

One hundred and forty-two copies of him—only those still alive—returned to the one vessel, which absorbed them. Skullcrusher Magnum was the original.

With my mindspace merged with his, my command overriding his own, I held him steady. With my physical arm, I braced his body around the back and hooked his sweater around his shoulders, baring his torso. With a magnitude of force far beyond what I knew before, I curled my hand into a fist and drove it against his breastbone. The skin split down the center as if hit with a mallet. His breastbone cracked in a long, jagged line, smaller fissures racing toward its edges.

My physical eyes remained closed. Later, I would think it was a little like Neo in *The Matrix*, when he fought the Smiths and saw the matrix itself.

A little like Neo, but far bloodier—Neo meets John Wick.

My fist was slick with Magnum's blood. With the *drash* nestled deep within his Magnum suit, his blood was human scarlet. He didn't even gasp his surprise. I released my supporting arm, allowing him to fall back with a heavy smack of his head. Instantly, I was perched over him, my fist hammering against that breastbone again, shattering it. I reached around its pieces, behind his ribs, to grip his heart.

It felt human but it wasn't. It was big enough to require two hands.

I slid my second hand alongside the first, cradling the pulsing, thrumming heart of my enemy in my palms.

I felt it beating.

Beating.

Beating.

I sucked the final threads of his energy into my own mindspace, where the *lushina* directed the entirety of his essence elsewhere, so that no part of him would taint me.

His mindspace went completely blank.

His heart, however, still beat.

*Dadum.*

*Dadum.*

*Dadum.*

Snapping arteries and vessels, I ripped it free of his chest cavity.

Blood rapidly pooled in my palms, trickled down my arms.

<*Eeeeeennnnnnnddddd drrrrraaaaaaashhhhhh*,> the *lushina* murmured.

No longer a command but confirmation of a task completed.

As if waking from a monthlong slumber, I blinked open my eyes. The afternoon light filtering in through the glass-plated window wall, largely broken out now, was too bright. The *tat-a-tat-tat* of nearby gunfire was too loud but rapidly dying down. The earth's shuddering rumbles were fading.

I blinked some more, and the office came into focus. With all the many Magnums now gone, the office was back to feeling cavernous.

Panic seizing me by the jugular, I searched for those who mattered most. The once luxurious space was more junkyard slaughterhouse than sophisticated office.

A few people were left standing: Orson and Porter, battered as if they'd fought in Armageddon; Armando and Yolanda, looking like they'd also fought a world-ending battle; and only slightly less battered, Sheriff Xander Jones and a scientist, still buttoned into her lab coat, a very blood-spattered white.

And Bobo. He'd reneged on his promise and was favoring the leg he broke when he and I were forced to jump from a runaway Clyde.

Beside Bobo stood a massive wolf, twice the size of my pittie, maybe more. His furry jaw was crimson-tinged, his legs painted with blood.

A few others around our age I didn't recognize leaned against broken surfaces, exhausted.

Still cupping Magnum's heart—no longer beating—blood dripped from my elbows and between my fingers. Slowly, I rose on shaky legs.

Once standing, I could better make out who lay on the floor. More bodies sprawled across the debris than remained upright.

My breath left me.

Entangled with Rich Connely's body and Zoe's, her alien head exposed—both still as only the dead were—lay Hunt, partially pinned beneath Zoe's calves, a chair leg jabbed through his gut. His eyes were open but vacant.

I couldn't breathe.

Brady lay nearby on his stomach. His empty stare pointed over a shoulder on a very broken neck. An arm stretched out to someone but didn't quite reach her.

Layla.

My friends . . . my magical friends.

All that truly mattered.

Layla was crumpled in a heap, her legs bent the wrong way at the knees. Her arms pulled the wrong way at both elbows.

Her chest rose and fell with shaky, barely there breaths. It was crushed.

My feet moved all on their own while my stare swept for Griffin. It trawled across bodies in the paramilitary dress of Magnum's zealous soldiers—and our similarly outfitted parents.

But Griffin—he was nowhere.

I stumbled, almost tripped over an upturned lamp, and when I slid to my knees in front of Layla, whose superior healing wouldn't be able to work fast enough to repair this level of damage, I caught movement over by the hot tub.

Griffin was dragging himself, trying to get to me.

Seeing only him, I careened forward.

His face was as beautiful as ever. Perfect. But blood dripped along an eyeball. One side of his skull was smashed in, dented and misshapen. Blood matted his hair. He'd used all his remaining strength just to reach me. He collapsed atop shards of glass and someone's blood—probably a Magnum's—they'd vanished but their blood hadn't.

Griffin strained to lift his head and couldn't. A cheek pressed into piles of glass, he gazed at me, blinking furiously as if he couldn't focus, couldn't really see me.

"Dream girl," he murmured so softly it was already like a precious memory. "Don't . . ." His throat bobbed as he struggled to swallow. "Don't bring us back." It was a garbled plea. "Live for us."

He blinked drowsily. His eyes closed to half-mast. "Live for me."

He must have heard Magnum.

"Fuck that," I said.

His eyes battled back open. "No. No . . . don't."

They closed again.

For the last time.

A strangled cry escaped my quivering lips.

Something nudged me.

I turned to find Bobo staring at me.

<*Bobo take*,> he said into my mind, into my unbearable grief.

He nudged the heart in my hands with his nose.

Vacantly, I extended it toward him and scarcely noticed when he snatched it with his teeth.

Not even wiping the slick blood from my hands before touching Griffin, I ran them over his face, trying to rouse him.

But Griffin, my love . . . *my* dream guy . . . he was gone.

Lowering down to my hands and knees, uncaring that glass sliced my blood-slicked palms, I pressed the tenderest of kisses to his lips, lingered for a few extended moments that had no chance of being enough, and bolted for Layla.

# 28

## On the Other Side of Death, Full Steam Ahead Down the Crazy-Town Line

Layla's eyes were glossed over by her tremendous pain, making the blue-gray of her irises stark beneath their glassiness. I skidded to her side, dropped to the floor, and clutched her hand with my own, Magnum's blood still wet in places along my fingers and palms. I kept my gaze fixed on her face and not on how her body was broken in so many places.

"Hang on, girl," I said around a choked sob. "Bad guy's dead now, so just hang the fuck on."

Her lips parted as if to speak. All that emerged was a weak, shuddering exhale that finished shattering my heart into a million fucking pieces.

No inhale followed it.

Desperation rocked me as I squeezed her hand. There would be no response, I already understood that. I'd witnessed death enough times by now to know what it looked like.

How it felt.

I squeezed anyway, calling her name, over and over again, until my voice grew raspy.

At some point I stopped trying. A deep, tremendous silence settled within me.

I was hollow.

Without my friends to love and fight for, I was empty—so, so empty.

Hands eventually descended on my back and shoulders. I didn't care whose, because I already knew they wouldn't be Griffin's or Layla's or Hunt's or Brady's.

This was why Griffin said he'd rather die time and time again than to have to watch the rest of us go. This cavernous hollowness so terrible it would consume me was why he'd been so haunted for being the sole survivor among us after the shooting at Ridgemore High.

As if I too had been speared through, smashed, and shattered, I shuddered at the very real possibility that I might never speak with any of them ever again. I pressed both hands to my chest, smearing my shirt and skin with blood most foul.

Ten thousand Magnums weren't worth these four.

All I wanted was these four people. Just these four.

"Joss . . . honey." It was my dad—or my not-dad, but what did any of that matter anymore?

His familiar hand soothed circles along my back. That was when I discovered I was shaking violently.

"Honey, come on," he said gently. "Let's get you out of here."

Numbly, I rose. My legs wobbled. My dad pulled me into him. Pressed a kiss to my head.

"I need their bodies together," I said in a voice I heard as if from far, far away.

"What? Honey, no. Leave them. We'll come back for them soon. We won't abandon them here, I promise."

I stepped free of his embrace. Crouched to grab an arm or leg of Layla's that wouldn't cause her further damage, decided there were no good options, and turned toward Brady instead.

I clutched his arm and tugged him toward her. His body caught on the wooden fragments of a chair, but I continued dragging him right over them.

"Joss, no . . ." my dad said.

"What's she doing?" Orson asked. When my dad didn't answer, he asked me the same question.

I didn't so much as glance their way. I was already staring at Hunt, calculating how far away he was and how to get him over here.

"I'm gonna save them," I said, my thoughts racing ahead. "Help me get Hunt over next to Brady and Layla."

"Are you thinking of trying to revive them?" my dad asked.

I didn't answer. Of course that's what I was going to do.

"Magnum told you doing that would kill you," he said, as if the *drash* hadn't been talking to me directly.

The mob of Magnums had concealed much if my dad had been here long enough to hear that.

"Magnum was a self-serving liar," I said, straddling Hunt's hips, examining the huge wound in his abdomen.

My dad crouched beside me. So did Orson. The hushed conversations of the other survivors in the room burbled like lapping waves.

"I don't think he was lying about this," my dad said. "From what we've gathered, he was telling the truth. If you try to revive them, you'll fail. And you'll die."

When I tried to grip it, my palms slid along the chair leg impaling Hunt. Too much blood. I wiped my hands aggressively on the thighs of my jeans until the blood was tacky enough that I could grab the chair leg and hold on.

"Sweetheart . . . you can't," my dad said. His tone was still gentle but firm, an imploring edge starting to sneak into it.

I adjusted my grip. Now that I had purpose again, my shaking had subsided.

Sucking in an inhale, I yanked the chair leg from Hunt's stomach. Its tip splintered and left fragments of wood inside his body, but I didn't clean them out. Who knew what might happen if Magnum's blood from my hands got inside Hunt, melded with his own blood? Maybe nothing would happen, but I wasn't sure it wouldn't.

If I could just get Hunt back alive, his preternatural healing—maybe with the help of a surgeon—would fix him up. I tossed the chair leg aside. It clattered and thudded.

Rounding Hunt's body, I squatted close and slid my arms under his, hooking them around his shoulders. I prepared to heft his weight on my own, but suddenly Orson was there, lifting his legs.

I glanced up at him. He offered me a grim, hardened smile that was as hopeless as my not-dad's words.

But when I stood with Hunt's body, so did he. A pool of blood marked where my friend had fallen. His shirt was soaked, front and back, and dripped as we moved.

We were sidestepping a pile of fallen hardcover books when my dad hustled over and helped me support Hunt's shoulders.

Gently, as if Hunt's open eyes weren't unseeing, we lowered his body to the floor beside Brady. Their legs touched.

Nodding at my progress, I aimed my attention in the direction where I left Griffin and found Armando and Yolanda already carrying his body.

They lowered him next to Layla, Armando cradling Griffin's busted head with a tenderness that made my heart clench and my eyes water.

His stare stuck on Griffin, Orson said, "Joss, your dad's right. As much as I'd like you to bring my son back to life . . . you shouldn't try. The five of you loved each other like I've never seen anybody else love each other. They loved you."

With filthy hands, he rubbed his eyes. His face was so bare without his usual tortoiseshell glasses. "They wouldn't want you to get yourself killed, too, trying to save them when they're"—his inhale shook—"when they're dead already."

My dad's hand was back on my shoulder. "There's no saving them, honey. The best you can do now is to save yourself. Live for them. Make it count."

"Griffin would want that," Orson said. "How he loved you . . ."

Each time they used the past tense was like a shovelful of dirt over their coffins, deep in a hole in the ground already.

I looked at my dad and Orson. Grief sagged across their features, making them appear a decade older.

So they hadn't lied . . . They did love us in their twisted ways.

I gazed from them to the two remaining ninja instructors, then to others whose faces were new, whose names I didn't know.

The formidable wolf was gone. In his place stood a naked, blood-soaked man who appeared to be in his midtwenties. His stance was strong. He wasn't defeated.

He nodded at me. A recognition that risks should be taken when the stakes were important enough. Either that, or it was what I wanted to see. It didn't really matter, regardless.

Armando, in his melodic Brazilian lilt, caught my attention. "*Me perdoa.* Sorry we not fight for you before. It was right thing to do."

"I'm sorry too," I said, the words still sounding foreign, like I was there in my body but also not. Like a part of me was missing.

"Sweetheart," my dad said, rolling on the balls of his feet, his hands clenched into fists, searching for a way to stop me when he had to know there was nothing he could do. "Please. Don't do this. You'll only die with them." Panic made his plea jumpy.

I had nothing to say to him or to anyone else. No final grandiose speech about the life-changing nature of love and friendship and loyalty, or about the nobility of sacrifice.

The only people I wanted to share anything with were on the other side of death.

I was going to cross that line to retrieve them. If I didn't succeed? If I didn't return? Well then, soon enough I wouldn't feel anything at all.

Bobo rubbed along my legs. Several smears of blood on my jeans were thick and goopy enough not to be fully dry yet, and they dragged across his dark fur. Not that it mattered. His muzzle was coated in the stuff, as were his front paws, like he'd used them to clamp down on the heart.

<*Did you eat Magnum's heart?*> I asked him privately.

<*Bobo eat. Bobo end. Danger.*>

Who was I to judge? I'd been the one to dig out the man's pumping heart with my bare hands.

<*I love you. Keep being a good boy, okay?*>

Bobo's tail was pointed. <*Bobo keep.*>

Knowing it was the last I might ever give him, I made myself smile at him. <*Okay, my sweet boy. You keep me safe.*>

Bobo jerked his head up and down, his ears flopping. <*Bobo keep,*> he repeated.

"Joss, no, *please*," my dad said while I stepped over my friends' bodies and lowered myself into the center of them.

I draped a leg over Griffin and another over Layla. I rested a hand on Hunt and the other on Brady. I made sure my bare skin touched theirs. Then I closed my eyes.

My dad began shouting. Orson soon joined in with quieter pleas that were just as insistent.

Man, had my life ever jumped tracks and railroaded down the Crazy-Town line.

Full steam ahead.

I wasn't exactly sure how I'd done it the previous times. I didn't know how to do it this time. So I did what had worked for me before: I got the fuck out of my own way and let that knowledge which transcended this form roll through me.

The floor gave a final rumble beneath my seat—was the battle not over everywhere, then? At least I heard no more gunfire.

I sank into myself, feeling where my skin connected with my friends. I reminded myself I wasn't just a human, I was also a *lushina*. What they could do, I could do. I was the one responsible for my crew's immortality. All I had to do was renew the spark of that everlasting life within them.

Give them a jump start.

Searching for that electric lightning juice cycling within my system, I found it crackling already, a part of me now.

My dad yelled some more. Other voices did too.

Then they faded.

Power, like an electric storm, crackled and arced and sizzled up and down my insides, jumping outward to coat my skin, making me untouchable by mere mortals.

I traveled back to my mindspace, relieved not to find any lingering remnants of Magnum within. I felt for my friends' energies, for their own mindspaces, and when I found them, all at once, I dreamwalked into them.

Then, like a defibrillator in the flesh, I pulsed my power into them.

<*Come back to me,*> I demanded—not through our telepathic link, which felt dead too, but of their very essences.

<*Return. Come back. Now.*>

The power of lightning and the *lushina* surged through me in long pulses.

In the same instant, the four of them responded.

Their energies came back online.

They turned on.

I imagined their essences as heartbeats, and, slowly at first, they began thumping.

*Ba-dum.*

Next, they sped up.

*Badum. Badum. Badum. Badum. Badum.*

Something bulldozed into my body.

*Bobo.*

Unable even to catch myself, I crashed backward onto my friends.

At some point, I left behind the physical for the dream—for another world, another dimension, whatever it was.

Bobo seemed to be barking or talking, others to be shouting.

It all slipped from my grasp, beyond my reach.

The dream claimed me entirely.

My own heart stopped.

The vessel that was my body unfurled like a blooming flower, releasing my essence.

The lightning storm that had raged within me calmed.

My soul floated free toward its source—the same for humans, *lushina*, and *drash*.

# 29

## Blink, Blink, Blink the Fuzz Away; the Red Was Here to Stay

### Griffin

It took major effort to wrench open my eyes, then everything was a watery red. I stared up at a red ceiling. I blinked. Blinked. Blinked. Still red. A filter over everything.

Someone was moaning. Someone else was yelling.

Blink, blink, blink. *Red.*

"Joss," someone was saying. "Honey, come back to me. Come back to me now."

Fuck, it was Reece.

*Sit up, Griffin.* My arms twitched, that was it.

*Get the fuck up.* My arms jerked but didn't obey.

Someone, maybe Reece, was crying. Others were whispering. Some were moaning more, grunting.

I tried to sit again, managed to move a tad, then collapsed back onto my head.

*Motherfucker! That hurt!*

"Griff, son . . ." my dad was saying from behind me. "Don't move. Whatever you do, stay still."

"Joss," Reece cried. "After everything, not now."

I flopped onto my side like a fish.

"Shit," my dad snapped. "Stay still, dammit."

*Blink, blink.* The fucking red wouldn't go away.

On my side, my head was way too fucking heavy. A pulse thudded through it. Pain, it was all pain.

More blinking. I saw Layla's legs. Next Brady. Hunt.

Then I saw *her*.

Then I really knew pain. A torment that'd have no fucking end.

Reece sat next to my friends with Joss across his lap, holding her against his chest. She wasn't fucking moving.

Bobo was leaning his front paws on her legs. He barked. Then again. Like he was calling her back.

Couldn't get my arms to work like I wanted. I rolled onto my stomach. My head hurt so fucking much I almost passed out.

Blink, blink, blink the fuzz away. The red was here to stay.

I pushed with my legs, slid across something sharp. Didn't care.

My dad yelled at me not to move. Cared even less. He called to others for help.

All anyone needed to do was help *her*.

Joss.

My dream girl.

Love of my life.

I held up my heavy-ass thumping head, pushed with my legs some more. It hurt. Fuck, did it hurt. Eventually my arms worked a little. Like a fucking seal, I dragged myself toward her.

Bobo barked. Made my ears ring. My head was a fuzzy ball of pain.

*Blink, blink.* More red. More hurt.

Joss was closer. I made my flippers work for me. Sliding. Dragging. Heaving. Crunching over shit.

Then I was close enough to touch her. My dad yelled at

me again. Reece did too. Bobo barked. My ears rang. My head squeezed and thumped and was about to fucking explode.

I ordered my arm to reach out, and the fucker didn't. I got my head up on her leg. My head might roll the fuck off, but I kept it there. My red vision swam.

"Joss," I tried, but couldn't hear myself.

<*Joss,*> I said into our link.

Damn. Even there, too soft if at all.

My vision blurred. Everything was red. Everything hurt.

<*Joss!*> I screamed into our bond.

Reece shouted at Bobo. Tried to wave him away from Joss.

Bobo jumped up. Pounded down on her chest, nailing her tits.

She gasped for air like she'd been drowning. Sat straight up. Jerked the leg my head was on. Smacked Reece on the chin.

I was falling. Falling. Falling. My head was tipping.

Her eyes popped open.

I held the fuck on just to see them.

She turned them on me.

Even red, they were the most beautiful eyes I'd ever fucking seen.

# EPILOGUE

## Forever

### ~Joss~

With its cherry-black, glossy exterior, all-black leather interior, and shiny chrome big block engine Brady the genius mechanical tinkerer had assembled just for me, Cleo was one sweet ride. He said he owed me, that they all did.

He didn't owe me a damn thing. I'd risked my eternal life for theirs, yeah, and it had majorly *sucked*. But it was nothing any one of them wouldn't do for me.

Still, I giddily accepted the unnecessary token of his appreciation. My 1999 Ford Mustang SVT Cobra coupe had gone from a junkyard salvage rust bucket to a wet dream.

Gliding my hands around the leather of the steering wheel, I admired Griffin as he stretched out his legs in the passenger seat.

Now he . . . he was a wet dream.

My dream guy.

He caught me checking him out, offered me that sly, sexy grin I'd never get enough of.

"What? Like what you see?"

I revved Cleo's engine, just 'cause I could—just like Griffin revved mine.

"*Love* what I see."

His grin softened, grew tender. "I love you, baby."

"Love you back."

At last, we could speak openly in our cars and know our conversations were private.

<*Bobo go,*> Bobo piped up.

*Well, almost private.*

<*Go, go, go,*> he said with a jump atop the blanket I'd draped across the back bench seat for him so he wouldn't scratch Cleo's leather. He'd only sprained the leg he'd previously broken and was back to his normal, energetic self.

With the *drash* vanquished, my pittie had gotten pushy. It was that same determination that had driven him to save me.

It had taken Bobo and Griffin urging me back to them, and a shove from the *lushina*, along with an infusion of their collective power, for me to pull a Lazarus.

Magnum hadn't counted on the *lushina* giving me a temporary boost. And he, thank fuck, was no longer around to regret his miscalculation.

Not only had the original Magnum absorbed every one of his duplicates before I killed him, but it seemed his freaky alieny companions couldn't survive without him, either—some sort of hive dynamic. Fanny, Zoe, Rich, a dozen more of our classmates, including the moron Pike Bills, lots of townies, such as a regular grocery store clerk and the dude who manned the counter at Hughie's Hoagies we'd thought was kind of our friend . . . their empty bodies and many others were found all throughout town—dead without a single outward sign of what did them in. Even Tracy Westwick, the scientist who'd served as the inspo for Griffin's supposed mother Mitzi, and Mr. Thompson, Ridgemore High's principal, had been hiding a nasty gray secret beneath skin suits.

To our surprise, however, the many mercenaries Magnum hired were plain ol' human. The soldiers genuinely bought into the Magnum worship he was selling. They actually believed he was the solution to the earth's many global problems. The misguided dudes were actually trying to help—and didn't mind killing a kid or five when they got in the way—making great money while they were at it.

Sheriff Xander Jones sent them packing, explaining that they'd served a terrible and devious archvillain—but not that he was some kind of creature from another world—while my crew and I were focused on recovering.

Although our physical injuries were devastating, with the help of some fine surgeons and some even finer preternatural healing abilities, in mere days we were back to normal.

At least on the outside.

New scars marred our flesh, but they were shrinking and fading quickly. Brady no longer sported any sign that rebar had once speared him through the chest at the Fischer House party, and the evidence of the five bullets that had ringed my chest at the high school gym had vanished entirely.

With time, there would be no indication that we'd battled for our very survival here at the institute either.

The lingering trauma of all we'd endured . . . that recuperation would take longer. But each day it got just a little easier to forget what it was like to have a predatory Magnum hunting us.

<*Bobo go!*> Bobo said, then barked.

Griffin chuckled easily, obviously not lost to heavy thoughts as I was.

<*Be patient, Bobo,*> Griffin told him. <*Lay'll be here soon, and then we'll go.*>

Next, Griffin broadcast into the telepathic link that only he, Brady, Hunt, Layla, and I shared.

<*Lay, dude, you comin' or what?*>

When seconds passed and she didn't answer from within Bonnie, idling directly behind Cleo, Brady grumbled, <*I think the problem's that Layla* is *coming, and she doesn't give a flying damn that we're waiting on her ass while she gets pleasured. Where's the fucking consideration, man?*>

I was about to say that Layla wasn't exactly big on consideration in general, much less so when sex was involved, when Brady spoke again.

<I *could be gettin' pleasured, too, but y'all see me here, don't you? Not making everyone else wait. And you guys know my sexy cougar's up for it. Yoli's always up for gettin' sticky.*>

Brady's "cougar" was no such thing. He was almost twenty-three—we all were—and Yolanda was twenty-eight. But there was no talking Brady out of his supposed "kink for the older ladies." We'd all tried, especially Yolanda. She didn't push the topic too hard though. The stoic, badass ninja instructor had fallen head over heels for Brady. She'd tried to play it cool; the dreamy looks she gave him on the regular gave her away. Not that it wasn't reciprocal. Brady had gone from a full-on himbo to an eager and devoted monogamist seemingly overnight. When he gazed at his girl, stars practically sparkled in his eyes, like a damn cartoon.

Yolanda was rarely far from his side nowadays, which meant it was a good thing the rest of us really liked her too. She perched in Bonnie's passenger seat.

Armando was stretched out across Bonnie's back seat. We wanted him along on our very first road trip out of Ridgemore, because Armando was just that cool. The Brazilian had turned out to be a feisty fucker, with a sharp mind and an even sharper tongue, who was just our style.

My Mustang wasn't the only one we fixed up. Making full use of the decked-out garage below the institute's mansion, we finally each had our own car. The long hours of dedication it had taken to convert three rust buckets into beauties was a soothing balm to our shredded insides. The familiar, regular companionship of my crew had gotten us through.

Behind the wheel of his sleek, red 1967 Mustang Shelby GT500, whom Hunt had named Bolter, he said into our telepathic link, *<If she's too far away to hear us, she hasn't even left the house yet.>*

He was in Bolter with a gorgeous powerhouse from the Aquoia tribe. Her name was Kaya Blue Cloud. Of all our new friends, she was secretly my favorite. Hunt's father, Joseph Waking Bear, had introduced them. Since that day they'd scarcely been apart, and they shared a bed every night. I'd never seen Hunt so happy.

*<I'm texting my annoying baby sister right the fuck now,>* Brady grumbled.

Not everyone knew my crew and I shared a telepathic connection, but Kaya, Yolanda, and Armando did, along with a few select others. They were accustomed to the silences when we spoke to one another inside our heads, though we did try not to be rude about it.

No one was aware the five of us could speak with Bobo, though, much less that he could talk back. We were psyched to finally be free of so many secrets, but there were those we held on to. Some things—like Bobo as my *compan*—felt too precious to share. Our circle of trusted friends was expanding, but our experience with Magnum had taught us a variety of lessons, prime among them: caution.

My phone and Griff's vibrated with Brady's messages into our five-way thread. We had a separate one for us and our extended crew.

**Brady:** Dude

**Brady:** WTF

**Brady:** Put it back in ur pants & get over here

**Brady:** Tired of waiting

**Brady:** Givin U 5 more then we're leaving ur ass behind

Of course, we wouldn't actually leave Layla behind while we exited Ridgemore for the very first time in decades. But since it was Brady texting, she maybe wouldn't be sure. If any of us would leave her, it would be him.

When I killed Magnum, whatever ability he was using to keep Ridgemore looping so that my crew couldn't escape its boundaries ended too. We discovered that Ridgemore squatted smack-dab in the middle of the vast Aquoia generational lands.

As soon as we were sufficiently recovered, we allied with the Aquoia to return the sacredness Magnum had tainted to its land. The tribe's leaders, which included Hunt's dad, believed my crew had worked with their ancestors from beyond to free them from the rich white man with the dark, evil heart. According to Joseph, a spirit-talker who saw and heard his tribe's ancestors almost as if they still lived, they were very pleased with our efforts and considered us great friends to the Aquoia. According to them, we were brave warriors who fought for their people. The tribe's elders extended us the great honor of officially inducting us into their tribe, with the appropriate ceremony soon forthcoming. Joseph and Kaya had been teaching us their ways.

And though Magnum's team had drugged and taken Joseph's sperm by trickery, and used his genetic material to produce Hunt without his consent, Joseph was eagerly embracing fatherhood. For the first time ever, Hunt had a parent who never lied to him, but who shared sage truths about the universe, daily existence, and most everything in between. Hunt threw out the silver hoop earring with the dangling turquoise that had never belonged to his father and replaced it with a similar earring that did belong to Joseph, who proudly wore its mate.

Hunt might have come about his Aquoia genetics in a questionable manner, but he was enjoying the sense of belonging to a larger community than just our crew. So were the rest of us.

Joseph said appearances didn't matter. Inside, we were Aquoia now, just as we were Sky People.

Together with the tribe, we decided to keep the institute and repurpose it: from a place that took advantage of its prisoners to a place that gave advantages to its willing students. My crew would live at the mansion Magnum built for us, making it our home base—to the absolute delight of the facilities-ho who lived inside me—while doing all we could to support the institute in becoming a safe haven for supernaturals.

When the dust of battle settled, we discovered dozens of young adults, and even some children, with paranormal abilities locked up in the underground bunker facility. They were only a small selection of the world's population of supernaturals, apparently. Several Aquoia, too, exhibited powers beyond this world, or at the very least, of its common comprehension.

With the resources of the institute, we had the opportunity to help all of them, ourselves too. We'd explore and learn about our abilities while we trained to wield them.

It was important that we understand more about the *lushina*, or the Sky People as the Aquoia called them, and about their great enemy, the *drash*. Perhaps Magnum and his creepy, gray "companions" were all the *drash* that had infiltrated the earth. But how could we be certain? By all appearances, Magnum Chase had been just another greedy human mofo who put his own desires above everyone else's. Megaelites like Magnum who took advantage at every turn because they could weren't uncommon enough on

Earth. But were they *drash* too? Were there more of them secretly plotting to bend humanity—and *lushina*—to their will?

Hoping it wasn't so wouldn't protect anyone. Better to be prepared, just in case.

We were far from alone in our mission. Already, we had a skeleton crew in place that would aid us, and it kept expanding. Yolanda and Armando would stay on to teach the students to defend themselves. Jude, aka Reece and my "dad"; Tobias, aka Orson and Griff's "dad"; and Marisa, aka Alexis and Hunt's "mom" were the only lie-rents to survive their fight with Magnum's soldiers. My not-mom and both of Brady and Layla's not-parents had been killed.

They'd gone down fighting for us up until the very end, just as they'd promised.

At least they hadn't gone out defending a lie but their love for us.

Jude, Tobias, and Marisa wanted to help make things right. For the first time in what felt like eons, I believed them. They would lead some other exemplary researchers in studying us—only to such extent as any of us felt comfortable, if at all; the choice was up to each individual—so we might begin to catalog the range of supernatural abilities and how it was that some of us "humans" had them and some didn't.

The institute would also teach academics of all levels to best prepare us for whatever the world might hurl at us. Marisa was spearheading the hiring, and already we'd drawn the attention of brilliant professors around the globe. Hunt was practically salivating at the chance to study with them. It seemed the more astounding the teacher, the more the idea of teaching such extraordinary individuals became absolutely irresistible.

I'd believed what we were building here was totally unique, a vanguard for a whole new world. I mean, I'd heard of no other institute for supernaturals anywhere, ever—outside of fantasy, of course.

Then we received a visit from a very scholarly, *talking* pygmy owl named Sir Lancelot—*so* bonkers—and two ancient wizard brothers named Albacus and Mordecai, who turned out not just to be ghosts—because *no*, that wasn't nutty enough: talking ghosts I could see and hear—but half ghosts. The brothers were equally alive and dead . . . somehow.

Sir Lancelot, Mordecai, and Albacus were responsible for several academies tailored to those with paranormal capabilities all over the world. There were more, they said, but by name they mentioned a Magical Arts Academy, a Magical Creatures Academy, and a Magical Dragons Academy.

*Dragons.*

I mean, *come on.*

Dragons!

My first follow-up question was: When do we get to see dragons? *Dragons.*

Sir Lancelot had trilled cutely, cleared his throat like a person, and assured us we'd set something up soon.

After our experience with the *drash*, I'd believed my mind incapable of blowing any wider open. My, how wrong I'd been. There were *magical academies* right under our noses all over the place—say what? How had I ever believed the world was so simple before?

We decided to name our new endeavor Ridgemore's Institute for Supernaturals.

Our mission was undoubtedly ambitious and far-reaching, and in this world that required moolah—lots and lots of it . . . good thing I'd torn out the heart of a bajillionaire, eh?

Sheriff Xander turned out to be a true ally. With the aid of some well-intended forgery and a few crossed and smudged lines, he figured out a way to allocate the entirety of Magnum's fortune to my crew. Xander said if anyone deserved that much money, we did, to make up for what that creep did to us.

Once we were in possession of the funds—and it was *so* much money; I'd never seen so many zeroes at the end of a number—we transferred it into a trust that my crew shared with the Aquoia tribe. Magnum had desecrated their sacred land—especially their lake, which they believed contained Sky People essence. He'd violated what was precious to the tribe.

The Aquoia deserved recompense too.

In union, we'd transform all that blood money into something amazing.

An incoming message vibrated my phone and Griffin's.

**Brady:** Time's up. Later!

Griffin rolled his eyes. "He knows we can't leave her. We're crew. We're not going on our first cross-country road trip without her."

I chuckled. "No, we'd never. He's totally bluffing. But I can def see why he's pissed." I waggled my brows, spoke in an over-the-top French accent. "Like he says, we could be getting . . . *pleasured*, too, instead of sitting around."

I ran my hands around Cleo's steering wheel. "Though it is one fine place to sit. Man, did Cleo turn out pretty."

"Nowhere near as pretty as you. No offense, Cleo." Griffin's eyes sparkled. "And . . . no one says we can't get a lil' busy while we wait." He slid along the leather of his seat, leaned forward. "Nowhere I'd rather be than with you, baby. I don't care where we are."

He pressed his lips to mine, kissed me gently, a precursor to so much more to come. "Clyde'll just have to forgive me for leaving him out of our first trip outside. No way do I not wanna be at your side for this."

I smiled against his lips, loving the taste of him. "That's nice of you."

"Cleo needs to feel the long stretch of road under her. She's brand-new. We'll go in Clyde next time."

"Deal," I murmured, my agreement vibrating between our mouths.

I kissed him.

In moments, his tongue was sliding along mine, my fingers clawing through his hair. His hands were gripping my thighs, guiding the one closest to him to bend onto the seat, opening me up to him.

We were dressed, but it was instinctive now. Our bodies were constantly finding ways to be closer to one another, more deeply connected. Our hands were on each other more than not. Since we'd survived Magnum, we'd slept together every night, entangled together.

My body was already flushed, wanting more of the sensations only he delivered. Already I'd half forgotten we were supposed to be heading out of town on a grand adventure.

Griffin's hands skimmed under my shirt, roving my skin. They slid upward, dipped under my bra, and caressed the bottom swell of my breasts.

He moaned and withdrew from our kiss just to smack his lips and stare at me. "My fucking dream girl . . . How'd I ever get so lucky?"

"You fought for me."

"Fuck yeah I did, baby. I always will. You fought for me too."

I leaned into his touch. Dropped my forehead to his. Closed my eyes.

"Yeah, my love, I did, and I always will too."

Bobo barked. I jumped.

"Shit, I forgot he was here," Griffin said.

<*Bobo go,*> Bobo said with a wag of his tail.

I laughed. <*Yeah, Bobo, we're going.*>

Our phones buzzed again.

**Layla:** F U, Brady

**Layla:** How dare U even think of leaving without me?!!!!!!!!!!!!!!

**Layla:** Almost there. Hold ur fucking horses. Talk Yoli into givin u road head or somethin while u wait. Make the most of it

**Layla:** Can't blame a girl for gettin the best sex of her life, now can u?

Laughing softly, I shook my head at the twins' antics. So much had changed in such a short time. But some things, it seemed, never would.

Griffin settled back against his seat. Clasped our hands together so our newest ink lined up along our inner forearms: *family* scrawled in a lowercase script, and immediately below it, *FOREVER*, in all caps, each letter a combination of pointy-sharp blades and thorns, dripping blood. And below that, from the biggest drop of blood emerge five rays as of the sun, shooting down from the sky—the rays were the Aquoia's representation of Sky People; the number five symbolized us.

Layla had made each stroke of art. She, Griffin, Hunt, Brady, and I all wore the same tats, forever linking us together—not that we needed ink for that. Turned out, our preternatural healing aligned with our intentions. We didn't want to erase our ink, so our bodies didn't.

<*Fuck,*> Brady's voice said into my mind from Bonnie. <*There she is. Fina-fucking-lly.*>

<*I heard that,*> Layla's voice said.

<*Good. You're in range. Dude, you took foreeeeeeever. What up?*>

*<Five juicy big O's, that's what up, my brother. Trent's unstoppable,>* she trilled giddily into our telepathic channel. *<Looks like I was a smart bitch to hold out for a wolfie. No regular man can satisfy me. But Trent . . . mmm, mmm, mmm, mmm, MMMM.>*

*<Okay, okay. Knock it off. We get the idea. Guy's got the stamina of a beast, we know.>*

*<And the cock to match.>*

*<We know,>* Brady whined.

Trent was the large wolf who'd joined the fight in Magnum's office. He was one of the few who managed to escape the underground bunker prison on his own, and even without knowing us, he fought alongside us. That automatically made him a-okay in my book.

Much to Layla's squealing astonishment—"Dreams *do* come true," she'd said—wolf shifters are apparently very real, as are other types of shape-shifters, as well as vampires. The world was so much more interesting than I ever guessed.

As soon as Trent got a good whiff of Layla, he'd claimed she was his mate, and he'd hardly left her side since. Layla was all "Trent this" and "Trent that." Her favorite topic of conversation was his dick, the best on the entire planet, she stated on the regular.

But absolutely not. No way. Griff's was. I'd gotten plenty acquainted with it in the six or so months since ripping Magnum's heart out.

In the rearview mirror, I watched Layla's Mustang approach, taking the final curve around the institute's private drive to where we waited just before the gate. Hers was a 1965 Fastback that she'd inexplicably named Judy. She'd painted her a satin white, but only as the base of her canvas. Brilliant artist that she was, Layla had hand painted streamlined tattoos all along Judy's body in sleek, black, winding lines. The result was so sexy that Brady hadn't stopped begging her to do the same to Bonnie. She said she was too busy gettin' boned at the moment, but maybe someday.

<*All right, guys,*> I said into our link. <*Y'all ready to bust outta this joint?*>

<*Hell to the fuck yeah!*> Layla said.

When she was close enough that I could make her out, and Trent in the passenger seat, I rolled forward.

<*Lie down, Bobo,*> I said. <*We're finally going.*>

<*Bobo go!*> he barked with an excited wag of his tail before settling down on the blanket.

I eased Cleo through the open gate. Bonnie, Bolter, and Judy nosed out behind me.

<*Colorado bound!*> Hunt called as we caravanned along the city road toward the town's exit.

<*Yeah, baby!*> Brady yelled.

Griffin grinned beautifully.

Just like there were schools for people with paranormal abilities we hadn't known about, there were also communities for supes peppered around the world. Trent was a member of the Rocky Mountain Pack, a wolf-shifter pack that spanned the length of the Rocky Mountains. Trent lived in a community in Colorado, nestled in the mountains. We were headed there first. He wanted his pack to meet his mate and her family.

After that, who knew where we'd go next? Trent had also lived with the Smoky Mountain Pack for a brief stint. Their territory aligned with the Great Smoky Mountains. We could visit. Meet more of this incredible supernatural community we'd been a part of and not even known it.

For the very first time in our lives, where we went, how, and when was entirely up to us. We had a home base and an important mission to accomplish.

We'd get back to all that soon.

Right now, what we wanted was the open road.

Expanse.

No limits.

*Freedom.*

The familiar undulating tree line of Ridgemore whipped by, and before long, there it was: the exit sign, the one we hadn't been able to escape.

I slowed Cleo to a crawl. Griffin linked our fingers together. He raised our joined hands and kissed the back of mine, then held on until I needed to shift gears.

I read the exit sign. <*We hope you enjoyed your visit to Ridgemore, where strangers become friends. Come back to see us soon!*>

<*Ugh*,> Layla said. <*Gross. So smarmy and manipulative.*>

<*We should set it on fire when we get back*,> I suggested.

<*Done deal*,> Brady said.

<*I so wanna light it up*,> Hunt added.

<*Ditto*,> Griff said.

Then I gunned Cleo. Shifted into third, fourth, then fifth, rocketing out of town.

My friends were on our tail as we zipped by a view that was already new and unfamiliar.

We were leaving behind so many lies—good fucking riddance.

Up ahead was the future—and it was wholly *ours*.

Here was our new beginning.

All fucking ours.

<*Family forever*,> Hunt sang.

<*Family forever, bitches*,> Layla echoed.

Our joint laughter rang into our bond as we zoomed forward into the unknown.

# About the Author

Lucía Ashta is the international-bestselling Argentinian American author of more than seventy young adult and adult fantasy and paranormal books including the Royals of Embermere, Smoky Mountain Pack, Witches of Gales Haven, Magical Creatures Academy, Witching World, and Six Shooter and a Shifter series. A former attorney and architect, Ashta lives in North Carolina's Smoky Mountains with her husband and three daughters. When she isn't writing, she's reading, painting, or adventuring.